About the Author

Michael De Stefano is from Philadelphia and makes his home in Cinnaminson, New Jersey. He is the author of *The Prodigy of St. Pete's* — the story of Andy Trumaine, an orphaned boy whose gift to others as he journeys through life is his good sense of the world; *In the Time of Their Restlessness* — a tumultuous coming of age story in urban America in the 1970s; and *The Gunslinger's Companion* — the story of a man born into a band of wheat belt migrants and his unlikely ascension into society.

For Kathy

Michael De Stefano

THE COURAGE OF EXISTENCE

AUSTIN MACAULEY
PUBLISHERS LTD.

A CIP catalogue record for this title is available from the British Library.

ISBN 978 1 78455 870 3 (Paperback)
ISBN 978 1 78455 871 0 (Hardback)

www.austinmacauley.com

First Published (2015)
Austin Macauley Publishers Ltd.
25 Canada Square
Canary Wharf
London
E14 5LQ

Printed and bound in Great Britain

Acknowledgments

The following articles, links, and videos were a valuable source:
Darfur − Region in Crisis: Childhood interrupted in Darfur's refugee camps. www.unicef.org/sowc/20297_30568.html
Sudan kills refugees in Darfur: news.bbc.co.uk/2/hi/Africa/7580778.stm
Daily Life in Kalma Camp, Darfur Sudan, April 2006: Uploaded to YouTube on May 17, 2010.
Missionary sees need firsthand during visit to Darfur refugee camp: by Erik Tryggestad/Christian Chronicle.
Genocide in Darfur: United Human Rights Council

Contents

PROLOGUE

A letter from a missionary working in Darfur, Sudan, written March 25, 2006: To whomever these words may find, be it you that has sent me, or God.

I am doomed to this place — this astonishingly bleak place from which I'm composing these words. When in moments of calm, I often recollect those times known as the past — that ever present demon who prefers to sneer at me and who takes immense pleasure in reminding me that I could never become all, or even a scrap of what I had once hoped. During the restless times, which are often, I consider the future. However, I'm not all too certain that I was sent here with the notion that I would survive. This may seem difficult to imagine, for I can scarcely imagine it myself, but not only am I able to consider such thoughts, but utter them without the slightest bit of regret. This place, albeit at times remarkable, was not all my own choosing. Mostly, it was chosen for me by another, whose wisdom, I believed, far exceeded my own. At this stage of my life, though, this place quite suites my needs, and it will continue to do so as long as I am in the flesh and therefore given to having needs. I wish I had the time to better explain my position, in the unlikelihood that this letter reaches its intended destination. But I must hurry, for soon my friend will wake and require my full attention. Should this letter go missing, or worse, get intercepted, I would ask that the reader of these words — words which could very well be my last, perceive them as the thoughts of a fellow human soul who tried — tried desperately and in their heart had the best of intentions, or at least believed that to be the case. And yes, I understand perfectly how weak my entreaty is, for we all believe that our causes are just and that we are fighting on the side of God. Be that as it is, and for whatever it is worth, I tried to be kind whenever presented with an opportunity. It is said that a place can change a person, that it can get under one's skin and afterward one is never quite as they once were. True, a place can change one's being, but can it erase and then rewrite their virtue? Or change the very essence of their nature? Perhaps it cannot entirely, but to a point it could knock it from its axis. With that in mind, when passing a mirror or anything that can produce a reflection, I permit myself a peek — a fleeting glance, and always am I astonished. Some days my appearance seems strange — even foreign, and so it never fails to surprise. At times, this revelation frightens me, though, most often I merely startle. It's an odd occurrence to not recognise one's own self. By now, though, I should be resigned to what I've become. I have been through many changes in my life and times, and at last I've reached the butterfly stage. Regrettably, I cannot imagine that my delicate wings would be long for the harshness of such a place, never mind that its hinterlands and vistas when in times of calm can be pleasing. The reason I say 'regrettably' is because my work here is far from finished. As I gaze out upon the landscape, I see the scaffolding of majestic acacia trees — the strange but magnificent baobab, whose branches appear as roots arching above their disproportionately wide trunks. Both, along with the palms provide a life source for those creatures who manage to exist harmoniously. Beyond the trees I see a multitude of texture and colour — layer upon layer on the way to Jebel Marra, known as the mountainous region. When I look to the left, off in the not too far distance I can see remnants of the Aouk, whose waters I have many a times dipped my hands and have cooled my parched cheeks. Though lurking by the water, behind the trees, and entrenched in the many layers throughout the landscape are those who have committed and will continue to commit unspeakable slaughter and treachery, and along with them, are others who maintain to know and understand God's purpose for humankind. Woe are those who serve the greater good, for their dreams may never be realised. Woe are those who maintain to fight on the side of heaven, for they are always outnumbered and have fewer swords. As for myself, I have never raised a hand, nor have I ever dared to make any existential claims as it might pertain to God's purpose; I am merely here to serve and serve I shall. But before I rest my pen, I will now end by saying these are the words of Jimmy — Saint Jimmy in Paradise, though you once knew me by another name. P.S. The blood stains on this letter belong to my friend. I know him only as someone who came willingly to this godforsaken land, and who like myself foolishly carries within him this ponderous affliction known as hope. Together we forged a friendship that could very well become his, and quite possibly my final act of humanity.

CHAPTER I
THE BOY IN THE CLOSET

London, England 1991:

Nestled in the Bloomsbury section of London, stands the charming and well patronised Ebenezer's Coffee House. The establishment opened in the year 1989; and if one were to confer with the locals, they would learn quite categorically that, along with being necessary (before 1989, there didn't exist a coffee house able to serve as a destination for locals and students of the university to gather) the establishment was an immediate success. Oddly enough, though, *Ebenezer* was an Aussie named Brian, who came to England to study agricultural engineering. However, during this worthwhile pursuit, a passion for coffee was developed. It has been noted by many that, when a passion is permitted to blossom into a career it can make for a happy life, and *toiling away* would never be how one would describe their days. Of course, no one truly believed that the blonde, ponytailed Aussie was named Ebenezer. Furthermore, after having been abroad for six years, his Australian accent, which was once as distinct as it was charming, was by then all but undetectable. It could be said of the young women of Bloomsbury, that they frequented Ebenezer's Coffee House because of the French Mug — a hot drink Brian crafted that contained French roast coffee, raw sugar, African coco, a speck of butter, and twist of nutmeg. Indeed, the young Bloomsbury women *could* claim to have passed by the area's more recently established coffee houses in favour of this concoction, along with Brian's other coffee-based inventions; their claims wouldn't be *entirely* wrong. And most would agree that the French mug was well worth walking a few extra blocks or driving an extra mile. But if truth be told, it was Brian himself that was Ebenezer's main attraction. After all, what young woman wouldn't want to look at a blond, ponytailed man in his mid-twenties possessing soft eyes, a rugged chin, bronze skin, and an intellect that was either equal to, and often surpassed that of the university students who frequented the coffee house. "He's like a surfer with brains," many of the female patrons would swoon. To his credit, Brian not only served the area's best coffee, but made every effort to educate Ebenezer's patronage on the virtues of his passion. And since reading and drinking coffee seem to go well together, he kept a shelf stocked with English classics, which folks were free to read and borrow on the honour system. The shelf included all the expected names: Jane Austen and the Bronte sisters, as well as the more modern D. H. Lawrence, and Oscar Wilde. There were even a few political nonfiction titles for those who enjoy indulging in such morass. And while one was reading, sipping coffee, or both, they were just as likely to hear the strains of a Haydn string quartet as they were the satiny crooning of Cleo Laine. On Friday evenings, there was live music, and musicians whose genres included either jazz, classical, or folk were invited to come and test their wares before the locals and university students. Brian preferred folk, but jazz and classical were welcomed. Whenever a jazz artist or combo appeared, Brian would dim the lights, and the coffee house seemed to transform into a night club. If still open, and if not too weary when through with his shift, a local named Jimmy Philips would happen by the coffee shop and relax with what was resolved a well deserved French mug. When not slated to work Sunday and his schedule had remained unchanged, Jimmy would come slinking into Ebenezer's coffee house at eleven o'clock a.m. sharp. The reason the term *slinking* is used to describe the manner in which Jimmy Philips entered the coffee house, is because he never came upon *any* room with *any* show of confidence, and furthermore, he would take his leave fully aware that he in no way would be missed. Therefore, Jimmy was given to *slink* in and out of rooms *or* establishments after never having favourably or unfavourably altered the dynamics. Those who frequent a particular coffee house do so as a matter of routine and therefore, tend to run into the same patrons. This is an occurrence that would usually result in a nod or smile, and often such simple acknowledgements could spark small talk, or a cordial but brief conversation. But this was never the case with Jimmy, as he was ignored entirely. Jimmy was a few years older than the college students who flocked to the coffee house and took up most of the seating. The students hadn't much if any interest in the nameless faceless working class shuffling through their day in search of their needed pick-me-up. But even those who went unacknowledged by the students also ignored Jimmy, despite *him* recognising many of *them*, whether it was by way of their faces or familiar outerwear. Regarding the university students, in his own mind, this ranked him as the most unworthy of the unworthy. It also begged the question, why did he continue to choose Ebenezer's Coffee House as a habitual? He could claim the coffee or the geography as valid reasons, but neither was the case. He also could have claimed that, in all likelihood he would have received the same lack of acknowledgement at another establishment, so why not Ebenezer's? The true essence of his patronage stemmed from the fact that Ebenezer's was an establishment where young intellectuals and intellectuals' wannabes gathered, and it was with them whom Jimmy wished to fit in— to desperately belong.

He first came to the coffee house presenting as a preppy sort with well groomed hair and conservative sweaters. But as time went by, the attire became more hippie-like and his hair grew to where he was able to gather it into a ponytail. That, along with a pubescent face incapable of sprouting a whisker lent to an appearance that was adolescently androgynous. Usually in those rare *is-it-a-he-or-a-she* cases, the voice was a dead giveaway, but even Jimmy's voice was genderless — not that anyone at Ebenezer's spoke to him and would know. As far as anyone could tell, Jimmy was without any outward traces of masculinity, obvious or otherwise. And he wasn't at all curvaceous like a woman, or how a woman would wish to be curvaceous. In fact, his only true *feminine* attributes were his soft and somewhat pretty facial features; otherwise he possessed the rigidity and stiffness of a man, and therefore, moved about like a man. There was much to Jimmy that one could wonder about, and yet he was largely ignored. In fact, the only words ever directed Jimmy's way were "excuse me" when having been accidentally bumped into when standing in line to place a coffee order, or when someone was on their way to the restroom and had to pass in front of him while he was in line. There were instances, though, when he happened by the coffee house when there wasn't such a crowd and therefore, was able to draw Brian into a conversation about his favourite topic: Coffee. Jimmy, for the sake of these rare exchanges, almost overnight became a coffee aficionado. The subject itself, he didn't necessarily find to be so much delight, and in fact, he regarded it as both tedious and unimaginative. However, it greatly pleased Brian to converse with anyone who knew why the beans of Guatemala were different from those of Kenya, and this Jimmy Philips *did* find delightful. Brian's eyes lit up whenever anyone spoke of humidity and elevation as how it pertained to a coffee bean, and why *this* environment produced a bean with notes of cocoa, versus another that produced fruit or nut flavours. For Brian, coffee was an earth science that was anything *but* unimaginative. Jimmy came away from their initial conversation in possession of the belief that the young females in the room would have a sudden interest in him, if for no other reason he quite possibly could provide them a handy liaison between themselves and the often ogled coffee connoisseur. After all, Jimmy must have acquired *some* personal information of interest that would prompt those giddy for Brian's attention to intercept him before reaching and then settling down in his chair? However, Jimmy took his French mug to a vacant seat in the corner of the coffee house (his customary spot) and did so without a single eye ever turning in his direction. Therefore, his countenance, which for a brief moment displayed a measure of pride and hopefulness (two expressions which for him must be considered a rarity) went entirely unnoticed. Jimmy was small in stature, and his smallness was to the extent of being boyishly scrawny. The few women who did take notice of him were fellow nurses from the hospital where he was employed. They described his face as not handsome but "pretty" and therefore, it was well suited to his "pettiness". However, these women fancied him only as someone who was "cute" in the way a "gnome" or "sprite", and among themselves they referred to him as "Puck", the fluttery character from Shakespeare's "*A Midsummer Night's Dream*". But none sought him out as a viable love interest. In fact, they were of the impression that Jimmy was the most nonthreatening member of a gender, which as times was given to behave overbearingly whenever in the company of women or in the pursuit of women. It was also fair to say that his female co-workers looked upon him as they would another female, only better, for contrivance was not something of which he was readily or at all capable. In fact, Jimmy played the role of *reliable confidant* and held firm to everyone else's little secrets. Nothing ever tempted him; least of all his own gain.

After having talked all that he could on the subject of coffee, Jimmy showed up at Ebenezer's with his fingers wrapped around a volume of short stories by Franz Kafka. He held it such that the university students would notice and hopefully form the opinion that he was an existentialist and intellectual worthy of knowing. He was certain that Brian took notice of the volume, but unfortunately, the coffee maven was too busy to pass along any judgment or commentary. This caused Jimmy to seem dismayed, and this led to a great deal of stammering and hesitation when it came time to place his order. Brian never let on that he was mildly annoyed that someone who had waited ten minutes in line, which was more than ample time to arrive at a decision, had suddenly and for some unknown reason lost their composure. As always, though, Brian maintained his Aussie charm.

"How about a latte?" he asked.

Jimmy agreed to the hasty suggestion, but when he walked away he was feeling utterly miserable, for despite all the conversations and exchanges he and Brian had on the subject of coffee, his usual order of a French Mug was not remembered. Despite what he chose to view as a rebuff, Jimmy brought the Kafka volume with him the next day, and then the next. But it wasn't until Sunday that Brian finally bothered to utter, "I didn't figure you for a morbid sort."

"Morbid?" asked Jimmy, as though wholly unable to ascertain what he had said or done to earn such an unflattering evaluation.

"I'd certainly say so," said Brian, who, with a nod gestured to the cover of the book that was well secured in Jimmy's hands.

"I take it then, you're not a big Kafka fan?" Jimmy asked.

"Studied him at the university," said Brian. "Half way through the semester I concluded that he was western civilization's leading cause for drug addiction and suicide. That's an opinion, incidentally, that others share. In fact, I almost went to the dark side myself. Finally, I told my professor, 'If this is education, I'd rather take up juggling.' He didn't see the humour in that, so I told him, 'I don't see the need for Kafka; so that makes us even.'"

"He does paint some rather gloomy pictures," admitted Jimmy, "but he also masterfully illustrates the parent-child conflict, does he not?"

"Perhaps so," said Brain, "and I certainly don't mind a good old-fashioned discussion based on existentialism, but not as it may pertain to alienation and psychological brutality. What could be more morbid? The most disturbing piece I ever read was "In the Penal Colony". After I was through reading and digesting every painful syllable, I spent the following three days whistling and humming songs from Mary Poppins, and I didn't give a hoot and a half who heard me. Although I must say, it takes much more than a *spoonful of sugar* to digest *good, old* Franz Kafka."

"I like Mary Poppins," Jimmy good-naturedly remarked. He smiled at Brian, and despite their differences on the subject of Franz Kafka, he thanked the coffee maven for the conversation, then he took hold of his French mug and located his usual seat in the corner of the coffee house. After he settled into his seat he opened the Kafka volume and peered over the page, surveying the room and occasionally sipping his hot concoction. He permitted his eyes to spy a quartet of female students from the university. He had seen them together many times in the past, and this morning while spying them, he began to recall with a measure of delight first noticing them back in the summertime. Then, they were sporting ponytails, sleeveless tops, sun kissed shoulders, and toe-loop sandals; their voices while engaged in their tête-à-tête seemed melodious in nature. That, along with their summer accessories had driven him to distraction and near madness, and what began as delightful reverie ended in frustration. How he longed to sit among them — to join in their tête-à-tête — it mattered not the discussion. Nor would it matter if they fancied him as one being cute in the way of a gnome or sprite; he would wait on them and pamper them if they so desired, *or* permitted — and for this he would rejoice. Oh, indeed, to gain access into the world of women — to sit among them — to know the scent of their lovely hair and soft skin — to hear their thoughts and to become familiar with and perhaps gain permission to celebrate their long coveted charms. But how their beauty intimidated him so, and left him a tortured wreck — perhaps more tortured and wrecked than Kafka had left Brian. Time and again this brand of torture had sent Jimmy to his bed, where he imagined himself a wanton filled with perversity and deviance. He went about this wantonness with a feverish craze, until he had at last erupted and sweat through

22

his night clothes. Only in his mind, though, were such inspirations accessible. Only in his mind could he indulge in such licentious reverence of women. When the dissolute ritual had concluded, his trembling ceased, and his shame fully subsided, he would reach for the photograph on his nightstand. It was with him for years, the photograph; it was never not by his bedside. He would gaze lovingly into the face of a young girl he once knew, and then press the photograph to his heart. Over and over, he would whisper the name *Mary Willow*. Often he would afterward drink himself to sleep. At other times, he would fall asleep with the photograph resting on his chest.

Jimmy became distracted from his lovely quartet, when to his right he heard a man his own age or perhaps a bit older droning on rather obnoxiously about the United States and "Operation Desert Storm". He seemed to be hollering at the newspaper that he was holding.

"Damn Americans! They think they own the whole bloody world and can do whatever they damn well please with it! And what makes matters worse, they come up with these media sensational names for their military manoeuvres, like they're video games or movies. 'Desert Storm?' Please! And there they are, all glued to their oversized television sets, like it's the damn World Cup, not that they know a bloody thing about soccer! And then here *we* are, like a loyal puppy dog with our poor, little snout stuck up the great big American asshole! Must we follow them every damn place they decide to go? There was a time, you know, when we were an empire that was actually capable of thinking for itself! Does anyone here remember those days?"

The man spoke as if he were armed with the benefit of wisdom and knowledge of history. (He perhaps had the latter.) Then he shoved his newspaper into the chest of the friend with whom he was supposed to be sharing a leisurely Sunday morning. "Here, what do *you* make of all this?" he cried out. The man expected his friend to concur and to do so by exhibiting equal vehemence, and that together they might stir up the whole coffee house. But the friend wisely elected not to engage his obnoxious companion. Instead, he read silently and sipped his coffee while his companion continued on with his rant. Obnoxious though he may have been, and Jimmy had a great deal of difficulty with loud people, particularly when their volume superseded the magnitude of their words, he had to admit the fellow made some good points. Continuing to peer over his book, Jimmy shifted his eyes to the right, in order to better see this man who was voicing such strong opinions. The fellow continued rebuking the United States, citing that their anti-Arab/Muslim sentiment was so strong that it perhaps clouded their judgment and made them exceedingly willing to want to take up arms against them — even at the slightest provocation. "It took them forever to get involved in World War II, but if an Arab/Muslim as much as takes a piss, than look out, it's guns blazing!" However, by that time, Jimmy had ceased listening — not that the fellow's words were no longer of interest (which they were) or he too boisterous, (which he was), but because the fellow had crossed his legs, and in doing so exposed the fact that he was wearing white socks with black dress shoes. For Jimmy, this was a dress code violation that could not be reconciled, no matter how well this particular fellow, or for that matter *any* fellow articulated his rage.

Jimmy made quite a habit of critiquing the appearance of men — how well they were or were not groomed, and in particular the coordination of their attire. This practice wasn't for the purpose of measuring himself against other men — at least not consciously — but rather, it was an exercise that he learned from his father, who was a stickler with regard to grooming and attire. Conversely, Jimmy wouldn't dare critique a woman based only on her appearance — he revered women to the point where they intimidated him so, and therefore, he was afraid that they would know what he was thinking. He feared that the intuitive nature of women was *that* strong. So whenever he noticed a woman whose eyeliner was applied too thickly, or a woman who had poured herself into an outfit better suited for someone a size smaller, he would quickly look away, not wanting to run the risk having noticeably passed judgment.

With regard to his own appearance, Jimmy's father was a most meticulous sort, and therefore demanded no less from his son. Jimmy's hair was to be combed a certain way; his shirts were always tucked in, no matter his activities; the proper socks to match the proper shoes were always worn; and his shoes always matched his belts. The importance of maintaining a meticulous appearance was paramount— an unwavering virtue that was drummed into Jimmy's head since the time that he was capable of thinking. It was his desire to please his father. In fact, he was quite steadfast in his desire to win the approval of *both* his parents. However, there was little or no reward; regardless of how successful were his endeavours. Jimmy's father was the more difficult to please — the standards he imposed on his son were less then reasonable, but at times he managed to display affection that could have been interpreted by any onlooker as genuine. His mother, it seemed to Jimmy, was the easier to please, (little did he know she expected less) however, she often seemed detached and at times acted put-upon whenever Jimmy sought out her affection. Time and again he tried desperately to win his mother's whole heart, but for whatever reason this was not an achievable feat. Perhaps his mother never wanted a child, but made the sacrifice for the sake of his father. Or, the idea of a child pleased her, but the effort of raising it was all too intrusive. Whichever the case, until an adult, Jimmy was never fully able to accept, nor would he become resigned to the fact that possessing his mother's whole heart was an unachievable feat. As the years went by, though, he wasn't sure if he loved to hate his mother, or hated that he loved her. Still, he went on trying to win her heart. It was when Jimmy was embarking on adulthood and had expressed the desire to become a nurse that his parents unilaterally opposed him — despite nursing becoming a field to which men were beginning to gravitate in good numbers. Jimmy's father was the more outspoken in the effort to beat down his son's aspiration, but his mother was right by his father's side, supporting him in both spirit and in tongue. Jimmy hadn't many friends, but those he had supported his ambition. So too did his Aunt Delia. After Jimmy wrote his aunt, she wrote back, *because of your caring and gentle nature, you would make the ideal nurse.*

In the past, Jimmy's parents were usually at odds with one another when it came to deciding how their son should be raised. The relationship of Nigel and Catherine Philips had a brand of tumult all its own, but when concerning their son, there was rarely peace and harmony within the walls of the Philips home. Instead, there was the writings of C. S. Lewis versus Tolkien; piano lessons versus the violin; polo versus cricket; industry versus becoming learned; and on and on. It was no wonder that Jimmy's parents rose up to oppose him when he dared to decide something for himself. *How dare he display a mind of his own? How dare he take initiative without consulting us? How dare he not trust our judgment with regards to what's best for him?* Jimmy was fully aware that choosing a field or vocation that both his parents would approve of would be an agonising endeavour producing a result that in all likelihood would leave him miserable for all of his days. He often wondered if subconsciously he hadn't chosen a field that would provoke both of his parents into beating their chests by way of threatening banishment and disownment — that in effect he was writing his own ticket out their lives. What better way to divorce his parents than to get *them* to divorce *him*? Even if to some extent it was unwitting, it was the first time in his life that he had ever done anything that could be described as shrewd or calculating. As far as the result of this unwitting shrewdness and calculation was concerned, it mattered not that overnight he had become poor and had to wear the same clothes for days on end, and eat food of little nutritional value — or, whether he had the resources to eat at all. After all the years of warfare and oppression, he was at last free — the cost, of which he was given to reconcile (not that he had a choice) was of little consequence. However, his childhood would remain a time from which he would never fully break free. Whenever his parents quarrelled, Jimmy would run for the closet. Every child has a special place, in or out of the home, where they feel protected from forces that possess the facility to overwhelm them. For Jimmy, his place of refuge was a closet. Nigel and Catherine never became wise to the fact that their son preferred a cramped dark space to the wretchedness of their company. However, had either or both became aware of this fact, it's doubtful an effort would have been made to discover the purpose behind their son's chosen asylum. The house had many closets, though, and on every floor: Some were for wardrobes, others were assigned for storage. One closet in particular was designated for outerwear. It was the closet for outerwear situated at the end of the hallway leading to the kitchen into which Jimmy would run and hide himself away. In was in that particular closet he felt the safest when in times of distress, and in almost every instance was his distress brought about by his parents' inability to settle their differences without the benefit of a lengthy shouting match. As a child, Jimmy wouldn't have been able to articulate why he felt safest in that particular closet; and if asked today his reply would be no more intelligible. There was nothing exceptional about the closet — its geography in relation to the rest of the house shouldn't have been a factor — it certainly wasn't any cosier. Nevertheless, the minute his parents began to raise their voices, regardless of in which room the quarrel was taking place, or where Jimmy was in relation, off he would go, dashing to the closet at the end of the hallway leading to the kitchen. Who knows how or why children develop ideas about such common places as a closet. He might have had hopes that the closet was passageway into Narnia, where waiting to befriend him was a faun, or a White Witch who would try and tempt him with Turkish delight, but because of his father, Tolkien had won out over C. S. Lewis.

The childhood of Jimmy Philips would pass without having experienced *The Chronicles of Narnia*. Jimmy couldn't recall with any certainty the first time he hid himself away in the closet, but the time that stood out above all others was when his parents quarrelled bitterly over which relative he was to stay with while they themselves were off vacationing. Jimmy had yet to meet any members of the Broxton clan (which was his mother's side of the family) or the Hughes' (his father's sister married a Hughes), and thus far had heard little about either. Moreover, he couldn't imagine what was so unique or fascinating about Vienna and Budapest that a five-year-old wasn't permitted to come along and witness firsthand.

Vienna and Budapest, as he could well ascertain, were faraway places with interesting sounding names — certainly more interesting sounding than Broxton or Hughes. When the battle began to rage, Jimmy took off for his dark, rectangular sanctuary, otherwise known as the coat closet. Once behind the door with it securely pulled shut, he lay with his cheek pressed to the carpet while clutching to two stuffed monkeys, which he had named Fish and Chips, proving that, despite his tumultuous home life, he was a young English boy in possession of some sense of humour. Fish and Chips were ten inches in length and came stitched with broad grins and big, round eyes that could only be described as happy. There were numerous opportunities for Fish and Chips to have accompanied Jimmy in the closet dedicated for outerwear, and their soft velvety skin had nearly as many opportunities to absorb many a silent tear. Jimmy closed his eyes and clutched harder to Fish and Chips when he heard his parents' voices raging. Moments later her heard angry footsteps pounding their way down the stairs. Through a small gap between the bottom of the closet door and the carpet, he managed with the benefit of one eye to peer out into the hallway. Although, the narrow crease was unnecessary; he knew the pounding on the stairs was caused by his mother, for it was belonging to one who was going about the house barefoot, which was something his father rarely if ever did; Nigel Philips almost always waited until bedtime before removing his shoes. Jimmy clutched firmly to Fish and Chips as he heard the angry smack of bare skin against the oaken steps. He couldn't imagine that his mother had given up so easily and went storming off before any resolution was reached, regardless of whose favour it was in.

Despite that Jimmy was able to see but an inch or so off the floor, while employing only one eye, the allotted space and a solitary eye was more than enough to recognise his mother's unsightly bunions, as Catherine Philips continued to pound her way down the hallway on the way to the kitchen, where the release of her tantrum was exercised on the dinnerware which had yet to be washed and put away. With nothing left to shatter that wasn't already on the table, Catherine Philips, with what appeared to be a renewed vigour to her frightened young son, returned to the stairs. Jimmy watched his mother's misshapen feet pound their way down the hall, while she herself, no doubt was on her way to resume what had already been the bitterest of rows. Jimmy loathed the sight of his mother's feet — he regarded them as monstrous deformities that he could never get used to, and were made in his estimation far too available. As an adult looking back, he likened his mother's feet to being in the same room with a morbidly obese person or a hunchback or having been a witness to a train wreck— it was difficult to look away, never mind not stare. We're told from early on that it's impolite to stare. But this particular etiquette is often found far too limiting, and therefore it only heightens our curiosity or desire to explore that which is deemed out of the realm of normalcy. Moreover, as is often the case with an accident or deformity, Catherine Philips's bunions became a grotesque source of fascination for her son. It was often that Jimmy's mother went about barefoot while in the house. Whenever she settled herself to read or involve herself in a television program, Jimmy, while accompanied by the ever present Fish and Chips, would surreptitiously drag either his building blocks, drawing paper and pencils, or whatever else he might have been using to amuse himself into the next room. During the time that he was permitted to play, which was far too infrequent, he didn't wish to have his mother's deformities as a distraction. However, no sooner would he settle himself in an adjoining room, invariably he would begin stretching his neck in order to peer into the very room which he had just left. Throughout the remainder of his days considered childhood, Jimmy was obsessed with human deformity; he made it his business to discover the multitude of sorts and to learn of their causes. He would routinely examine his own person for bumps that might later on result in unsightly protrusions. This peculiar obsession ended with the beginning of puberty, which launched an altogether new variety of examinations. The day following his most memorable night in the closet, Jimmy wearily slinked into the kitchen where he discovered his mother barefoot at the stove, but then all at once perked up when realising that Catherine Philips was preparing a family favourite: mushroom and barely soup. "*Good old* mushroom and barely soup", was what Nigel Philips affectionately called it; his endearment on behalf of the hot tasty concoction was genuine, despite all the tension that existed between him and Catherine. Often the soup was made upon request, but at times it also served as a peace offering and the weary five-year-old arrived at the conclusion that in this particular instance it was likely the latter. No matter the reason, it made Jimmy glad, as he was inclined to believe that the soup would facilitate the passing of a peaceful evening. Jimmy took a moment to deeply inhale the worthwhile result of his mother's effort, but before his presence was made known he executed an abrupt about face and went dashing off to his parents' bedroom. Moments later, he returned to the kitchen after having fetched his mother's slippers. "Here, Mother," he said, handing her the slippers. "It's still quite chilly outside and the kitchen floor is cold. See, I needed my slippers, too." He pointed downward in order to draw Catherine's eyes to the floor where she took appreciative notice of the aforementioned slippers.

"That was awfully thoughtful, Jimmy," his mother remarked, as Jimmy positioned her slippers on the floor such that she was able to easily slide into them.

Jimmy smiled that his mother was agreeable to the slippers, and then went to fetch his milk and cereal for what was his customary breakfast.

"Incidentally," his mother continued, "you'll be staying a fortnight with the Broxton's, while your father and I are away on our vacation. They live out in the country, do the Broxton's."

"You and father are going to Vienna and Budapest?" Jimmy sulkily asked.

"Cheer up, Jimmy, you're finally going to get the chance to meet your Aunt Delia — my sister!" Catherine's voice lilted when disclosing to Jimmy that his Aunt Delia was in fact her sister. Perhaps Catherine was craftily trying to plant the seed in her son's head that this was a meeting he had always anticipated. But Jimmy, who was ever intuitive, recognised his mother's use of subtext to try and influence him. "And Mr. Broxton — or, Uncle Peter, as you should probably call him, is an awfully nice fellow. Well, at least that was the impression I was left with the few times that I've been in his company." From his position in the closet, Jimmy didn't recall anyone having been declared the winner of last night's shouting fest. He wondered if his mother wasn't making an impetuous assumption that his father was prepared to relent on the issue of *Broxton versus Hughes*. The aroma of the soup began to envelop him in a most unfriendly manner. What if *good old* mushroom and barely soup wasn't requested or would later be presented as a peace offering? What if this dutiful retreat to the kitchen was his mother's way of disarming his father before she unleashed her fangs and claws? The result of which would be another night of warfare. It then occurred to Jimmy that, perhaps it was sometime after he had fallen asleep in the closet that his father had relented.

But what would cause his father to relent after championing for the Hughes' with such vehemence, Jimmy wondered. Jimmy may have been exceptionally intuitive for one so young, but knew nothing of a woman's facility to be wickedly submissive, or the remarkably effective results such conduct could produce. However, of his parents, with regard to the *Broxton versus Hughes* affair, it mattered not which was victorious; after all, what did Jimmy know of the Broxton's or Hughes' other than they weren't so nearly interesting sounding people as Vienna or Budapest were places.

"Oh, and you also have two cousins named Colin and Douglas," his mother told him. This information was added well after the fact, but brightly, as if it had slipped her mind and then with a sudden burst was remembered. The knowledge that he had two cousins served to brighten Jimmy's mood, until moments later when he learned that his cousins were twice his age and that in all likelihood they wouldn't have much if any interest in him.

"Ten, by all accounts is still a child," said Catherine. Then she added, though more to herself, "I'm sure that three young boys can find *something* in common.

"Mother, where's Vienna and Budapest?" Jimmy asked. Until just recently he had never heard of these two famous European cities, less knew their location. The extent of his geographical knowledge was, he knew that he lived near London, New York was a city in America, Rome was in Italy, and that the pyramids were in Egypt; these facts were all taught to him by his father.

"Vienna is a city in Austria," his mother told him. "It's a beautiful place, I hear — charming and with a great deal of musical culture. I believe Schubert was from Vienna — or maybe I'm thinking of Haydn. Well, I'm fairly certain they're both Austrian." Catherine grimaced, for whatever musical knowledge that she had absorbed through the years (which was more limited than she realised) was eluding her. "Anyway, Budapest is in Hungary. At one time Budapest was two cities, Buda and Pest, and the Danube River flowed right between them. I suppose it still does." Catherine's last remark was added before chuckling at the absurdity that a river situated between two cities could wander off on its own and then later return. "Either way both cities were ruled by the Habsburgs and were part of the Austro-Hungarian Empire and go as far back as the Huns, King Stephen ... or maybe even the Stone Age! However, I'm not quite sure how they both came to be *Budapest* — perhaps it was all Emperor Franz Joseph's doing, but I'd only be guessing. Your father is quite the historian, you know; perhaps you should ask him?" Jimmy slinked away from the breakfast table having decided that not only did the Broxton's and Hughes' *sound* less interesting than Vienna and Budapest, but, in fact, *were* less interesting ... *infinitely* less interesting. Still, he knew it would be useless to clamour that he would much rather visit Vienna and Budapest and to see the Danube River, wherever it happened to flow, than to spend two weeks in the country with relations who were essentially strangers. So when he did slink away from the breakfast table, he did so despairingly and without uttering a word. He hadn't made to as far as the arch leading to the dining room, though, when his mother called to him, "Did I mention to you that Colin and Douglas were twins? *Are* twins?"

"No, Mother, you did not," replied Jimmy, struggling to sound grateful that his mother bothered to correct her oversight. He tried to summon a note of enthusiasm regarding the whole affair, but the fact that Colin and Douglas Broxton were twins was hardly a game changer. In his estimation, however scarce were his references, the Broxton's and two weeks in the country remained infinitely less interesting than Vienna, Budapest, and a 2,872 kilometre river known as the Danube.

****

It was a two-hour car ride from Bayswater (a London suburb) to the Cotswolds, which was a collection of villages lining a fairly sizable, scenic, and to the opinion of many, the most charming portion the English countryside. During the first hour, five-year-old Jimmy Philips was treated to a detailed dissertation on the timeline of Budapest, beginning with the Ottoman Empire's capture and looting of Pest, moving on to the Turk's capture of Buda in the 1500s, then on to the Austrians driving the Turks out in the 1600s. The lesson continued and led to the establishment of a dual monarchy in what would be known as the Austro/Hungarian Empire in 1867. As Jimmy learned, this all came together under the Habsburgs and Emperor Franz Joseph — the result of which was the combining of Buda and Pest into what became in 1872 and today still *is* the capitol of Hungary. It didn't take very long for Jimmy (less than five minutes) to regret having asked his father how Buda and Pest became Budapest. He never imagined that his curiosity would require such an involved history lesson. Had he known that his father not only was able, but was more than willing to speak in such volumes on the subject, he would have never mentioned the word *Budapest* and simply looked out the window in silence as he had on most car trips. Neither Nigel nor Catherine Philips could be described as automobile chatterboxes — they rode mostly in silence, enjoying the scenery while immersed in their own thoughts, and Jimmy was always accommodating by seldom asking questions as children often do from the rear seat of automobiles. Worn out from listening, Jimmy spent the remaining hour asleep while clutching to both Fish and Chips. When they were nearing the Cotswolds, his mother began pointing out the rolling hills that were brought to life with the brilliance of the late spring; Catherine thought such scenery was worth noticing. She asked Nigel to stop at Rodborough Common for a view of the trees, which appeared as if they were spiralling into the base of a valley. Jimmy was shaken awake so that he could stand in the foreground of the panorama and have his picture taken. It wasn't often that the Philips' afforded themselves time to trek to the countryside, and they couldn't remember the last time that they had done so in spring, therefore Catherine wished to have a portion of the journey captured. While clutching to Fish and Chips, a droopy-eyed Jimmy forced a smile until Catherine and Nigel were each satisfied that they had captured sufficient documentation of their drive into the countryside.

When at last permitted to reposition himself in the rear seat, Jimmy once again managed to doze, but it was only moments later that the car drove up alongside a grand old Tudor on the left. "This is the place!" his mother called out. "I can see the address!" Unless engaged in a shouting match, it was seldom that Catherine Philips displayed such emotion. Nigel wondered, *was she that eager to see her sister, or to be rid or her son?*

After skirting along an impressive stone retaining wall, which was well draped with an abundance of sedum in full bloom with its vibrant yellow stars (mixed in with the sedum was a smattering of spent periwinkle — also, sprouting from a multitude of crevices where mortar had gone missing from in-between the stones were hens and chicks and Irish moss), Jimmy's father pulled into a driveway. After a sharp ascension, which might have confounded any emergency brake, the driveway took the car to the level of the wall, where began a circular drive, which was amply lined with English boxwoods. Nigel rolled down his window in order to treat his senses to the mildly pleasing fragrance of what was his favourite broadleaf evergreen. The car coasted along slowly until having reaching the Broxton's front door. It wasn't but a moment that Nigel had rested the motor, when a woman, whom Jimmy presumed to be his Aunt Delia and whom must have been waiting patiently by the door, came bursting out into the sunshine. She was glowing, and her glow along with her enthusiasm seemed to overwhelm the springtime and all the loveliness that was present as a result. She hadn't made it very far past the door, however, when she came to an abrupt stop, then turned about and called, "Peter, Peter, the Phillips' are here! Colin, Douglas, come quick!" After the driver and passengers uncoiled themselves from the confined cabin,

Delia Broxton went charging toward the car with arms spread wide and appearing as though she might engulf anything in her path. She charged with short choppy steps to accommodate the flimsy white sandals, which were selected to match her flower printed summery frock — a frock which, despite the reckless animation that it was made to suffer, looked lovely. The smacking sounds that were produced by several choppy, hurried steps drew Jimmy's eyes to the ground, where his attention was gathered by his Aunt Delia's feet, which he noticed right away were *normal.* In fact, they were better than normal; they were dainty and pleasurable to look at. For this, he was relieved, but then he felt badly that his mother was forced to walk through life with such deformity. Throughout her fervent exercise, Delia Broxton was calling out, "Catherine, Catherine; it's been much too long! But you look wonderful! Just wonderful!" Delia embraced her sister with much more fervency than was returned. Nevertheless, to embrace her sister after so long a separation caused Delia Broxton's mouth to crease into a grin that was as wide and happy as the grins that were permanently sewn onto the faces of Fish and Chips. Her eyes were all a flutter and she jerked from side-to-side the way a young girl might when hugging a ragdoll. Catherine seemed dissimilar — even inconvenienced by all the bestowed affection, and she remained perfectly upright throughout what was mostly a one-sided exchange. Her lack of display was even too palpable to have escaped a five-year-old, who began to wonder why his mother bothered quarrelling so vehemently in favour of the Broxton's if she didn't feel all that affectionately toward them; but sometimes Nigel and Catherine Philips quarrelled just for the sake of quarrelling or to merely win a point. Championing opposing sides of a given issue was a cornerstone, or perhaps the most defining feature of what had all along been a dysfunctional marriage. After observing his Aunt Delia presented with only a cheek to kiss, and having had her embrace returned in a manner that, at best could be described as half-hearted, Jimmy failed to understand why it should have mattered so much to his mother that he stay with the Broxton's instead of the Hughes'. Ruminating the matter led him to wonder, had he done something wrong? Were the Broxton's awful people to whom he was sent to be punished? No one would mistake Catherine Philips as a warm person, but a sister who hadn't been seen for so long must have been counting on a more affectionate reception. Jimmy couldn't imagine his father acting so distant toward the Hughes'; though he didn't know the Hughes', perhaps they were monstrous. Despite the multitude of notions running round his head, he couldn't fail to acknowledge his Aunt Delia's affable and affectionate nature, especially when having the opportunity to observe it while juxtaposed with his mother customary impassiveness. At last Jimmy concluded, if his Aunt Delia was in any way indicative of the Broxton clan, then he would be most grateful for his mother's victory and enjoy a lovely two weeks in the Cotswolds. What Jimmy wasn't yet aware of, was that his Aunt Delia was his mother's younger sister, and that *she,* or Delia Cromwell as she was known then, had won the heart, or as Catherine Cromwell had put it, smothered Knightsbridge's most eligible bachelor into a hasty submission. Catherine had a difficult time (as an older sister might) watching a sister four years her junior not only wed first, but do it so exceedingly well. Not to suggest that the Philips' were poor — far from it— but the Broxton's wealth was decidedly superior, and Delia was already with twins and living in the countryside by the time Catherine had at last come upon the radar of one Mr. Nigel Philips. Until courted by Nigel Philips, Catherine Cromwell was miserable and had herself well convinced that the world had all but left her behind. Until Nigel, she was lonely and chose to believe that Delia not only moved on with her new husband, but had abandoned her sister. Jimmy was an only child, and therefore hadn't occasion to concern himself with underlining causes for sibling rivalries. He didn't care to dwell *too* long on why his mother's greeting of a sister that she hadn't seen for quite some time lacked any measure of genuine affection. Instead, he chose to dwell on his first impression of Delia Broxton — an impression that led to the notion that she was someone of whom he could easily grow fond — a woman who by all indications was every bit as lovely as the flower printed frock that hung so delightfully on her form.

"Nigel, oh, Nigel, how is my dear brother-in-law?" gushed Delia. "Is my big sister taking good care of you? I can see that she must because you look quite well. And *you* must be Master James! Or would you prefer that I call you Jimmy?"

"Jimmy would be fine, Miss … I mean, Aunt Delia," said Jimmy. Delia Broxton's eyes had a smile all their own and Jimmy found this an even more pleasing feature than her well formed feet.

"Catherine, he's a darling!" Delia continued to gush. "We're going to get on just fine, I can tell." She then knelt down and gave her nephew a big, affectionate squeeze — it was an overt gesture — the intention of which was to dispel any concerns there might have been to the contrary. Delia Broxton's gregarious nature might have overwhelmed one who had never been squeezed or openly fussed over, as relatives are wont to do when receiving the youngest among their clan, but Jimmy didn't seem to mind it all that much. And despite never having spent time with relatives, he would have had no trouble recognising disingenuous affection — after all, he had plenty of practice. However, in his Aunt Delia, he found her clear, bright eyes and affectionate nature not only pleasing but the most genuine of any he had ever encountered. Suddenly Vienna and Budapest, if not having lost their luster entirely, they didn't seem nearly so interesting as his father made them out to be during the first hour of their car ride from Bayswater.

A moment later, Peter Broxton appeared. As Jimmy might have expected, his Uncle Peter was more subdued than the woman of the house. After all, how much celebration could one household endure? Peter Broxton first approached Catherine. Perhaps it was his desire to begin with what he might have anticipated as the more awkward encounter. Next, Peter moved upon Nigel, whom his feelings for were entirely ambiguous. This in no way should suggest, however, that during either encounter Peter Broxton wasn't warm and friendly — he most certainly was — and as Jimmy was easily able to establish upon *their* introduction, his uncle seemed both genuine and kind when acquainting himself. At last the twins, Colin and Douglas Broxton made what one who was given to the practice of understatement might describe as a disinclined appearance. Jimmy was able to acknowledge upon his initial examination, although it was made briefer than was his wish, and by eyes that appeared menacing when glaring back at him, that his cousins weren't quite so identical as were Fish and Chips, but they were close — close enough that at a glance one could easily conclude that they were *entirely* identical. Both boys were rather fair in complexion, their hair was a striking towhead blonde, and they possessed equally striking blue eyes that for reasons unknown to Jimmy appeared to fill with contempt when glaring at him. It wasn't a simple *Look who showed up to spoil out first two weeks of summer vacation* glare. That, Jimmy might have expected and even understood. But the twins' glare was more a *What are you doing here, you scrawny little nothing?* sort of look. *Go back to wherever it was you came from or we'll make you wish you had!* Jimmy felt himself shudder. He pressed Fish and Chips to his person, and for fear his weakened knees might give way and cause him to tumble to the ground, he leaned against the door of the car. The eyes of the Broxton twins narrowed as they appeared to zero in on Fish and Chips. A keen observer might have presumed that tearing the big, round eyes and happy grins off the faces of those well clutched figures was likely to be their first order of business. *If you think those silly little monkeys can protect you, or you, them — think again!* Jimmy hardly expected his cousins to make a big fuss over him the way his Aunt Delia had, or to act as warmly toward him as had his Uncle Peter, but what he hadn't expected was for them to leave him with a sinking heart and wishing for two weeks with his parents in Vienna and Budapest. *Where is my Aunt Delia's smiling eyes?* he had the proclivity to shout out, but the menacing glares of Colin and Douglas Broxton left him weakened in form and mute of tongue. At a glance, Colin and Douglas Broxton appeared quite identical, but when given the advantage of examining them more carefully than a mere glance would permit, it was apparent that Colin (who was the older by minutes) was an inch taller and a touch slimmer. What, too, was apparent, regardless of careful examination as opposed to the benefit of a mere fleeting glance, was that the Broxton twins were beautiful — there was no other word that could accurately describe them — cute or handsome fell dismally short. When seen apart from one another, they appeared as angelic, fair-haired youths too delicate for whatever coarseness the world might have in store. But when together, they seemed to possess a unique single-mindedness — it was as though they were opposite ends of a rarefied entity that derived pleasure in its ability to threaten — a well unified pair capable of all sorts of malevolence, and *this* the young but intuitive Jimmy Philips recognised immediately. Jimmy looked over at his parents and wondered if they, too, had recognised the vileness that emanated from the striking eyes of the Broxton twins, but Catherine and Nigel were too engaged with his aunt and uncle to have noticed any such subtlety. The twins separated on the way to meeting their adult relations — and as they did all the malevolence that only seconds ago caused Jimmy to shudder seemed to dissolve into the midday sunshine; all that remained were two cherub-like faces, which when gazed upon invoked feelings of beauty and innocence — as beautiful and innocent as springtime and the flower printed summery frock that hung on the form of their vivacious mother. Colin advanced toward their Aunt Catherine. Douglas, their Uncle Nigel. There appeared the be no exchange between the twins, be it a ruling or some prevarication with regard to the assignment of introducing themselves, but Colin, who perhaps sensed that Catherine Philips was the more difficult acquaintance, broke first in her direction and did so exceedingly confident in his charms. The twins' welcome of an aunt and uncle they hadn't seen since the earliest days of childhood and of whom they had no clear memory, was remarkably gracious and seemed rehearsed to the extent of being polished — their movements were almost as adroitly choreographed as their words were chosen. Nigel Philips looked over at Delia Broxton. He said nothing, but his nod was a clear indication of his admiration. *Well done* was what he might have said had he chose to communicate verbally. *You're raising two very impressive young men.* The look and nod didn't escape the intuitive five-year-old, who along with his two monkeys further receded from the now well acquainted group. Jimmy clutched to Fish and Chips, and with the benefit of the car door at his back, he managed to remain on his feet. He had the disquieting sensation of one cast adrift and it made him long for the four walls and dark space of his closet. The idle chatter, which at first was careful, but when aided by Delia Broxton's gaiety it became more relaxed, also became an indecipherable murmur to one who felt so far removed. He was dangling out on the fringe of the world — a place he had been to before. But not for the smiling eyes of his Aunt Delia occasionally glancing in his direction and reeling him in, Jimmy might have slipped over the edge, or worse, wished he had. The lonely sea of Jimmy Philips was made more unbearable when he observed the manner in which his mother comported herself with the Broxton twins. Catherine had smiled, and for the first time Jimmy was able to recognise a resemblance between his aunt and his mother. For Jimmy, this was a rare occasion, indeed, to witness a genuine smile appear on the face of his mother. Catherine's smile wasn't the usual calculated gesture to which Jimmy had often been the recipient, but a reaction to an exchange with one of the beautiful boys, and this served to introduce Jimmy to a new plateau of isolation. Jimmy was desperate for his parents to leave — that in their absence he at last might come to understand a world whose dynamics could shift in his favour. Even the malevolence that only moment ago was evident in the eyes of the beautiful twins seemed kinder than the forsakenness he had come to know. Jimmy plummeted further into despair and was certain of having to endure yet more isolation, when his parents were invited to stay for lunch. However, both Nigel and Catherine were quick to insist that they needed to get back on the road.

"We have quite a drive back to Bayswater and we leave bright and early in the morning and Catherine still has plenty of packing to do," said Nigel. "You know how it is?" He directed his words toward Delia, with the hope that the excitable younger sister wouldn't become too insistent or overbearing on the subject of lunch.

"But we haven't seen both of you in so long and we've just gotten started," Delia sulked. "I made so much food …"

Catherine Philips glared at her husband that he might falter at the hands of her younger sister's fervent entreaties but Nigel managed to hold firm to the original reasons stated for their needing to make a hasty departure. "Promise me, dear sister, that you'll send postcards," begged Delia. "I want to see all the fascinating places you intend to visit on your journey. Nigel, you'll see to it, won't you?"

"Will do," he readily agreed, while leaning in the direction of the car.

After Catherine and Nigel drove off, the Broxton's, along with their anxious guest and his two monkeys entered the house. They all marched directly to the dining room and the lunch that was awaiting them and which was already laid out on the table. "All this food," Delia said, rather sulkily.

"I certainly hope you feel that your own family plus Jimmy was worth all this time and effort," said Peter.

"Of course," said Delia. "Nevertheless, it's a pity that Catherine and Nigel weren't able to stay. Well, hopefully I'll get to spend some time with my dear sister when they return."

"A pity, indeed," was Peter Broxton's disingenuous remark. Then he shot his wife a look that was meant to imply that, her sister and brother-in-law surely could have afforded themselves a measly half hour to join them in a lunch — that was *if* they really wished to, but for whatever reason it was settled upon that the idea was a disagreeable one. In an obvious attempt to deflect from her husband's intuitive assessment of her sister and brother-in-law, Delia added, "Jimmy, I prepared the bedroom directly across from mine and your Uncle Peter's; that way if ever you need anything in the night we'll only be three short steps across the hallway; and with tonight being your first night away from home, I would urge you to come to us for anything big or small and not dare to assume it an inconvenience."

"Your Aunt Delia is right, Jimmy," said Peter. "You can't feel too save on your first night spent away from home. But you should find the accommodations comfortable and us Broxton's easy to get along with. Right, boys?"

"Mother, if I'm not mistaken, isn't that the bedroom where last summer our guest, the Duke of Somerset was found strangled?" asked Colin.

"Most definitely that's the bedroom," added Douglas. "In fact, at night when the wind isn't wuthering too loudly you can hear his ghost struggling to get out. And now that it's summertime the nights should be quite still."

"How the poor Duke must have struggled on that night last summer," Colin continued.

"And the awful sounds he must have made! For whatever reason his poor ghost is still struggling to get out, and it must be repeating those same terrible moans because they always sound the same. Perhaps it's doomed to remain there for all eternity? Or perhaps it's waiting for just the right person on whom to take out its vengeance?"

"Could very well be," added Douglas. "I know that if I were strangled to death *my* ghost would *surely* seek vengeance … on anyone!"

"Boys!" cried Delia. Her eyebrow was raised sharply as she appeared poised to dish out a scolding. "My dear sister, your Aunt Catherine, has entrusted us with her only son. I repeat, her *only* son. Let us make certain that we don't return him damaged, or worse, scarred for life by what *you two* may see merely as a harmless prank, but could very well be perceived by one younger and more impressionable, as an act of terror. Jimmy, I'm afraid sometimes your cousins can be downright monstrous, so whenever they begin to act up you're not to pay any attention to them." Turning toward the twins, she added, "Now what do you say we get Jimmy acclimated to the house and grounds, then tomorrow we can drive to Winchcombe and tour Sudeley Castle and the secret garden. I can't think of a more perfect way to begin a summer vacation; and I hear the foxgloves, daisies, bluebells, and poppies are positively bursting in their full bloom and that they make quite a display!"

"The garden can't be much of a secret, Mother, if you already know so much about it," said Colin.

"It was in the castle's earlier days, when inhabited by Queen Catherine, that the garden was a secret," said Delia. "Now it's a tourist attraction waiting to be seen — by *us*."

"Borrrring," crooned Douglas.

"Gardens and castles a bore? I should think not," said Delia. This was one instance when Jimmy wished he wasn't imprisoned by his own introversion — if not, he would have clamoured on behalf of gardens and castles. What could be more fascinating? But he remained quiet and trusted that his Aunt Delia would prevail on the subject of what they would do on the first official day of summer vacation. "I suppose, then, Douglas," she added, somewhat acerbically, "that you would rather be back at school? It shouldn't be *too* much trouble to get you enrolled, if in fact you prefer to forgo your summer vacation."

"As a matter of fact, Mother, Douglas would love for the summer to fly by so that he could be back in school," said Colin. "Haven't you heard? He's in love with Mary Willow. There's no place he'd rather be right now than back at school."

Douglas frowned that his twin had exposed him so. Colin, conversely, seemed quite pleased with the effect his unexpected announcement had on his brother. "Mary Willow?" crooned Delia. "You mean our darling little girl from Bibury, Mary Willow? Perhaps, then, we should ask her to come along. What do you say, Douglas?" A delightfully wicked grin formed on the faces of Colin and Douglas Broxton, that yet again they had succeeded in a ruse — that their single-mindedness had prevailed, and the result would see them spending the first day of summer vacation with Mary Willow. "And how fitting," Delia went on, "that we should tour Sudeley Castle, considered by many to be the most romantic in all of England." Delia's voice became low and mysterious, and she drew everyone closer to the table the way one would when about to reveal a story about ghosts or legends. "Apparitions have been known to wander about the halls of the castle— particularly at night — and when they wandered they've been heard revealing all sorts of secrets from the past — from hundreds of years ago — secrets of treachery that would have gotten people hanged — or worse!" Delia paused in order to give everyone a moment to imagine what might be worse.

This led Douglas to wonder aloud, "Mother, what could be worse than being hanged?"

Continuing in her low, mysterious voice, Delia responded by telling them, "Back in Elizabethan times they had all sort of monstrous ways torturing and executing people, including beheadings!" She put her hands to her throat as though protecting herself from the possibility.

"Mother, you said the object was for us to return Jimmy to your sister undamaged," said Colin. "Well, he looks awfully frightened to me!"

"Oh, Jimmy, dear, I'm so sorry," said Delia, who wasn't aware that she had been tricked by the twins into revealing what was worse than death by hanging, all in order to frighten her young nephew. "From now on I'll stick only to the facts." She composed herself for a moment then added, "Queen Catherine, the last and surviving wife of King Henry VIII, was said to have been seen wandering the halls in search of her lost child. Many over the centuries have reported seeing a tall, slender woman all dressed in green with a likeness to Catherine …"

"Aren't you a bit young to be in love, Douglas?" Peter Broxton interjected. The entire time that Delia was going on about ghosts and castles, Peter was mulling over his son in love. His wondering aloud of the subject came so well after the fact was made known, and in a voice so entirely dissimilar to Delia's story telling voice, that it effectively shattering the current mood in the room. Everyone (including Jimmy) was eager to learn what became of Queen Catherine and her lost child, but they threw themselves against the backs of their chairs and let out a collective sigh. Peter, seemingly ignorant to the fact that he had spoiled the general mood in the room, continued with, "I was more than twice you age when I first fell in love with your mother. A boy your age shouldn't be concerned with that sort of nonsense."

"Nonsense!" shrieked Delia. "Since when is *love* thought of as nonsense?"

"When it involves ten-year-old boys. That's when!" was Peter's retort. He wasn't angry that Douglas was in love — or though that he was — or that Delia found the notion agreeable; he simply subscribed to the theory that the heart of a ten-year-old boy shouldn't be occupied with romantic love; nor should such love be encouraged.

"Romeo and Juliet weren't much older than our dear son and darling Mary Willow," said Delia.

"This is all too true," said Peter, "but as I recall, their situation didn't end very well. Perhaps if they were a little older and more capable of understanding such feelings, they might not have taken their own lives." Delia Broxton's shoulders slumped and her face became a great big frown that was pointing down toward the table. Peter's point was undeniable: When children are forced to comprehend adult feelings, situations are likely to become quite muddled.

"Perhaps had they better understood their feelings, they might have gone on to murder one another, instead," Colin chimed in. Colin seemed perturbed for having been forced to listen to his parents' quibble over whatever love might exist between his twin and Mary Willow, and whether or not is was appropriate. He wanted to move on from it — or rather back to the subject of Queen Catherine, her lost child, and Sudeley Castle, and he as much as demanded that it happen. "Mother, you can't begin a story, especially one so interesting, and then leave us all hanging!" Jimmy was certain that he saw anger flash in Colin's eyes and that it had far less to do with his Aunt Delia abandoning a story and much more to do with Douglas's feeling for Mary Willow. Perhaps Colin also was in love with Mary Willow and was jealous, or worse — tormented. As Jimmy observed, there was no trace of anger in the eyes of Douglas Broxton; he appeared quite serene. This led Jimmy to the notion that, although Colin and Douglas Broxton were well capable of single-mindedness, they were also capable of possessing thought that was entirely separate from one another — thought that not only lacked accord, but that at times could produce conflict. Jimmy now held to the belief that whatever symbiotic malevolence existed between his twin cousins stemmed first from Colin and trickled into Douglas.

"You're right, Colin, dear," said Delia, whose frown disappeared in favour of her smiling eyes. "It's wrong of me to begin a story and then leave everyone hanging. So here goes it. Queen Catherine: Queen Catherine was born Catherine of Aragon and was the youngest surviving child of Ferdinand and Isabelle of Spain. It was the custom in those days that shortly after a child of her station was born, the parents would begin looking for a political match that would be to their advantage …"

"What your mother means," Peter interjected, "when you were high up on the social ladder, particularly royalty, your spouse was chosen for you as early as when you were a small child." "How awful," cried Douglas. "What if the person that was picked for you turned out to be monstrously ugly, or a dwarf? What then?"

"The boy has a point," said Peter. "All that betrothal business must have gotten plenty messy at times, especially when you consider the way royals were given to intermarrying. I'm sure there was an instance or two when someone ended up with a spouse that they considered grossly objectionable. Of course, in the good old UK, a king could simple claim that his wife was guilty of some sort of crime and then have her beheaded. Then afterward he would be free to marry the hottie with whom he had been cheating with all along."

"Father, could we please let Mother finish the story," begged Colin. Peter sighed that his son found his humour so tedious that he preferred a centuries old story of royalty. (Peter found the royals old *and* new to be a humdrum affair.) "Alright, dear," he said to Delia, "carry on. I've been booted off the stage; the audience has spoken and they want you!"

"Thank you, Peter," she began. "As the story goes, Queen Catherine was three years old when she was betrothed to Arthur, the son of Henry VII; Arthur wasn't quite two. Twelve years later, in 1501 when Catherine was sixteen, she made the journey to England. It was said the journey took three months and many storms were weathered, but she arrived safely in Plymouth sometime in October. A month later, she and Arthur were married in St. Paul's Cathedral in London. Unfortunately, their marriage didn't last long; Arthur was dead within a year of sweating sickness …"

"Sweating sickness?" asked Jimmy. He quick put a hand to his mouth, afraid that he had spoken out of turn. The twins shot him a menacing look, that perhaps he had stolen their question.

"Indeed, it was an awful illness, sweating sickness," said Peter. "Its symptoms were headaches, profuse sweating, fever, terrible pain, and difficulty breathing. Often you were dead within a day. But not to worry, the illness never made it beyond the Tudor period; there haven't been any recent outbreaks or isolated cases that I know of."

"Anyway," Delia continued, "Henry VII didn't wish to lose Catherine's dowry, so a year after her husband's death she was betrothed to the king's next son, the future Henry VIII, but Henry wasn't yet of age. By the time young Henry *was* of age, his father was no longer too keen on a Spanish alliance. This left poor Catherine with a very uncertain future. But kings don't live forever, you know, and upon his father's death, Henry VIII's first order of business was to marry Catherine. At last, Catherine of Aragon was Queen of England!"

"And what of the lost child?" wondered Colin. "The one Queen Catherine's ghost is still looking for?" The legend of the lost child seemed a genuine concern for Colin; his eyes swelled with hope that he might learn something that would cause him to feel in some way connected to this lost youth, who centuries later was still sought after. His swollen, hopeful eyes embodied all the innocence that could be wished for childhood days, and such hopefulness also served to provide one already in possession of angelic fair-haired youth incomparable beauty.

"Queen Catherine's first child was a stillborn daughter," Delia went on. "That's when a baby's born dead," she added, while looking Jimmy's way. She assumed correctly that *stillborn* was a new word for him. "A year later, though, Prince Henry was born. There were great celebrations for the birth of the young prince, but the poor little thing, his life was over in less than two months. Next, Catherine miscarried, and that was followed by another short-lived son."

"Not the happiest of stories, I should say," Peter Broxton wryly interrupted. "This Queen Catherine surely wasn't the luckiest of sorts."

"Some of us do have most unfortunate lives," said Delia. "That's why we should all be grateful for whatever blessings come our way; for instance, my dear nephew coming to stay with us."

"But what of the lost child, mother?" Colin again urged to know. It was though, for him, nothing else of the story mattered.

"A few years after the tragedy of Prince Henry, a daughter named Mary was born and she lived!" Delia continued on. "But Henry was growing frustrated that after all this time he still was without a male heir. At last the time had come when Catherine was no longer able to conceive and Henry had fallen in love with Anne Boleyn. Unbeknownst to poor Catherine, Henry petitioned the Pope for an annulment. Eventually, though, Catherine found out about it and so began a long political and legal battle. Catherine sought not only to retain her own position, but also Mary's. But then Anne Boleyn became pregnant. The news compelled Henry to reject the power of the Pope in England and seek the Archbishop of Canterbury to grant the annulment. Well, as they say 'it's a man's world' and things broke overwhelmingly in favour of Henry and against Catherine. Poor Catherine was forced to renounce her title of Queen and then was separated from Mary, when also forced to leave the court. As a child Mary was often ill, but was never permitted to see her mother. How she must have yearned for her and called out. I can't imagine the despair a young girl must feel when often ill and separated from her mother. In less than three years from when they first became separated, Catherine was dead, no doubt of a broken heart."

"How awfully sad," said Douglas. "If I see Queen Catherine's ghost tomorrow at Sudeley Castle I won't be afraid and I'll tell her how sad I feel for her."

"How about you, Jimmy?" asked Delia. "Would you be afraid if you saw Queen Catherine's ghost?"

"I might have, Aunt Delia, if you hadn't told us her story," said Jimmy. "But now I'm sure that I wouldn't be afraid; and I would hope to see her so that I could tell her how very hard I wish that she finds Mary because that would make her happy."

"How very thoughtful, Jimmy," said Delia.

"But whatever became of Mary?" wondered Colin. "What did she do after she grew up?"

"Well, as it turned out," Delia went on, "Edward, Mary's half-brother and son of Henry VIII and Jane Seymour, upon Henry's death became King Edward VI. Years later when Edward became mortally ill, he tried to have Mary removed from the line of succession. As the story goes, there existed religious differences within the family, and I suppose Edward didn't wish to see a Catholic sitting on the throne."

"Ahh, that's right, Queen Catherine was from Spain. You won't find many Protestants over there," Peter chimed in. "I suppose with Mary being a daughter, Henry didn't give a hoot and a half what religion she was, and so he allowed Catherine to raise her Catholic."

"Anyway," Delia continued as though not in the least bothered by the interruption, "Lady Jane Grey was initially proclaimed queen, but Mary assembled forces and had Lady Jane ousted. (Delia was well aware that Mary had Lady Jane Grey beheaded, but decided the well known fact was unbecoming to include in a story told to children.) So as it turned out, dear Colin, Mary, the lost child of Queen Catherine, became Queen of all England!"

"So in actuality," added Peter, "she was Mary I, the one they called ..."

"Mary I, Queen of England and Ireland, my *darling* husband," Delia alertly broke in, and with emphasis. "*That's* what they called her; nothing more. That was her *only* title." Delia didn't wish for Jimmy or the twins to know that Queen Catherine's lost child grew up to become not only Mary I, but was dubbed *Bloody Mary,* for having hundreds of Protestant leaders executed, including the Archbishop of Canterbury. "Now let's call darling Mary Willow and make our arrangements for tomorrow, shall we." The mere mention of Mary Willow brought a smile to the faces of all three boys, but Douglas's smile was the broadest.

"Queen Mary I; was she the one for whom the rhyme *Mary, Mary, quite contrary,* was written? Or would that have been Mary, Queen of Scots?" wondered Peter. As was often the case, Peter's wondering aloud came too long after the fact. Delia had moved on to the business of contacting Mary Willow, and as long as Delia was involved with anything that had to do with Mary Willow, neither Colin nor Douglas cared which Queen Mary was the notable contrarian. Jimmy had a passing interest, but was much more interested in the Mary who was on the other end of the telephone.

****

To go with its rooms and hallways of which there was abundance, the Broxton Tudor had a multitude of nooks and crannies, which aside from lending to a home already rich in charm, had no real practical purpose, especially with only a family of four occupying its space. For Jimmy, though, this was a great source of fascination to know that one could hide themselves away, and if so inclined they could remain hidden away for days. However, when his Aunt Delia came to tuck him into bed, he wasn't entertaining any thoughts of where he might hide from his cousins should they display any inclination to misbehave toward him or tear to shreds his monkeys; nor was he considering Queen Catherine or any other apparitions that might be wandering about Sudeley Castle. Nor for that matter, with any measure of delight, was he mulling over the secret garden with its profusions of foxgloves, daisies, bluebells, and poppies. The only thing, or rather, *person*, that Jimmy was unable to pry from his thoughts once he was alone in his room, aside from the strangled Duke of Somerset and his ghost, was Mary Willow. Once Jimmy was through performing a comprehensive search of his room and was satisfied that he wasn't cohabitating with a strangled Duke, who may or may not have ever existed, or his ghost, which he wouldn't have been able to see no matter, all that was left to do was to wonder about a girl whose acquaintance he had yet to make. *And what could be lovelier,* he lay in bed wondering to himself, *than a girl named Mary Willow?* After all, his Aunt Delia kept referring to her as

Darling Mary Willow. And how lovely was Aunt Delia, with her smiling eyes, long flowing hair which she wore as carefree as a child, and well formed feet? If only his mother could possess some of Aunt Delia's loveliness. He right away dismissed his mother from his thoughts in favour of repeating over and over again in his mind the name *Mary Willow, Mary Willow, Mary Willow*. The name itself lent to enchantment — it was like something from out of a fairy tale ... *Mary Willow, Mary Willow*. And how fitting that tomorrow they would be visiting an old enchanted castle, thought of by Aunt Delia as being the most romantic ... *Mary Willow, Mary Willow*. It seemed wholly unbefitting to simply say *Mary* or *Willow;* not even in his mind was Jimmy able to separate the two words, which when said together or merely thought of, seemed to possess a measure of loveliness and poetry. Indeed, Mary Willow was either the girl who was lost and wandering alone in the woods at the onset of nightfall and was praying for her knight or prince to come and rescue her — or, she was the heroine of a fairy tale. Jimmy was given to these imaginings until at last too tired to hold a thought in his head. When morning came, Jimmy creased his eyes open just enough to see the earliest rays of sunlight breaking through the window. Those early rays were a clear and illuminating indication that he was still in bed, not on the floor of a dark closet, for there had been no angry voices from which he needed to escape. He made it through his first night away from home having slept straight through until morning without once having to tiptoe across the hallway and disturb his Aunt Delia or Uncle Peter. He felt proud of this modest accomplishment, and his mouth creased into a drowsy smile that indicated as much. However, no sooner his eyes widened and he rouses himself to where he was fully awake, he became quite agitated. He tossed the bed pillows about, and with vigor he shook the blanket. Then, as if struck by an unsettling notion, he became fearful and so he stayed kneeling in the middle of the bed — he remained quite still and without making a peep. He even ceased from breathing for fear someone or some*thing* was lurking about the room. He permitted his eyes to travel about — they were thorough in combing every inch of the floor, walls, and ceiling. But there was yet the closet; he couldn't rest his fears until it too was searched. He jumped down from the bed, scampered over to the closet, flung open the door, and then went lunging back to the bed. From the middle of the bed he stretched his neck in order to peer into the closet and then shakily called, "Is anyone in there?" When he at last determined that his room was quite free of apparitions, monsters, or anything else that could cause a young boy any measure of distress, he ran to the window to see if what, or whoever was responsible for his current predicament was still hovering about. Of course, it was a spare bedroom that Jimmy was occupying. The room was seldom used, and who knows when last the sash was disturbed; it was century old wood that had endured the shrinkage and swelling of a century's worth of seasons and was no doubt warped. Jimmy struggled mightily — he pried and pulled and pushed — he even banged on the sash without a thought to whom he might be disturbing so early in the morning. He wasn't well endowed with an ample degree of masculine strength, but he wasn't short on determination, and it was his determination that enabled him to overpower a century old sash. It was that time of morning when the dew was still thick and the air was quite cool. At once, Jimmy felt the coolness and moisture on his face. He tilted his head toward the ground just below the window. All that could be seen was undisturbed shrubbery — no evidence that anyone had escaped from his room — not by way of the window. He looked off in the distance, but all was peaceful — the heavily dewed grass, flower beds, and groundcovers too appeared undisturbed. Next, he had the notion to investigate what could be lurking underneath his bed, but hesitated, until arriving at the decision that raising the bed skirt to peer into a dark area was too frightening a proposition — even more frightening that the closet. With some trepidation he sauntered over to the door which he cracked open to see if any of the Broxton's were up and about. All was quiet and so he waited while peering through the slightly ajar door. It might have been a minute maybe ten, he was too out-of-sorts to accurately measure how much time elapsed before he watched his Uncle Peter emerged from his bedroom well dressed and looking very prepared for the day. Jimmy wouldn't bother his Uncle Peter about his predicament; he would wait for his Aunt Delia. He peered around the doorjamb, his eyes following his uncle until he disappeared after reaching the end of the hallway. When all was clear, he went tiptoeing across the hallway and rapped gently on the door.

"Is that you, Jimmy?" asked Delia; her voice was still groggy from sleep.

"Aunt Delia, could you please come to my room?" urged Jimmy. "I'm afraid something has happened — something very strange."

"I'll be right there, Jimmy," she said. "I just need a minute to pull myself together." Jimmy went tiptoeing back to his room, where he sat on the edge of the bed, though he didn't dare dangle his legs; he kept his whole person atop the mattress while he waited. When Delia Broxton, in her nightclothes and with hair that was messy from sleep entered her nephew's bedroom, she saw at once that he was quite out-of-sorts.

"Aunt Delia, I'm afraid the Duke of Somerset was in my room last night — or, at least his ghost was." This, Jimmy declared as if there was no other explanation for his current condition. "When I woke up I was soaking wet and then I found this bowl of water on my nightstand. I'm certain it wasn't there last night before I fell asleep. And now both my monkeys are missing!"

Delia glanced at the bowl on the nightstand, and what followed was a sigh of exasperation. "Oh, Jimmy, I'm so sorry," she went on to say, "but the Duke of Somerset wasn't in your room last night, nor was his ghost; though I wish he had been, you might have fared better. You see, I'm afraid that you've become the victim of a most idiotic prank."

"A prank?" asked Jimmy.

"Yes, it's a trick that older boys play on younger boys to make them feel unsettled," Delia told him. Delia spared Jimmy the knowledge that his nightclothes weren't soaked with the water from the bowl, but that in fact it was the water from the bowl that caused him to urinate all over himself. She drew him a bath and assured him that when he was through and had reported to the breakfast table, his monkeys would be there waiting for him, and that never again would he wake in such a condition. "Peter, you must have a talk with your sons," said Delia. "They've behaved positively monstrously toward my dear little nephew."

"Uh oh, what have they done now?" Peter wondered; though his wondering didn't occur without him also rolling his eyes, and this was done in a manner that would lead any observer to believe that his wife was given to frequent exaggeration.

"It seems that sometime during the night, poor Jimmy became the victim of the old hand-in-the-bowl trick!" cried Delia.

"Really?" said Peter, as though he was altogether overwhelmed by the incredulity that his two fair-haired angels were not only capable of, but even knew of the old hand-in-the-bowl trick. "You mean like I did to ol' Willoughby back when we were at the university?" Peter leaned back in his chair, and a wicked smile began to form on his face. It was if remembering the juvenile event brought about a measure of satisfaction that hadn't been felt in years but was missed.

"Yes, Peter," acknowledged Delia with a note of condescension, "just like you did to *ol'* Willoughby when you were back at the university; however, *ol'* Willoughby was an adult, as you were, or at least you two were both old enough to have made such a claim, whereas Jimmy is a dear and sensitive little boy, not at all ready to become the victim of such pranks."

"He *is* quite the sensitive sort, isn't he?" Peter acknowledged. "One might even suppose that he's been bullied a good bit in his five years. It makes one wonder how things *really* are over in ol' *Bays*water."

"Peter, what are you suggesting?" cried Delia.

"Don't you find it just a bit odd that Jimmy is five-years-old, closer to six, in fact, and that this is the first time we've met him?" Peter was fully aware that this was an issue that caused Delia a great deal of distress, but one that was never openly discussed. "Are you really blind to the fact that we've never once been invited to Bayswater?" With Jimmy finally at the Broxton home and now becoming an issue, Peter seized upon the opportunity to say all that he had been wanting to say on the subject of the Philips'. He intended to take full advantage. "We've invited them to our home several times in the past, for every holiday and other occasions, and each time they've either vacillated — they're *good* at that— or cited some lame excuse for why they needed to back out at the last minute — and at *that* they're even better. For crying out loud it's only a two-hour drive! And Catherine is your older sister. You'd think she would've wanted to show off her son at the first opportunity." Delia's eyes travelled to the floor. She tried to poise herself, that at last she was about to receive an earful regarding the Philips' and all their suspected peculiarities. "I have a good hunch that Catherine and Nigel aren't traveling to Vienna and Budapest to vacation, but to see whether or not they can salvage their marriage; or worse, they've dumped poor Jimmy in our laps and never intend to return!"

Disregarding the latter part of Peter's last remark, Delia wondered aloud, as if reaching to establish a case for why she believed him to be wrong: "If that was the case, then why not travel to some place more romantic, like Paris, or Venice? I've never known Budapest to be a destination for rekindling a tired marriage. It certainly wouldn't be *my* first choice."

"The reason they haven't gone to Paris or Venice," Peter maintained, with a measure of condemnation, "is because *we've* already been there. We have *not yet,* however, been to Vienna or Budapest. No doubt your sister if nothing else, wants to return with bragging rights."

"Oh, Peter," cried Delia, "do you really believe that my dear sister is that shallow?"

"Whether you choose to acknowledge it or not," Peter went on, "very quietly and in her own strange way, your *dear sister* has been competing with you since the day we met. I'd be willing to wager my last pound, if ever I became so unfortunate, that we were deprived of Jimmy infancy and the following years because she thought the poor boy wouldn't hold up well in comparison with Colin and Douglas."

"Oh, Peter," Delia again cried out.

"Why, good morning, Jimmy," called Peter. He made certain that his cheery a.m. greeting was loud enough to have drowned out Delia's cry. "Your breakfast and monkeys young man, just as your trusty Aunt Delia had promised."

"Feeling better now, Jimmy," asked Delia.

"Much better. Thank you," Aunt Delia," he replied. The warmth and sincerity of Aunt Delia's smiling eyes helped put the matter of Colin and Douglas's execution of the old hand-in-the-bowl trick and two kidnapped monkeys, if not behind, than momentarily aside.

Delia glanced up at the clock on the wall. "I better go and wake Colin and Douglas. Darling Mary Willow will be here any minute."

The mere mention of Mary Willow caused Jimmy's droopy eyes to brighten. And despite his cousins, whose antics thus far were a clear message that he should expect two weeks of utter torment, he greatly anticipated Sudeley Castle, its secret garden, and his first meeting of a girl whom Aunt Delia never failed to refer to as *Darling* Mary Willow. "I wonder if one of us will spot Queen Catherine?" Jimmy seemed genuinely hopeful of the possibility.

"You never know," said Peter, who laid down his newspaper, abandoned the remaining coffee in his cup and was off.

When the Broxton twins appeared at the breakfast table they sneered at Jimmy, but with Peter already gone and Delia otherwise occupied preparing breakfast, their intimidating tactics, as was often the case, went unnoticed.

"I trust your first night was a pleasant one," said Colin. Both he and Douglas wore satisfied grins, and then erupted into a chorus of laughter that could only be described as both menacing and antagonistic. Jimmy recoiled and clutched his monkeys. The twins stifled their laughter when their mother returned to the table.

"We're going to have such a lovely day together," she said.

"In a secret garden that's no secret at all," Colin drolly added. The remark drew a chuckle from everyone, including Jimmy, who figured it was prudent to acknowledge his cousin's wit. The doorbell rang. Jimmy knew at once that it must be Mary Willow, and so he set aside Fish and Chips, and then sat up as straight and tall as his limited figure allowed.

****

Jimmy continued peering over his Kafka volume; he had been spying on the quartet of female students — the same quartet that in the past left him a tortured wreck, when out of the corner of his eye he saw Brian come out from behind the counter and make his way toward the boorish man who had been droning on and on about the United States and "Operation Desert Storm" and how fossil fuels will be the eventual cause of World War III if not Armageddon. In the past Ebenezer's Coffee House had been the venue of many a political discussion — discussions that had even leaned toward debate, but never had anyone mounted their high horse and carried on about a particular issue to the extent that their voice drowned out the rest of the coffee house. Jimmy wasn't certain whether the fellow was attempting to incite a revolution or was daring some bold coffee lover to challenge his ideas. Whichever, Brian appeared determined to accost the man with regard to his boorish behaviour. Jimmy was afraid the result of Brian's action would escalate into a scene that would send Ebenezer's patrons spilling out onto the sidewalk — an early and abrupt dismissal from their late Sunday morning routine. Despite Brian's determined look, to Jimmy's astonishment *and* relief, he merely presented the boorish man and his quiet companion (who had all along had remained with his nose in the newspaper) with a fresh cup of coffee. "My very first shipment of Tanzania Peaberry," Brain proudly stated. "And I would like you two to be the first to try it. And since you will, in fact, be the first to try it, I expect an honest and detailed critique." A perplexing but thoughtful look came over the face of the boorish man — it was the sort of look that often occurs when one has given a subject or object all their fervor, but then something else of interest arises and throws them off balance, leaving them torn on where their focus should be aimed. The man's companion, who had his nose in the newspaper, had no such dilemma. He folded up the newspaper and was most grateful that Brian's generosity, at least for the moment, had silenced his friend. At last, a smile formed on the face of the boorish man that he had the distinction of being the first recipient of Brian's newest flavour of coffee and that he was respected to the extent that he was required to supply a *detailed critique*. As the men sipped, Brian explained that peaberries were the result of coffee fruit developing a single oval bean instead of the usual pair of flat-sided beans, and that botanists have observed that a peaberry develops only when one of two ovaries in the flower is pollinated. "Arabica coffee is self-pollinating, so peaberries are a sign of infertility. Most coffee mills don't bother weeding out the peaberries, but those who are into peaberries use special screens to weed them out. My friends, you are drinking pure, one hundred percent peaberry coffee straight from Tanzania!"

"Smooth and mellow," said the boorish man.

"With a hint of chocolate, too," his companion added. Both men agreed that it was every bit as tasty as the Sumatra that they had been enjoying and hoped it would become part of the rotation of coffees that get served daily. Jimmy smiled admiringly at the crafty manner in which Brian handled the boorish man and what potentially could have escalated into a volatile situation, and all it cost him was two cups of coffee — wholesale! Jimmy even managed to catch Brian's eye despite that his face was mostly hidden behind Kafka. Brian's smirk was subtle but its message was clear: *It's true what they say about dogs; they'll forget all about whatever it was they were barking at as long as you show it some food.*

Jimmy shifted his eyes over to where only moments ago the quartet of young women had been sitting — the same young women he had hoped would have thought enough to accost him following his conversation with Brian — or, when hopefully having noticed him entering Ebenezer's wielding a Kafka volume. To his dismay, though, they had gone — upped and disappeared sometime during Brian's attempt to educate the boorish man and his companion on the virtues of peaberries; Jimmy never heard any zipping up of coats, shuffling of feet, nor any chairs being pushed back in place, all which *had* occurred. *If only that boorish fellow hadn't distracted me*, Jimmy thought. But who was he kidding; had the boorish man not garnered but a shred of his attention, the quartet, just as they had in summer while sporting ponytails, sun kissed shoulders, and toe-loop sandals would have waltzed out of the Ebenezer's Coffee House without having given him a second look. Jimmy set down his volume and went to order a second French mug. When he returned to his seat in the corner, no longer was he hiding behind his book and peeping — or, as *he* preferred to think of it ... observing. This time he began to read. *To hell with the girls and "Desert Storm" and peaberries*, he thought with a measure of disdain. He pretended that none of those subjects mattered — that he didn't care, and so he began to pour over Kafka, reciting passages in his mind as though performing them on a stage —

and on that imagined stage he became a mesmerising orator and gateway for those desperately thirsting for a darker sense of reality. It wasn't until he finished his mug that once again he bothered to peer over the book. The coffee house had turned over entirely; he recognised no one. He watched Brian wielding his Aussie charm on who for Jimmy were perfect strangers. He felt further removed than ever before when within the wall of Ebenezer's, and this imagined distance caused him to feel a despairing sense of abandonment, or worse, a queer sense of isolation. Either was unbearable; so with his plummeting spirit, he closed up his book and decided that taking to the cold streets of Bloomsbury was the friendlier proposition. It was one o'clock — eighteen hours yet until Jimmy needed to report to the hospital. However, tomorrow he would not be reporting as part of a capable staff as he had so many times in the past. Instead, tomorrow he would be reporting as a patient. How many times in the past had he held the hands of those bearing the weight of anxiety and distress that often accompanies being a patient? How many times had he told those who were frightened not to be afraid and that they should have every confidence in a favourable result. But now it was his turn to be admitted and to understand just how weighty anxiety and distress could be. Eighteen hours. Eighteen long hours. How would he fill them? What would he do? Where could he go? His first inclination was to drink himself into a coma, but then he considered the likely prospect of sleeping through the alarm all the way until the afternoon and missing his appointment, and who knows how long he'd have to wait for another. So instead, he tore his hair from the ponytail in which it was gathered, shook his modest chestnut mane and went walking in the cold January air. He would walk until the verge of collapse — or so he decided — and even then he would press onward until bleary-eyed and incapable of rational thought. He would walk until so utterly exhausted that he couldn't care less if the next day he was to be executed, never mind that his gathering storm of fear was over having surgery. Throughout the day he would find throngs of people in which to lose himself — his random thoughts dissolving into their bustle and murmur. However, the same reoccurring thought kept invading and would chase away all the random thoughts he had and thus ruin any chance he had of attaining the tenuous or false sense of peace to which he aspired. The thought being: It was mid-January and yet another Christmas, another New Year, another holiday season had come and gone without a word or card from Catherine and Nigel. Both Jimmy and his parents stopped trying to understand one another long ago, and the prospect of discovering or manufacturing common ground from which a relationship could flourish no longer existed. Nevertheless, it bothered Jimmy that Catherine and Nigel Philips, despite the dysfunction and damage that routinely flourished from their union, and which Jimmy detested and on many levels was glad to be rid of, were able to let go of him so easily. As a child he had always imagined, had all three of them been in a lifeboat weighted with too many supplies, good old Catherine and Nigel wouldn't think twice about casting him adrift. That was the story of Jimmy Philips — a boy born into the world only to be cast adrift upon a lonely sea that seemed ever eager and was always threatening to swallow him up. At times he even wished for it to happen. Delia Broxton had sent Jimmy Christmas card. Then again, she always had — rarely did she miss a holiday and would often call, and Jimmy was always thoughtful and reciprocated. He so enjoyed talking with his Aunt Delia; she had such a lovely voice and always had kind words to say. Though, as the years marched on the phone calls became less frequent, but it was more Jimmy's doing than Delia's. There was much of Jimmy's childhood, both in Bayswater and the Cotswolds that was so disturbing that it ruined any chance he had for peace in his adulthood. With these remembrances came bouts of melancholy which caused him to further retreat from the world. He would spend one ponderous day after another organising his thoughts onto paper and then he would mail them off to his Aunt Delia. So instead of chirpy phone calls, which earlier on had been the custom, their correspondences were done with thoughtful letters. Delia always read Jimmy's letters alone, for she knew that his words, whether at the beginning, middle, or end would cause her to weep. Jimmy had an open invitation to the grand old Tudor in the Cotswolds, but often declined.

The Cotswolds had become home to nearly as many bad memories as Bayswater. Jimmy never went anywhere near the place on holidays; he figured that Colin and Douglas were sure to be there, but from time to time, he did manage to drop in on Aunt Delia. He would usually come by unannounced; he preferred it that way and would make the two-hour drive with no guarantee that Colin and Douglas wouldn't be there. He would wait in the car until it was determined that his cousins were scarce, and then he would go and ring the bell. If it was determined otherwise, he chalked it up as a pleasant drive in the country, where he was alone with his thoughts while having the benefit of fresh air.

Jimmy had always believed that it was by some awful twist of fate that he was born the son of Catherine and Nigel Philips and that Colin and Douglas were born the sons of Delia and Peter Broxton. *It was suppose to be the other way around! God made a mistake! An awful, egregious error! One that can never be corrected!* Those were words that he wrote once when in a fit of anger, but wisely elected not to mail them off to his Aunt Delia. Though he so dearly wanted Delia to know how badly he desired to belong to her, and also to intimate to her how undeserving Colin and Douglas were. But how does one say such a thing? He read the angry words over and over again until he concluded that the risk of how his words might get interpreted was too great, and Delia Broxton was not a bridge that he would dare burn. Without her there'd be no one left in the world to whom he could pour out his heart, so he crumpled up the paper and tried to masturbate his way to a better humour.

Jimmy pounded the cold sidewalks of Bloomsbury, from Bedford Square to Tavistock Square to Brunswick Square, until quite unintentionally he discovered himself standing in front of the Church of Christ the King. He had a notion to enter, if no other reason than to appreciate the physical warmth it might provide, but the early English Neo-Gothic edifice and confines begged that one enter for the purpose of genuflecting and to contemplate, two things Jimmy had no desire to do. At last, he decided that it was offensive to enter a house of worship with the same base motives as would a homeless wretch, and that there would be plenty of other places along his ramble with which to achieve warmth — if that was all he so desired. It was four o'clock in the afternoon, the sun was hanging low and causing the air, which all day long had been plenty cold, to possess an extra bite. Fifteen more hours for which to account. Jimmy's fingers were frozen, his face was numb, yet still he refused to enter the church. *How many people on the earth*, he wondered, *were forced to exist in an endless and unforgiving wilderness called 'the streets of London in winter.' How dare I enter God's house only for the purpose of warmth! How dare I even think it!* He ignored the cold and journeyed on until he came upon Lord John Russell's, a pub he walked by numerous times in the past, but had never thought to enter. Given his current mood he figured a drink would be more useful to him than prayer. It took a moment for Jimmy's eyes, which were bleary from the cold, to grow accustom to the warmth of Lord John Russell's, which was supplied by an efficient heater along with the heat emanating from an ample supply of humanity. Soon after he rubbed his eyes to some level of clarity, he noticed that the pub was crawling with students from the university. This prompted his eyes to go roving the area in search of his female quartet, whom he began hoping had traded a popular coffee house in favour of what appeared to be an equally popular pub. During his survey of the area, which caused him to become more preoccupied then was realised, twice he needed to be asked what he was drinking. Both times he stammered and vacillated and was altogether vague — his words were as vague as did appear his countenance. His thoughts, though, were anything but vague. He wished to catch the eye of just one member of the *quartet* and to see in that eye a trace of recognition. He would know for sure, then, that he had been taken notice of, and that he was largely ignored in favour of the importance of the studies they brought along, their private female conversations, not to mention their pursuit of Brian. It was in this mother of all delusions that he took comfort. After all, a pub was not a coffee house — the element, the dynamics, everything was different, and these differences seemed to lend to a more favourable result, or so he believed. But the quartet was not spotted. Jimmy had searched very inch of Lord John Russell's twice, but the popular pub wasn't a destination of the quartet, at least not on this particular Sunday afternoon. Moments later, he was presented with a mug of Old Speckled Hen that he had no memory of ordering. Jimmy wasn't much of a beer drinker, but just last week overheard a co-worker raving about this particular brew, mainly for its remarkable smoothness. "It was so smooth I had to keep reminding myself that I was actually drinking beer," the co-worker had stated. Somehow amid all his stammering and vacillating the words Old Speckled Hen must have wiggled their way free and made it to the surface. Jimmy sipped amid the pub's clamour, and as best as he could tell no one was droning on about ill-advised Wars or bad politics. For this he was grateful, as otherwise he would have felt compelled to make every effort to listen, if for no other reason than to ascertain whether his own opinions on such matters were in accordance with the pub going public, but he had already received quite an earful at Ebenezer's and wasn't eager for more.

Empty chatter was spewed about and Jimmy allowed the onslaught of verbiage to travel throughout the room without any effort on the part of his ears to try and catch them, and all the while he remained with his eyes fixed on the dark words of Kafka. He wasn't actually reading but merely staring at the words — or in other words, he was occupying space and breathing air. He became just as he had so many times in the past when in a public place — a nonentity. Jimmy departed Lord John Russell's at seven o'clock. Only twelve more hours to go. It was dark and frigid, and on the streets at that dark, frigid hour on a Sunday folks were scarce. Without the benefit of the sun, the air *was* and *could* be described, if one were to be kind, as unfriendly. Nevertheless, he walked swiftly through the cold, and both his swiftness and the cold made him feel uncommonly alert and alive. He welcomed his frozen cheeks and eyes, both which stung from the bitter cold of a London January. His eyed produced tears which froze before they had a chance to roll down his cheek — or, perhaps it was his frozen cheeks that caused him not to feel his tears; he couldn't be sure of which. Through the dark, desolate night the smallish figure of a soul often thought of by his professional peers as an androgynous sprite journeyed on, step after step, until at last he reached his dwelling. He became weak in his knees and light in his head once he stepped inside, for in doing so he allowed the cold air in his lungs and his frozen skin to meet the warmth within the walls. He rushed over to a seat into which he readily collapsed, and there he waited for his skin to thaw and his bleary eyes to settle and focus. When at last he established that he was in reasonable possession of his wits, he permitted his eyes to rove about a dwelling that he decided was a complete falsehood and misrepresentation of who he was. This wasn't the first instance that such a notion was arrived at, but it was the first time that Jimmy felt poised or empowered to act upon it. *Who lives here?* he wondered aloud to himself. *What poor, pathetic soul dares to exist within these walls? Who is the occupier of this space? Show him to me!* Jimmy ran to a mirror into which he glared with nothing less than contempt. He allowed his contempt to simmer and froth until having reached a peak, at which time he smashed the mirror with both fists, though only managed to lacerate one. With aggression that was frantic, but within the realm of understanding its purpose, he went from room to room taking pictures down from walls and ridding the area of all its trinkets and artefacts. "To hell with the girls from the coffee shop!" he shouted as he went about tossing articles into bags. The quartet, with their delicate charms and chirpy conversations had owned far too many of his nights —

nights which saw him erupt with delight, but then afterward plummet into despair. "To hell with Catherine and Nigel; may their next twenty-five years be just as fucking jolly as the first!" No longer would Catherine and Nigel Philips hold any part of Jimmy hostage — there would be no more dominion held — he would break free entirely. "To hell with that boorish imbecile, who was droning on about America!" Other than the fact that he was obnoxious, Jimmy had no viable reason to include the boorish man into what was an emotional paradigm from which he intended to divorce himself, but he was on a roll going room to room deconstructing his life and figured why not condemn as many people to hell as possible before having collapsed and was all out of breath. Besides, the boorish man was one more example of the countless who had gone before with the wielding of opinions deemed worthy of airing in public space, and Jimmy, on this frigid Sunday in January, decided that had heard enough. At last, he stood back, and with his heart thumping in his chest he gazed at the bare walls, empty shelves, and clear table tops. The place where he slept and ate and dwelled looked like a tornado had sucked everything into its vortex. By the door, bags containing what thus far had been the life of Jimmy Philips were lined up and ready to be discarded. But Jimmy wasn't through; there was still more work to be done. He made for the cabinet underneath the sink and located a bucket, scrub brush, and some detergent. *Monday, January 14th is as good a day as any to be reborn,* he thought. He attacked the floors with the same frantic aggression that he had asserted upon the walls, shelves, and table tops. He would scrub them free of the stain that thus far had been his life, and tomorrow and every day thereafter, he would christen them with feet that would walk through the world in such a way that he would be entirely unrecognisable to all those who for years looked passed him. It was one o'clock; only six more hours to go. At last spent, Jimmy crawled into bed. He reached over to his nightstand and took hold of the only artefact that was permitted to remain. Within the picture frame was evidence of a bright summer afternoon — as lovely a summer's day as there had ever been. In the background of the photograph was the secret garden of Sudeley Castle, with its profusion of foxgloves, bluebells, daisies, and poppies. In the foreground stood five-year-old Jimmy, Colin and Douglas Broxton, and Mary Willow. In one hand Jimmy was clutching to Fish and Chips. His free hand was occupied by the tender hand of Mary Willow.

"My dear, sweet Mary Willow," he cried, pressing the photograph to his chest. "Why did you have to leave me? How different it all might have been. How very different my life's journey would have been had you been permitted to remain in the world."

CHAPTER II
THE CLOCKMAKER'S SON

Finn stretched out his arms and tossed back his head in order to better look skyward. He walked slowly and in a swerving sort of manner and it caused him to appear as though he might have been slightly inebriated or was simply moving about for the sake of moving. A man with no particular destination was how he appeared — at least no destination that he was in any hurry to get to. However, on his face he wore a grin indicative of one experiencing a fair measure of satisfaction. There was no trace of wickedness or deviance to his grin, it was purely idyllic, like that of a man welcoming a new day by inviting the sun to shine down on him and infuse his weary body with all its celestial properties and having every confidence that such harmony between man and nature would occur. However, not only was Finn well rested, but by then he had already been up for hours. Those around him, many of whom were shuffling about in every which direction, for they were in the habit of keeping quite busy as a matter of their daily ritual, took a moment to looked at him and wonder. This, Finn had suspected, but gave their wondering no regard — at least none that would prompt him to tilt his head forward and spoil his period of idyll. Mr. Charles Finn was having what is often referred to as *'a moment'* and intended to remain in that moment for as long as his ample neck would support his head in such a position. He further reached and stretched as far as his arms would allow — his eyes were wide open, as wide as they could go, taking in the blueness of the sky, the garish brightness of the sun, and the lacey white clouds — their randomness and beauty were scattered throughout the atmosphere. Were he to continue pointing his face skyward, and as such, remain throughout the day, he could go on pretending that he was at a ball park with the smell of hotdogs filling his nostrils and making his mouth water, or lying on a blanket in the park alongside Caroline, the only woman he ever loved that could make it all the way from the opening bars to the finales of both Bruckner and Mahler without dozing— *and*, like himself, discovered her soul when first listening to Shostakovich's 11th Symphony. But Caroline was also the only woman ever to scorch Finn's poor heart. *Oh, Caroline, where are you now? What might you be doing today?* Finn wondered. *Are you on some golf course, just out for a drive, or at a matinee?* He chuckled at his lame attempt at poetry and it caused others nearby to wonder at what he was chuckling.

It was Saturday — a day that Finn and Caroline usually spent together. In his mind he permitted himself to run through the litany of all their old Saturday activities and to revisit all their old Saturday haunts — but mostly he tried to imagine, to which activity or haunt a new love interest was being treated; he couldn't yet allow himself to believe that with a new lover might come new activities and new haunts. He took great comfort in the notion that Caroline was dragging Bruckner, Mahler, and Shostakovich into her next relationship — that she was enlightening a new love interest with that which he had once enlightened her. To believe this was more than a comfort, but affirmation that quite possibly Caroline hadn't moved on so easily as once was suspected. He hadn't taxed his mind *too* much with the reminiscences of Saturdays past or those of the current, before he remembered that the east coast of the United States was a world away, and that Saturday had either yet to arrived or had already past — he wasn't sure which. This prompted him to concoct scenarios for whatever Caroline might have done Friday or is about to do Sunday.

Caroline was a needy sort — at least she seemed so in the beginning, and Finn was always of the notion that her neediness in due course would provide the relationship its undoing; nothing like writing the end of a story while you're supposed to be enjoying the journey. However, as it turned out, it was Finn's own neediness that paved the way to the love affair's eventual demise. What he needed, no woman *could* or was *prepared* to give, and as a matter of routine he began to wrestle with questions that couldn't be answered. He tirelessly went in search of a *"path"* or *"way"* that would allow his soul to flourish without there existing the possibility of a spiritual dead-end. He became existential in his accepted wisdom and adopted philosophies that caused him to become ponderous and plaintive for days on end. Caroline was patient and believed that Finn was going through some sort of phase that would eventually pass. A full year had gone by, though, when Caroline concluded that she hadn't miscalculated the length of a *typical phase*, but that Finn, in fact, had made a paradigm change and not necessarily for the better, and moreover he wasn't about to return anytime soon, if at all. At last, Caroline freed herself from a man who had become an emotional burden. She wasn't bitter, only sad, and she wished Finn well and hoped that the *"path"* or *"way"* he sought would soon get discovered and led to a life of fulfilment.

Finn's neck was beginning to stiffen. The sun, which for a while accommodated his folly and thus had aided in producing many curious stares from those shuffling about the camp, had moved more directly overhead and was causing his eyes to sting and then tear. No longer could he imagine the ball park and the aroma of hotdogs, less the nearness of Caroline and her lovely scent. No longer could he transport himself to anywhere in the world he wished to be by simply looking up at the sky — the great equalizer. As long as it's only the sky that we see, we can pretend to be anywhere more favourable than where we are at the present time. Finn tilted his head forward and wiped his eyes. Once his eyes were clear and he had brought his swerving, meandering gait to a halt, he discovered that he was pointed to the north, as his eyes were resting on the peaks of the mountainous region of Jebel Marra. At last, he brought his eyes nearer to the ground and the city of tents and the displaced multitude that dwelled within the tents. He was back. Both his body and mind had fully returned to what he once dubbed *hell on earth* — Darfur, Sudan. "Back from our little trip, are we?" asked Owen Somersby, an Englishman and fellow teacher with whom Finn worked at the schoolhouse nearby the Kalma refugee camp.

His chirpy inquiry was followed by a friendly pat on the back. "Unfortunately," replied Finn.

"Am I to take it, then, that you had a pleasant journey in a pleasant place and that you had someone pleasant whom with to share the experience?" wondered Somersby. "Perhaps you were the beneficiary of a calm sea and prosperous voyage?"

"No one goes to unpleasant places in their own mind unless they are a masochist," said Finn. He leered at Somersby as though he were wondering whether his colleague was an advocate of masochism as well as one who involved himself in its practice. "But I appreciate the Mendelssohn reference," he added. "It's good to know that I'm rubbing elbows with someone who's cultured in the way of the arts."

"Mendelssohn?" said Somersby. "And here all along I thought 'A Calm Sea and Prosperous Voyage' was a Beethoven opus."

"Did you have to completely shatter my lofty assessment of you, Mr. Somersby?" Finn drolly remarked. "Would it have killed you to let it stand?"

"I'm very sorry, Mr. Finn. But I imagine you're quite right on the subject of traveling to unpleasant places in one's own mind," said Somersby. "To do so, one would *surely* need to be a masochist. I, on the other hand, often imagined hiking into a forest, where waiting for me is a long, flowing-haired virgin who has all but been convinced, by yours truly of course, that my semen is an elixir for eternal youth and beauty. The reason I say all "*but*" convinced is because I like to imagine the variety of scenarios with which she can be coaxed into service. Nothing like winning them over you know."

"Mr. Somersby, you truly *are* a scoundrel," said Finn. "Virgins in the woods? You actually masturbate imagining that you're the big bad wolf? Did you have your hand in your pants when you mother read to you Little Red Riding Hood?"

"I don't deny it," said Somersby. "But do tell me, Mr. Finn, where were *you* in those moments of reverie, when you were disconnected from our all-inclusive resort — our vacation destination featuring all the aseede, gurassa, and makhbaza you can eat. I mean *really*, Mr. Finn, what sort for fellow would allow himself to drift away from such a place? You shouldn't want to seem as an ingrate, you know; it wouldn't go over well with the locals."

"I see they taught comedy quite well back in England," Finn mockingly acknowledged.

"There was no bigger fan of *Fry and Laurie* than yours truly." Somersby swelled with pride when mentioning the British comedic duo.

"Nevertheless," said Finn, "I'll try and remember to adhere to your advice on not appearing as an ingrate. Though if you must know of my reverie, I sailed the ocean blue all the way back to my homeland. Actually, Mr. Somersby, that was a silly embellishment, and one that didn't come out nearly as poetic as I would have liked. But the fact is when one is engaged in reverie, one has no need for any means of transportation. One instant I was here, and in the next I was able to adeptly transport myself to a ballgame."

"A ballgame?" Somersby broke in, wholly incredulous that the dreamy look that came over Finn was brought about by bats and balls and the smell of grass.

"Yes, a ballgame," replied Finn. "You know … baseball? That grand old game we Americans invented, but have been accused by you English to have copied from cricket or rounders — or, some other silly game which you try and pass off as a *real* sport?"

"Alright, alright, enough rubbish about baseball," implored Somersby. "It's difficult to imagine how such a game, when at its speediest is like watching a sewing circle, ever became a spectator sport. Who in their right mind would be interested in inflated men like your Barry Bonds, who cheated in order to hit a silly ball a greater distance. Get on with the good parts of your reverie, my good fellow — the parts that would interest a scoundrel!"

"Since you're so insistent, I suppose then that I should get right on with it. Well, after I left the ballpark," Finn went on, "I went in search of a former lover, who incidentally was also my last lover. And I shall now admit to you, that it was *she* who made the decision that we should become *former* lovers."

"Was she a hottie, at least?" wondered Somersby. "Because it's a real bummer when even the plain Jane's of the world start dumping you. A real ego killer, you know."

"She had this sexy bottom lip piercing thing going on," said Finn. "Yes, you could say she was *'a hottie,'* but in that *Indy-rock, I sleep on a futon* sort of way. (Somersby nodded as though he understood the outlandish description entirely; though he did envision let-it-be hair and toe loop sandals — perhaps the woman in Finn's reverie was even a vegan who also had a politically revealing tattoo, albeit abstract, that warned all suitors that she was a tree hugging radical. Perhaps, also, the tattoo was in an area where one would need to work to get to see it, and depending on one's political affiliation, it would either serve to intensify or wilt an erection. Nevertheless, Somersby grew to enjoy, and would look forward to Finn's outlandish descriptions; he laughed hardily when Finn described Dr. Soderberg, a Swede with the Doctors Without Borders healthcare clinic at Kalma, as being *handsome in that, even too clean and preppy to fuck Doris Day sort of way.*) "Anyway," Finn continued, "naturally, because I had the advantage of existing in a daydream, or *reverie* as you called it, I found her and in due course managed to redeem myself. There's a certain satisfaction that comes with redeeming yourself to a former lover. And I must say it's amazing how well you can choreograph a scenario in your own mind — ever the most sensitive confrontations fall into place and always to your advantage. Anyway, after she recognised and then grasped the err of her way, I simply walked away from her. I left her a shattered mess to ponder a once in a lifetime opportunity lost forever. What a pity."

"No!" cried Somersby. "You didn't! Did you?" His eyes were swelling with disbelief. "You mean to say, that idyllic expression you wore had nothing to do with love? Nor, all the imagined sex that you wanted to have with some hot school teacher you had way back in the day when you were a pimple faced freshman, but instead it was all about revenge?" This, Somersby wondered with a fair amount of the incredulity, before adding with a note of exasperation, "And you referred to *me* as a scoundrel?"

"For crying out loud, Mr. Somersby, we're men!" Finn declared. "From time to time, we're permitted to act base and to travel the low road. I should think it's not only expected, but depending upon the situation, highly acceptable."

"I suppose you are right about that, Mr. Finn," said Somersby. "Acquiring too much gentility isn't good for the gender; it's best that from time to time we err on the side of our primal nature, as long as it isn't so often to where we're seen as bestial sorts entirely unfit as lovers. We still need to show a romantic side, though, if for no other reason than to fool those whom we pursue into believing that we're trainable. But more to the subject, I can well imagine that one time or another we've all wished the worst for lovers who once managed to make confetti out of our poor heats. But this is beginning to evolve into a conversation that would be much better suited when equipped with full glasses in hand and a bottle with which to refill them. And speaking of bottles, today I was planning to take a drive to Nyala with the hope that I'll get lucky and meet our connection. The fellow did us a good turn with that Chevis Regal, never mind his mark up. And since you paid the last time, I thought I'd pony up for the next go-around. After all, it's not as if I can squander my money on a round of golf — so contraband liquor it is!" By then, Finn was only half listening and was looking over Somersby's shoulder over to where Sister Ignatius appeared most diligent in administering care to a Darfuri woman whose tribal origins he was unable to determine. Finn and Somersby each had professed failure to recognise any discernible traits among the Sudanese of African tribal origins, but *were* able to detect differences between the African and Arab tribes of the Sudan. Neither saw this as so egregious a shortcoming that it warranted any admonishment, which was why they so readily admitted to it, but it was one which Sister Ignatius never let slide.

"She takes entirely too much delight in reminding us of things," Finn had once acknowledged. Finn didn't begrudge the fact that Sister Ignatius had made such a quick study of the landscape and was more abreast of the logistics and the numerous complications that has served to make Darfur what he dubbed *"hell on earth"*, but instead wished that he himself had. In his life and times he had never come across a nun in possession of such a fierce intellect, nor one to be so astute concerning so many matters. He found this fact all too surprising and at times even a source of frustration.

Since arriving at the Kalma refugee camp, Finn and Somersby were said to have been *as thick as thieves,* along with the other overused idiom *two peas in a pod*; yet the slight but apparent tension that existed between Sister Ignatius and Finn, did not also exist between the sister and Somersby. Finn was inclined to attribute this slight tension as being sexual in its nature, and that he, in fact, must possess a manner which effectively has forced Sister Ignatius to regard herself more a woman than nun, therefore it had become necessary for her to invent reasons to repel and to rebuke him. This was a most generous assessment for why Finn believed Sister Ignatius looked to cut him down. The more accurate assessment, though, was that Sister Ignatius was of the impression that Finn was a man filled with American arrogance and who sought recognition for having become a missionary. She wasn't *entirely* wrong. And although Finn's motives for becoming a missionary were pure in his own mind and lately were approaching purity in their actuality and essence, he at times appeared to meander about in a manner that served as a testimony to all others: *I am a product of a capitalist democracy considered the highest in rank — an industrial nation of the highest order capable of providing its citizens with luxuries none of you could imagine, so therefore my sacrifice for the cause must be considered greater than anyone else's.* This was the opinion that Sister Ignatius formed when observing Finn's strut, which she perceived as possessing too much confidence even for an American. Though, despite the sister's judgment, she didn't necessarily find Finn an irksome sort, only that he needed improvement, which given the opportunity, she would see done. "So what's her story?" asked Finn.

"Sister Ignatius?" asked Somersby, after having followed Finn's eyes over to where they were resting. "As we already well know, she's a Franciscan who was sent here to assist Doctors Without Borders. A fairly worthwhile organisation, wouldn't you say? And I don't believe there's a harder working pair of hands in the whole camp — a real multi-tasker, she is."

"Multi-tasking is a bullshit term invented by a society that has gotten so soft it sees the need to pat itself on the back for having the ability to do two things at once. A couple generations ago women were running entire households while pregnant with their seventh child. What kind of tasking would you call that?"

"Spoken like a true Irish Catholic; and despite my English Protestant heritage, I mean that in the kindest way; we should all be proud of our heritage," said Somersby. "But I do see your point."

"Really, Mr. Somersby," Fin went on, "we've takin the time to invent all sorts of terminologies and catchphrases and all for the purpose of patting ourselves on the back for doing nothing more than what should be expected. But back to my original question: What I mean is, what's her *story*?"

"Oh, *now* I see what you mean," said Somersby. "But you posed the question as though you suspect that there's something unseemly in Sister Ignatius's past that drove her to her vows, or perhaps some sordidness that she's been concealing from the world, but that *you've* been itching to uncover. She seems an awfully genuine sort, though, if you ask me."

"No one is *that* genuine, *that* good, not even a nun," said Finn. "Everyone has got a story, and so must she."

"Quite right, Mr. Finn, everyone *has* got a story," agreed Somersby, "but not every story has to be a messy one. Or, are you the sort who believes the more upstanding a citizen appears — or, in this case *a nun,* the more they must be hiding? Surely, you can't be *that* jaded? Or can it be that our dear Mr. Finn has the hots for Sister Ignatius?" Somersby paused in order to observe how Finn reacted to his epiphany, then exclaimed, "That's it, isn't it! You're hoping to find a crack in the sister's armour and exploit it with the idea that you can bed her! And you called *me* a scoundrel!"

"If you leave now, Mr. Somersby, you can be back from Nyala before nightfall," urged Finn. "You don't want to be out on the roads in darkness. By all means have a pleasant journey, and do make every effort to procure us a bottle of Chevis Regal; we wouldn't want to find ourselves out of desperation having to sample any of the native potions."

"Will do, Mr. Finn, will do," said Somersby, who was feeling no trace of indignation over a dismissal that was mockingly subtle. "But while I'm gone you had better tread carefully. I don't want to return and find you all curled up in a ball with an acute case of swollen testicles, if you know what I mean."

"I'll bear that in mind," said Finn.

Finn eyes followed Somersby until he had all but reached the boundary of Kalma; he was glad to be rid of his friend and colleague so that he could turn all his attention to Sister Ignatius — the very busy Sister Ignatius. The sister worked tirelessly, dividing her time between refugees who sought comfort through means of spirituality and the overcrowded healthcare clinic of the Kalma camp of which there never seemed to be any downtime. (The sister was a nurse by trade.)

Despite her smallish stature and seemingly frail appearance, she moved about with remarkable agility and possessed what some had observed to be surprising strength. Her arms and legs, though, seemed incapable of sinuous motion — they were rigid and seemed only to understand abruptness, as evidenced by the manner in which they hammered away minute after minute, hour after hour in their staccato-like fashion. One could exhaust themselves just by observing Sister Ignatius when engaged in her duties. "She reminds me of a piston in an engine," Somersby had once said. Finn advanced a few subtle paces in the direction of the sister. When having achieved a certain distance he found himself drawn to her hands. He also found it odd that he hadn't noticed the sister's hands before — or, perhaps he had, but failed one way or another to honour them with any regard. For Finn, this must be considered atypical, for he saw every part of a woman, regardless of her vocation, as possessing the facility to trigger sexual potency, especially in those who have no qualms in celebrating their baseness. They were surprisingly small were the sister's hands, even for one so diminutive, and Finn spent an exorbitant amount of time observing them. But what was more surprising than the smallness of their size, was how utterly unattractive he found them. This was an unexpected disappointment, for he imagined one so petite possessing dainty extremities one would long to touch or be touched *by*. Instead, what he discovered were rigid, industrious hands that might have belonged to a mechanic or stone mason, albeit a small one — hands that were not at all in accordance with the ankle of which he had just last week caught a glimpse — or, more accurately was presented with the opportunity to spy. The sister was reaching for something overhead that couldn't be gotten to without the benefit of rising up on her tiptoes. The effort caused her calves to flex and her slim, shapely ankles to from a favourable pose for anyone seeking to admire them.

Later that night those well admired ankles sent Finn to his bed where he masturbated furiously. *It was the end of a hot, exhausting day; there were no other kind at Kalma. The sister's face was glowing with perspiration — her eyes were weary, but they also contained a sparkle from all that was accomplished. She permitted herself to collapse into a chair and extend her legs onto Finn's laps. (He happened to be seated beside her.) "You wouldn't mind being the footstool for a weary nun, would you, Mr. Finn?" she asked.* In his altered state the sister's conduct didn't seem nearly so irregular as it no doubt would have otherwise. *He was thrilled to accommodate the feet of this weary, petite soul who had laboured so long and hard. When the sister extended her feet onto Finn's lap, her pants, which were cuffed to mid-calf rode up nearly to her knees. Finn gazed lustfully at her weary and well perspired form and how well it all flowed together down to the bareness of her slim, shapely ankles. He lifted one to his mouth.* Afterward, he paced about for several minutes attempting to grasp how the slim, shapely ankle of a nun could serve to inspire such a scenario, and from it unleash such intense sexual fury. Every muscle in his body ached from the strain it was forced to endure; never had he experienced such an immense ejaculation. When his breathing returned to normal and his body cooled, he returned to his inadequate mattress unable to attribute anything to the experience other than the ankle itself. This was a notion that seemed somewhat bizarre. Not that a woman's ankle was beyond the reach of loveliness or unable to provide the gateway for inspiration; Finn was well aware of the multitude of ways a man could become motivated by a woman; but to be brought to such a place — such a threshold led him to the precarious notion that perhaps forces of nature existed between he and the sister — forces that might get explored. There was another theory that occurred to him — one far more base and thus proving Somersby right, that Finn was a devious sort whose goal was merely to "bed a nun". Though the only thing Finn knew with any amount of certainty, it would not be the last time that he would ever pay tribute to Sister Ignatius's ankle. While remaining in the throes of his ardent preoccupation, Finn thus advanced further in the direction of Sister Ignatius. He hadn't gone about in that familiar, confident strut that often caused the sister to raise a disapproving eyebrow, but instead, moseyed along in a fashion that begged that he remain undisturbed — that his thoughts, whatever they were, be permitted to flourish. He continued his examination of the sister's hands, hoping to discover something that would stir him — some redeeming quality aside from the fact that they were the hardest working pair of hands at the Kalma refugee camp. He observed her applying an ointment to an abrasion on the neck of a Darfuri man whose tribal origin he could not ascertain. At last he was upon her. "Sister Ignatius, might I have a word with you?" His overture was exceedingly polite and had all the chirpiness of a child seeking approval, however, on the heels of his stupor the sound of his own voice was jarring to him, but to no one else.

"As you can see, Mr. Finn, I'm very busy at the moment," replied Sister Ignatius. "Perhaps we could talk later." There was no mistaking her condescending tone, which was held in reservation for no one other than Finn.

"You don't like me very much, do you, Sister?" Despite the question, Finn's tone remained polite, nor missing was any chirpiness.

"All things considered, Mr. Finn, I believe I tolerate you just fine," the sister told him.

"How awfully nice to be tolerated, Sister," said Finn. "When I find the right words to express how it warms my heart, I'll be sure and convey them to you. Meanwhile, try not to act too disappointed if the words are a long time in coming."

"Alright, Mr. Finn, perhaps we should put our guns back into our holsters and begin again," was the sister's witty recommendation. The man whom was receiving care from the sister let out a chuckle. He didn't understand her last remark entirely, but understood it enough to realise that it was clever and that it was intended to be humorous without necessarily being impertinent. "Mr. Finn, meet Hadil. Hadil, meet Mr. Finn. Imagine Hadil, Mr. Finn was good enough to come all the way from United States to grace us with his presence," said Sister Ignatius. "How lucky can we get?"

"I thought our guns were to be returned to our holsters?" Finn's indignation wasn't nearly so strong as his words might have suggested. This, Hadil clearly recognised and therefore laughed hardily. "I'm very pleased to make your acquaintance, Hadil," said Finn. He smiled broadly that the Sudanese gentleman had displayed appreciation for his humour.

"I'm most pleased to make your acquaintance as well, Mr. Finn," said Hadil. The words of the Sudanese man, although mechanical in their cadence were well-spoken and sincere.

"Sister, I've come to speak to you about some of the children in my charge," said Finn.

"The children?" asked Sister Ignatius. Despite her wariness of *Finn the man*, she admired the work that he and Somersby were doing with the children of Darfur. At once, any suspicions that she might have had for why Finn sought her out were altered, as was her demeanour. Her busy hands were brought to a respite and her face registered concern along with being flattered for having been approached in the matter of the children in Finn's charge.

"Yes, the children," returned Finn. "Two in particular. Something very disturbing happened yesterday. I'd like to run it by you. Your opinion would be most valued."

"Well, don't keep me in suspense, Mr. Finn!" begged Sister Ignatius.

"You are, as you've said, very busy, Sister," said Finn, "and what I have to show you would require your full attention. Perhaps it would be best if we meet sometime later this evening — over by the tress just after the sun goes down; it's usually pleasant about then. Good day, Sister Ignatius. Good day, Hadil."

"Good day to you as well, Mr. Finn," was Hadil's cheery return.

"He's a good man," Sister Ignatius told Hadil once Finn was no longer within an earshot. "A little rough around the edges as most men tend to be, present company excluded, but then again he's only been here a few short months. In due course he'll be just as happy as the rest of us." The remark caused Hadil to laugh more vigorously than before, and with that vigour came a twinkle in his eyes.

This prompted the sister to throw her arms around Hadil and laud, "God bless you my good man!" for every morning she would rise and remind herself that she was fighting the good fight and that it would one day be worth it, and the twinkling eyes and noble face of the thoughtful Sudanese gentleman was confirmation in the middle of what thus far had been a trying day.

"You are more kind, Sister," said Hadil. "And may God bless *you* and all your good work. On behalf of my family and many others, we are most grateful that you are here." Hadil's gratitude caused the sister to look away and to endure a moment of discomfiture.

Moving right along she said, "He does have a good heart, though, does our Mr. Finn." Looking over Hadil's shoulder at the sea of tents within Kalma — tents that were pieced together with whatever material was handy, and the multitude of refugees that occupied them, she whispered the words, "He would have to. Anyone who comes anywhere near this place would have to." Her words were faint, and as was intended, they fell short of Hadil's ears.

Finn decided to retire to his quarters for the remainder of the afternoon. He had forgotten all about Somersby and the trip to Nyala in pursuit of Chevis Regal — a trip that Finn easily could have made, but for the sake of a few words with Sister Ignatius he chose to remain behind. He made himself comfortable with his copy of Dostoevsky's "The Idiot". Over the past several days he had become quite enthralled with the saintly Prince Myshkin. After reading a fair sample of each, Finn concluded that he preferred Dostoevsky to Tolstoy. He himself was more in line, or at least familiar with Dostoevsky's Christian understanding of sin and redemption, and like many he revered Dostoevsky as a prophet crying out in the spiritually barren west. Conversely, he concluded that Tolstoy was a liberal intellectual, who viewed Jesus only as a divine teacher of moral truth and that Tolstoy also was a man who agonised over rationality. Finn had done more than his own share of wrestling with rationality and it came at the cost of Caroline, the only woman he ever professed to have loved. Dostoevsky, as Finn came to learn, had little use for rationality. Finn closed the book and settled it down onto his lap once he had become cognizant of the fact that he was reading the same passage over and over. It wasn't a riveting nor profound passage worthy of such review, but rather, he was stuck in the same place because he was busy reflecting upon how he had been so struck by Hadil, and now he found himself more preoccupied with this man whose tribal origins he couldn't begin to guess, than he was earlier with Sister Ignatius's stone mason-like hands. *How dare he smile, laugh, and display any measure of cheerfulness,* thought Finn. *How dare he act affably toward anyone! Can it be that he doesn't realise that he's been herded into a refugee camp filled with thousands of others who are displaced?* Finn tried to reconcile the tall, slender Hadil — his sparkling eyes, noble face, and a smile filled with warmth and sincerity despite the trying circumstances of a refugee camp, juxtaposed with having come from a place, where it's not all that uncommon, or perhaps even routine for someone to wish death on your children and your children's children for having held them up at a green light, Heaven forbid, for three whole seconds! It made Finn chuckle disdainfully to remember all that he once believed were inconveniences. He didn't know the true meaning of the word; no middle class American could; certainly not as Hadil understood it. Hadil was one of the sedentary of Darfur — a peaceful farmer of millet and sorghum, who had his land scorched and home set ablaze by the Janjaweed. He and his family narrowly escaped with their lives. This was a fact that Finn had yet to learn about Hadil, however, the Sudanese gentleman's story was not an uncommon one; many of the sedentary of Darfur now residing at Kalma and other camps could share a similar story. What Finn did know, however, was that in a matter of mere minutes he became quite fond of this man whose tribal origins he did not know — more fond than he had ever become of any colleague he once knew and cared to remember from his former life. He looked forward to their next meeting and hoped it would come soon. He was eager to extend his friendship and, in turn, gain Hadil's.

It was dusk — no remnant of the sun was apparent when Finn finally woke. Sitting on the floor besides the Dostoevsky opus that had slipped from his fingers was a bottle of Chevis Regal. Somersby, as it turned out, had a fruitful trip to Nyala. Finn had no memory of dozing off, or of the book falling to the floor. Somersby, who at times was given to noisy entrances, this time must have been respectfully quiet, but for whatever reason chose to leave the book on the floor; perhaps he wanted Finn to go reaching for it and instead find his hand resting on the bottle. Finn and Somersby behaved like two college roommates devoid of any social contract; there were no rules written, nor any regard for one another's time and space; everything was acceptable, and with the job that they were doing and in the place they were doing it, you might say they were the perfect couple. Finn checked the time and at once sprang from his chair. He knew the always dependable Sister Ignatius would already be there waiting for him. He dashed off hoping that she hadn't given up on him and retired for the night, but then he figured correctly that the sister wouldn't hold *him* to the same rigid standards to which she would hold herself. He eased his pace when he spotted her in the distance alone and in front of the Acacia trees, where earlier he had suggested they meet. She didn't exude the appearance of one who had been kept waiting *too* long. "How very interesting, Mr. Finn, that you should show up a few ticks on the tardy side and with a bottle and two glasses," said Sister Ignatius. She struck a haughty pose, pursed her lips, and raised an eyebrow before adding, "Is it your intention to corrupt me or to simply mock me? *Or,* do you actually plan on making such good use of that bottle that you're afraid you might misplace one of the glasses?"

"Such a sense of humour," remarked Finn. "But I must say, Sister, you surprise me."

"How so?" she wondered.

"Clearly, you underestimate my baseness," Finn told her. "I plan to get you plenty drunk and to take full advantage of you." He narrowed his eyes as though he were a monstrous entity fully prepared to scorch her soul with unredeemable corruption, then he playfully added, "You can't say that you haven't been warned." It took a few months, but Finn at last succeeded in bringing laughter to the mouth of Sister Ignatius. He grinned victoriously when he saw that his remarks also caused her to blush — that behind her vows there remained the vestige of a woman. Then he went on to add with a measure of sincerity, that her current state, which until the present hadn't been known by him, enhanced an already pretty face.

She, in turn, lurched forward and uttered, "What darkness lurks in the souls of evil men."

"What darkness, indeed," returned Finn. Then he proceeded to uncap the bottle and pour out both glasses. He examined the colour of the liquid in each; though missing was any sunlight or candlelight by which to lend any enhancement — there was only the duskiness of the earlier part of evening, and warm, heavy air that seemed reluctant to surrender to the lighter, cooler night. Finn put his nose to the glass from which he intended to drink, which incidentally had the greater volume. Of course, this was all an inane display to tempt the sister into reaching for a glass.

"Surely, Mr. Finn, you can't expect me to partake in the drinking of contraband spirits?" Sister Ignatius put forth her objection as though, were it not ill-gotten or unlawfully acquired gains, she might have been enticed into taking the plunge. In other words, she thought it best to refuse citing the law not her vows, that way she would be less open for ridicule.

"Correction, sister," said Finn. "Black market spirits. You wouldn't want any parts of the contraband spirits that from time to time come floating around our luxurious environs. Have you even caught a glimpse of Merissa — what the locals call beer? It's sour and cloudy and can cause Mahdi's revenge. That's the Sudanese version of Delhi belly, or so I'm told. And then there's this wonderful concoction known as Aragi — it's distilled from dates, which sounds pleasant enough, but it's potent and sometimes is contaminated with methanol, or worse, embalming fluid! Can you imagine? Methanol and embalming fluid? No thank you! I much rather pay the exorbitant mark-up for true and trusted black market booze; at least I can drink with the confidence that my insides won't shrivel."

"Mr. Finn, please be sure to pass along to Mr. Somersby, for I'm sure that he has been informed of our meeting, being that you two are as thick as thieves, that although I appreciate his effort and will continue to pray that neither of you end up arrested and carted off to a Sudanese prison, I wasn't able to enjoy the fruits of his journey to Nyala. But please go on and enjoy, Mr. Finn," she added. "I promise to be a most agreeable spectator, while you aspire to whatever level of inebriation you wish to achieve."

"First off, Sister," Finn went on, "Mr. Somersby has not been informed of our meeting. Not that it *was* or *needed* to be a secret; I simply hadn't the opportunity to inform him. But enough of Mr. Somersby. I'd like to tell you a story if I may; although it's not entirely without relation to Mr. Somersby's trip to Nyala and the two of us standing here together. I'm sure you'll see the relevance."

"Oh, please do, Mr. Finn," Sister Ignatius implored. "It was a long, tiring day and I think I should like to hear a story, even if the goal of its allegory is meant to corrupt me."

"You're to be commended for your insightfulness, Sister, but I assure you this is no allegory, but a story of truth, and one which as I've already stated has relevance." Gone from Finn's countenance was the smirky confidence that was apparent when he strolled up to Sister Ignatius with a bottle and two glasses. "My mother wasn't merely a frequent church goer, she was ardent about attending," he began. "Come Sunday morning she was the first one in the pew. This was a weekly occurrence that to my dismay never wavered. She would drag me along until I had thankfully, or from her perspective, regrettably reached an age when I was old enough to rebel. I was never fully certain whether my mother's aim was to instil her only son with the virtues of the Catholic doctrine or if she merely wanted company. As a youngster I always suspected the latter, for my father was a man who professed having no time for the church. But as I grew I came to suspect that within our family of three, my mother's desire was to nurture a religious ally. Lucky me. Anyway, after my thirteenth birthday, except for the all important Christmas eve and Easter Sunday masses, my mother, with equal frequency and ardency went to church alone. "During the years when I *was* going or was dragged along, I never missed an opportunity to complain bitterly about having to get up so early on my day off from school. To her credit, though, my mother never made any speeches about *what I owed the Lord,* or that, in comparison to what others less fortunate in the world must endure, getting up early on Sunday morning didn't exactly qualify as *a sacrifice*. If she had gone that route, as some parents were known to do, it would have been unbearable. For a child, listening to such drivel is unbearable; seven-year-olds don't ponderously go about their days wondering what they owe the Lord; nor can they sit still long enough to care about those less fortunate. And I'd be willing to wager that most sever-year-old feel that way, not just the American ones. Instead, she would routinely remind me that it was Father McKinley who oversaw the early mass, and that he was her favourite priest. I can still remember thinking, if I was entitled to have a favourite baseball player, then my mother was entitled to her favourite priest. Of course, this didn't make my Sunday morning wake-up call seem less like drudgery. Though I must admit, Father McKinley was a compelling orator; even as a youngster that much I could tell.

But now, Sister, let us fast forward a few years. That would bring us to my high school graduation party. My father knew that I was a talented student, but underachieved because of laziness and lousy work habits, and therefore was undeserving of a party. He lost that battle to my mother, who, in turn, extended an invitation to Father McKinley. Because he considered himself a friend of my mother's, he gladly accepted. However, before the night had reached its conclusion, *my* father, along with my Uncle Bill were picking my mother's favourite priest up off the kitchen floor because he had drank himself into a stupor. The poor man was slurring his words, never mind his inability to stand. My father and Uncle Bill had to carry poor Father McKinley back to the rectory. Thankfully for them the rectory was only a short distance from our house. It was late and well past dark, still my mother found it necessary to blanket Father McKinley's collar for fear someone would recognise him as a priest being carried away from our house. She saw it as her solemn duty to spare him, who had lost all sight of his limitations, any shame. "Uncle Bill was carrying Father McKinley by the legs. *My* father, on the other hand, had the unfortunate task of holding him by way of under hooking his arms. The reason that I say "unfortunate" is because along the way Father McKinley twice vomited on my father's shirtsleeve; nothing like a little priestly puke to top off the evening.

When they arrived at the rectory, they managed to clean up the poor father, got him to rinse out his mouth, and then put him to bed. By the time they arrived back at the house, the few guests who had remained long enough to witness Father McKinley's condition had gone, and my mother was upstairs in her room crying. My father, who wasn't ordinarily a consoling type, went to her and asked, 'Why are you crying.' My mother held Father McKinley in such high regard that, seeing him in such a state left her shattered — her moral compass was pointing in every which direction except the one where it had become so steadfastly fixed. It was as if all of a sudden the world became a hodgepodge of uncertainty and with an un-navigable landscape — a monster filled with all sorts of treachery. My poor mother had been set adrift on an unfriendly sea and was fearful that any second she would be swallowed up. My father, a man who had no time for the church, assured my mother that tonight *hasn't*, nor *should* it change the fact that Father McKinley *was* and still *is* a most worthy advocate for God, and that we are mere mortals, and that even the most exceptional among us are prone to make mistakes, never mind sin. By the end of the night he did manage to convince her that one blemish in what thus far had been a fifteen year relationship was hardly a deal breaker, and that other blemishes could likely follow, and that with all the good that Father McKinley had done for the parish, he shouldn't be judged so harshly less condemned, especially over something so simple as forgetting his limitations. My father urged my mother to maintain her lofty and well-earned opinion of Father McKinley, which she did. "I guess what I'm trying to say, Sister, is that you've been sent to *hell on earth* and at the very least you have conducted yourself admirably

— more admirably than anyone *I've* noticed. You've already passed the test even by your own ridiculous standards, which are much more stringent than God's. *He*, I would imagine, is reasonable. Besides, and I beg your pardon for sounding grim, but who knows how much longer you'll be permitted to hang around this place. I mean, haven't you heard; Darfur can be bad for one's health, or so I'm told. So I say live it up while you still can, or before you lose your wits entirely drinking nothing but that damn hibiscus tea you've grown so fond of."

"Perhaps you're right, Mr. Finn," the sister admitted. "And I must say, your father sounds like a most rational man and one in possession of more than his share of wisdom."

"You're very right about that, Sister," said Finn. "If nothing else my father was a most rational man who enjoyed sharing his wisdom. With that in mind, perhaps we should raise a glass on his behalf."

"Alright, then, Mr. Finn," said Sister Ignatius. "To the senior Mr. Finn it shall be."

The amber-coloured liquid had just begun to trickle down the sister's throat, when Finn decided to ask, "Incidentally, Sister, have I yet to inform you that I hated my father?"

Sister Ignatius coughed up the Scotch whiskey and began to choke. Some of the spray that was launched from her mouth reached Finn, who alertly grabbed her glass before it went tumbling to the ground and spilled out all its pricey black market contents.

"But, Mr. Finn," she managed to cry out between coughs and also in spite her burning nostrils, "you just got done telling me the most splendid things about your father! How is it possible that you hated him?" Once Sister Ignatius appeared to have regained her composure and Finn was fairly convinced that her feet squarely beneath her and would remain so, he handed her back her glass.

"The truth is my father was too old to be my father," he went on. "He was well into his forties by the time I came along, and when I reached the age when young boys clamour to participate in activities such as playing little league baseball, he was right there to point out that I shouldn't waist time on such frivolous pursuits. Of course I'm paraphrasing; he used simpler and harsher terms such as *silliness* and *nonsense*. But there have been many men, I suppose, who believed wholeheartedly that they had *what* to offer the world, and whatever others clamoured for in their estimation was mere silliness and nonsense. My father made a life trivialising that which my mother and I saw as worthwhile. He was a clockmaker, my father, and he saw his craft as some sort of noble calling. Can you imagine — a clockmaker actually believing that his vocation was a calling?"

"It may not be so far a stretch as you think, Mr. Finn," Sister Ignatius broke in. "Time has been mankind's most important element ever since — well — the beginning of time! It has marked the years, decades, and centuries — time is historical. And when you think about it, we live entirely by the sun, the moon, our calendars, and therefore, time — or, as you father would have it — our clocks."

"Well, I suppose when you put it that way it does seem rather noble," Finn admitted. "Although, my father didn't regard his craft as how it could relate to history and the solar system, and certainly not of the time space continuum; his perception was much simpler. He was of the belief that somewhere trapped within its fibres or hidden in its grain, wood possessed a soul, and that artisans who once shaped and polished wood into fine cabinetry were, in fact, bringing it to life; and those who built mechanisms to be placed into those fine cabinets were giving that life a purpose. I can't deny that my father was a true craftsman, and if there was one thing he admired it was the craft end of industry. Indeed, he lived for his work did my father, but in doing so he largely ignored my mother. The poor woman spent her best years starving for affection that he wasn't inclined to give. There was even a period when she took to doing bizarre things with the hope of gaining his attention, including making the most exotic dishes belonging to foreign cultures, while my father was the sort for whom you could alternate chicken and meatloaf at every dinner and he would be perfectly satisfied; food didn't excite him. Once she came home from a department store having purchased an outfit best suited for a native American, but even *that* didn't rouse my father — not even enough to utter *what the hell do you think you're doing parading around like that*! Then one day he woke only to discover that the world had something called an internet and devices called cell phones. Indeed, Sister, the world had gone entirely digital and no longer had any use for an old clockmaker. Suddenly my mother became very important to him. Sadly, though, he was thirty years too late, as her libido, as she had confessed to me, was all but gone. Nowadays they spend their evenings in close proximity, sharing only the nonsense that comes into their living room by way of television, and not many memories."

"How very tragic," said Sister Ignatius, "— for all of you."

"He didn't *mean* to smother my childhood with his middle age pragmatism, nor drain the vivacity from my mother's heart," said Finn. "I'm fairly certain he wasn't aware of what he was doing; it was just his way. I suppose I shouldn't hate him. Hating him makes it *my* problem. Instead I should feel sorry for him. But now I've gone and gotten completely sidetracked from what I planned on talking to you about."

"The children," the sister reminded him.

"Oh, yes, the children," said Finn, as he refreshed both glasses; this time he was more generous with Sister Ignatius. "Aside from the usual learning and studies, Mr. Somersby and I have been teaching the children how to draw, and I must say some have drawn delightful pictures — rudimentary of course, but delightful nonetheless. Some depictions are of stories that have been learned, while others have relied on their ability to imagine. However, some have expressed themselves in a most disturbing manner."

Rolled up in Finn's back pockets were two samples of drawings. He handed them over to Sister Ignatius, along with a pen — it was a fancy sort that came equipped with a miniature light bulb on the end; it was needed to better examine the drawings, for darkness had fallen. As Finn had stated, the drawings were typically crude and rudimentary in there execution — exactly what one would expect from children not considered budding Picassos, but they, nevertheless, were profoundly effective in their message. The first illustration that the sister examined was of a helicopter dropping heavy artillery on a hut. The second saw a man on horseback brandishing a sword and was about to slash the throat of a defenceless woman. "These *are* very disturbing," admitted Sister Ignatius, "but they're hardly surprising. Children tend to draw what they know. When you were a youngster, I imagine you drew pictures of your house, your mother's garden, and produced a fairly recognisable image of your father's automobile, and when you went to display your artwork you were made to feel proud of your efforts. Perhaps you also drew a picture of the neighbourhood playground with all its apparatus and with stick figure representations of you playmates scattered throughout; the perfect childhood scene. These are all common things most children draw because it's what they know. *These*," and she handed the drawing back to Finn, "are what the children of Darfur have come to know."

Finn rolled up the drawings and returned them to his back pockets. He began to recall an incident from only a few years ago, November of 2001, when a first grade teacher entered the teachers' lounge all worked up over an illustration done earlier that day by one of her students. The boy had drawn a tall, narrow structure covered with windows — a well-done likeness of a skyscraper with a spire piercing through the hovering clouds. Raining down from the upper windows of the structure were small mammals of every sort: squirrels, rabbits, mice, and so forth; a childlike, but obvious depiction of 9/11. As the drawing was being passed around the lounge all were taken aback and were trying to determine the correct course of action: Should the boy be approached by his teacher? Should the principal get involved? Should the boy be sent home with a note so that his parents could deal with him however they saw fit? They decided unanimously on the latter, that the school should wash its hands of the "incident" as it was described and allow the boy's parents to deal with him directly. Finn attributed the incident to a world that had fast become an unrelenting multi-media circus — a frenzy of twenty-four hour a day news networks run amok, releasing an unending deluge of words and images that infiltrate society until they have at last reached the eyes and ears of those we have sworn to protect. *There is no way to battle against this well-equipped machine — to slay this ugly monster,* Finn knew. Finn also was aware that, while the children of western cultures may have learned of the world's atrocities while running past television sets on their way to play in their backyards, the children of Darfur, particularly those whose drawings he carried in his pocket, have come to know atrocities having witnesses them firsthand. "Do you know why, Mr. Finn, that what's happening here in Darfur to the farmers, villagers, and the sedentary ones *isn't* considered genocide?" Sister Ignatius posed the question, while Finn once again refreshed their glasses. Before he could speculate in his mind, or aloud venture a guess, the sister added, "Genocide by definition is the intent to wipe out an entire group based on either national, ethnical, racial, or religious grounds. The ethnically African Darfuris aren't being killed because their African, you see; nor are they being killed for religious reasons; for those doing the killing are also of the Muslim faith." Sister Ignatius's words became tremulous — her composure, as Finn observed, was beginning to slip when she further added, "You see, Mr. Finn, it isn't sufficient to merely get wiped out, you must get wiped out for a specific reason. After all, rules are rules and we mustn't bend them nor deviate in any way. Heaven help us when madness has no definable purpose, or when *we* the supposed rational ones fall short of determining its goal!"

"So direct intervention isn't forthcoming because of a damn technicality?" Finn punctuated his disgust with a derisive chuckle, though it wasn't the least bit contrived. Sister Ignatius responded to his disgust by casting her eyes downward and remaining silent, for had she done otherwise it might have resulted in further rage and frustration reaching the surface. She wished very hard for those feelings to pass, but they were simmering inside and for a long time now they were yearning for a voice. "So how long do you plan on remaining in the region?" Finn wondered.

"I'm here for the duration," the sister replied. Her words were quick and curt, as though she had anticipated the question and had a well prepared answer already to unleash.

"That's awfully ambitious, don't you think?" asked Finn. Before Sister Ignatius could reply, Finn rather drolly reminded her that Darfur wasn't exactly good for one's health. "But really, Sister," he went on, "you could end up mad before it's all over, or worse, and then you won't be good to anybody including yourself. Was this your decision?"

"The very day that I arrived in Darfur, I penned a letter to my fellow Franciscans back in England stating that I would remain here for as long as it took to restore order or a sense of wellbeing to the region," the sister told Finn. Her words were direct, but she was beginning to sway, perhaps from the contents of her glass, the topic of conversation, or both. "You see, Mr. Finn, on the day that I arrived, I saw something. Do you understand me, Mr. Finn? That I saw something? And that it was even worse than those drawings you've been carrying around in your pocket?" It was clear to Finn that Sister Ignatius was well in the throes of the alcohol she had thus far consumed, along with whatever hysteria that was brought about from her initiation to Darfur, which she all along had been trying to block out, though without success. She was no longer attentive of any decorum she thought necessary to uphold, or any virtues of the like. Finn didn't ask what it was that she saw, for he sensed an answer was forthcoming regardless of any solicitation. The sister threw back her head and emptied the remaining contents of the glass into her mouth as though it might better prepare her for what she was about to say. Finn watched as her eyes swelled as if belonging to one crazed; she was reeling and appeared that at any second she might unravel. "I saw a woman, Mr. Finn," she went on. "She was pregnant — far along, like she might deliver any day, or *that* day. She was a villager, a sedentary one carrying a basket, but I was too far away to see its contents. Men came upon her. She tried to escape but was limited by her condition. These men seized her and held her down. I heard her screams, her terrible screams, I can still hear them. And while she was being held down against her will, one of the men *cut* open her womb. Her *womb*, Mr. Finn! Her fucking *womb*! Then they ripped the baby from her and killed it! And then they killed her! Dear God! Oh, dear God, may this place drain me of my life, take every drop of my blood, but I swear I will remain until it's rid of such atrocities!" Sister Ignatius was unable to control her sobs. Soon after her sobbing subsided she became dizzy and her head grew hot. She jerked away from Finn, and in doing so, her glass went flying from her hand, though it landed intact, while she herself appeared to twist in the air before falling to her knees — her condition far worse than the glass. Finn went and knelt down by her side and held firmly her shoulders while she tried to brace herself; he could feel her innards convulsing. Afterward she said to Finn in a most self-deprecating manner, but too ashamed to look his way, "They say it's the party girls who are the most fun. Isn't that what they say, Mr. Finn? But when they end up vomiting all over your shoes, then they're just a pain in the ass. My sincerest apologies, Mr. Finn, for having ruined your ambition." Finn thought it prudent not to comment either way regarding the sister's last remark. *What darkness lurks in the souls of evil men.* Finn wasn't feeling very evil about now and had all but forgotten the "ambition" he had hoped might come to fruition with the aid of a few sips of Chevis Regal.

The evening had drifted dramatically away from having never mind cultivating such thoughts. He did, however, assist the sister to her feet and asked, "Would it be alright if I walk you back to your quarters?"

"I appreciate you kindness, Mr. Finn, but perhaps it would be best if I made my way back to my quarters alone," Sister Ignatius told him. "I'm sure you would agree that I caused more than enough trouble for one night."

Finn elected not to press the sister on the matter of her walking back to her quarters alone or whether she had, as was suggested, "caused more than enough trouble". He remained by the acacia tree, as unsteadily she went wandering off. She hadn't gotten very far, though, when she turned and called, "Did I satisfy you tonight, Mr. Finn?"

"I beg your pardon, Sister," was Finn's curious return. "Could it be possible that something happened tonight that I was not aware of?"

Sister Ignatius managed an ironic smile that ended up a grimace. "I meant in regards to the drawings, Mr. Finn — the children's drawings."

"Right, of course, the drawings; I had almost forgotten," said Finn. "Indeed, as expected, Sister, your input was most — *satisfying*."

When Finn arrived back at his quarters, he discovered that Somersby had made himself quite comfortable and was taking the liberty of fanning through the Dostoevsky volume.

"Deep reading I should say, wouldn't you, Mr. Finn?" asked Somersby. "One would think a place like this would require comic books. Anyway, earlier on I spied you and the sister over by the acacia trees. You seemed to be getting on quite nicely the two of you, but then it became too dark for me to see. I thought about employing my trusty flashlight by pretending that I was looking for something that I might have dropped outside earlier, but that would have been terribly obvious not to mention rude."

"Yes — on both counts," said Finn.

"I don't disagree. But now don't keep me in suspense, my good fellow," implored Somersby. "Who claimed victory? Who won the night, God or ol' Satan himself?"

"Neither," said Finn. "It was a draw. If anyone, or rather, any*thing* can lay claim to victory it was the Chevis Regal." Finn acted as though he didn't care to elaborate and hoped that the conversation would end there, but Somersby's wheels were beginning to turn, and in no time he formulated a scenario, and of its accuracy he was enormously confident. "You see, there's where you're wrong my good friend," he told Finn. He set aside the Dostoevsky volume and assumed the posture of a man who was quite pleased with himself "If that was indeed the case, than the Chevis Regal is not only proof that God won, but won in a landslide. *He* sent me to Nyala and made certain that I successfully acquired spirits that would ultimately protect our good sister from the devil that seems so well manifested within you, and to a far lesser degree, Sister Ignatius herself. So she got too drunk to bed, is that it? Perhaps she even threw up all over the trunk of one of those majestic acacia trees? Score one for the Man upstairs!"

"Goodnight, Mr. Somersby," said Finn.

It wasn't long after Finn went to his bed that he began to dwell on the notion that he and Sister Ignatius had each granted one another a peek into the other's soul, and with that peek came a level of intimacy neither could have anticipated or only yesterday imagined possible, and furthermore it was infinitely more gratifying than what Finn had otherwise imagined. He wondered about tomorrow, when sober and back to task, would Sister Ignatius once again see him as just another arrogant American? Would he once again hope to glimpse her ankle or go in search of other reasons that would send him to his bed to lay awake and to tremble with delight? Meanwhile, Sister Ignatius went to her bed mortified over her display. She wasn't angry that Finn had encouraged her to drink and succeeded, but that like Mrs. Finn's favourite priest, she strayed well beyond her limitations. She assumed that it would be useless to try and resist from appearing shamefaced tomorrow when seeing Finn. She prayed that he wouldn't grin victoriously in the face of her shame. After the remaining ill-effects of the Chevis Regal had passed, her thoughts turned to the unfortunate clockmaker and his wife, then to her own parents, whom she hadn't seen for years, but were far more damaging.

CHAPETR III
THE BOY IN THE CELLAR

By day, Catherine and Nigel Philips avoided any direct companionship by a method known as entrenching themselves in groups taking tours. Both pretended to be ignorant of the fact that they were using crowds as buffers or as a means of comfort, and what better buffer and means of comfort than the affability of vacationers taking tours — folks who are on their best behaviour and who are at their most at-ease state in the calendar. From nothing easy conversations were struck. After all, Vienna and Budapest were fascinating places that provide much to talk about, and Catherine and Nigel were able to effectively talk through whoever was handy — it all seemed so natural. By night the two of them hid behind menus in which they pretended to be far too engrossed, appearing as if they were reviewing an itemised checklist of unparalleled importance. When the emptiness in their stomachs at last became too unbearable, they made sure to order food and wine that was well worthy of, and therefore certain of sparking discussions. For two people who, when they weren't shouting at one another struggled for words, the complexity of wine and the preparation of foreign cuisine aided in avoiding any awkward silences that no doubt would have otherwise occurred. While waiting for their wine they repeatedly told one another how hungry they were. So there they sat, night after night, Catherine and Nigel Philips in restaurants all over

Vienna and Budapest, sipping, chewing, and people watching — discussing the benign with more than its due treatment, but no issues of any real poignancy were ever raised. They each chose to play it safe and not take any chances by provoking one another. Neither was prepared, as originally thought, for the prospect of passing or failing — sinking or swimming; therefore, the threshold or precipice or whatever name best suites those who have reached a crossroads with a large measure of fear and timidity, was wholly avoided. In other words, the well planned getaway that was intended to serve as a referendum on their marriage, ended up a cordial vacation with two cautious people, who managed to agree that the cuisine was "superb", the architecture was "grand", the Vienna Boys Choir was "lovely", Budapest was "an education", but that the Danube was "just another river".

Catherine and Nigel Philips returned to Bayswater no more or less broken; although, as is the case when harmony becomes the custom, disrepair can also be gotten used to. So much for the benefit of an Austro-Hungarian getaway. During the drive back to Bayswater, Catherine was not only surprised, but found it quite odd that without the benefit of solicitation Jimmy hadn't uttered a single word regarding Colin and Douglas Broxton. Furthermore, when asked, he had little to say on the subject of his twin cousins and how they got along, and what was said seemed an effort and a painful one at that. However, he gushed on and on about his Aunt Delia and Uncle Peter; although, about them he wasn't asked to comment. Also, his eyes always possessed an extra sparkle whenever mentioning the name Mary Willow — a name that got mentioned often. In fact, Jimmy's first order of business was to show his parents the photograph of him, Colin, Douglas, and Mary Willow standing in the secret garden of Sudeley Castle. However, when showing off the photo, he had his thumb placed over Colin and Douglas — it was well eclipsing their faces when he asked brightly in regard to Mary Willow, "Isn't she just the most beautiful girl, Mother?"

"Oh I'd say she's *quite* pretty," Nigel was quick to chime in. "A real looker if you ask me." It was Nigel's belief that he was a much better judge of beauty regarding the female sex and therefore should have been consulted first. He didn't go so far as to articulate the issue of being slighted, though his alert response to his son's overture spoke for itself. Nevertheless, Jimmy was glad for his father's lofty appraisal on a girl he had grown to admire, but it was his mother's opinion that he truly sought. Perhaps because she was a woman, Jimmy desired to know in what regard, or in what realm his mother held Mary Willow, but all Catherine could manage was a half-hearted shrug — the kind of shrug that one usually gives when they see no real harm in agreeing but are not necessarily in agreement. Jimmy was dismayed by his mother's apparent disinterest of a girl he couldn't stop thinking of, and furthermore, he had a clear sense that even if his mother had been enamoured with Mary Willow, she wouldn't have admitted it. Jimmy put his mother's disinterest of Mary Willow behind him, just far enough to where he could gushed on about Sudeley Castle. Despite not capturing even a glimpse of Queen Catherine's ghost, there was still plenty to talk about — not only of the castle but of the entire day. In return, Catherine Philips found it necessary to inform her son that, while Sudeley Castle was capable of impressing a child, it paled wholly in comparison to the grand architecture of Vienna and Budapest. In fact, she referred to the Cotswolds as being part of the "Humdrum English countryside". With having no experience with which to compare it, Jimmy decided not to dispute his mother's meagre claim of the Cotswold villages, but in his heart he believed differently. Despite his menacing twin cousins, for him the Cotswolds was heaven on earth, for tucked away in one of its charming villages was a girl named Mary Willow.

****

It would be five years before Jimmy would make a return to the grand old Tudor in the Cotswolds. Another five years had come to pass and did so without the Broxton's receiving a single invitation or having been provided any reason at all to drive to Bayswater. Within those same five years the Philips' repeatedly found excuses to turn down invitations sent to them by the Broxton's. Jimmy missed his Aunt Delia and spoke of her with brightness, with fondness, and often, and at times all this enthusiasm for his mother's younger sister would cause Catherine to look away and wince, or to snootily turn up her nose. But every now and again, Jimmy was granted the opportunity to speak with his Aunt Delia on the telephone, and cards without fail were traded on holidays and birthdays. He thought often of Mary Willow, and over the past five years he spent a great deal of time wondering how often he had crossed her mind. Whenever he spoke with Aunt Delia he never failed to ask about Mary Willow and would beg his aunt to remember him to her.

During the course of the past five years Jimmy managed to take an enchanted day spent at Sudeley Castle and its secret garden, along with a Sunday picnic at Cleeve Hill and romanticise them into an enduring friendship for the ages. How he so loved and was consumed by the mere idea of Mary Willow, and just knowing that she existed lit his every day — even the dark days weren't without some brightness. So many nights he took to his bed remembering the touch of her hand when together they walked through the halls of a centuries old castle, and on each morning he woke to the loveliness of her smile — he kept the photograph of all of them together at the secret garden on his nightstand. Then, Mary Willow was a ten-year-old girl befriending a young boy clutching his monkeys. But Jimmy had long since left behind Fish and Chip. Now he was a ten-year-old himself, and whose perception of that time was greatly altered. However, as were both Colin and Douglas, Mary Willow was now fifteen.

This time Catherine and Nigel were headed for a two-week vacation to Singapore. Delia and Peter agreed not to act put-upon that Jimmy was being dumped in their laps with the notion that a romp about the Malay Peninsula was the recipe for saving a marriage that, as a matter of routine was contentious. "Wouldn't counselling be cheaper?" Peter snidely wondered. But this time Delia and he both agreed that they cared nothing of Catherine and Nigel's motive for a getaway; they were thrilled to once again have the opportunity to look after Jimmy, and he, in turn, was thrilled when learning that he was going to be spending two weeks in the Cotswolds. By then, Delia had given up on the notion of having a true sisterly relationship with Catherine. She also developed the predilection that, were Catherine and Nigel in fact running away from life in England and had secretly planned to remain in Singapore, that was a scenario that would suite her just fine; she would wholly embrace the opportunity to finish raising her dear and only nephew. After the Philips' arrived at the Tudor, Delia and Jimmy embraced as though they were making up for every day ever spent apart. For Jimmy, his Aunt Delia was like an ocean of affection he was free to dive in to — he needed no invitation to experience its luxury of warmth and softness. Afterwards Delia greeted her sister and brother in-law cordially, then informed them that lunch was available if they so desired, but made no real fuss about it. When Catherine and Nigel readily declined for reasons that were nothing less than predictable, Delia was quick to bid them farewell.

Mrs. Delia Broxton was even lovelier than Jimmy remembered — her bright, smiling eyes were a joy to see, and far as he could tell, his Uncle Peter hadn't changed all that much in five years. The same, however, could not be said for Colin and Douglas. Being that they were virtually identical, Jimmy wouldn't have known his cousins had he not spotted them together. Colin was still an inch taller and a touch slimmer than Douglas. Both were still fair-haired and could fool anyone into believing they were angels that possessed irresistible charms, but nowadays they also possessed the physiques of ruddy, athletic young men. What remained the same as five years ago, though, was that when in tandem the Broxton twins could prove to be quite a menacing duo. Conversely, Jimmy was considered just as scrawny for a ten-year-old as he had been for a five-year-old, though intellectually he had grown by leaps and bounds, and he spoke beautifully. Nevertheless, when sitting across from his twin cousins, who had typical teenage appetites, and therefore were anxious to dig into their lunch, Jimmy felt himself reverting back to the same bullied sad sack that the Broxton twins remembered from five years ago. The twins' eyes filled with mischief and malevolence, and they smirked across the table at Jimmy, who at first sat tall and proud in his chair but then cowered and sank. Nothing had changed; with a look the Broxton twins were able to psychologically shred their young cousin, and what's more, at fifteen they exuded a lustiness that was magnetic and sexual and commanded attention — Jimmy couldn't look away from them. The smirks of both young men clearly suggested that their young cousin didn't, nor wouldn't stand a chance, and that he would be much better off were he to hitchhike back home to Bayswater or hop the next plane to Singapore. *You do understand, Cousin, that this isn't going to go well for you* the eyes of the menacing duo seemed to shout out from across the table. Jimmy swallowed nervously. Finally, he managed to shift his eyes away from his cousins and over to his ally — the always pleasant and lovely Aunt Delia; however, she wasn't paying attention to her sons to notice any nonverbal threats that they might have been making. She was too busy gazing at Jimmy. "It's been so long, Jimmy," said Delia. "Too long, in fact. Would you be needing another tour of the house?"

"Not at all, Aunt Delia, I remember exactly where everything is," he proudly chirped. It was true; he remembered every nook, cranny, alcove, and passage way.

"Well good, then; and I prepared your bedroom," said Delia. "I want you to feel perfectly at home here — as at home as you ever felt anywhere. Oh, Jimmy, we're so excited to have you here with us again. Aren't we, Peter?"

"Indeed we are," agreed Peter, with his much more tempered male version of enthusiasm. "But do tell us, Jimmy, where are your two friends?"

"My two friends?" he wondered. His countenance twisted in the familiar fashion that usually occurs when one is confused by a question, despite his Uncle Peter having asked the question in a manner which suggested that the answer was something that Jimmy should have known right away without thinking. He struggled to get a handle on to whomever his uncle might be referring, but his search for an answer was a fruitless one.

"Indeed, your two friends," Peter continued. "Now, what were their names?" It was Peter's turn to have a twisted, confused look.

"Why, Fish and Chips, of course," Delia broke in. "As I remember, Jimmy, you three were inseparable." Jimmy flushed with embarrassment and wished that his Uncle Peter hadn't chosen to rehash his early childhood folly, especially while in the presence of his menacing cousins. He might have taken pleasure in the recollection otherwise, but certainly not at the present. Instead, he shrugged to indicate that Fish and Chips, along with fairies, dragons, beanstalks, and other things of storybook enchantment *were* and *had* been outgrown for some time — half a lifetime ago, in fact, and they wouldn't be returning. "So what are your plans for this afternoon?" Delia directed her words toward Colin and Douglas. It was summer and the boys were free to roam about as the wished.

"It's a nice day, Mother, so I thought we'd hike on over to Bourton-on-the-water and see what's cooking," said Colin.

"We'll hike slow so that Jimmy can keep up with us," added Douglas. "What do you say, Jimmy? Up for a hike?" A hike sounded like the perfect remedy for someone who had just been through being cooped up in an automobile for two hours with Catherine and Nigel Philips and all the uneasiness that they could provide. Moreover, Douglas had promised his mother that her nephew would be well accommodated — a consideration to which Colin had readily agreed. Jimmy hadn't a valid reason for being less trusting of Colin and Douglas in the present than he had been five years ago, but his intuition was screaming for him, despite the fact that the eyes of his cousins were suddenly devoid of any mischief and malevolence, to be on his guard! Nevertheless, and despite the validity of his misgiving, he felt encouraged that his cousins were willing to make allowances for his diminutive size. Maybe things had changed, after all.

"Jimmy, you'll just love it!" chirped Delia. "Bourton-on-the-water is lovely this time of year! I wish Uncle Peter and I had the time to come along."

"Since when do *we* hike?" wondered Peter, as though the very notion was an absurdity.

"That's quite right," Jimmy," said Delia. "I'm afraid your uncle has an aversion to walking. He seems to avoid it at all costs, like one avoids the plague or certain vegetables." The wry remark drew laughter from Colin and Douglas, but when Jimmy joined in, their laughter ceased at once and they shot their young cousin a hard glare. They were permitted to laugh at their father's expense, but not their young cousin. *You haven't earned that right* was the message.

"What was the point of having all these roads built if we're going to leave the car home and go for silly hikes?" wined Peter. "Really, where's the sense in that?"

"It's not about what makes sense, Peter, it's about exercise. Perhaps you've heard of it?" Delia winked at the twins; it was an unneeded signal for them to laugh at their father. Jimmy, meanwhile, remained quiet.

"As a matter of fact," retorted Peter, "I *have* heard of exercise, despite that there are those in this room who believe that I'm not as fit and trim as I once was. Nevertheless, I intend to honour the men, who by the sweat of their brow gave us these roads, by driving on the roads, not hiking."

Delia turned her smiling eyes on Jimmy and said, "Well, no matter how one chooses to arrive at Bourton-on-the-water, being there makes for a lovely day and one you won't soon forget. I think we can all agree to that." Then she turned to the twins and added, "Not one more second of this glorious summer sunshine that we're having should go to waste. It's on days like this that one should desire to rush outside and leap and skip and twirl about in wide open spaces."

Who could be lovelier than Delia Broxton? a woman possessing within her eyes all the life that Jimmy so desperately longed to discover when searching his mother; but time and again, Catherine Philips, who was too severe, failed to thrill her son with the joy of simply being alive, or to infuse in him the desire to want to leap, skip, and twirl about on a perfect summers day. But how can anyone think to doubt or dispute that Bourton-on-the-water was lovely at this time of year after Aunt Delia had said so. Of course, Jimmy would love it! Thanks to Delia, Colin, Douglas, and their young cousin began their hike with full bellies.

In the beginning, Colin and Douglas were true to their word, they walked a pace that made it easy for Jimmy to keep up. They past the Almshouses, a row of homes built in1612 for the purpose of accommodating six poor men and six poor women; these twelve folks were also given weekly allowances for basic survival along with a frieze gown, a ton of coal, and a felt hat annually. The Almshouses still provide homes for twelve elderly poor and they remain as they were, save for the modern kitchens and bathrooms. Colin and Douglas also gave Jimmy an education on Market Hall, a rectangular stone structure with several open arches highlighting the centre of Chipping Campden. It was built by the town's benefactor, Sir Baptist Hicks, the same man responsible for the Almshouses, and for the purpose of providing shelter for traders. Jimmy clamoured to visit Market Hall, but Chipping Campden was too great a distance for a hike. They came through Northleach, whose town centre is completely unspoiled, having changed little since 1500. Afterward they arrived in Lower Slaughter, for the purpose of showing Jimmy The Old Mill. Colin and

Douglas seemed to enjoy playing tour guide for their young cousin. However, as they were leaving Lower Slaughter for the wide open spaces and fields of lavender, they picked up the pace and then began to scold Jimmy for being as they called him, "A slowcoach!" Jimmy struggled mightily to keep pace, and all the while his cousins snickered at his effort. When no longer within an earshot, the twins decided that it wasn't much fun if their young cousin couldn't hear all their clever deriding and insults. With that in mind, they more than slowed their pace in order to allow Jimmy to catch up, they actually stopped and waited him. Jimmy was relieved, believing that the silly game was over and that his cousins had well proved their point, that in comparison to them he was physically inferior, and now they would return to being informative tour guides. But when he was permitted to catch all the way up to his cousins, they seized hold of him and rolled him down an embankment. He cried, "Please don't," for all the good it did, as his cries only served to further encourage his brutish cousins.

"How was that, Jimmy?" they called down to him — their voices accompanied with the same wicked laughter that Jimmy remembered all too well from five years ago. "Would you like to go for another ride? No cost; you only need to make it back up the hill." Jimmy knew it was useless to protest. He was also afraid that should he do so, or in any way not act a sport, his cousins might wind up tossing him down the embankment instead of merely rolling him, and turn an already brutish activity into a medieval game of midget toss. Jimmy made it three quarters of the way up the embankment before its pitch proved too daunting a test for his young legs. Colin and Douglas went to meet him at that point, though they were hardly accommodating; they were rough when seizing hold of Jimmy's arms and even rougher when marching him the rest of the way up the embankment. Once at the top they rolled him down again and again and again — five times in all! Thank goodness, though, for Jimmy's sake, the twins grew tired of marching him back up the hill. After each turn, Jimmy's legs would falter closer to the base of the embankment and Colin and Douglas would have to go further in order to fetch him. The labour, they at last decided, wasn't worth the thrill of watching their young cousin's frail little figure rolling down a hill. Thank goodness for small favours. After five trips down the embankment, Jimmy's hips and shoulders were quite banged up and bruised. "We're so awfully glad you came to stay with us, Cousin," said Colin. "You just can't imagine all the amusement you're about to provide; the word boredom will never escape our lips." Colin's mock cheeriness nearly caused Jimmy to burst into tears; though somehow, despite his ravaged body and frayed psyche he managed a stiff upper lip.

"No need to look so glum, there, Jimmy," said Douglas. "It's only two weeks. The time will fly by just like that; you'll see." Douglas snapped his fingers to indicate how quickly he thought the time would pass, and then let loose the wickedest of chuckles.

"Easy for you to say," remarked Jimmy, "you weren't the one being rolled down the hill."

"No need to sound so cross, Jimmy," said Colin. "We were just having a bit of fun — at your expense, of course. But you might as well know from day one, that's the way things are going to work; we have all the fun and you get to bear all the cost. It's only fair that we warn you. Now, don't you feel a whole lot better knowing where you stand? That you should expect anything at any moment and nothing should surprise you?"

"Now that you put it that way, how could one *not* feel all warm and fuzzy?" Jimmy drolly remarked.

"Brother, our cousin has a sense of humour, after all," said Colin. He acted genuinely surprised, for he *was* surprised by Jimmy's drollness, but his tone exceeded *surprised* on the way to *astonished* or *flabbergasted* or whatever else would serve to surpass *surprised* in order to mock the fact that Jimmy was found in possession of a sense of humour. Then Colin added, with regard to the cost that Jimmy must bear for the sake of his and Douglas's entertainment, "Just think of it as charity, Cousin, or community service, that way these two weeks won't seem so gruelling. You're a charitable sort, aren't you, Jimmy? Besides, I hear charity's good for the soul — a ticket into Heaven. You want to wind up in Heaven, don't you?"

"At my age I have plenty of time to earn my way into Heaven," Jimmy told his cousins. "At least I think I do," was what he added warily when examining their faces in order to determine whether or not in their hearts there existed enough evil to commit murder. "And I'm fairly sure one can gain Heaven without several times having been rolled down an embankment. Besides, the way I see it, or *feel* it, charity works out much better for the receivers than it does for the givers."

"Brother, he's a real sharpie, I tell you." It was clear to Colin that his young cousin was the owner of a worthy intellect, but nevertheless, he chose to mock in his praise.

"Well, if charity isn't your thing, Jimmy," Douglas added, "then just think of us as a couple of hungry lions on an African plain, and you're a poor, fragile gazelle or young wildebeest that strayed from the herd and is all alone. Oops, I guess that wasn't very comforting, was it?"

The menacing duo took turns giving Jimmy's back a hardy slap, then they broke into a chorus of laughter. "Don't worry, Cousin, we can't very well kill you," Colin managed to utter through his contrived chortling.

"The very best that we can do is come close," Douglas added.

The colour drained from Jimmy's face, leaving him a pale and pasty victim of intimidation. He winced as though any second he might become sick, but still he managed to ask, though rather shakily, "Will we be seeing Mary Willow today?" As much as he desired to see Mary Willow (aside from his Aunt Delia, Mary Willow was all that he was able to think about since learning that he would coming to the Cotswolds), it was his wish to steer the conversation in a direction other then how he was to spend the next two weeks doling out charity that would no doubt come in the form of torture. Jimmy remembered how Douglas fancied Mary Willow, and Colin also seemed to favour her as well. It was his hope that the mere mention of her lovely name might summon a softer and more civilised side of his otherwise brutish cousins.

"Why the sudden interest in Mary Willow?" wondered Colin. Jimmy had a clear sense that his cousin's wondering contained little in the way of innocent curiosity; nor was it at all apathetic. Furthermore, he needn't have been in any way intuitive to detect the sudden change in Colin's demeanour at the mere mention of Mary Willow. The lovely girl from Bibury sparked *something* in his cousin, but what? Jimmy stiffened, as Colin's tone made him feel more threatened than when he was being rolled down the embankment. He was searching for an innocuous answer to a probing question that carried an unmistakable edge and perhaps even a tone of warning.

"I remember that day at Sudeley Castle and the secret garden just like it was yesterday," said Jimmy. "We all had so much fun together, and I just got to thinking that Mary Willow might want to join us on our hike."

"You'll get your chance to see Mary Willow, alright," said Colin. "Won't he, Douglas?"

It seemed to poor Jimmy that every word coming from Colin Broxton's mouth was a carefully planned assault — a psychological assault that was designed to leave him shattered. *You'll get your chance to see Mary Willow, alright. Won't he, Douglas?* Colin's words left Jimmy to wonder whether some awful misfortune had befallen Mary Willow, and that his cousin wished for the time being that it remains a surprise. But Jimmy dared not ask. Douglas's answer to *Won't he, Douglas* came in the form of a smirk. Colin followed with a smirk of his own, and behind each was a sordidness and evil that caused Jimmy to shudder and wish that he had never mentioned the words *Mary Willow*. He struggled to understand how his Aunt Delia could be so blind to the single-minded monster that was her twin sons. How was it possible for them to have fooled her for so long? Like all the Cotswold villages, Bourton-on-the-water can inspire enchantment. One can cite its charming cafés, tea rooms, and abundant shops of varying interests as reasons for wanting not only to visit, but linger for hours and perhaps even days. Aunt Delia, as far as Jimmy could surmise, understated Bourton's loveliness and allure. However, many agree Bourton's greatest attractions are its honey-coloured architecture and the peaceful River Windrush. The River Windrush is a catchment of the Thames. Shallow in its depth it peacefully meanders through the village of Bourton and at some segments its well lines with trees. There are several arched, stone foot bridges by which one can cross the Windrush — in most cases they're three arches to a bridge. Most cross where the village shops and eateries are densest, while others cross where the landscape is more pristine. It was over the side of one of *those* stone bridges that Jimmy was hung upside-down by his ankles. Given the earlier events of the day, this *should* have seemed, if nothing else, a predictable manoeuvre and one Jimmy should have seen coming. But until seized by his brutish cousins, who were beginning to display a kinder side as they had when touring Jimmy by the Almshouses, Old Mill, and while describing Market Hall, he hadn't suspected, nor was of the slightest suspicion that he would be turned upside-down and dangled over the side of a bridge. Jimmy spent those first moments of being dangled upside-down angry with himself for having been so easily baited. Colin and Douglas Broxton and a bridge — even a moron could put together a jigsaw puzzle that included only three pieces — three obvious and oversized pieces. But Colin and Douglas, as Jimmy had the misfortune of experiencing in his earlier youth, had the decided advantage of single-mindedness — a subtle glance, a slight shifting of the eyes was all that was needed in order for them to concoct elaborate schemes — or, in this instance, spur-of-the-moment mischief. What chance was there for poor Jimmy? If he had any chance of surviving the next two weeks, he would have to learn to think along with his cousins, and when possible, anticipate the road ahead. His only other options were to fake illness so that he could remain locked away in his room, or cling to Aunt Delia — he could remain in the house and never leave her side.

When Jimmy was led across the first bridge they came to, which placed them amid much of Bourton's hubbub, he stood wide-eyed with fascination; he had never seen a more charming village and couldn't imagine why Colin and Douglas were leading him away from such delightfulness; though he didn't dare protest — Heaven forbid he convey any thoughts or judgments that might get interpreted as disinclination. In one respect, though, Jimmy was fortunate: The arched, stone bridges that spanned the Windrush were low; therefore, if someone, for instance, was let go of while hung upside-down, survival was close to a near certainty — the worst likely scenario was that one might emerge from the river soaking wet with silt filled pockets. However, the bridges were *so* low that those dangling a certain unfortunate party upside-down were able to entirely submerge their head in the river. With that sort of villainy literally at their fingertips, Colin and Douglas Broxton developed a sudden fascination with how long their young cousin could hold his breath when held upside-down under water. They decided to make it a game or a challenge, and they assured Jimmy that should he reach an entire minute they would take him to see Mary Willow and had promised prompt delivery. Colin and Douglas suspected that Jimmy, despite the passing of five years (half his life), was quite smitten with Mary Willow and wondered to what lengths he would go to see her, or what atrocities he would endure in her name. However, given the latest turn of events it was doubtful that Jimmy would have any desire to see Mary Willow, especially after having been half-drowned and soundly defeated by his brutish cousins. Besides, he imagined prompt delivery to have meant rudely deposited on a doorstep a wet, beaten, and haggard mess to be discovered by a girl he had spent the past five years in one way or another dreaming about. *Some* discovery! That's not exactly how Jimmy imagined his reintroduction to Mary Willow, therefore he would not give his cousins the satisfaction of watching him struggle under water to reach a whole minute — he would not play their insane game. And why should he? He was to spend two weeks in the Cotswolds and figured there would be other opportunities aside from today to see Mary Willow; his Aunt Delia would surely see to it. Jimmy's head had been submerged no more than ten seconds when he curled his torso, and in doing so he was able to remove his head from the cool river water — though barely. However, this was an enormously difficult position for one to maintain for any length of time, especially while hung upside-down. Even had Jimmy been an athletic sort, which he was not, the abdominal muscle can withstand only so great a strain and for only so long before requiring rest. Jimmy struggled mightily to remain in a curled position — he fought as best he could against his own weak body, but in the end the strain proved too great and he was forced to succumb and allow his head to once again become submerged in the cool River Windrush. Before surrendering, though, he was provided adequate encouragement, which came in the form of his unified tormentors informing him that, if he didn't promptly uncurl his body he would be dropped into the river altogether or perhaps forcefully plunged. In short intervals, Jimmy alternated between the water and the air. His cousins looked on with amusement as he emerged gasping for air, and then once again submerged himself after having filled his lungs with an ample supply of the atmosphere. On and on this continued, though his dwindling strength and stamina became the influence for the increasing amount of time that was spent submerged. However, as it turned out, the water became the friendlier proposition, as it served to drown out the mocking words and hideous laughter of Colin and Douglas Broxton. At last, his body faltered altogether and the cool river water became his only option. Jimmy remained at rest, his arms and muscles limp, his head fully submerged in the calm River

Windrush — the same river that, only a short distance away was providing delight to the multitude that had chosen Bourton as their destination for a lovely summers day.

Jimmy's fate was in the hands of his two sociopath cousins, who thus far had managed to charm everyone and in particular their parents, and perhaps now were prepared to do-in the only person that was ever suspected of seeing through them and that understood their single-minded malevolence. If, in fact, it was Colin and Douglas Broxton's aim to return to the grand old Tudor a set of twins minus their young cousin, then so be it, for Jimmy was rendered powerless in regard to his own outcome. And as his eyes were closed and his head remained submerged in the cool, dark river, he thought *what did it matter, anyway*? After all, it was just recently that his father had informed him that he was different from all the other boys, and that he was weak and frail, and that in all likelihood wouldn't grow to become a man — at least not like any of the men with whom Nigel Philips was acquainted, and Catherine Philips did nothing to dissuade Nigel from his meagre opinion of their son. That was Jimmy's very last thought before being yanked from the cool River Windrush and planted upright on the bridge. When Colin and Douglas let go of their young cousin, he wobbled only a second or two before his legs gave way altogether and he fell to his knees. There, prostrate on the hard surface of the bridge, and with desperation, he tried to draw all the available air in the vicinity into his terribly distressed lungs. Jimmy couldn't be certain whether or not he was grateful to be alive (he was still too consumed with the effort it took to recover from the experience), but it could surely be said that he was surprised. When he regained but a fraction of his composure after having been helped back to his feet, Colin and Douglas each slapped his back in a congratulatory manner and informed him that he was a good sport. Jimmy thought that after having been rolled five times down a fairly steep embankment and then nearly drowned, "good sport" was a meagre compliment at best, and that a much more glowing tribute could have been spared.

However, Douglas went so far as to lend Jimmy his shirt to dry his face and hair — a magnanimous gesture, and one to say the least took Jimmy be surprise. And why wouldn't it given the events of the day; though, Jimmy, in turn, informed his cousins that if having been hung upside-down over a bridge until nearly drowned was the mark of a good sport, he would much prefer to be otherwise. Colin and Douglas saw the humour in their young cousin's wit, as was evidenced by their laughter.

"We always knew you had it in you, Cousin," was Douglas's praise. Shortly afterward, Colin and Douglas met up with friends from school and introduced Jimmy as their cousin from Bayswater and seemed fairly proud to do so, and with their stamp of approval no one dared to scoff at the idea of a ten-year-old tagging along. This remarkable turn of events roused Jimmy into wondering whether having been hung upside-down over the side of a bridge until nearly drowned was some sort of initiation — a test that he in fact passed, though he didn't dare ask. He figured that if he was *in the club,* as they say, then he would learn so in due course. He spent the remainder of his time at Bourton-on-the-water a well treated mascot to five older boys and whose opinions on whatever matters were raised were not only welcomed but enjoyed. There were even instances when Colin and Douglas exhibited affection for their young cousin; but Jimmy knew better than to turn his back on a snake — especially one with two heads. "I should trust that you had a good day, Jimmy, and that your cousins were good in showing you around?" Aunt Delia asked, when they were all assembled at the table for supper. "No one got into any mischief today, did they, Colin?"

"Yes, Aunt Delia," replied Jimmy, "Bourton was just as you had said it would be, even lovelier."

Delia Broxton's questions regarding the boys' hike to Bourton were, if nothing else predictable, and Jimmy had long since prepared his answers. Therefore, when his answers surfaced they did so sounding a bit hurried, monotone, and were also doused with the sort of anxiety one might feel when having over rehearsed for a part in a play or an interrogation. Aside from briefly wondering about any mischief that was gotten into, Delia directed all her questions toward Jimmy. His cousins had the sense that under fire he might falter and so they narrowed their eyes when glaring in his direction. *Don't you dare mention the embankment or what was done to you on the bridge, or much worse will surely follow! That you can count on!*

"And what did you think of the River Windrush?" chirped Delia. "Isn't it the most charming river you ever saw?"

"Of course it is, Mother," Colin answered. Meanwhile, Douglas held his glare on their young cousin to make certain that, until his brother was through speaking, the sufficiently intimidated Jimmy continued to hold his tongue. "Everyone knows that the Windrush is the most charming river. Right, Father? And we made certain that Jimmy had the best view of all. Didn't we, Jimmy?"

Jimmy looked down at his plate and winced as though the mere thought of agreeing with Colin was worse than any misfortune that might befall him should he not agree. But afterward he did manage to convey to Aunt Delia that he had in fact departed Bourton-on-the-water having seen the River Windrush in all its splendour, coming and going, and from every angle. Delia Broxton smiled warmly at Jimmy — her beautiful, bright smile that taught him the true meaning of loveliness — then, in what was meant as a display of affection, she reached over and playfully tousled his hair. Afterward she informed the three boys that her and Peter would be leaving in the morning shortly after breakfast and wouldn't be returning until the late afternoon. Those were not words that Jimmy longed to hear, that his Aunt Delia would be scarce for the better part of an entire day and that he would be left alone to battle against evil! He could think of nothing more disconcerting. After all, the embankment and bridge were spontaneous events, at least they seemed so to him; but now he would have hours and hours to anticipate and to ponder the malevolence of his cousins, and they would have hours and hours to concoct elaborate forms of torture. He sat down good and hungry from a day of hiking, but now lost was any stomach for his dinner. "We'll be meeting some of your father's associates and their wives at the Norwich's home for one of those teas, Mrs. Norwich is so fond of hosting. You know how much Mrs. Norwich enjoys showing off her wares?" Colin and Douglas sighed to convey, *what could be more tedious then a day at the Norwich's?* However, missing in their exaggerated sighs was any trace of sympathy. "Yes, I'm sure it will be deadly dull, but somehow we'll manage to muddle through. We usually do, don't we, dear?" Delia punctuated her last remark with a playful poke of her elbow into Peter's side. Peter, in turn, sighed as though he had already struggled to determine what *was* more tedious than a day at the Norwich's, but to his dismay he came up empty. Addressing her sons and nephew, Delia further added, with all the loveliness of her bright smile and with a fair amount of confidence, "I'm sure you boys will manage just fine without us." Jimmy had his one eye fixed on his Aunt Delia while she spoke, but with the other, he was certain that he saw a glance pass between Colin and Douglas — the same sort of glance that must have passed between them right before he was rolled several times down an embankment and then later on right before hung upside-down over the side of a bridge. One glance and that quick their plans were already made, their scheme well thought out, every detail in the correct order. It was uncanny all that could pass between Colin and Douglas, all that they were able to accomplish without the benefit of even a single word or any sort of verbal exchanged — not even a clearing of the throat. But Jimmy knew it was so, that they were *that* unified, *that* cohesive, by the satisfied, bordering-on-evil grins they now proudly wore — grins that time and again, and for some inexplicable reason always went overlooked by Delia and Peter Broxton. Despite his dwindling desire to eat, Jimmy forced food into his mouth one morsel at a time. Tomorrow, he knew, was a ways off and he would starve should he honour his dread and not the need to fill his belly. But tomorrow, he also knew, would not be the bringer of kindness, nor provide a scenario in which he would find himself a well treated mascot to older boys — a welcomed tagalong whose opinions were both well received and enjoyed. The look that passed between his twin cousins and the grins that followed told a much different story — one prompting him to wonder exactly how early his aunt and uncle would be leaving for the Norwich's, and more importantly, what was his Aunt Delia's interpretation of *late afternoon* regarding their return. Jimmy grew more and more anxious until at last too paralysed with worry to raise a fork to his mouth. He stared at his plate, visibly solemn and ponderous as he tried to determine how many hours he would have to survive alone in the house with his brutish cousins. When Delia placed dessert on the table, he began to inquire about the Norwich's, particularly Mrs. Norwich and what he gathered to be her impressive array of wares. In Listening to Jimmy, one would come away wholly convinced that he possessed a keen interest in such things, but not Colin Broxton.

"They're no children at the Norwich's tea," Colin told his young cousin. "Children aren't permitted." Colin saw right through Jimmy's attempt to get himself invited *to* the Norwich's and *away* from him and Douglas. He grinned a most victorious grin before having added, "Nice try, though, cousin."

"I'm afraid Colin is right, Jimmy," said Delia, who didn't take notice of what transpired between her older son and nephew. "But I promise we'll plan an exciting outing for the day after."

Later that night, Jimmy lay awake in his bed wondering how he could slip away from the breakfast table unnoticed in order to go off and hide in one of the many nooks and crannies the grand old Tudor thankfully provided. It was a house that could well accommodate anyone who desired — or, in the case of Jimmy Philips, *needed* to hide out for a good stretch of time. Jimmy remembered some of his favourite spots and where they were positioned. Five years ago, on more than one occasion, he, while accompanied by Fish and Chips, recognised the need to take refuge in one of those favourite spots. Now it was his hope that, after the passage of night, Colin and Douglas Broxton would wake to discover a day worthy of seeking adventure and not bother about where their young cousin might be hiding, that they would leave him alone and permit him to remain undisturbed in a cramped, dark space until sometime in the late afternoon he heard his Uncle Peter's automobile rolling into the driveway. Tonight would also be the first of thousands that would follow, which would see him with great vigour, spring into an upward position after having dreamed the sensation of drowning. He woke gasping for air just as he had after having been yanked from the river and planted on the bridge. When he at last settled himself, he summoned only thoughts of those things which he knew as lovely, and the first that came to mind was Mary Willow. He tried to imagine how she might look today, but all that he was able to envision was the ten-year-old girl, who five years ago stood beside him in the secret garden; his mind wouldn't allow him to travel beyond that point. But his Aunt Delia had promised an exciting outing on the day after tomorrow. It wouldn't be long.

In the morning when Jimmy woke, before reporting for breakfast, he abandoned his nightclothes in favour of dressing for the day. It was his wish to be well attired, alert, and prepared when he strolled into the kitchen, not a droopy-eyed pyjama clad sad sack that he usually was at home or how he might have been remembered five years ago by his cousins. There, he discovered his Uncle Peter, also dressed for the day, though he wasn't sitting upright, instead he was spread about in his chair as though *it* was wearing *him*; his uncle's appearance put Jimmy in mind of a blanket that was carelessly thrown onto a piece of furniture. Perhaps Peter was trying to accommodate an ache he developed from the fretful night sleep he had thinking about the boredom of a day spent at the Norwich's. Peter preferred that any socials involving his associates take place on a golf course with fresh air and pristine views, and more importantly, without wives, not cooped up at the Norwich's *with* wives. He sipped coffee and poured over the newspaper; he appeared as if he hadn't a care in the world, and that if he was any more sprawled out on the chair he might slip onto the floor. Meanwhile, Aunt Delia, as Jimmy observed, also was dressed for the day — and, as expected, was her usual chirpy self. However, she moved about in a disjointed fashion and seemed alone to bear whatever urgency there might have existed in regard to the day's preparations; for clearly, whatever those preparations were, they were not being shared equally among the Broxton hierarchy.

After typical morning pleasantries were exchanged, Colin and Douglas, just as Jimmy had moments ago, came waltzing into the kitchen alert, prepared, and dressed for the day. Their shining and well freshened appearance caused Jimmy to slump into a posture that screamed defeat — that no matter how far ahead he thought, not matter his preparation, he was no match for his cousins. "Good morning, Cousin," Colin pleasantly called out, as he was the first to make his disingenuous offer. "I trust you had a good night's sleep? That there was no bowl of water on your nightstand or visitations from ghosts?" Then he grinned his smirky, menacing grin to let Jimmy know that, no matter how far ahead he thought, or how careful were his calculations, he didn't stand a chance.

Douglas followed by also calling "Good morning, Cousin," then joined his brother in wearing the same smirky, menacing grin. Jimmy wanted to scream out to his Aunt Delia, *how do you not see this! Don't you realise what I'm up against! Have you no clue of the torture that I'll have to endure while you're away sipping tea! Fuck the Norwich's!* Like most woman about to find themselves in the company of

124

other women, Delia Broxton was far too absorbed with the state of her own appearance to concern herself with whatever misgivings Jimmy might be experiencing at the hands of Colin and Douglas. Nevertheless, she managed to continue along with the task of making breakfast, though her preoccupation with regard to her hair, application of makeup, and how well her dress fit caused her to seem, as Jimmy had already observed, fragmented. *And*, unless someone tampered with his coffee or set his newspaper on fire, Peter Broxton wasn't about to divert his attention enough to trouble himself over his sons and whatever sinister plot they might have in store for their young cousin. Moreover, when asked by his wife what he thought of her appearance, Peter's reply was agreeable, but too truncate and more tempered then Delia would have preferred. However, Peter's lack of enthusiasm hadn't at all to do with Delia's appearance, which, incidentally, was quite pleasing as always (Delia was the sort of woman who rolled out of bed looking fresh and lovely), but rather, he was looking *ahead*, but not necessarily *forward* to tea at the Norwich's. Peter considered some of his associates, friends, but didn't care for what he described as "humdrum teas", where he was held captive all afternoon and forced to listen to the Cotswolds more fortunate's droning on about their travel plans or where they had already been — especially where they had already been. Peter found nothing more tedious than finding himself in a position where he had to pretend to maintain any level interested in what others were doing and what they already did. He sipped his coffee and remained hidden behind his newspaper until it appeared that Delia was ready to go. During this time, he pretended not to hear Delia whine about the advantages of being a man. Jimmy tried to eat quickly, but Colin and Douglas were faster and finished first, despite having eaten more and arriving at the breakfast table later. Delia offered to make more toast and to dish out the sausage and scrambled egg that remained in the pan, but everyone maintained to have been satisfied, so she excused herself from the kitchen. She returned several minutes later much more relaxed and confident in the presentation that she would make at the Norwich's. With the heels she was sporting and with her hair done up, she appeared several inches taller. The few ringlets that she kept down to lay upon her one cheek softened what might have been too much severity. Her ensemble — everything in combination transformed her from a fresh-faced beauty to one whose allure could inspire the devil. "The town MILF (mothers I'd like to fuck)," Colin whispered to Douglas. Even Peter peeked over his newspaper. On the way to the front door, Delia fussed over Peter, primping his shirt collar and rumpled suit jacket — both which had been victimised by the poor posture he exhibited at the breakfast table. As soon as they heard the car engine turn over, Colin and Douglas closed the front door and seized their young cousin, who made what was determined as a feeble, even laughable attempt to sneak away. Each had taken an arm, which they gripped much more firmly than was necessary and rudely marched poor Jimmy through the house back to the kitchen, then down a narrow corridor which led to the cellar door. They flung open the door, marched him down the stairs, and then rudely threw him to the ground. After which, they pirouetted back to the stairs, which they promptly and with agility climbed — it seemed to Jimmy that only a second or two of mad rumbling was heard before his cousins disappeared. He still had his face to the floor when he heard the cellar door close and then lock.

"Have a nice day, Cousin!" called Douglas. "And don't worry, your eyes will adjust to the darkness before you know it."

"And when they do, you'll be able to see the rats coming for you," Colin added. "And trust me, Cousin, they *will* come. And you won't believe the size of them! Some of them are big enough to put a saddle on and ride! But there is a silver lining to all this, Cousin. The truth is, we have a surprise planned for you, one you're sure to appreciate. So while you're alone in the dark with only rats for company, know we're out there in the world, in the fresh air and sunshine thinking of you." The twin's hideous laughter burned in Jimmy's ear. He remained face down on the cellar floor, weepy and wondering what satisfaction could exist for the well-endowed in conquering that which was decidedly weaker? Where was the thrill? He felt less a person and more a *thing,* which his cousins were free to mistreat for the sheer purpose of amusing themselves; he had no notion that their cruelty toward him stemmed from the fact that they feared his intuitive nature, that they saw him as a threat that they needed to break and if necessary destroy. His weepiness and wondering turned into anger and he flew up the stairs and began pounding on the door. He demanded to be let out, but Colin and Douglas had already gone; they were on their way to Ladyhill Covert in Bibury, and as expected, neither had bothered to inform their frightened, young cousin of their plans. Despite that Douglas had mockingly wished Jimmy a nice day, the frightened young boy was angrier with Colin for having taken immense pleasure in warning him about the rats. It wasn't enough to merely be locked in a dark, musty cellar and to be ridiculed by Douglas, Colin found it necessary to apply the finishing touch by putting the idea of rats large enough to saddle and ride in poor Jimmy's head; it was always Colin, it seemed, who was all too willing to insert the final dagger and thus demoralise an already broken opponent. Jimmy always maintained the notion that Colin was the brain and the crueller of the two, and that if a heart existed between them, it beat inside Douglas. But there was no separating them — they were a conjoined entity able to strike fear in the hearts of those approaching even the most basic understanding of their essence.

Jimmy continued to shout and cry, until at last he became resigned that a dark, locked cellar was his destiny for however long his cousins wished it, which would likely be until they heard his Uncle Peter's automobile roll into the driveway. He perched himself on the top cellar step with his arms folded tightly in front of his chest and with his back firmly pressed to the door. He strived to feel enveloped, to feel things near him, and so he imagined that he was back in the closet at the end of the hallway leading to the kitchen — a place of refuge and solace into which he used to disappear with Fish and Chips when came the loud voices. How else could he reconcile that

Catherine and Nigel were vacationing in Singapore, that Delia and Peter any minute would be sipping tea at the Norwich's, that Colin and Douglas were off to Ladyhill Covert in Bibury (Jimmy was only aware that his cousins had left the house, but nevertheless, were out and about on a lovely summers day), while he was locked away in a dark, musty cellar? Why was it *his* existence, he wondered, that had to be a struggle? Was it that way for all the weak and frail of the world? Did they all suffer abandonment and isolation? From as early as he could remember, Jimmy wanted his life to be different from what it was, but nothing ever changed. When at last he was able to settle himself and with a measure of calmness summon thoughts that were more balanced, Jimmy resigned himself to the fact that being locked down a dark, musty cellar was only marginally worse than repeatedly being rolled down an embankment — the result of which produced only mild bruising and dizziness — but it was far less worse than being hung upside-down over the side of a bridge with his head submerged in cool river water until nearly drowned. He concluded that he was no worse or better off than yesterday — a day that he ultimately survived. He was also able to conclude that, his Aunt Delia wouldn't spend a single night in a house where large rats — or, for that matter, rats of any size were permitted to roam freely.

Before he became fully aware of it, just as Douglas had promised, Jimmy's eyes adjusted fairly well to the darkness; with each passing minute he was able to penetrate further and further into the musty cellar, until at last he was able to spot high up on a wall and just inches below the ceiling, a curtain This was a most promising discovery and one that precipitated him relaxing his tightly folded arms and lurching forward on the top step. It mattered not that the curtain was dressing only a small rectangular window — it would supply sufficient daylight along with providing an effective portal through which to view the outside world — a most vital feature for one trapped alone in a cellar. He descended the stairs and carefully stepped his way to the wall. There, he discover piled up against the wall were wooden crates — four stacks of two in all. The stacks, as Jimmy dolefully discovered, were taller than his person. He made several attempts to hoist himself up and onto the top crate, but he hadn't the strength nor agility to accommodate this modest ambition; his body, as was the case when trying to maintain an abdominal curl in order to keep his head out of the cool River Windrush, was too frail and weak. On his final attempt, his hands slid down from the dry, warped wood of the crate, and when doing so they managed to gather several splinters. With his back to the crate, he despairingly sank to the floor, where with his teeth he managed to dislodge many of those gathered splinters, though some were too deeply embedded for the use of teeth and for the time being they would have to remain. But Jimmy wasn't through — not just yet. His determination began to swell and it became greater than his fear; he refused to accept defeat at the hands of his own weak, undersized body. He managed to get his small fingers between one of the top end crates and the cellar wall, and after doing so, he began to yank. At first it was a futile exercise in which he managed only to scrape his fingers against the roughness of the cellar wall. Nevertheless, he continued on. He yanked and yanked until one derisory inch at a time the top crate began to shift over the bottom crate. He was nearly all out of strength, when at last, and with only one desperate and mighty yank remaining in his weary arms, the crate came toppling to the floor, where thankfully it remained wholly intact and could be climbed on to. Jimmy collapsed beside the crate, where he huffed and puffed and tried to gather himself for one final show of strength. His stood behind the crate and leaned such that all his weight could be applied, then he began to push. He pushed and pushed until he was able to suitably position the crate in front of the stack that was directly in front of the window, then he promptly began his ascend. Once the window was achieved, he seized hold of the curtain as though it were an entity out of which he was preparing to choke the life (perhaps he imagined the curtain was the Broxton twins or his parents); then in a fit of anger, which seemed to augment his strength, he ripped the curtain away from the window and did so as if he was blaming the object for the effort that was required to get his hands upon it. What Jimmy didn't know, but perhaps should have suspected, and might have if not for his haste, was that the curtain had been fixed into place for years and perhaps even decades, and therefore it had collected more than its share of dust. His foolish, angry manoeuvre produced quite a cloud that stung his eyes and launched him into an attack of sneezing which nearly toppled him from the crate. When he, along with the dust had finally settled, there came the satisfying discovery of daylight, which had gushed through the window and flooded the cellar — most objects could now be seen with a fair amount of clarity. He quick turned toward the window, and when peering through it, he delighted in the multitude of shrubbery, trees, and slopes that made up the rambling landscape behind the grand old Tudor. Then he turned back toward the cellar, and for his own benefit he sighed loudly to further convince himself that having been locked in a dark, musty cellar wouldn't be the ordeal that Colin and Douglas had hoped. Jimmy sat atop the crate and permitted his eyes to rove about the now somewhat illuminated cellar. It didn't take him long to determine that the artefacts, equipment, and supplies stored in the cellar were not at all representative of the folks who currently dwell upstairs, but of a family who long ago had taken up residency in the grand old Tudor. The cellar had the smell of mustiness and of oil, and most everything it housed was well cobwebbed if not ancient. The supplies had been sitting in place for decades; the antiquated though functional equipment had gone undisturbed for at least that long; only the artefacts, such as the old-fashioned, ornate balance beam scale once used for weighing silver and gold, which Jimmy regarded with a fair measure of fascination after having peeled away its ample veil of cobwebs, and a phonograph, which still had on its turntable a vinyl record thickly covered with dust of Sir Edward Elgar's "Enigma Variations", had been introduced to the cellar in more recent times. Remembering the sneezing fit that tearing away the curtain had produced, Jimmy was much more careful when removing the dust from the vinyl record; though he soon discovered that both the composer and selection was entirely unfamiliar. Aside from storing outdated artefacts left behind by residents past, or perhaps by those who originally occupied the Tudor, Delia had decided on a more practical purpose for the grand old Tutor's attic — a sewing room; and being that the attic was somewhat removed from the rest of the house, she figured that it would make an ideal room where she could work undisturbed. After this was decided, so began a steady three-day parade of carrying from the attic to the cellar, that which she described to Peter as "useless old junk", but what her nephew now saw as treasure. It didn't matter to Delia that Peter believed that some of these artefacts, if matched with the right collector, might fetch a fortune, or that they belonged to those who lived at the Tudor a hundred years ago and therefore were historical. To her it was all dusty, cobwebbed junk, and she preferred that it all get stored in a part of the house where she never planned to visit.

Delia didn't care very much for the cellar; it gave her "the willies" was what she often told Peter, who, in turn, told her that her feelings regarding the cellar were "drivel". Nevertheless, once the attic was through being emptied of all its wares and transported to the cellar, she never again returned. Peter kept his wine in the cellar and joked that it was also where he kept his mistress, and that there was only one way for Delia to prove whether this claim was true of false. But nothing could entice Delia to venture down into the cellar, and she would often respond to Peter's outlandish methods of enticement by making a childish noise known to some as *a strawberry*.

Jimmy meandered through the cellar careful not to miss anything, and as he went about he tinkered with all its forgotten and unwanted treasures. He found a great deal of delight in handling and trying to deduce the purpose of all these interesting objects of old — so much so that he had all but forgotten that he wasn't down the musty cellar by his own choosing, but had been locked away by his brutish cousins, who, for awhile now, he had stopped thinking about. As he continued on, what began as a dark, musty cellar, became a sort of after-hours museum that he was permitted to tour alone and which contained articles that he was able to touch and to tinker with; everyone at one time or another has found themselves in an interesting place and wishing that they could have it all to themselves.

Next, Jimmy stumbled upon several kegs of nails, and beside those kegs were two old-fashioned rectangular wooden tool boxes, the kind with a long cylindrical bar for a handle. He was sorting through one of the boxes when he discovered a manual drill press. He was fascinated by its configuration, with its flat, round wooden knob on the top, crank handle in the middle, and a shaft in which to place a bit on the end. Despite all the years of inactivity the tool still smelled of oil and Jimmy didn't find the smell unappealing — in fact, it helped inspire him to imagine the sort of man who might have used such a tool and how he might have used it. He concluded a manual drill press to be a tool that would require powerful, steady hands and a fair degree of skill. This led him to further conclude that it wasn't a tool all too familiar to his Uncle Peter; Jimmy didn't imagine Peter Broxton as the *tool type.* Nearby were two sawhorses and a workbench, and above the workbench was positioned a simple light fixture — the kind with a pull chain, though missing from its socket was a bulb. Jimmy made a thorough search of the area, but there were no bulbs to be found. Still, he took the trouble of positioning one of the sawhorses alongside the workbench — he would use it to climb up onto the workbench should he stumble upon a light bulb while rummaging through the remaining array of fascinating but neglected treasures. Jimmy couldn't understand, but in the future would remember to ask his Aunt Delia and Uncle Peter why they had such little regard for the eclectic array of treasures he spent the past two hours discovering and which caused him to wonder and to imagine. Why were none of these fascinating artefacts used or displayed, but instead were stored in a cellar and allowed to collect dust and to grow cobwebs? Every inch of the musty old cellar either marked history or had a story to tell, and history and stories, as is often the case, have romance, but not at the Broxton Tudor — all the history and stories were going to waste! From the landscape, to the architecture, to the its many nooks and crannies, the grand old Tudor possessed more than its share of charm and interest, but the most fascinating part of the old place, according to Jimmy, was dying from neglect.

After Jimmy had winded his way back to his starting place (the cellar stairs), he discovered an ornate, claw footed walnut bookcase; however, the case displayed not a single volume, old or new, which came as a disappointment; he would have delighted in positioning himself on the crate, just below the window with the company of an old volume to fan through; reading books was a hobby of a sort, if you could call it that — it was how he spent most of his time when at home while isolated in his room. Instead, the bookcase was home to several bottles of wine. What Jimmy found most peculiar, though, was that unlike everything else that had occupied his mind, kept his hands busy, and stroked his imagination; the bottles were free of cobwebs and thus far had collected very little if any dust. Jimmy had no way of knowing whether the bottles were recent purchases, or items of old but of some interest; both the former and latter would explain why they appeared to be so well looked after. He brought one of the bottles nearer to the window to better read the label. There, he discovered that it was the former. So in a dark, musty cellar that housed more history than most antique shops, Jimmy had finally stumbled upon the only items actually purchased by a Broxton and in which a Broxton had any interest.

He made his way back to the wooden crates, which he climbed atop in order to be nearer to the window. The view of the outside reminded him that he was a prisoner in the cellar, but the warm midday sun was pleasing in a soothing sort of way on his shoulders, and after awhile his eyes began to flutter as he became drowsy. That he had more than dosed off, but fell into a deep sleep came as a surprise — a surprise that wasn't realised until there came a loud rapping on the window. The rapping startled him. It took a good moment or so for him to get his bearings. He woke in a sweat and had forgotten where he was, which was perfectly understandable — it's not often when one has occasion to nod off while atop wooden crates in a musty old cellar. After thoroughly rubbing his eyes, Jimmy squinted through the glass, but aside from the rambling landscape he saw nothing — at least nothing that could have produced such a sharp sound on a window pane — there were no tree branches in plain sight and no evidence that any objects had blown against the glass — everything appeared tranquil and undisturbed. What he had yet to realise, however, was that Colin and Douglas had returned from Ladyhill Covert and were flanking the window. Neither boy from the vantage point of inside the cellar could be seen. Jimmy's face was pressed up against the windowpane, when there came an arm swinging down into view. At the end of the arm was a closed hand, which again rapped loudly on the glass. This time Jimmy jumped back and nearly fell from the crate. He was too startled to prevent himself from yelling out. "I take it you're still down there, Cousin?" Colin called. "That you weren't able to escape?" The chuckle that followed the rhetorical questions was one of immense self-satisfaction and wickedness. "We knew from the terrified yell that it must still be *you* stuck down there. And I'll bet you're good and hungry about now, unless you're too white from fright to consider your growling little tummy." Despite the hours of enjoyment that the cellar had provided, Colin's mocking tone caused Jimmy to view it as a place of banishment or of the worst kind of imprisonment. "So how'd the rats treat you, Cousin? Did they behave themselves today? They can be darn right nasty when they're good and hungry, you know. We're surprised you didn't break the window and escape; scrawny little shit that you are, I imagine you could fit through the window quite easily. So either you're a stranger sort than we imagined and enjoy dark, musty old places, or you just didn't think to do it. So tell us, Cousin, which was it?"

Jimmy figured it prudent to play along with all the nonsense about large cellar dwelling rats, else the brutish twins might busy themselves cooking up yet another scheme to try and terrorize him. He also admitted that he didn't find dark, must old places favourable and simply hadn't considered the window as a means by which to escape. "Cousin, we want to let you know that we didn't just go thoughtlessly running off this morning," said Douglas. "We actually considered you a great deal today. It could even be said that you were on our minds most of the time that we were gone and so we brought you back a surprise. We're quite sure you'll enjoy it."

"Douglas speaks the truth, Cousin," added Colin, "you *were* on our mind a great deal and we *do* have for you a *wonderful* surprise. You might say it's your reward for being such a good sport. And, Cousin, make no mistake, you *have* been a good sport — a very good sport — even better than we could have hoped."

"I'm glad that I was able to exceed your expectations," remarked Jimmy, whose drollness was equal to Colin's derision.

"We do love that sense of humour, Jimmy," said Douglas. "Keep it coming, because you're going to need it."

"Once again Douglas speaks the truth," Colin added. "A sense of humour can be like a best friend, and everyone needs a best friend. Don't you agree, Cousin?"

First praise, then warning. Nothing was ever simple with Colin and Douglas — every message or thought had a secondary meaning — behind every act of kindness was looming an act of terror. There was no getting ahead of them, and poor Jimmy wasn't up for the challenge. Though he didn't care if Colin and Douglas kept him locked away in the dark, musty cellar after having been reminded of his hunger — he was accustom to long periods of isolation, and where they took place, as he saw it, was of no great consequence — all he wanted was for his cousins to go away from the window and for him not to hear their voices. *I'll gladly remained banished to the cellar and my afterhours museum, just let me be!* was what he wished to shout but remained silent. Following Colin's words, a figure was pushed in front of the window and then was held there firmly in place. Until then, Jimmy wasn't aware that a third party had been present and with this new knowledge he became mildly intrigued. He was only able to observe the figure from the knees on down. He permitted his eyes to travel to the ground, where he saw feet that were bare and unmistakably feminine. This caused his interest to swell even further. The knees, which he also noticed were bare, were pressed together in a manner that might give one the impression that their owner was filled with a fair amount of dread and disquietude. Had Jimmy's eyes been able to travel farther upward, he would have also witnessed hands, which, when in a relaxed state possessed much loveliness, but now were rigidly clasped together and were dangling in front in order to preserve what little if any modesty that remained. "What do you think so far, Cousin?" asked Colin. "Would you care to see the rest? If you're *normal* you would want to. But I understand "if" is an awfully big word — isn't it, Cousin?"

All at once, Jimmy went numb with fright — perhaps as much fright as the knees which his eyes helplessly beheld from behind the stationary casement. He was unable to respond to Colin's overture; though, had he been capable of any words, this was an occasion when he might have elected to remain silent. His frightened silence, however, was perceived by the menacing pair as bold ungratefulness, and it prompted Douglas to unleash an assault on his ears by yelling, "You little shit! We went through a lot of trouble for you today! You better start showing some fucking appreciation!"

Jimmy jerked away from the window, when at first the girl who was believed rigid with fright was positioned sideways and then forcibly pushed down to her hands and knees, exposing for Jimmy every bit of her nakedness. The girl was visibly trembling and Jimmy could sense the magnitude of her shame — shame for her nakedness and how it was presented — shame for being handled as if she was less than a person, but a thing. "Don't you look away, Jimmy!" yelled Douglas. "Don't you dare look away, or we'll come down there and give you a thrashing you'll never forget!"

"You had better listen to Douglas, Cousin," warned Colin. "You were told yesterday that we couldn't kill you, that we could only come close. Big shock, Cousin. We lied! We're fucking liars!"

The eyes of Colin and Douglas Broxton would usually sparkle with the very devil himself, or their mouths would form a grin filled with derision when addressing their young cousin. Never before had they actually *shouted* words of anger — never before was there belligerence in their tone, only in their intention. Something was different — something in only the space of a few hours must have changed to have brought about this deviation in behaviour, this notable distortion. But there was no mistaking it — their malevolence, which customarily was subtle and crafty had turned violent. He was slow and reluctant, but Jimmy did as ordered and turned back toward the window. He refused to take in the girl's nakedness — he would not allow his eyes to travel beyond her flaxen hair, which hung prettily about in loose wisps alongside her face. The girl looked straight ahead, not daring a peek in the window — nary did she shift her eyes. She remained an object — a nonresponsive *thing* to be preyed upon.

Jimmy felt his heart sinking, his frail, little body becoming limp; for worse than fright, he sensed the girl's resignation — the sort of resignation that's brought about by helplessness — by succumbing to forces you haven't the power to resist. Jimmy didn't recognise the girl, for she had changed a great deal over the past five years. No longer was she the young girl who filled with wonder when exploring Sudeley Castle, or who skipped and twirled through its secret garden, exhibiting all the gaiety and freedom that childhood allows. She had since become a young woman, but there wasn't a shred of doubt, only certainty of who she was.

Despite the inability to see their faces, somehow Jimmy knew that it was Douglas who was kneeling behind Mary Willow and Colin kneeling in front of her. Both had remained shirted; they were only as naked as they needed to be. At last it was all becoming clear to Jimmy; he understood the game: Viewing Mary Willow's nakedness was his reward for having held his breath under water for a whole minute and for being as his cousins said, "a good sport", and that perhaps it was his lack of gratitude that caused his cousins to go so far afoul. How he wished that he hadn't intimated his eagerness to see Mary Willow, but it had been five years, half his life! He wept silently that Mary Willow was shamed for his benefit and that her egregious ill-treatment was partially his doing. He looked away. *Let them come down here and thrash me*, he thought. *Let them kill me if they wish, at least they will have let poor Mary Willow alone.*

Jimmy's theory for why Mary Willow was paraded before him and then so ill-treated was only partially correct: He had no way of knowing that, unfolding right before his very eyes was the un-holiest of trinities — a trinity that began five years ago in subtle stages and progressed to what he was now forced to witness, and if taken further would result in certain destruction.

From the age of ten, five years ago, Douglas began professing his love for Mary Willow, whereas Colin, for the sake of his twin, had always denied having been in possession of such feelings — until in more recent times. Early on, though, Colin would loom in the background whenever Mary Willow was present; he would peer at her over Douglas's shoulder as though he was making every effort to determine whether or not she was right for him (them). If it was, in fact, Colin who led the brain in their single-minded dynamic, then perhaps it was Douglas who led the heart. Nevertheless, Colin chose to proceed in a more guarded fashion and to see to it that their heart didn't go astray or venture off into places where it couldn't be controlled. However, the heart lacks obedience, and in matters of love and war, there can be no ties, only winners and losers. But in the case of the Broxton twins and Mary Willow, there were three very distinct scenarios; all were bleak, and all would arise without any declaration of a winner: Colin and Douglas could come undone and destroy one another; for the sake of their own survival they would destroy Mary Willow; or, they would force Mary Willow into destroying herself. All three knew the stakes and that their alliance would not end well. Despite all three being *in the know*, they continued to play their dangerous game. Today, though, was the first time that Colin and Douglas Broxton had forced themselves on Mary Willow. The game, as they themselves might have predicted, was spinning out of control, and swept up in this twister of madness was a ten-year-old boy who was trapped in a cellar. Nothing in the world made any sense to Jimmy — certainly not his controlling father, and less his mother, who seemed to possess little grasp in the way of human affection; nor, too, did his Aunt Delia, who he adored and perceived to be the essence of loveliness and virtue, but who in the matter of her monstrous twin sons was unable, as they say, to see the forest for the trees. His judgment of his Uncle Peter, however, wasn't nearly so harsh: After observing his uncle and the carefree manner in which he comported himself at breakfast, sprawled out on a chair and supplied with his coffee and newspaper, Jimmy dismissed Peter Broxton as an absentee lord, who despite providing a manor over which he professed to oversee, he had limited if any knowledge of its goings-on. Nowhere, not even in his own mind could Jimmy find even a shred of peace and comfort. Every bit of the darkness that enshrouded him in Bayswater was present at the grand old Tudor in the Cotswolds; there was no escaping it — it had travelled, and with its new geography, and with uncommon vigour it intensified to new heights — unbearable heights.

Hurriedly and with a great deal of agitation, he climbed down from the wooden crates. Once on the ground and having worked himself into a frenzy — a dizzying frenzy, he began kicking the crates and pounding his small, tender fists against the warped wood. His frenzy began to surge and swell and soon he began launching himself into the wood, battering his shoulders until well bruised, and then the sides of his face until welted and bleeding. During this manic display of masochism, he screamed repeatedly as one might when forced to withstand torture; although, in his current state he had become all but immune to any and all physical pain — his screams were those belonging to one who had at last broke from a blitz of mental torment. The depth of his torment and his brokenness was sensed outside — at first by Colin, who began to thrust with more vigour into Mary Willow's mouth, then by Douglas, who followed his brother's lead from behind Mary Willow.

Not only had Jimmy's pain become tolerable, but it was welcomed, as again and again he launched himself into the stout, wooden crates, leading with his shoulders, sometimes with his face. He was wild and frenetic and he appeared to teeter out on the edge of utter madness, though his madness had a goal with one very definable feature: Whatever pain and torment Mary Willow was forced to suffer at the hands of his brutish cousins, he wished for his own pain and torment be as great if not greater. He was powerless to rescue her and to take away her shame — that much he knew — so instead he would break himself for her sake and in her name — darling Mary Willow. Unless shared equally, or what was perceived in his own ravaged mind as being equal, there was no other way for him to accept such a profound and utter defeat. After gathering himself for another mighty lunge (his last as it would turn out), he didn't merely run, but launched himself, and in doing so, he made ringing contact with his face and chest. The force of the blow was so that it sent him reeling and stumbling away from the crates and across the cellar floor over to where stood the claw footed walnut bookcase. Not without an effort, he got back to his feet but was a wobbly, exhausted, and a battered mess. Continuing with his frenzy, he took hold of a wine bottle by the neck and hurled it — end over end, the bottle travelled across the cellar until it met a wall; the explosion of glass both looked and sounded spectacular, and he found it satisfying. So he threw another, then another, then another, adding to the red-stained wall until he became alert to the fact that the cellar door had been unlocked and the door was swung open, though not a word was called down to him. He went tearing up the cellar stairs, through the house, and then he exploded through the back door and out into the rambling sundrenched landscape behind the grand old Tudor. He yelled for Mary Willow, but she was nowhere in sight. He stood alone among the shrubbery, trees, and rambling slopes a battered and disoriented mess. Colin and Douglas had already retreated to their rooms, where they planned on remaining until summoned for dinner. When Jimmy re-entered the house, he was met unexpectedly by Delia and Peter, who had just returned from the Norwich's. Seeing his aunt and uncle served to restore him to a state of calmness, though vividly apparent was his battered condition.

"Jimmy, what on earth happened? You look an absolute mess!" cried Aunt Delia.

"For crying out loud, he looks like he's been put through a grinder," remarked Uncle Peter.

Peter Broxton wasn't trying to be droll, he was every bit as taken aback by Jimmy's condition as was Delia. Jimmy remained fixed in place, and on his battered face he wore a faraway gaze and offered no explanation regarding his astonishing appearance; nor did he have any memory of repeatedly launching himself into large, stout wooden crates. Though had he remembered, he might have determined that such absurdness — such bizarre masochism was grounds upon which to concoct a false account. "How was the tea?" he managed to ask.

Delia and Peter peered in at the ten-year-old, whose composure seemed all too remarkable for one who appeared as if having been recently and perhaps only moments ago was traumatised. Stranger yet, as they observed, Jimmy seemed hardly aware of his condition.

"The tea?" replied Delia. She was clearly accusing Jimmy of deflecting. She couldn't imagine that under the circumstances he could remember his manners otherwise. "Good Lord, Jimmy! Your face! Did you get injured? Were you attacked? Where are your cousins?"

"My cousins?" he asked. With the mention of Colin and Douglas he quickly put his hands to his face. Afterward he appeared genuinely astonished by the sight of blood that appeared on his fingertips. In a burst of clarity he wondered to whom else could the blood belong but to himself? With the sight of blood, though, came an onrush of pain — his shoulders, chest, and face began to throb. His composure, which only moments ago, was thought to have been remarkable, began to slip precipitously. This sudden and sharp slippage caused him to sway disjointedly about the room and to murmur words that were indecipherable to both his aunt and uncle.

Then, in a sudden burst, he remembered why he was feeling a wreck, and furthermore, what caused him to repeatedly launch himself into stout, immovable wooden crates stacked flush in front of a wall. However, neither the former nor latter did he intimate to his Aunt Delia and Uncle Peter, but instead, he turned away from them and once again went charging through the back door and out into the rambling landscape.

Delia called after him, but Jimmy heard not a word; he was once again swept up in the throes of the same frenzied state that only minutes ago had gripped him when still locked away down the cellar. Delia looked back at Peter and was about to suggest that, since he was better suited that he should run after Jimmy, but before she could say as much, Peter alerted Delia to the fact that the cellar door was left wide open. Both agreed this was peculiar, for the cellar wasn't a choice place for recreation, and that perhaps in some way the dark, musty area was related to the condition in which they found Jimmy *and* his strange behaviour. However, they also agreed that Jimmy wasn't the sort, who on his own accord would go investigating dark, musty, unfamiliar places. Nevertheless, Peter was of the notion that whatever happened to his wife's beloved young nephew must have occurred down in the cellar. Peter went in search of what he referred to as his "trusty flashlight" and then headed straight away for the cellar. He didn't expect Delia to follow, but that's exactly what she did; her curiosity over how her nephew came to be a battered mess was greater than her fear, though she was still filled with reluctance, and therefore kept her hands gripped tightly to Peter's shoulders as together they descended the stairs. Peter was surprised by how well lit the cellar was, but then he became alert to the fact that, where once was positioned a curtain, now there existed a bare window through which was pouring the late afternoon sun, and a sun flooded cellar was proof that some activity had taken place in the seldom ventured to area during his and Delia's absence. Below the window he noticed that a crate had been rearranged, and on the floor nearby the crate was the discarded curtain. He shined his flashlight and saw the bloodstained wood of the crate, which explained the "how" of the mystery, but not the "why". Next he permitted his eyes to travel about the cellar before they came to rest at the shattered glass below the wine-stained wall.

"What on earth happened here?" Delia wondered aloud.

"Who could have done such a thing?" asked Peter. He looked to Delia as if there existed the hope that she could offer an explanation. When none was forthcoming, he shone his flashlight on the near empty claw footed walnut bookcase, then shook his head in despair. This was too much mystery and destruction to accompany so little in the way of explanation.

Meanwhile, Jimmy, giving no regard for either his hunger or pain, ran wildly and at times stumbled through the sloped acreage owned by the Broxton's. Beyond the Broxton land were multitudes of wild brambles through which his barely adequate legs had to weave. It had been five years, half his life, but he was fairly certain in which direction was Ladyhill Covert in Bibury, but cared not how long or how much village he might need to search before finding Mary Willow. He was determined. Weaving his way through the brambles, which were easier to negotiate than the slopes, Jimmy stumbled once more, this time skinning his knee on an earth embedded stone. He wasn't impervious to the pain, though by now, he had grown accustom to the sight of his own blood. Undaunted, he picked himself up and continued on his quest. He crossed a road and entered into a field. There were more slopes over which to stumble, and brambles through which he needed to weave, but at last he reached a clearing. There, well off in the distance, though very much visible, was a bedraggled girl walking with an unnaturally narrow gait and with her arms folded tightly to her chest, much in the manner Jimmy's were when he first found himself locked away in the cellar. She would have given anyone the impression that she preferred disappearing over being discovered, even if the discoverer was an innocent ten-year-old boy. Indeed, everything about Mary Willow's countenance and manner screamed that she would rather be left alone with her thoughts, her misery, no matter how unbearable. Jimmy's eyes widened and he sprinted into the clearing. "Mary Willow! Mary Willow!" he cried out.

Mary Willow didn't turn toward the direction of the excitable voice, but maintained her narrow gait and kept her head held low.

"Mary Willow! Mary Willow!" Jimmy continued to call. At last Jimmy caught up with her. "Mary Willow — it's me — Jimmy Philips! Don't you remember?"

"What is it that you want?" she tersely asked; though not for a second did she waver from looking straight ahead, nor did she slow her pace. "Are you alright, Mary Willow?" Jimmy thoughtfully wondered aloud as he bounded alongside her.

"Of course I'm alright! Why shouldn't I be alright?" Mary Willow's words continued to sound terse and snapping. This caused Jimmy to recoil, but then a moment later, he managed to gather himself and stammer, "B-but Colin and D-Douglas ..."

"What about Colin and Douglas?" was Mary Willow's sharp return. "What about them? What are you trying to say?"

"Back at the house outside the cellar window," said Jimmy. "Remember?"

"Stop being so damn cryptic, Jimmy, and just say what's on your fucking mind!"

Five years, half a lifetime of waiting, only to be caught in a storm of justifiable rage, for which Colin and Douglas Broxton were responsible. Nothing could have been more contrary to all that was imagined. After her angry words were blurted out, Mary Willow turned toward Jimmy and brought an open hand down across his face. It wasn't until after she felt and heard her open hand smacking against his soft cheek that she noticed his terribly battered condition. She jumped back and shrieked at the sight of Jimmy's face *and* for the sake her own violence, which came to her as a shock (never before had she struck anyone), and perhaps was even more a shock then Jimmy's messy condition. Despite the sting of the blow, Jimmy didn't as much as put a hand to his face, but hung his head that his caring and concern had produced such an anger reaction. Mary Willow fell to her knees, where she burst into tears, and then she crawled over to where Jimmy stood. She threw her arms around his waist and cried, "Forgive me, Jimmy! Please *do* say you forgive me! I don't know what I'm doing!"

"There's nothing to forgive," said Jimmy. "You're upset and I ran after you because I was worried. You do remember me, don't you, Mary Willow?"

"Oh, Jimmy, dearest Jimmy, how could I forget you," cried Mary Willow. "How could I ever forget are picnics together and that lovely day at Sudeley Castle and the secret garden. Those are days I'll always treasure, and I have a picture of us all standing together in the secret garden. Your Aunt Delia gave it to me in a lovely frame. I keep it on my nightstand, where I'm certain that it's the first thing I'll see when I wake up each morning and the last before I turn off my lamp and go to sleep."

"Aunt Delia gave me the same picture as well, also in a lovely frame," chirped Jimmy. "And guess what, Mary Willow? I, too, keep it on my nightstand, and for the same reasons!"

There's nothing all too profound or ironic about two people having shared an experience each in possession of a keepsake photograph displayed on something as common as a nightstand, but it moved Mary Willow to, once again, burst into tears and to throw her arms around Jimmy. The two remained fixed in an embrace and for awhile neither saw the need to utter a word. Their silence seemed to magnify their breathing and the sounds of chirping birds in the meadow. How wonderfully uncomplicated to sing, tootle, and chirp all day long in a meadow and to be perfectly content to do so. It's not all that uncommon for a person to desire to be a bird or anything other than a human being, especially when human life has reached the lowest of points and the world has been stingy in its ability to show any kindness. It's exactly what Mary Willow and Jimmy Philips were both thinking and eventually intimated to one another — to be a bird or any creature able to live free of all human torment.

"It isn't going to end well, you know — Colin, Douglas, and me," said Mary Willow. "I've lain awake at night trying to imagine all sorts of ways how it *could* end well, but I don't see where it's possible. "I had no idea what they had in store today when we were hiking back from Ladyhill Covert. When we were nearing the back of the manor, I heard Colin say that a curtain was missing from a cellar window. I didn't think anything of it; after all, what could be so extraordinary about a missing curtain? But then I saw a look pass between him and Douglas. I've seen that look before, but I never imagined ..."

Cutting her off, Jimmy asked, "Do you think that they're evil? I mean ... *really* evil?"

"You might think me quite mad, Jimmy, but I think Colin and Douglas Broxton is one person existing in two bodies," said Mary Willow. "That's crazy, isn't it? I must be plenty mad myself to even think such a thought, but sometimes I really wonder." Jimmy's head jerked upward to where his eyes met Mary Willow's. Despite the notion of "crazy", her belief of what the Broxton twins were was what he had suspected all along, but he dared not mention it for fear *he* would be thought crazy. "They're never in conflict with one another; they're always in perfect agreement; in a way it's unnatural," Mary Willow went on. "And it's strange, even eerie, how quickly they can move from caring to destructive, or from kind to threatening, and the efficiency with which they do it — that, too, is unnatural. Somehow, though, I'm drawn to them; and when I'm with them it's both thrilling and frightening — like something wonderful or awful is about to happen and you're not sure which, but you feel compelled to stay around long enough to find out. Being with Colin and Douglas is kinda like standing in line waiting to board a big, scary rollercoaster and your turn is coming up next and you're not sure whether to go through with it or turn and run the other way. I suppose if I had any sense, I would lock myself away in my bedroom and not come out until I'm an adult. "I'm glad you're here, Jimmy. You'll protect me, won't you?"

"Yes, Mary Willow, I *will* protect you," he said. "I'll do my very best."

Everyday Mary Willow and Jimmy would sneak away and meet in the same clearing. It mattered not how much time each may have spent pacing and wondering, neither became fretful, for there existed supreme trust that the other would show, and neither was ever disappointed. They were both only children, with one suffocating from more attention than any one human soul could tolerate, and therefore had unwittingly begun walking the path of self-destruction, while the other, who thus far had lived a life of abandonment and isolation, was starving for attention, and in a way was equally susceptible to the likes of the Broxton twins. As the days unfolded, for the sake of one another, Mary Willow and Jimmy Philips became the one good thing upon which they could rely. When together in the meadow they felt insulated by the trees, slopes, and the wild brambles that helped shape the area. For two people who seemed to exist out on the fringe of a world that has had little in the way of kindness to show them, and where true friendship was in short supply, insulation and the comfort of company that was both thoughtful and forbearing was all to which they had aspired. What developed, though, over two weeks of clandestine meetings, was a friendship and bond, the likes of which no earthly tragedy would ever break.

****

Nothing much changed for Jimmy upon his return to Bayswater: Catherine and Nigel's trip to Singapore did little in the way of strengthening their rifted marriage, and shortly after all three were assembled under one roof, the warfare, which had been a common occurrence, continued with its usual regularity and vigour. As for Jimmy himself: As was the case before summer vacation, upon returning to school he was shown the same lack of regard by his male peers, who by virtue of their advanced physicality were much closer to manhood. Luckily for Jimmy, for awhile he was befriended by many of the girls at school, who weren't yet enamoured with the sight of male perspiration, along with any the signs of budding manliness that began to surround them. However, this unexpected but well enjoyed favourability was short-lived, as one by one, the girls all got their periods and were swimming in hormones, and with their newly found maturity they sought out the larger athletic types, leaving Jimmy, once again, largely ignored and very much alone. Shortly after his return to Bayswater, Jimmy and Mary Willow began corresponding on a weekly basis by way of written letter. Their letter writing would last for years and would never falter — not once for any reason would it take a week's vacation. Those written words on sheets and sheets of paper were not in any way calculated, nor were they carefully chosen, but were an outpouring of honest emotion, which at times would serve as a lifeline whenever one sensed that the other was going too far adrift or needed the reassurance that they were well loved and cared for, and that no matter how far out on the fringe they existed, they were not alone. It was during those times, when they were putting pen to paper or reading one another's words, that they were able to exist on another plain or feel safely enveloped in an alternative reality. With words alone, they could transport one another back to the meadow where they were insulated by the trees, rambling slopes, and wild brambles. In the meadow, there were no loud voices or scary roller coasters — only soft voices and the sound of chirping birds, and a boy and girl who longed to escape the world.

CHAPTER IV
WE'RE NOT SO DIFFERENT AS YOU THINK

As Sister Ignatius was discovering, there was no greater enemy of tired, bloodshot eyes and a pulsating cranium (each having been brought about by an ample amount of Chevis Regal), than a bright, unrelenting morning sun. Finn, however, was no stranger to coping with tired, bloodshot eyes and a pulsating cranium, and he was also well familiar with their cause and common enemy, therefore when he moseyed on over to the Doctors Without Borders healthcare unit within the Kalma refugee camp, he did so supplied with a pair of sunglasses and a ball cap after having consumed a sufficient amount of coffee and aspirin.

Sister Ignatius pretended not to have spotted Finn as he was approaching — or, *moseying*, which was how her spying eyes interpreted his gait. Along with having to cope with the irregularities that occur when one has surpassed their limits, she woke this morning fearing that she might have to contend with Finn's smiling eyes and the satisfied grin she figured him to wear on the morning after having influenced a nun to surrender to alcohol. Of all the earthly pleasures or evils over which to suffer a momentary lapse, succumb, or with which to run afoul, the consumption of alcohol could be regarded as one of the less egregious. Nevertheless, Sister Ignatius, with her bloodshot eyes and pulsating cranium was certain of having to suffer through the company of a smirky Finn. He had yet to utter a word, but she had already grown agitated assuming she would have to endure his supercilious tone. Although quite busy, the sister tried to appear busier than she actually was, and when at all possible she performed her duties with her back to Finn. Finn had a clear sense that Sister Ignatius was embarrassed over last evening's escapade, which saw her deposit most of what she had eaten that day onto the raised, bare roots of an acacia tree. After the sister bid Finn a hurried "Good morning," which carried with it little in the way of welcome less an invitation to converse, he replied by stating: "Just came from having my morning coffee with Mr. Somersby."

"Oh?" said Sister Ignatius. She truly didn't begrudge that Finn had thus far enjoyed a leisurely morning sipping coffee with his English colleague, and that he troubled himself to *mosey* on over to the camp's healthcare clinic to inform her of this fact, but that's how it was interpreted.

"The two of us were pouring over a newspaper that he purchased yesterday when he was in Nyala in pursuit of *you know what*." Finn sighed, and then in a manner that could only be describes as self-deprecating, he added, "The U.S. central command has portrayed Iraq as edging toward chaos, was what we learned from this one particular article. Well, what do ya know? Oh, and did I mention that violence is at an all-time high? And last but not least, urban areas are experiencing ethnic cleansing campaigns to consolidate control? God bless the good old U.S. of A. Where would we ever be without them?"

Sister Ignatius saw right through Finn's attempt to overwhelm any embarrassment she might be feeling over getting sick last night from drink. Nevertheless, she smiled warmly that his magnanimity and thoughtfulness stretched to where he would speak disparagingly toward his own country for her sake. She didn't know with any degree of certainty

Finn's position on the war in Iraq — it wasn't a subject they discussed personally, nor had she overheard any relative conversing on the subject that he might have had with Somersby, and there was ample opportunity to overhear the two colleagues, for when together, if nothing else they were a chatty pair. Nevertheless, Sister Ignatius had always assumed, mainly because she viewed Finn as an arrogant sort who never let anyone forget that he was from *the great land of opportunity and of plenty*, that The United States' efforts in what was dubbed 'Operation Iraqi Freedom' was something that pleased him. Either way, she appreciated his thoughtfulness. "Well, Mr. Finn, regardless of what may be going on three thousand kilometres to the north of us, I should welcome you to the a.m. version of the Kalma healthcare unit," said Sister Ignatius. "And if you think this is something, if you can afford the time, just stick around; the most crowded pub in Soho has got nothing on us!"

"I don't doubt it, Sister" said Finn. "And for sure, you'll never hear me clamouring that I'd rather have your job to do than my own. And if you ever do, you'll know I've really 'gone off the rails' as Mr. Somersby likes to put it." That Finn had acknowledged how hard and long the sister laboured brought a warm smile to her face. After all, everyone from time to time enjoys a bit of acknowledgement or an occasional pat on the back; no one is immune to the satisfied feeling that comes when told they're appreciated. Besides, it mattered not to Finn that the Franciscan sister was serving God on behalf of humanity; long hard hours were still long hard hours. Finn wished to have a word with the sister regarding last evening: It was his hope that the way it ended wouldn't adhere as a deterrent from future discussions, and if that much was agreed upon, then he would assure her that the next time he would be much stingier with regard to doling out spirits. For the time being, though, he chose to linger along the perimeter of the open air facility until he could have a full moment of her attention. While lingering about he noticed a picture that she had displayed on a tabletop. He hadn't noticed it yesterday when he met Hadil, the Sudanese gentleman with the noble face whom he desired to befriend, but now that he had, he decided that it looked entirely out of place among all the hospital paraphernalia, which given the makeshift conditions, looked remarkably organised. As far as Finn could see, there were no other photographs in plain view. He wasn't sure of what led him to assume that the only personal artefact in sight belonged to Sister Ignatius, but he was near certain that it did. When examining the photograph more closely, he judged the age of the film as *decades old*, therefore the children in the photograph couldn't have belonged to Sister Ignatius, and so there went a theory of one of the many secret lives he had always suspected the sister of concealing. Finn couldn't pinpoint Sister Ignatius's years, but knew that the two of them along with Mr. Somersby were very close in age and that the photograph went back to a time when they were all prepubescent.

"Be careful Mr. Finn," called Sister Ignatius, when she spotted Finn reaching for the photograph. "It's my most valued earthly possession."

"Not to worry, Sister," said Finn. "Never was there a more sure-handed fellow that I — even on a morning after."

"Ah, I was wondering when you would get around to mentioning last night." The sister narrowed her eyes as though she was preparing to greet the devil that she assumed was about to surface in Finn.

"Last night?" said Finn. "What do you know; I have no memory of last night. That's so unlike me, though perhaps some time you'll be kind enough to fill me in. I do, however, remember falling asleep reading Dostoevsky. The next thing I knew, Mr. Somersby was shaking me awake. Afterward we had 'a few pops,' as he likes to say, and that's the extent of what I can remember. I surely hope I didn't miss anything *too* exciting."

Again, Sister Ignatius smiled warmly that Finn, albeit with humour, was thoughtful and had considered her feelings. "I don't doubt you, Mr. Finn, that you're sure-handed — even on a morning after indulging, but it's a very sentimental photograph," she told him. "It's travelled with me throughout the years and seldom has it been out of my sight."

"And what an enchanting photograph it is," said Finn. "Where was it taken? And just who *are* these lovely children? I've never seen such a lovely quartet."

"To answer your first question, it was taken at the secret garden of Sudeley Castle," the sister told him. "England, as I sure you're aware, has its share of castles, and Sudeley Castle, I was once told, was the most romantic."

"And this beautiful young girl standing between the two boys who appear to be twins and the much smaller boy? That wouldn't be you, would it, Sister?" wondered Finn.

Sister Ignatius clearly understood that Finn had paid her a compliment, and one which should have been received with a smile or some other measure of delight, but instead, it caused her to stammer, "Y-Yes. I mean, n-no." That Finn's eye went straight for the girl in the photograph caused her whole demeanour to shift. She was all of a sudden well out-of-sorts.

"Well, which is it?" asked Finn.

Sister Ignatius took a deep breath and then another, and with it came the return of some composure. "Her name was Mary Willow," she went on. "No girl was ever lovelier than she. She was the sweetest of the sweet, the kindest of the kind, and she was someone whom I once loved very much."

"Was?" said Finn, who right away jumped to the conclusion that this person called Mary Willow was someone with whom Sister Ignatius had a lesbian affair.

"Yes, Mr. Finn. *Was*." Both the sister's tone and countenance became solemn when adding, "She died tragically some years ago. We all have had events in our lives that have tested our faith, our resolve — events that we must move on from so that we ourselves can survive and maintain some sanity. Mary Willow's death, I'm afraid, was an event that I was never able to fully get beyond. Some suspected that the twins killed her, but not enough evidence was gathered and so it never went to trial. The police investigated diligently, or so I was told, but her death was declared a mystery — a tragic and gruesome mystery."

Finn wondered the method of murder, but elected not to force Sister Ignatius to delve further into a subject that clearly caused her distress. Instead he asked, "And the small boy?" "Jimmy Philips was his name, and he loved Mary Willow as much as anyone — perhaps more so than any one human soul has ever loved another." Sister Ignatius seemed proud to state such a claim. "I realise that that's a bold statement," she went on to add, "but believe me, Mr. Finn, it's not said with a light heart — I believe this to be an absolute truth. They say he went mad once he learned of Mary Willow's death. No one has seen or heard from him since."

"How awful," said Finn. He gingerly set the photograph back down on the tabletop. He appeared a superstitious sort who believed the photo was cursed and that there existed the possibility that any lingering tragedy it possessed, if held too long, could be transferred to his person. "And the twins?" he added; although at that point he was almost too afraid to ask.

"I lost track of them." The terse reply made it clear to Finn that having lost track of the twins didn't come with any measure of regret for the sister. "Although, you could say I wanted to lose track of them," she went on to admit. Despite all the suspicion over Mary Willow's death, we were never that close to begin with, the twins and me. They lived in the Cotswolds, which is a lovely stretch of the English countryside, and they were of a certain privilege. Anyway, it was their mother, Delia Broxton of whom I was most fond. Since Mary Willow's death, though, I haven't spoken with her or written to her with the same regularity as I once had. The whole sordid incident caused us to drift apart; though I suppose it was more my doing — that it was me who did most of the drifting."

"This story just keeps getting cheerier and cheerier, doesn't it?" remarked Finn. "It's a wonder you haven't taken the photograph and tossed it into some river or had someone dig a hole and bury it somewhere where you'll never think to look."

"My apologies, Mr. Finn," said Sister Ignatius. "I don't mean to be so morbid, especially first thing in the morning.

"Please, Sister, don't apologise," said Finn. "The lives of those children in the photograph make for the perfect campfire story in such a place as Kalma."

Finn's mild sarcasm, in turn, drew somewhat of an ironic smile from the sister, who assumed that the subject was brought to a close and would have preferred that be the case. She made an abrupt move to indicate her wish to return to her duty, when Finn asked, "So I take it then, that it was *you*, sister, who took the photograph, since you're not one of the subjects *in* the photograph?"

"Y-Yes — I mean, n-no," the sister once again stammered. She apologised for again acting out-of-sorts and cited last night's ill-advised activity as the cause, though Finn suspected otherwise — that there was far more to the photograph then meets the eye, but figured it would take another quiet evening out by the Acacia trees to get to the whole truth of a photograph that, on the surface was already quite a story. Nevertheless, he played along with the sister and assured her that her behaviour was perfectly understandable given the amount of Chevis Regal that was consumed.

"The twins' mother, Delia Broxton took the photograph," Sister Ignatius went on. "She must have taken it, for I believe that was the summer I was travelling through Austria and Hungary with my parents."

"Ah, travelling through Austria and Hungary, you were?" said Finn. "No doubt Vienna and Budapest? Fascinating places, I hear. Some time you must tell me all about them. Though it sounds to me that the twins weren't the only ones who were of a certain privilege." After having been mistaken that Sister Ignatius was a self-loathing lesbian, Finn now theorised that she was guilted into her vows by entirely too much privilege. It seemed a logical leap.

"Unfortunately, I was quite young and don't remember very much at all, and what little I do remember is vague at best. Most of my recollections are from what I was told later on." The sister's tone and countenance revealed a bit of testiness when adding, "But I assure you, Mr. Finn, I did not have what most would consider a privileged upbringing. In fact, I had anything but …"

"Anyway, Sister, I sought you out this morning because I couldn't wait to tell you how much I appreciated your insights and enjoyed our talk last night. I hope it won't be our last." Finn words were followed with a smiled. It was the sort of smile that forms on one's face when they've discovered humour of which no one else had been made aware. "However," he went on to add, "if you don't mind, from now on I think I shall like to retain Mr. Somersby as my drinking buddy."

"A most wise decision, Mr. Finn," said Sister Ignatius. "Most wise, indeed."

****

The Kalma refugee camp is believed to be one of the largest and more heavily populated camps in the Sudan and perhaps in all of Africa. It's home to an estimated 90,000 displaced Darfuris, many whose homes were set ablaze. One of the more common occurrences within the camp are young men pushing poles into the hard ground to erect frames on which to drape anything that could serve as a shield from an unforgiving sun. Huddled together and stretching from horizon to horizon are a multitude of tents and mud huts. As Finn and Somersby have acknowledged, "This is a scene that would give anyone pause no matter how many chances they have had to bear witness."

Despite the overcrowding and poor sanitation, within the multitude of tents and mud huts there still existed hope, and along with that hope were men and women who continued to apply their industry, and children who remained thirsty for education. "Children tend to draw what they know," was what Finn relayed to Somersby, but not without afterward crediting Sister Ignatius. Finn had showed Somersby the alarmingly violent drawings done by the children in his charge — the same drawings he had showed Sister Ignatius. The two colleagues who grew up an ocean apart would go on to work diligently to try and unlock the *child* in Darfur's children. If the potential was there, and they believed that it was, then success was not only attainable but a very real possibility.

"So bedding a nun wasn't your only objective, after all?" Somersby had incredulously remarked. "You actually had, dare I say, a secondary motive that could be understood as — honourable?"

"Mr. Somersby, you say that as though my having honour is out of the realm of possibility — a rare turn of events."

"Could it be then, that our dear Mr. Finn isn't the scoundrel that some of us had originally thought? And that there is ownership to *some* scruples and *some* morals regarding, at least, *some* of our species not having come endowed with a vagina?"

"I wouldn't go so far as to say all that," Finn had replied. "My scoundrel hood, I'm proud to say, remains very much intact. After all, Mr. Somersby, I wouldn't want to disappoint you, nor make you feel *too* alienated from the rest of the Kalma population."

"Mr. Finn, your opinion of me goes straight to my core and warms my heart," Somersby had told his kindred colleague.

"What are friends for?" was Finn's reply.

A few weeks had come to pass before the opportunity for Finn to reacquaint with Hadil had presented. Finn had been keeping an eye out for the handsome, well-defined features of the tall Sudanese gentleman that had left such a favourable impression, but in a refugee camp that was home to 90,000, it was more likely that luck or some coincidence would supply the scenario if they were to meet again. It had been a few days since Finn and Somersby saw Sister Ignatius. They wondered if she had found cause to avoid them, and so the two cronies decided to pay her an impromptu visit at the Doctors Without Borders clinic within the camp. When they arrived, the sister wondered aloud, "I trust that thus far you two have enjoyed a leisurely morning with your mugs of coffee?"

"She can't help it," Finn told Somersby. "It's that whole Catholic guilt thing — it's so ingrained that they themselves aren't even aware of it."

After the snarky exchange, Finn began reading titbits about the war in Iraq from a newspaper he purchased the day before in Nyala, while on a mission to procure (successfully) another bottle of Chevis Regal. As it was the case for many, the war in Iraq had become somewhat of a sore subject for the sister. The bombardment was a military manoeuvre that many had cheered, however, the minute the boots hit the ground there came a pouring of outrage. When Finn finished the passage that he was reading, he paused to raise an eyebrow, then he uttered rather superciliously, "That wouldn't be a bit of crossness that I'm detecting from our good sister, would it? After all," he continued, (although his words were entirely for the benefit of Sister Ignatius, they were directed toward Somersby) "*your* poor Tony Blair is just as up to his proverbial neck in this sordid affair as *my* George W. Bush. They're both on the hot seat for sure."

"You're quite right about that, Mr. Finn," agreed Somersby. "Never mind who pushed for this bloody war, they certainly *are* both up to their necks, as you well put it — or, as some like to say, they really *stepped in it* and are now *knee deep* — I'll leave the euphemisms to the imagination." His last remark was followed by a covert nod in Sister Ignatius's direction before giving Finn a smirky sort of wink. "You may refer to the war in Iraq as a sordid affair with your mere words, Mr. Finn, but your tone seems to suggest something else entirely — or, could it be that you're merely trying to get my goat?"

Sister Ignatius turned squarely toward Finn and rather firmly stated, "And if you were to take your nose out of that damn newspaper, you'll see that I'm looking squarely at *you*, not Mr. Somersby!"

"Sister, you wouldn't be accusing me of being a warmonger, would you?" The tone of Finn's inquiry was overwhelmingly condescending with a near undetectable trace of indignation. Nevertheless, he did as the sister suggested and removed his nose from the newspaper; although his aim wasn't necessarily to honour the sister's wish as much as it was to better observe and perhaps even delight in her agitation.

Sister Ignatius tried to appear hurried and overly burdened when she went on to mutter with a measure of disgust: "Greeted as liberators, indeed. Isn't that what your dear Mr. Cheney had said? I wonder how those *once well chosen* words taste about now. Not very good, I'll bet. I imagine we'll be in Iraq until kingdom come if we don't first run out of money." She raised her voice when adding somewhat superciliously, "You see, Mr. Finn, there's a rumour going around that this war is costing a few greenbacks, some of which could get allocated for loftier purposes, and Lord knows I can certainly think of *one*. How about you?" She waved her armed about somewhat derisively; it was as if she was trying to alert to Finn of the obvious, in the event that he had become insensible. He removed his eyes from the animated sister and rested them on the sea of tents that stretched from horizon to horizon. Somersby did the same. This was a scene that never ceased to sober, and when juxtaposed to the context of their exchange it was nothing less than astounding. It was right then, when Finn and Somersby were looking out over the landscape that Hadil appeared. His appearance seemed sudden, as if he came squirting out from the multitude. His appearance came before anyone had the chance to utter something they might truly regret. And whether it was for Hadil's benefit or his son, Mozamel, who was right by the Sudanese gentleman's side, the mood which was bordering on confrontational quickly shifted to pleasant. "It's Mr. Finn, correct?" asked Hadil.

Finn smiled broadly and acted genuinely pleased that Hadil not only remembered *him*, but also his name. He took great pleasure in introducing to Somersby the Sudanese gentleman, whose face appeared to portray a world of kindness and who was able to lend a quiet grace and nobility even in the most trying of circumstances. "My oldest son, Mozamel." Hadil had a hand at his son's back, encouraging the young man to step forward.

Both Finn and Somersby placed Mozamel at about fifteen years of age. They took a moment to examine the young man's well-defined features and determined them to be as handsome and also possessing the same sort of gracious nobility as his father.

"My son has a rash, Sister," said Hadil.

Mozamel frowned in a manner that suggested that his father was overprotective and too much an alarmist and that there were many others with far more pressing issues. He made light of his rash, but his father's persistence prevailed. "It may very well be nothing," said Sister Ignatius, "but it won't hurt to let us have a look."

Hadil was very proud that in a time of great crisis, Mozamel had exhibited strength and every sign of becoming a man.

Hadil no longer had land on which to farm, but he did have some tailoring skills, which he applied in Nyala. Mariam, his wife, volunteered her services as an assistant at the Doctors Without Borders nutrition clinic within the Kalma camp. Mozamel saw to it that his younger siblings were being educated, and he also learned to concoct meals from the most meagre of provisions.

"He has become a master chef!" Hadil declared of his son. With only wheat, beans, oil, salt, and powered food mixes at his disposal, Mozamel was managing to fill the bellies of his siblings. As for himself, Hadil, and Mariam, they ate whatever was left, and more often than not, it was barely enough to keep up their strength. Throughout the course of conversation, Finn, Somersby, and Sister Ignatius learned that Hadil's land had been scorched and that his house burned to the ground. The family only narrowly escaped with their lives, particularly Mozamel. During the ordeal, Mozamel witnessed his dear friend, Sumaya, gunned down. He held her hand until her life had fully expired.

"I knew that she was going to die, and I knew the danger of staying with her," Mozamel told them, "but I wanted the last thing Sumaya saw in this world to be the face of someone who cared for her."

"I can't think of a greater act of courage and kindness," said Sister Ignatius.

"Nor I," agreed Somersby, who along with Finn, tried to remember life at fifteen years of age and how they might have coped under such impossible conditions. To ignore all warning and self-preservation so that a young woman wouldn't die alone on an open field staring up at an empty sky was beyond admirable. Their lives were too far removed from that of Mozamel's, and like most, they were never presented with the opportunity to exhibit such courage. "All we need is another two or three billion like you Mozamel, and we might actually have a shot at world peace," said Somersby.

Finn and Somersby looked on admiringly at Hadil's oldest son — not as much for his courage, which was extraordinary, but that at the ripe old age of fifteen, Mozamel already knew something of himself that in a lifetime many would never learn. How does one react when the wolf is at their door? *Courage under fire* is what some call it. We all would like to believe that if ever a situation were thrust upon us, like Mozamel, we would seize ownership of such an attribute and employ it admirably. Finn couldn't learn enough about Hadil, Mariam, and the impressive young man that they gave the world. With each passing day, Darfur, a place Finn once dubbed "hell on earth", along with the Kalma refugee camp, were no longer a mere mission or a job, but it was becoming his life and it filled him with more purpose than he had ever imagined. Slowly but unmistakably, the old clockmaker who had stolen the joy from his childhood, and the young and beautiful Caroline who had broken his heart, together were sliding down a slope and about to drop into the *pool of insignificance*, where they would swim for their lives, but ultimately drown. No longer was Finn's spirit weighted with malice or resentment, but it floated about with a greater sense of wellbeing. A sudden inclination came over him to embrace Hadil and he felt strong in his desire to inform the Sudanese gentleman of his admiration, and that the reason Mozamel was such an impressive young man was because he has such an impressive father. "There, that should take care of it," said Sister Ignatius. "But you'll be sure to come back in a few days and let us have another look, won't you?"

Mozamel was unable to resist the sister's good nature, and therefore readily agreed to return. Although, no sooner did he received the good news of his rash and was enjoying the company of his new acquaintances, a faint rumbling could be heard in the distance. *It can't be thunder,* Finn thought to himself. He looked curiously at Somersby. The two men then looked skyward and saw the same blue, cloudless atmosphere to which they had earlier woke and under which they had sipped their morning coffee.

Moments later, the faint rumbling grew louder and it seemed to be bearing down on the camp. Also the ground began to tremble, and what followed was a murmuring throughout the camp that at the very least put it on-edge. The collective murmurings of such a multitude along with the tense gesticulations that accompanied them, created a curious sense of dread for those, who like Finn and Somersby, weren't in the *know*. Ninety thousand men, women, and children simultaneously were stirring for a reason that was not yet apparent. Finn and Somersby first looked at Hadil. Then they shifted their eyes over to Mozamel and Sister Ignatius. They studied their faces of all three, hoping that somewhere hidden in their countenance was an explanation or at least a hint of what ninety thousand people seemed to be preparing for. The faces of all three were grim, but they also appeared poised. This led both Finn and Somersby to the understanding that, the faint rumbling and trembling terrain and whatever was to follow, Hadil, Mozamel, and Sister Ignatius had experienced in the past, and therefore knew how to comport themselves. Finn gazed out upon the restless multitude, and then, once again, brought his eyes to Hadil, with the hope that the Sudanese gentleman would sense his misgiving and lend some perspective to why tensions throughout the camp were escalating on what seemed a second-to-second basis. "What's happing?" wondered Somersby, as he watched Sister Ignatius loading up a backpack with medical supplies.

The camp seemed to shift and sway, and here and there clouds of dust appeared. Finn could sense the collective urgency throughout and likened it to the activity of birds and insects in the waning moments before the arrival of a storm. "I'm not sure what's happening," said Sister Ignatius. She made every effort to remove any alarm from her tone, although her countenance and actions revealed having had some suspicion.

Conversely, Hadil and Mozamel hadn't much if any doubt, and no sooner the sister was through gathering up her medical store, a group of children, who only moments ago were playing and chattering about, were now running wildly through the camp yelling, "Janjaweed! Janjaweed!"

As they passed by the clinic, Hadil gravely whispered, "Devils on horseback." The term "Janjaweed" is a colloquialism meaning "a man with a gun on a horse". For years the Janjaweed acted as horse-borne bandits swooping in on non-Arab farms to steal cattle. Today, they are a well formed militia acting on the behalf of the Khartoum government, pillaging towns and committing mass murder.

Within moments the Kalma refugee camp was no longer a place where here and there clouds of dust were being kicked up, but instead it became one massive cloud of dust, and within that cloud the camp's frantic inhabitants were scurrying about in every which direction — the sheer volume of their collective movements and murmurings were deafening. Finn, Somersby, Hadil, and Sister Ignatius, all at once though unwittingly began to converge toward Mozamel until they had formed a protective barrier around him. Soon they themselves were all enveloped by the pounding of hooves on the hard, dry terrain, and the sound of gunfire. The Janjaweed, along with the shifting of thousands under siege became a clamorous stampede of violence and terror. In a matter of seconds an already trying existence transformed into a caldron, where taking place was the worst kind of human behaviour.

Unlike the crimes against humanity in Kosovo or the genocide in Rwanda, subjects that on numerous occasions Finn had discussed with a colleague over a drink or a latte safely and from afar, he now found himself firmly entrenched within the worlds latest atrocity. No longer was Darfur merely a place where sedentary tribesmen and women were herded into camps. No longer did its depiction lie wholly within the crude drawing of children. And despite the pain and burning that was shooting through his body, he felt not a shred of regret that he elected to come to this region of unrest and torment. Instead, his mind raced with concern over the wellbeing of Hadil's other children, though this was not an issue he chose to raise aloud while beside the Sudanese gentleman and his brave son. Amid the confusion and escalation of violence, Finn felt a hand take firm hold of his wrist.

"Come!" yelled Sister Ignatius, and she began to pull him along. The two began to sprint off, although they hadn't gone but a few paces, when Finn stopped to observe Mozamel, who was forced to the ground and shielded from the spray of bullets by the brave and alert Hadil.

"Was the boy hit?" Finn managed to call out above the panic. "Was Hadil?"

"It wasn't Mozamel who was hit, nor Hadil!" cried the sister. "Now, please, Mr. Finn, we can't wait around any longer!"

With the pounding of hooves and the sprays of bullets waging an assault on their ears, the sister and Finn managed to weave their way through the multitude and its collective hysteria. It wasn't until they had reached the point of being in the clear that Finn realised who had been hit.

"We have to keep pressing on, Mr. Finn!" urged the sister. "It isn't but a kilometre in that direction, an old abandoned shack. If we can make it there, I can safely treat your wound."

The Janjaweed tore through Kalma, shooting and butchering — they looted the medical supplies and other critical provisions that managed to find its way to the camp by way of UNICEF and other charitable organisations. What they couldn't take with them they would set ablaze, just as they had to the homes of the many who were herded into Kalma. "I didn't know nuns to be such athletes," Finn huffed and puffed. "Couldn't we walk the rest of the way?"

"Fine, Mr. Finn, but we should walk quickly," implored Sister Ignatius. "You're bleeding, in case you hadn't noticed, and we can't very well stop in the middle of a clearing to patch you up; and had we stayed, I was afraid that if you took another bullet your situation would have become too critical. I'm sorry to tax you so, but I really did have to get you away from there.

"But do tell me, Mr. Finn," the sister continued, but with a noticeable edge, "was that enough chaos for you? Is the old heart pumping good and fast? Is the adrenalin flowing rather freely? Do you feel more alive?"

"What are you suggesting?" The sister's line of questioning caused Finn to become agitated, and despite the pain that with each breath and step was surging through him, he managed a clear note of indignation. "A while ago you seemed quite pleased with what was going on to the north of us in Iraq," Sister Ignatius reminded him. "There was even haughtiness to your tone — or was that just for *my* benefit?" Before Finn could answer, she went on to add, "So, what do you think *now* that you've gotten a healthy dose of what actually goes on in the world? It's much different up close and in person, don't you agree, Mr. Finn? Kosovo, Rwanda, and now here: I imagine the perspective was altogether different from the other side of the Atlantic? Am I right? The world is easy when it only comes to you by way of a newsreel; you need only to change the channel and it's right back to sports or comedies or whatever else *we* westerners choose to entertain ourselves with, and Lord knows we have a multitude of choices. But you *did* have your 9/11 debacle, we surely mustn't forget *that*."

"You sure picked a fine time to make your point," said Finn.

"90,000 people have been crammed into Kalma, Mr. Finn," said Sister Ignatius. "90,000 people who use to have lives, and homes where they greeted one another good morning and kissed one another goodnight. How many of those 90,000 do you think are lying dead in a pool of their own blood? Perhaps as many as were killed in the trade centres, I would imagine! And how many women do you think are being raped right as we speak? Perhaps as many as get raped in New York City in any five year period! Would you say that's a fair estimate? But that's just today. What about tomorrow, next week, or next year, not to mention what might be going on in other camps near and afar!"

"Sister, you can bludgeon me all day long with your words, but why should I apologise for the United States being civilised? Or, for that matter," Finn added, "the whole western hemisphere being overall more civilised than the east? That's a fact one can hardly deny, less dispute."

"Really, Mr. Finn? Civilised?" The sister shrieked, as she thought Finn much too haughty in his rhetoric. "You're actually of the opinion that, because shots are never fired on American soil, and because your military reeks its havoc overseas, while the citizens that it has sworn to protect are able to exist wholly above the fray, that that makes you more civilised? Mr. Finn, really?

"And to make matters even worse," the sister went on, "is that you give these media sensational names for your military manoeuvres, such as "Desert Storm" and "Shock and Awe." Indeed, "Shock and Awe". I believe that it was your dear Mr. Rumsfeld who came up with *that* beauty, and naturally it prompted all you Americans to gather around your oversized television sets, where you were glued to "Shock and Awe" like it was some damn video game that you were all trying to ace, or the latest empty-headed reality show. You all watched your bombs drop and those missiles you're all so proud of hitting targets, and it was like a great big Fourth of July celebration! But then the aerial bombardment ended and "Shock and Awe" simple became "The War in Iraq" and suddenly it wasn't so much fun anymore. It became terribly complicated very quickly with unexpected insurgence, didn't it, Mr. Finn? And now young men are coming home with missing limbs or in body bags!"

"What do want from me, Sister? The United States is in a lose/lose position," Finn tried to argue. "The United States is *always* in a lose/lose position. Whenever we act it's, 'There goes those damn Americans again, sticking their nose where it doesn't belong.' We have good ears in America, you know; from across the pond we can hear what you Europeans are thinking. And when we sit back and mind our own business, these same ill-equipped boobs begin droning on with, 'Well, why aren't the Americans doing anything about it? Why aren't they getting involved?' Jacques Chirac begged the U.S. to intercede in Kosovo, but then lambasted them for Iraq. Instead of the United States of America, they should call themselves *The United States of We're Damned If We Do And Damned If We Don't*. Since we're constantly getting flack from the rest of the globe, it would most fitting, wouldn't you agree, Sister?

And while we're on the subject, if you were to stop the average American on the street and asked what he or she thought, it's likely they'd tell you that they would prefer that the rest of the world simply go on with the exercise of ass fucking itself to hell or into oblivion, since it always seems to be striving for either place! And as I'm sure you know, Sister, nowadays things aren't all that peachy in the good old land of opportunity. We may not have refugee camps occasionally getting sprayed with bullets, but we have plenty of other issues. I sincerely doubt that England any time recently have been inundated with Mexicans and Cambodians and all the other no-wants and undesirables America routinely takes in. The U.S. is beginning to resemble the liver of a stage four cancer patient with the burden of all that it has had to filter."

Silence was what followed Finns last remarks. What also followed was their arrival at the abandoned shack of which Sister Ignatius had spoken. It didn't appear to be the safest of structures, for it had long since fallen into ruins, both from neglect and vandalism. Once they stepped inside, Finn apologised for his remark about what he believed the average American preferred that the world do — citing that, although likely accurate, it was most uncalled for.

"We're not as different as you think, you and I, Sister," Finn went on to add "After all, we're both Existentialists, are we not? I mean, we wouldn't be here if we didn't believe in shaping our own destiny or existence by way of asserting ourselves into the world. And I must say, we've certainly chosen quite a lofty path upon which to assert ourselves. Unfortunately, the high road to heaven, I would imagine, is a rather short one. Bumpy as hell, but short. Of course, when one has a bullet sufficiently lodged in their body they can stake such a claim with utter confidence. Anyway, I pegged you for an Existentialist awhile back, when within an earshot I overheard you going on about Kafka with one of the doctors — that handsome Swede — I believe his name is Soderberg."

"You were lurking in the bushes?" the sister accused Finn.

"Sister, we're in Kalma; there *are* no bushes," was Finn's droll retort.

"It's quite alright, Mr. Finn, it wasn't a private conversation. But perhaps in a way we are Existentialists, but you more than I," Sister Ignatius maintained. "Where we truly differ, though, is that you aspire to change the world in order to better accommodate you *own* views — you *own* perception of the greater good — the world according to a westerner — whereas I am willing to bend and if necessary, break, in order to accommodate the world."

"Is that your profound and philosophical way of reminding me that I'm a selfish bastard spawned from the milk of American arrogance, and that you're an angel of mercy sent here by the Franciscans with no agenda other than to serve humankind and are perfectly willing to die for the cause? Really, Sister, must it always end at the cross for you Catholics?"

"*You're* Catholic, Mr. Finn! Or have you forgotten?"

"Non-practicing," Finn replied. He didn't utter it proudly, but as a matter of record.

"Still, there's Catholic ideals ingrained in your soul that perhaps you're unaware of."

"Maybe you're right, Sister; but can there be no other alternative other than to break for the cause?" At first Finn sighed, then he began to swell with agitation before adding, "Well, be that as you believe; but how hollow must it be to wake each morning only to launch yourself into a world that can never love you back the way you assert to love *it!*" Finn's tone was more scathing then the sister for the moment could bear, and so she turned her back to him.

"I have God's love," she muttered, "and that is more than I could ever need and perhaps even deserve. I much prefer to exist as a soldier seeking to serve and to please God, than one who goes about with swagger mocking Him because they think they have it all figured out."

"It's not that I mock God or ridicule the Catholics or the importance of those entities in our lives; I understand perfectly that within them there is value," Finn began. "It's just the way I see it, God is given far too much credit and nowadays too much blame — especially too much blame. I'm fairly certain that the idea of God originally came about, because the belief that the world is a random, ungoverned place was entirely too terrifying. Indeed, Sister, God has become a handy means in which us *good old* human beings can exorcise ourselves of any real responsibility; and clever species that we are, we went ahead and concocted a omnipotent being to whom we can assign blame. 'It's not our fault; it must be God's plan.' 'God must be angry, so He sent us a hurricane or a tsunami to show us who's really in charge of the asylum.' How unfortunate for us that we're saddled with a supreme being that has a flair for communicating by way of devastating forces of nature. Of course, it couldn't be that these forces have come about because we keep punching holes in the atmosphere with space programs and a multitude of pollutants; it's God's fault! I'm sorry, Sister, but I have little patience for the half-baked relationships that have been manufactured between man and the omnipresent."

"The *idea* of God? *We* concocted?" Unlike her playful accusation that Finn had lurked in the bushes, Sister Ignatius seemed genuinely dismayed in his belief that God was born merely out of human shortcomings. "My apologies, Sister, if my choice of words offends you," said Finn. "Perhaps this will resonate better: A man purchases a hotdog from a food vender on a street corner. He walks away with his mouth-watering over the delicious but unhealthy midday meal, then he goes into swoons as his teeth pierces through the bun, mustard, and then lastly the juicy dog itself. In fact, he's so entirely distracted by his appetite and by the aroma of his fast-food selection, that he makes it all the way to the end of the street before he realises that the vender had short-changed him. So back he goes to teach the vender a thing or two about arithmetic as it pertains to money. However, on his way back to the vender a piano plummets from a third story apartment building and crushes him. Dead as a doornail and flat as a pancake he lay as folks from all angles begin to converge on the scene. 'When your time's up it's really up,' the Catholics in the crowd had murmured. 'Poor fellow,' uttered the Jews, 'when God point his finger He doesn't fool around.' But you see, Sister, this wasn't an omnipresent event; this was simply the result of a cheapskate who decided that he couldn't live without his dime and decided so while movers mishandled a piano."

"I must admit, Mr. Finn, you have quite a flair for anecdotes or speculative prompts as we use to call them back at school," said Sister Ignatius.

"Thank you, Sister," said Finn, "but more to my point, God is a great big, wondrous force that keeps planets from being sucked into suns and stars from colliding, but He's hardly a being that involves Himself in the day-to-day decisions of our silly little lives."

"So you believe that God had no influence over us at all?" asked the sister. "That He is merely a bystander who provides little to nothing in the way of guidance?"

A smirk formed on Finn's mouth before he replied: "Why would He bother exercising any measure of governance over a species that provides Him with such amusement?"

"Amusement?" Sister Ignatius found the implication offensive.

"Why of course," said Finn. "Amusement. The universe is only interesting to astronomers and others who have the time to sit around and wonder about it; but *we're* without a doubt the most amusing sideshow in ten galaxies. Haven't you heard, Sister, we're God's very own reality show! Whenever He tires of cosmic energy going off here and there, or supernovas, there's always good old reliable *us* to provide the comic relief."

"You know, Mr. Finn, I beginning to think you're full of it," said Sister Ignatius. "I don't think you believe a single word of what you just said. In fact, I believe that you're trying to smite God in order to make certain that He'll pay attention to you because you're afraid."

"You got me, Sister. That *must* be it." Finn had clearly mocked Sister Ignatius's intuitiveness, but then he began to wonder whether there was more truth to her insight than even he himself was aware of. "Incidentally, Sister," he went on, "I hang on your every word, and I'm being perfectly sincere when I say that I truly admire your intellect. You're more scholarly then any Jesuit that I've ever come across; perhaps you should've tried to become the world's first female priest. However, your theory a little while back before we engaged in our *Almighty* dialogue also seemed to suggest an alternative philosophy: that while *I* may be in constant conflict with the world, which I don't deny — *you,* dear Sister, are in constant conflict with yourself. Perhaps you could teach me to be more wavering, whereas I could teach you to be less? But there is no doubt, Sister, we are two very conflicted souls. So you see, we're not all that different, after all, you and I."

"I need to take care of you now, Mr. Finn," said Sister Ignatius. "Your wound."

"Of course," said Finn. The tone of his reply might have given one the impression that it had slipped his mind.

Sister Ignatius gave Finn a mild sedative to better help him to remain calm while she treated him. While rummaging through the shack she discovered some old blankets. She went outside to shake off the months of dust that had settled on them. When she returned, she laid them down and helped guide Finn to the floor. She took a towel and some water from her backpack and patted down his face, then went to work on his wound. "So many times I watched you while you were working; at times close up, at other times from afar." Finn was already becoming a bit groggy. "Even when you weren't aware that I was watching you, I was watching you. I never imagined that I'd become one of your patients."

"Try to relax," said Sister Ignatius. "Then when all is calm, I'll go and fetch Mr. Somersby and we'll get you back to the clinic."

"Sister, amid all the confusion I lost track of Mr. Somersby," said Finn.

"I am sure Mr. Somersby will be fine," said Sister Ignatius.

"And Hadil? I'm worried about him," said Finn. "He was separated from his wife and other children when those savages came upon the camp. And what was that threatening word they kept chanting over and over?"

"Zurgha," said Sister Ignatius. "It's a term the Janjaweed use for a black African."

"They're some bunch of cowboys, the Janjaweed," said Finn.

"Hadil once told me that he saw them chain together a group of villagers at a marketplace and then set them on fire," said the sister. "There isn't a level of atrocity or torment that they haven't reached. Sorry, Mr. Finn." The sister momentarily withdrew her hands when she saw her patient wince in pain.

"I'm grateful, Sister," said Finn, "that you only wear a wimple, or cornette, or whatever you call that thing on your head, instead of a full habit, because you're really quite a pleasure to look at, you know."

"Please, Mr. Finn, try and rest," begged Sister Ignatius. "And take that dreamy look off you face."

"That dreamy look, in the event you're interested, Sister, is otherwise known as bedroom eyes," said Finn. "Perhaps in your former life you encountered them a time or two."

"Call them what you wish," said Sister Ignatius, "but right now they're an unwelcomed distraction."

"What a killjoy," muttered Finn, as his shoulders slumped and his eyelids began to sag.

CHAPTER V
THE GIRL ON THE BARSTOOL

London, England 1993:

Heads turned whenever Claire Damien entered Bruno's Café, and tonight was no different. It couldn't be said that she frequented the establishment, but whenever she made an appearance it was treated as a happening. Even the eyes of all those who had opted for a booth instead of a barstool were resting on her, never mind that to ogle from such a disadvantaged position one needed to be obvious about it; some (men and women alike) were stretching their neck in order to gain a view to her entrance. Men who were shooting billiards momentarily paused their game, until Claire Damien's confident and purposeful strut came to its glorious end, which was the acquisition of a barstool. Bruno, who himself was keeping bar, stopped to acknowledge her presence well before she reached her destination. He seemed genuinely pleased, but was also anxious that Claire Damien's destination was a stool at the bar; though this was often the case. Also, Claire Damien never once entered Bruno's Café accompanied; she was always alone. She came alone, and alone was how she would leave — in every instance.

Claire Damien was a statuesque figure who, as the only other female seated at the bar observed, possessed the poise of the many characters played by Lauren Bacall; there was even a striking likeness to the once famous femme fatale who often was Humphrey Bogart's leading lady. To look at Claire, one might half expect her to say, *You know how to whistle, don't you Steve? You just put your lips together, and blow.* The other female, who by comparison was unimpressive and with no remarkable features other than her diminutive size, tried not to appear too in awe of the stylistic manner in which Claire Damien asserted herself, but failed, and did so to the extent of being the most obvious gawker in the room, including the men who were playing billiards. Claire Damien appeared the sort that, not even the building catching fire would prompt her to lose an ounce composure; her affect, which wasn't infused with a bit of falseness or pretence would remain wholly undisturbed. However, those who knew her, and there few, were of the opinion that her impervious nature was a by-product of the dangers of her job, and that the role she created, in time, became her "real" persona. When she took her seat, a look came over her that could only be described as *one of disinterest* — it was as if once she settled herself with crossed legs, perfectly erect posture, and took a second to survey the room, it was concluded that visiting Bruno's Café was certain to be a ho-hum affair she could have sooner done without. Although initially dismayed, Claire Damien's seemingly unapproachable manner served to further arouse the interest of the only other female seated at the bar. The woman became fascinated by the fact, that without the benefit of making any sort of eye contact or uttering a word, Claire Damien was able to shift the dynamics of an entire establishment. She was a happening, and one that pretended not to notice the buzz that she was able to generate. Claire lit a cigarette, blew a cloud of smoke into the air, and said, "Hello, Bruno." Her voice was husky, and as always it oozed with the kind of confidence that most men would find threatening. In those rare instances when her coolness was challenged, the result was the point of a knife put to the throat of one perceived as having acted too boldly. The moral of the story: Walk by a snake; say hello if you so desire; but under no circumstances press your luck.

"Been awhile, Claire," said Bruno. "Where you been keeping yourself?" Bruno's tone was friendly and unassuming, and more to the point he was careful not to sound as if he was prying into Claire Damien's affairs.

"Around," was Claire Damien's vague reply. The reply was followed with a swift stream of smoke blown in Bruno's direction. The barkeeper interpreted the femme fatale's not so subtle gesture to mean it would be wise not to challenge her vagueness. However, it should be duly noted that such consideration did not work both ways; if so desired, Claire Damien reserved the right to probe into the affairs of others. Whether you were a friend, a colleague, or mere acquaintance, that was the terms of the social contract; though these terms were never explained, they were always understood and understood with unmistaken clarity. "So who's the newbie?" she added. Claire subtly shifting her eyes toward the other end of the bar, where sat the other female — the woman who gawked with awe.

"Don't know — it's her first time here," replied Bruno. "And you know me, I never forget a face."

"Of course," said Claire Damien, acknowledging the barkeeper's asset for which he seemed so proud. "Though, I don't believe she's from around here. She doesn't look the type."

"Would you like her removed?" asked Bruno. The barkeeper wished for nothing or *no one* in his establishment to cause Claire Damien any sort of displeasure. "Not at all; she intrigues me." Claire Damien blew another thin stream of smoke, then told the barkeeper, "Be a dear, Bruno, and ask her where she's from." The woman clearly overheard the conversation as it had developed. Nevertheless, she thought it prudent to wait until the barkeeper posed the question. Bruno did as instructed, but did so without giving the woman the courtesy of looking in her direction. Perhaps it was his desire that the unfamiliar woman conclude that he wasn't merely some minion who did Claire Damien's bidding, but that they in fact were cohorts, equals, and with a common goal. He reported back to Claire Damien that the woman was from Bayswater, but now lives in Bloomsbury.

"That's curious," said Claire Damien. "From a quiet suburb to Bloomsbury; must be one of those liberal intellectuals or maybe some sort of artist; although she doesn't look the type." She took another moment to regard her cigarette, and then said to Bruno, "Ask her what she does."

Again, without bothering to look the woman's way, the barkeeper did Claire Damien's bidding. She was surprised to learn that the unfamiliar woman was a nurse. "Hmm," she said, narrowing her eyes as she looked the woman's way. "A nurse from Bloomsbury turns up for the first time at an east end bar." Looking back at Bruno she added, "The plot thickens." She went on to further add, "Either she plays the part of a prim and proper sort by day, and therefore doesn't wish to be spotted in such an establishment by her friends or colleagues, which could mean that she's some sort of deviant — or, she's the quiet, neurotic sort and she's here stalking someone." Bruno reported back to Claire that neither was the case.

"Well, Bruno," she said, "I suppose it's time that we learned the name of our mystery guest. Don't you?"

"The lady wants to know you name," Bruno called out. A moment later, the barkeeper dutifully repeated the words, "Mary Willow."

"Really?" said Claire Damien. She acted as though Bruno's parroting of the unfamiliar woman's name was the first time that she heard it uttered. "Mary Willow? Why, how enchanting," she went on. "Surely there must've been some fairytale with a young girl named Mary Willow; perhaps it was one of those stories where a lass wanders off and gets lost in the woods and encounters all sorts of dangers, but in the end she meets a prince. Bruno, be a dear and tell our new friend that my name is Red Riding hood."

"The lady said her name is …" The barkeeper was cut off, when Mary Willow abruptly and rather firmly interjected the words, *"I heard"*. The barkeeper looked back at Claire Damien. He swallowed nervously wondering whether Claire would let the brusque utterance pass or whether this impertinent young woman, who perhaps wandered too far from Bloomsbury, would come to an unfortunate end. Bruno uttered rather meekly, "I don't think she wants to play the game anymore."

"Tell her to go fuck herself!" was Claire Damien's hostile return. "If there's anything I can't stand, it's a self-loathing lesbian. Really, Bruno, can you think of anything worse?"

Initially, Bruno was inclined to wonder what made Claire Damien so certain that Mary Willow was a lesbian, never mind a self-loathing lesbian, but ultimately, and perhaps wisely, he elected not to issue such a challenge. After all, what did it matter to him what this woman was, so long as she was a paying customer and wasn't a troublemaker. In regard to whether there was anything worse than a *self-loathing* lesbian, he replied, "The Spanish Inquisition is what first comes to mind."

"You spoil sport, Bruno; you really know how to go for the early kill." Bruno sighed, as Claire Damien's droll reply to his quirky witticism showed her more easygoing nature and that perhaps there wouldn't be any trouble. The barkeeper then respectfully excused himself from having to give Claire his undivided attention. In fact, he all but asked permission so that he could begin busying himself with other patrons around the bar who were in want of refills.

Meanwhile, Mary Willow quietly withdrew herself to her drink, and while sipping, she also tried to recapture whatever thoughts were rolling around in her head before Claire Damien strutted into Bruno's, but it was all too futile, as she remained more than mildly intrigued by Claire, despite her discernment of likening the femme fatale to a snake, a fox, or any other creature of which one who was decidedly vulnerable should be wary. With the corner of an eye, she continued to observe Claire Damien, and what happened next, Mary Willow found most curious and it led to her being further intrigued. Claire blew a stream of smoke into the air, stamped out her cigarette, then merely glanced in the direction of the billiard table. By no means was it a stare or gaze of any sort, only a fleeting glance. What followed this subtle to near undetectable gesture *or* signal, prompted one man to lay down his billiard cue and another to raise up from a chair; everyone else in the establishment, from those seated at the bar, to those chattering away in booths, to those billiard observers gathered nearby the table sipping drafts from pilsner glasses remained as they were — only the two men who were engaged in a gentleman's game (they weren't playing for money) had reacted to Claire stamping out her cigarette and her fleeting glace. And only Mary Willow, who hadn't taken her eyes from Claire Damien, took notice of what might have been a prearranged summons.

The two men approached Claire Damien — not in a cautious manner, but with a casual stroll, and when having arrived at her side, their mood brightened and they began acting as if they were old schoolmates thrilled to have at last stumbled upon one of whom they were once so well fond — a true, welcomed, and overdue reunion was how this curious farce was portrayed. As the two men were flocking about the femme fatale, she took her shoulder bag from the bar and placed it on her lap. Then, in what could only be interpreted as a gesture of affection, she placed a gentle hand on the one man's cheek. The man then took hold of her hand and kisses it in a manner that seemed to display utmost reverence. While this was transpiring, the other man lifted a fairly sizable envelope from her bag and exchanged it with another, which all along had been hidden in an inside pocket of his jacket. This was a deft manoeuvre, the execution of which the observant Mary Willow hadn't a suitable vantage point to witness. Nevertheless, her instincts were telling her that something bordering on the nefarious was unfolding.

Following the exchange of envelopes came a brief exchange of pleasantries, and that was followed by wondering *whatever became of so-and-so,* along with wondering *what they each had been doing for the past ten years*; they were speaking in indiscernible code and it seemed very well scripted, though it was all a deft improvisation.

Afterward the men returned to the billiard table, while Claire Damien repositioned herself so that she was once again facing the bar. All three had played their part well, right down to pretending to exchange telephone numbers and promising of following through with keeping in touch. Claire lit another cigarette and right away resumed her conversation with Bruno, which earlier had ended with the absurd comparison of the Spanish Inquisition to self-loathing lesbians. Never once, though, did Claire look in Mary Willow's direction. For that matter, neither did Bruno. They had a bit of fun, though, making all sorts of absurd comparisons in an effort to try and top the quick-witted *Spanish Inquisition to self-loathing lesbians* juxtaposition, but as far as the newbie at the other end of the bar herself was concerned, the subject was closed — they had moved on. Whatever interest or fascination that Claire Damien might have had in Mary Willow, apparently ended with the staged interruption of the billiard players. Nevertheless, Mary Willow continued to sneak peeks at the other end of the bar, and she noticed that during the course of conversation, Claire Damien had taken a pen from her bag, which she utilized on the back of a coaster. Her hand appeared to squeeze the pen firmer than was necessary and she applied it in an abrupt and authoritative manner, despite maintaining an easygoing effervescence, which was indicative of the conversation.

As the night wore on, the smattering of patrons seated about the bar became a crowd whose denseness and demands of its sole keeper made any ongoing conversation between Claire Damien and Bruno, difficult. Mary Willow began to feel enveloped by the multitude of voices and also by the music, which along with the crowd increased in its volume. She became restless and arrived at the notion that it might be best to leave behind what was left of her second drink and make for the exit; after all, she was a Bloomsbury girl in an east end bar — perhaps she had bitten off more than she could chew. The crowd, the music, and the blitz of white noise that it produced was closing in on her from all sides and causing her to feel displaced and unsettled, and with these feelings came a queer sense of isolation and abandonment — the same sense of isolation and abandonment that had been the albatross of her childhood. She tried to fight through the impenetrable miasma of clamour and humanity in what for her was an unfamiliar atmosphere, all for the purpose of remembering why she ventured to the east end of London in the first place, and furthermore, what she hoped to accomplish by entering Bruno's Café, but no sense of clarity seemed within her grasp. She went reaching for her glass and what was figured to be one last sip of her drink before she made her departure, when everything all at once altered: The music became muted (or so it seemed), the clamour from the crowd became a mere mummer, and the sheer mass of humanity, which only seconds ago seemed an insidious entity, became an unobtrusive and modest gathering of no particular consequence, and all because Claire Damien rose up from her barstool. The femme fatale, as Mary Willow observed, appeared irritated by the sudden alteration in musical volume and additional patronage. However, instead of making for the exit, as Mary Willow had suspected she might, Claire directed herself toward the end of the bar. *She headed straight for me!* Mary Willow thought nervously. Mary Willow was of the notion that Claire Damien was prepared to give her a piece of her mind for no longer wanting to *"play the game"*, as Bruno had put it. She knew that her reply was filled with impertinence, but that her impertinence wasn't wholly unwarranted — she had been toyed with and felt that she was perfectly within her right to take exception. She looked away, for she had made up her mind that she would act startled if or

183

when Claire Damien accosted her. *I'll pretend that I didn't notice her approaching,* she thought. The sea parted for the tall, broad shouldered femme fatale as she made her way toward the end of the bar — no one dare caused her in any way to veer or to alter her gait. This sort of reverence served to heighten Mary Willow's uneasiness, who, with the corner of an eye still managed to maintain a point of observation. However, when the moment of truth was upon her, Mary Willow couldn't bring herself to act nearly as startled as she had hoped. The nearness of Claire was more imposing than Mary Willow had imagined; she felt cloaked within the woman's shadow, and this cloak caused her heart to sink and it rendered her limbs motionless, numb entities over which she had little or no command. She wisely chose to remain silent — she wouldn't dare an utterance until there came a clear solicitation — an unmistakable summons; though she did allow her eyes to meet those of the looming presence. This wasn't done, however, with a mere shifting of eyes, but with a face turned upward and filled with admiration, for Claire Damien, as Mary Willow was easily able to ascertain, was even more beautiful and impressive up close. Claire was also tastefully fragranced, and this caused the girl on the barstool to swell with curiosity and the proclivity to ask what she wore, but again she wisely elected to remain silent.

Claire, in turn, looked down at the smaller, less impressive female, and when she did, her mouth formed a smirk — the sort of smirk that would have conveyed to any onlooker, that she was of the notion that Mary Willow wasn't worthy of much consideration, less having abandoned her drink and barstool. Claire reached into her bag for the coaster to which earlier she had authoritatively taken a pen. She placed the coaster in the palm of Mary Willow's hand and then wrapped her fingers around it.

Bruno, whose curiosity was well aroused by whatever might be transpiring, invented a reason to saunter to that end of the bar. He picked up a most capable ear and heard Claire Damien say, while maintaining a firm grip on Mary Willow's hand: "On this coaster you'll find my address and the time that you're to arrive there. If you dare to be tardy, or worse, not show, I'll hunt you down and slit your throat, and with whatever time you have remaining, you'll be provided a front row seat to your very own castration. Have I made myself clear, *Mary Willow*?" Mary Willow's astonishment was such that, she became momentarily paralysed and was unable to either sink in her stool or recoil from someone, who earlier toyed with her, but now was perceived as a tormentor. Furthermore, she was unable to summon a single word, not that any in particular came to mind. Her means of conveying to Claire Damien that she understood the terms and conditions should she fail to appear at the said place and at the said time, came by way of a wide-eyed and frightened nod and with her mouth slightly agape. Before she was able to recover but an ounce of composure from having been so stricken, she watched Claire Damien walk away, this time making for the exit. Once again the sea parted for the tall broad shouldered woman. "Is she fucking kidding?" was Mary Willow's desperate appeal to Bruno, once the dangerous woman was out of sight. "She *is* kidding, right?"

"She not much of a kidder." Bruno seemed delighted to inform one who was already burdened with worry regarding such fact, then he went on to added, "I can't claim to know her *well*, but that much I *do* know."

"You mean to say that she would actually follow through with such awful intentions?" Mary Willow was all but pleading with the barkeeper to inform her that it simply couldn't be so, that it must be a show or a farce, or perhaps some sort of test. *That must be it*, she thought. *The newbie from Bloomsbury must pass some sort of initiation before she can be accepted as a regular here at Bruno's Café.*

"Look Missy, whatever Claire Damien says, Claire Damien means," said Bruno. "I don't claim to know much in this life, but that much I can assure you."

It seemed to give Bruno enormous pleasure to have enlightened Mary Willow with regard to Claire Damien's character. The prideful manner in which he spoke also led her to the notion that the barkeeper was a lackey who wouldn't dare pass up an opportunity to flatter the dangerous femme fatale.

"What does she want with me?" Mary Willow cried out.

"Couldn't say," said Bruno. His brief and abrupt reply was a clear indication that he was losing interest in what Mary Willow could only describe as a development that surpassed any known absurdity. This served to make her feel even more frightened and alone. Seeing this, Bruno tried to sound reassuring when he said, "Cheer up; maybe she's taken a liking to you; although you'd be the first. Come to think of it, though, I've never seen her leave here with anyone, nor has she ever showed any interest in anyone — not the sort of interest I have in mind; but we're a *take all comers* sort of establishment, and I can tell you firsthand that stranger things have happened. I've spent a good many years behind this bar, and if there's one thing that still rings true, it's that human beings never cease to surprise me, and I've never judged a one of them."

"Tell me what I should do!" begged Mary Willow.

"Exactly what she told you to do," was Bruno's firm reply. "In case you haven't already figured it out, the Lady is no one to trifle with."

Given her current vicissitude, the atmosphere, which was dense and clamorous and only moments ago was perceived as unfavourable and had adversely enveloped Mary Willow, was now a source of comfort — a haven. She scanned the multitude that was a menagerie of human sexuality, and within her surged the desire to embrace it — to embrace it all, with all its quirky and peculiar aspects, and without any regard for which quirks and peculiarities she was best suited. She became a fascinated observer while sipping the remaining liquid in her glass, but did so with a keen eye fixed on the time, which was an element that suddenly became paramount. After her last swallow she made for the exit, but not before

Bruno wished her luck. That the barkeeper deemed it necessary to do so was cause for Mary Willow to wince as one would when about to confront something unpleasant.

For awhile, she walked about the East End rather aimlessly; she kept only to herself having lost any and all desire to interact or to observe. Though, if the truth be told, she was afraid to allow anyone or any*thing* distract her from Claire Damien's very specific instructions. Occasionally, she stared fixedly at the coaster as though she was willing it to produce some sort of evidence or reassurance that she, in fact, wasn't about to enter into a world of perversity and deviance, but there were no lines to read between or language to interpret — there were only pen strokes that appeared hurried, indicating a place and time.

She was ten minutes early when she arrived at the address indicated on the coaster. She didn't wish to appear overeager, and she also wondered whether or not Claire Damien frowned upon impatience in a like manner that she did tardiness. With that in mind, she thought it prudent to remain put until nine of the ten minutes had ticked away; she didn't want to run the risk of her wristwatch being more than a minute slow. She spent the time pacing about the sidewalk in tight circles while attempting, however futile, to collect her scattered thoughts, which included first and foremost: *Why am I here?* She glanced down at her wristwatch a final time, and then began to climb three flights of stairs after having been buzzed in.

Owing to more misgiving than was ever before imagined, she rapped most gently on the door. There was no answer, though she suspected that the gentle rapping was heard, but that Claire was choosing to make her wait, either to see how long she was willing to do so, or to enjoy the dominion that she was wielding over the situation. Mary Willow managed to summon the courage to rap a bit louder, although this was done with trepidation, for fear that such action could be interpreted as impertinence. Still, there was no answer. She stood alone in the narrow corridor with mounting disquietude, while contemplating whether or not she was to enter on her own accord — that all along, *that* had been the expectation, despite it not being made known. Her next thought was to imagine how a woman, who had already displayed the willingness to threaten, would admonish her for having dared leap to such an assumption. Her mounting disquietude had all but overtaken her, when at last she took the doorknob in her hand and gave it a slight twist. At first it gave her a start that it turned freely; although she had no expectation that it wouldn't. She pushed the door open but an inch, and then paused to gather whatever little composure she might have possessed before venturing any further. Though before doing so, she attempted a peek into the room, but saw only darkness. She pushed further on the door, allowing the light from the hallway to permeate into the darkened area. This timorous action prompted the husky voice from within to issue an invitation. The confident manner in which Claire Damien uttered the simple words "come in" caused Mary Willow to stiffen. Still, she managed to push further on the door, but only enough to permit the passage of one so slight, as was her own figure. She maintained her grip on the knob until the door was quietly and respectfully returned to its closed position. There, still, and perfectly upright, Mary Willow stood enshrouded in the darkness of what was a modest vestibule, though the room to which it led was no less dark, and this, in turn, led her to wonder whether Claire Damien found artificial light objectionable, or had simply chosen darkness as a method of intimidation — as if the threat of a slit throat and castration wasn't intimidating enough.

Without yet the benefit of an invitation to advance, Mary Willow remained a rigid figure in the doorway; although by now her eyes had discovered across the room, Claire Damien's remarkable silhouette positioned upright in a chair and with one long, shapely leg draped over the other. Next, she heard the flick of a lighter, followed by the appearance of a bead of yellow light and a trail of smoke heading toward the window. Indeed, as Mary Willow acknowledged, Claire Damien, even in mere silhouette was a happening — a dynamic occurrence that commanded no less than one's full attention.

Meanwhile, Claire's well-adjusted eyes read clearly in the face of her guest the sort of fear that can often accompany uncertainty. She found this mildly amusing and it caused her mouth to crease into the supercilious smirk that was her hallmark. In turn, her guest had never known anyone to possess such poise and confidence, and the result was a mixture of dread and admiration.

"Come closer," Claire demanded. A voice in the darkness needn't be raised to possess authority — it need only be direct, and Claire's was most direct. She punctuated her order with a stream of cigarette smoke blown in the direction of a sparsely dressed window through which was breaking the muted light of the moon and the more intense light of a streetlamp.

With only a slight measure of hesitation, Mary Willow did as instructed and advanced further into the room. "You follow directions well," Claire told her. "There's a lot to be said for that — it's admirable. But that was some display back at the bar. 'I heard?' Those were your words, were they not?" Mary Willow hung her head and was plausible in her attempt to sound remorseful for her terseness. "Those who challenge me don't usually fair very well. That's not fiction, dear, that's a fact," said Claire Damien. "And those who challenge me in public often come to a regrettable end. But in the past I've made an exception or two. The fact is, Mary Willow, you intrigue me. I could become very interested in why a Bloomsbury girl turned up at an East End bar all by her lonesome. I like the challenge of a good mystery, and unless I'm very wrong, this one has some promise. But tonight isn't the night for probing into who we *really* are. There are other things that must be learned first. Now take off your clothes … all of them."

"Take off my clothes?" peeped Mary Willow. "All of them?"

"Do you usually repeat all that's requested of you verbatim, or only that which you find disagreeable?" There was a discernible chortle to Claire's voice, which was a fair indication that she found some amusement in her own question.

"No," replied Mary Willow.

"*No*, you don't repeat all requests? Or, *no*, you don't find my latest request disagreeable?" Mary Willow had the sense that Claire Damien was beginning to toy with her much in the way she had back at the bar when using Bruno as her liaison.

"Both," she said; though she was quite taken aback by the woman's highly irregular request.

"Good answer," said Claire. "Though I'm particularly grateful for the former. You see, I'm not one for conversations having to last longer than they need to. It's an annoyance to hear one repeat your questions because they have difficulty formulating answers. Now, if you don't mind I'd like you to proceed."

Claire turned her head away from her subject and blew another thin stream of smoke toward the window. The manner in which she did so seemed a clear indication that she was nearing the end of her patience. So, despite the irregular request, and also the uncertainty of whatever were Claire's intentions, Mary Willow did as instructed and began to undress. Despite having the luxury of darkness, she felt no less clumsy and awkward throughout the manoeuvre than she might have otherwise. The removal of one's clothes from one's body must be considered nothing less than routine — a commonplace exercise that's done at least once daily. However, with another present, it has all the makings of become a happening — a pathway to discovery. But in darkness, and at the behest of a stranger posing as a spectator — perhaps a lecherous spectator — it provided Mary Willow ample cause to feel both clumsy and awkward.

She began by removing her shoes and didn't achieve full nakedness until at last having removed her stockings. When she returned to an upright position, she discovered herself standing in the middle of a well-illuminated room. The sudden onset of light caused her to shriek with astonishment and to shrink from the harshness of the glare.

Moments later, she peeked out from behind her hands and discovered that the room's lone spectator was still posed in her chair — still with the same unflappable poise and confidence that she had displayed earlier on at Bruno's Café. Mary Willow felt a remarkable surge of both shame and exhilaration pass through her as she stood naked before Claire Damien. To be so exposed, in knowing such vulnerability, there came a rare synthesis of thrill and danger. Claire, subsequently, seemed more interested in her cigarette, and especially her drink, which until then had gone untouched, than the nakedness of her guest. But that was how Claire Damien comported herself — she never showed her cards — she always demonstrated the upside of control. Those were the means by which she conquered not only her adversaries, but the few soles in the world that she considered friends. *Please,* Mary Willow was pleading inside, *look at me for God's sake! Judge me if it's of your proclivity, but don't just sit there! Don't ignore me!*

Claire rattled the ice cubes around in her glass, then raised the glass up to the level of her eyes, where she could better examine its amber contents. She wanted there to be no mistaking that her drink took full president over her guest, whose time of abeyance was beginning to quell her heightened sense of thrill and danger, and in its stead introduced a level of distress that soon bordered on the unbearable.

Finally Claire had finished with her charade. She rose up from her chair and made her way over to her guest. Within her strut, there existed an air of confidence and certainty that she had broken Mary Willow — that Mary Willow was prepared to submit and, if required, give herself over entirely.

"I hope I'm not too disappointing," she meekly uttered. Claire walked a tight circle around her guest, pivoted on her heel, and then repeated the manoeuvre in the opposite direction.

"A bit on the small side," she said, "but I suppose you'll do."

Mary Willow wasn't certain whether Claire Damien was referring to her overall stature, which admittedly was slight, or her adolescent breasts. However, this was not a question she cared to pose; nor was she particularly keen on gaining confirmation regarding what another perceived as her inadequacies. For the moment she was satisfied to learn, for whatever it was worth, that she would "do". And whatever "do" meant, it was decidedly more favourable to having her throat slit before an eventual castration. When Claire Damien returned to her seat, she instructed her guest to dress, and then informed her that she was dismissed. Mary Willow wasn't sure whether she should act relieved or disappointed over a dismissal that was delivered impassively and was nothing less than unexpected. Once again Claire rattles the ice cubes in her glass. She returned to her perfectly upright pose with one long, shapely leg draped over the other, and she appeared to be scanning the room for a focal point other than Mary Willow. Mary Willow took her leave of Claire Damien entirely uncertain of whether she had already reached the end, or was merely at the beginning of the most bizarre encounter/relationship of her life. From the moment she saw Claire enter Bruno's Café, she felt the world and everything in it shift, as if she had slipped into an altered state — and irresistible but dangerous distortion of reality. But should this bizarre encounter, in fact, place her at the beginning of whatever just began, she could easily conclude that tonight was as perplexing an inauguration as was ever imagined. Whether at the beginning or end was a matter she mused over while making her way back to Bloomsbury. The only resolution that was reached was the one that already was suspected: Should this mad encounter blossom into anything resembling a relationship, its "terms" or "rules of engagement" would be determined wholly by Claire Damien.

"I suppose you'll do?" she muttered to herself along the way. "Do for what — a maid? An errand girl? Or maybe a doormat?" She was fully cognizant of the notion that Claire Damien hadn't merely toyed with her, that instead, she had been put to some sort of test, which only by the skin of her teeth she passed, for it was only *supposed* that she would *do.* "Now there's a real confidence booster if I ever heard one." She was somewhat droll in uttering these words of irony, and did so with a shrug of the shoulders and while turning her head toward an imagined listener, for there wasn't another soul on the sidewalk. She went out of her way to walk by Ebenezer's Coffee House, though it was figured to be closed at such an hour. Still, she lingered on the sidewalk, further contemplating her vicissitude to which was owed either to a well or poorly chosen tavern. She began to consider how many similar establishments were passed on her quest to drink in public as an unaccompanied female, and why it was Bruno's Café that was eventually settled upon. Was it fate? Luck? Were there forces at work? She remembered setting out with an objective, but was aimless in its pursuit and vague on what her hopes were for an outcome. She didn't tax herself too long, though, before deciding with a measure of antipathy, that to wonder about such things was a pointless exercise. She retired to her bed, but had great difficulty sleeping. Every warning sign imaginable kept going off in her head: Be wary! Tread carefully! Be on your guard! Don't be a fool, run away! They were all going off all at once and turning her tired head into a crowded pinball arcade. In the end, though, she ignored her instincts, as danger can be a powerful aphrodisiac, along with being an elixir for a life thus far sentenced to nothingness. She surrendered to her arousal, which silenced and superseded all warnings.

****

On the following morning, despite having thrown herself into her a.m. routine with more than her customary vigour, Mary Willow was unable to dispel any and all thoughts of Claire Damien — the femme fatale had crept into her head and there she would remain. Intermittently, Claire had surfaced throughout the course of the night, into the wee hours of the morning, and she was right there to greet Mary Willow in the twilight of her slumber. Though Mary Willow wasn't necessarily inclined to exorcise Claire Damien from her thoughts, and in fact she had spent a great deal of the night reliving the bizarre encounter, while repeatedly reaching for herself. It drove her near the brink of madness to imagine herself once again standing naked before Claire Damien — to be wholly exposed in both the flesh and soul and willing to submit to whatever profane pleasures were desired. It made her tingle with both danger and excitement to understand the depth of control that Claire Damien had maintained over her throughout their encounter. In a way it all seemed so illusory, and yet not only was it an occurrence, but one that for Mary Willow was defining: the control, the helplessness — it stroked her sexuality in ways never before imagined, and it would become a drug — the effect of which would border on obsession. That morning she had the sensation that she was gliding through space, and as she went about Bloomsbury, she dissected crowds with her eyes, and all the while she wondered, was it possible that Claire Damien was among the thousands — the over caffeinated multitude, who piloted themselves through the day — or, was she indeed a phantom, who from dusk until dawn preyed on the weak?

****

Heads turned when a magnificent bouquet of long stemmed red roses was paraded through the University College Hospital in Bloomsbury. The man doing the parading was wearing a shirt that read *Bonny Blooms*, so it was only natural for hospital staff members to assume that the bouquet was for a patient, and one with a young, thoughtful lover, who for whatever reason couldn't make bedside. When in doubt send roses. However, it wasn't long after the man arrived at the nurses' station asking for a Mary Willow, that the entire third floor was buzzing. A great deal of talk was made and conclusions were already drawn before Mary Willow was even in possession of the magnificent bouquet. Though once having gained possession, flocked about, fussed over, and then questioned, she went on to profess ardently that she hadn't a suitor, nor had she an admirer near *or* from afar — at least none of which she was aware. Some accused her of being less than forthcoming, while most allowed themselves to become swept away in the mystery of a secret admirer. After all, who doesn't fancy the idea of a secret admirer? There was a less than significant minority, however, that acted envious that someone had deemed Mary Willow worthy of such a magnificent bouquet; and make no mistake, it was all that and more. Either way, the third floor, minus the sour minority, spent the remainder of the day giddy over the prospect that Mary Willow either already had, or was soon to have a lover.

Despite all the good-natured urging and encouragement, Mary Willow waited for a private moment to pluck the envelope from the bouquet. Ordinarily Mary Willow wasn't one for showing up for duty distracted. Admittedly, today she was all in the throes of a dither, though she had good cause. But it wasn't until witnessing the giddy effect that a bouquet of roses had upon her fellow nurses, that she herself was at last able to locate her own composure. In fact, it was she who had the task of restoring order to the third floor of the University College Hospital. But then there arose the uncertainty of what was in the envelope. Unless mistaken, for she truly hadn't a love interest (stripping off one's clothes and posing naked in a strange woman's flat didn't qualify as such), Mary Willow was all but certain that the arrival of the magnificent bouquet of long stemmed red roses was a direct result of last evenings bizarre encounter. No matter, the gesture was thought to have been an impressive one — it certainly made a good impression among most of Mary Willow's fellow nurses, but the note inside the envelope was no less impersonal than the hurried pen strokes that last evening were scratched out on the underside of a coaster. In fact, the only distinction between last night and the current effort was an upgrade in stationery, thanks to Bonny Blooms, and the signed initials *C.D.* Aside from that, all Mary Willow had to stare at was a date and time. As she acknowledged, with both a measure of perplexity and dismay, there was a remarkable disconnect between the bouquet of red roses, which were accented with baby's breath and were well fragranced and could only be interpreted as a gesture of affection, and the note, which was nothing more than an instruction informing her of the time and date that she was to appear. Red roses — an unmistakable symbol of romance, accompanied by a note that had all the warmth and spark of a court summons. For Mary Willow, there was no wrapping her mind around this enigmatic woman, who possessed the unique ability to frighten her into arousal. What's more, there were fifty hours between now and the time of her "appointment". Fifty hours to wonder, to imagine, to fear — or to ache. Mary Willow left the hospital with her gather of blooms and headed straight away for her home.

Along the way it never once occurred to her to happen by Ebenezer's Coffee House with the idea of providing some of the regulars, who of late have taken some notice of her, the chance to fuss over the impressive bouquet. Despite strutting along the sidewalks of Bloomsbury in good spirits and with a curiosity that was soaring, tonight she sought the company of no one. Last night had been a long and eventful one, and her body was tired; although it hadn't occurred to her until having retreated to within her four walls, that she hadn't, in fact, disclosed to Claire Damien her place of employment. She could well remember the farcical manner in which Claire probed her, and that in doing so Claire involved Bruno, and that it led to her disclosing that she was a nurse, but never once did she let slip where she practiced her nursing. In one respect this flattered Mary Willow, that Claire Damien took the trouble of locating her whereabouts in order to send roses and arrange what was hoped to be a tryst. In another respect, she found it quite disconcerting that a woman, who thus far had threatened castration and the slitting of her throat was able to procure information with such alarming expedience. Once home and after having found a suitable place to admire her bouquet, Mary Willow arrived at the conclusion that she had too many thoughts rambling around inside her head — thoughts that were colliding and causing her to feel restless and discordant. Within her walls there lacked the peace she sought, and from this modest disillusionment grew a yearning for space and movement. She would escape from within her four walls and take to the streets and night air, and she would do so with the notion that it would bring her being back into some semblance of harmony. But the night air, open space, and those shuffling along the sidewalks couldn't provide nearly enough distraction to rid her of the vision of Claire Damien's smirk, nor of having been informed that she was *a bit on the small side, but would do.* This led her to wonder whether she had, in fact, made the final cut — or, was she merely invited back for a second tryout.

Along her travels she saw the blind man playing his flute— the same blind man she saw a thousand times in the past, but had always walked by without giving a thought to what he might be playing. Tonight, without any understanding of why, she decided to linger and to listen. *This poor soul was a musician, or at least though so, and that has to count for something*, was what she thought to herself. Furthermore, the man hadn't a hat, cup, or any sort of receptacle into which to toss change, and in Mary Willow's mind this somehow legitimized him — a man who brought music to the squares and sidewalks of Bloomsbury for the sheer joy that it gave him and hopefully others. The man was playing an obscure passage that Mary Willow established was either modern-classical or avant-garde jazz. Although not recognised, the music maintained some sort of shape, and subsequently her interest. In the past she was of the belief that the man was a burnout who knew a tune or two, but mostly piped out random notes to passersby with the hope that they would stop long enough to dip into their pockets. It pleased her to learn otherwise.

Afterward, Mary Willow asked the man what he had played, and he informed her that it was a sonata by Anton Webern, composed originally for cello and piano, which he transcribed for solo flute. She confessed to having limited musical knowledge, particularly in the more highbrow, artful genres, but that she enjoyed his playing just the same. Before taking her leave of the man, she expressed genuine regret for having left her home penniless, to which the man replied, "I give private lessons by day for flute and piano. By night I take to the open air and play for Him (the man pointed skyward) for having given me such a good life. Whenever folks stop and listen it's a bonus, but I couldn't take a cent."

"I wasn't expecting to make any stops," Mary Willow told the man. "I came out walking only with the idea of clearing my head, but something told me to stop and listen."

"I hope I was able to help," the man replied. "But a clear head in today's world is almost too much to hope for. Though this can help," was what he added while holding up his instrument. "But it begins first with Him." Again the man pointed skyward.

Had Mary Willow chose to comment on the flutist's insightful remark, he might not have played another note for the remainder of the evening. The modern world, as it has many times been accused, does not a clear head make, but instead it's likely to provoke lengthy discussions without clear resolutions. She apologised again for having left her home penniless — not that the man would accept a monetary gift, but she felt the need to give, to give something, *anything*, for clearly she was the beneficiary of this fortunate acquaintanceship. The flutist thanked her for listening and wished that her life become a peaceful journey. She couldn't remember ever hearing a better and more well put sentiment.

As she journeyed on, Mary Willow thought less about Claire Damien, and more about a man who was able to hold remarkably complicated music to memory. *Why,* she wondered, *does one with such ability have only the streets for a concert hall and passersby for an audience? Why does the world, although it praises talent, look only to reward industry?* She considered the thousands, who each day in every which direction race through their lives and invariably pass the flutist, never affording a moment to consider the depth of his soul or the extent of his virtuosity. She decided that the world was a place for which one must weep. Though by journey's end, the prevailing questions were ones that she believed the flutist and He to whom the flutist had given praise would find objectionable: Why did she demean herself by putting herself on display before a perfect stranger? And why was she so desperately in want of doing it again?

****

On the following evening after her shift, Mary Willow sought out the flutist with the notion of atoning for having been penniless the night before; she knew that he wouldn't accept money for his musicianship, so she came by bearing coffee from Ebenezer's and also to listen. She wasn't so bold as to assume he'd care for a French Mug, so a light blend of regular coffee with cream and sugar on the side it was.

She learned that the flutists name was Elijah, and that his earliest childhood memory was of his grandfather, who was a violinist for the London Philharmonic, playing him into a nightly slumber. "It's been over fifty years," he said, "but sometimes at night I can still hear those gentle strokes coming from his bow. If I could ask God for one thing, I'd ask Him that those peaceful strokes be just the thing I hear when it comes time for me to leave this world." Mary Willow felt sympathy for Elijah, but in a way she also envied him. He was unable to look up and see the grandfather who so dearly must have loved him and who gave him the gift of music, but he had fond and lasting childhood memories. The flutist asked her for a request, but she hadn't the knowledge to ask for anything by name that wasn't well beneath his ability, so she asked that he choose for her.

"Like you, Schubert had a kind and gentle soul," he told her. Then he began his serenade.

Mary Willow would have enjoyed nothing better than monopolizing all of Elijah's time — for his music *and* his conversation; but as they say, the show must go on, and the flutist was just getting warmed up. Mary Willow thanked him for sharing his music and for the story of his grandfather. She walked back to Ebenezer's, but it didn't take her long to regret having entered the popular coffee house. She tried to keep Schubert playing in her head, but as luck would have it, there was a man droning on about how the United States was all up-in-arms over a truck bomb that was detonated under the north tower of the World Trade Centre, and this same man was also of the opinion that the U.S. would "no doubt be looking to wage war"! She had heard it all day long at the hospital, and Elijah had been a most welcomed distraction, but now it was back to reality — the modern world — most of which had little or no time for Schubert. She got her coffee to go.

"Twice in the same night? And to go? This certainly is a switch," remarked Brian. "On your way to some hot engagement, I hope." Over the past few months, Brian and Mary Willow have had numerous exchanges over numerous subjects, and with those exchanges developed a familiarity beyond the usual barista/coffee lover relationship. Brian still enjoyed that Ebenezer's was a university student hangout, but nowadays he's no longer so enamoured with all the pretentious intellectual snobbery as he once was; he frowns whenever he hears a young man, whose still popping zits, or a young woman, who has yet to be properly satisfied going about quoting Aristotle or Schopenhauer, or regurgitating some obscure passage from a piece of classic literature and doing so as though they now own the secret of life. Of late, he's developed a kindness toward the commoner — the labourer — those who from sunup to sundown apply some sort of industry so that the world would still turn.

As a nurse, Mary Willow was certainly no stranger to the application of industry, but she was also learned— so like Brian, she bridged both worlds. "I am," she lied in regard to Brian's hope that she had *some hot engagement*, then was quick to take her leave. She appeared aimless in the manner in which she meandered along the sidewalks of Bloomsbury, until at last she was no longer *in* Bloomsbury. She walked and sipped coffee and all the while she was trying to reclaim Elijah's gift of Schubert. She wasn't as successful as she had hoped, but kept the vision of him playing in her mind's eye. Elijah was middle-aged and with a well-weathered exterior — it was as if he had lived his whole life on the sidewalks and squares of Bloomsbury, but when he played he looked like an angel — and now having spoken with him, Mary Willow felt ashamed for having so many times been part of the hurried, over caffeinated multitude that pretends not to notice one another and who had passed by the flutist without an acknowledgement of any kind — a human stampede that has all but forgotten that it was born with a soul. But she found some solace, in that a blind man is unable to see ignorance, and that perhaps blindness is God's way of eclipsing the godless world from the true angels on earth.

Some time had passed when she discovered herself standing outside Bruno's Café an hour before closing and with no memory of how she got there. "This makes two nights out of three," Bruno said, with a measure of surprise. "Working your way up to becoming a regular, are you?"

"Maybe," said Mary Willow. Though the manner in which she uttered the one word reply suggested that the idea wasn't all too appealing.

"Well, I see you survived," he said. "And from what I can see, everything appears to be intact." He shifted his eyes as to give Mary Willow's slight form a quick but thorough examination.

"Oh, I survived alright," she said. "Then of all things, I was sent a magnificent bouquet of long stemmed red roses that came with an invitation. I never told her where I worked

— *or* lived. What do you make of it? And what's her deal, anyway?"

"She comes in from time to time and has a drink," Bruno told her. "Sometimes she meets someone, sometimes she doesn't. She talks, I listen. If she wants to converse, I engage her. If she happens to tell me something, it's understood that I don't repeat it. She's never once uttered the words *'don't repeat this'*, she would never talk to anyone who needed such reminding." Mary Willow found if amusing, that in attempting to explain Claire Damien's 'deal', Bruno couldn't resist a bit of self-praise. "But what I don't do," he added, "is go probing into the lady's business. I tend not to put me nose where it don't belong, if you what I mean. So I can only tell you what she's like when she's sitting on this stool, but I can't very well tell you what her 'deal' is." After watching Mary Willow sigh from having learned so little, he further added: "Granted, she ain't Mary Poppins, but she ain't Jack the Ripper, neither."

"That's just peachy." Mary Willow frowned. "You just described everyone in this bar, if not all of London."

"Here," said Bruno. He placed a double shot glass of Crown Royal on the bar. "This'll take the edge off those nasty ol' worries." Mary Willow eyeballed the glass as though it supplied more danger than Claire Damien. The last time she put whiskey to her lips, although it was of the bottom shelf variety, she had done shots with fellow nursing students, the result of which saw her projectile vomiting onto someone's shoes.

"I don't know whether I should just roll with the punches and see what comes of it, or move to a foreign country, where she's sure not to look for me." Mary Willow tried to sound droll in her remark, for it wasn't her wish to burden Bruno with all her dread, but she also wanted to play the part of the *damsel in distress* with the hope that the barkeeper could help form her decision.

"Look, the lady sent you a bouquet of red roses," he told her. "Take it at face value. Why does anyone send red roses?

It's not likely that they'll lead to cement boots." It was hard to dispute, that when red roses are sent it's a sure sign of romantic interest, but then Mary Willow showed Bruno the note that came with the supposed romantic gesture.

"I agree," he said, "it does have all the warmth of an appointment card. But I've always known her to be a woman of few words — says only what she has to and not a syllable more. Hey, now don't you go on thinking so hard about things. Nothing'll put years on a person faster than thinking too hard." Mary Willow agreed that not thinking so hard was sound advice. She thanked Bruno for his ear and for having been supportive to someone who was essentially still a stranger. She finished her drink in silence, and then made her lonely, nocturnal trek back to Bloomsbury. Admittedly, though, the following day was spent enshrouded in the throes of distraction — there was nothing to occupy her thoughts that were capable of superseding the excitement and anxiety generated by the anticipation of a second meeting with Claire Damien.

The entire day was spent on the first car of a roller coaster tantalisingly ticking its way up its initial incline as it prepared to make its sharp, terrifying plummet. At last, there she stood, posed, but not as *poised* as she had hoped, in the corridor outside Claire Damien's door. Timidly, she rapped on the door, and as was the case three nights ago, no one seemed all too anxious to answer. She twisted the knob and pushed on the door; she created an opening, just wide enough through which to pass. She sighed when discovering not darkness or harsh glare, but a dimly lit flat. The softness of the light was both pleasing and inviting; still, she found it necessary to hold firmly in her hand the note that had accompanied the bouquet of roses; she wanted the comfort of confirmation so there could be no mistake or any dispute over the date and time that she was to appear. She held the note in an outstretched hand as to offer it to Claire Damien — she seemed of the belief that there existed the necessity of having to validate her appearance. *This means that I'm supposed to be here, doesn't it?* was what the gesture was so desperately trying to convey.

Claire Damien ignored the gesture entirely and went forward with grandly stating: "It's said that the Pinot Noir grape is complex and temperamental — that it takes an exceptionally caring hand to get it to grow and for it reach its full potential. That would make it very much akin to our own species, would it not?"

"I suppose it would," agreed Mary Willow; though she knew nothing of the effort needed for wine to reach its full potential. Moreover, Claire's ignorance of the note caused Mary Willow to become embarrassed for having brought it along. She began fumbling the note in an effort to fold it such that it could be better concealed it in her small hands. During this fretful exercise, which Claire also chose to ignore, she was encouraged to put the rim of a glass to her lips.

"It's also said that it takes a sophisticated palate to appreciate the Pinot Noir's complexity," Claire Damien went on. "Is this true?"

"I'm afraid that my palate is quite pedestrian," admitted Mary Willow, "but if it means anything at all, I do find the taste rather pleasing." Claire Damien smirked as if not all that surprised that the true character of the spirit was lost on her guest. "And the roses were quite lovely," Mary Willow went on to chirp. "I never saw such a robust bouquet; I imagine they'll remain in all their splendour for some days." She spoke with a lilt when frothing over with regard to the roses. It was a rather transparent effort to mask her uneasiness and also to deflect from having limited knowledge and experience with wine.

"Roses are not at all without relation to wine," Claire Damien went on to state.

"They're also temperamental, they require exceptional care, and like wine they're capable of extraordinary results. I believe it's fair to say that many of the finer things share those traits. Don't you agree?" Mary Willow tried to reply, but all at once her mouth went dry, and therefore she became frightened that her words would come out all in a jumble.

It was clear to her, however, that Claire Damien's brief monologue on the virtues of wine and roses was some sort of allegory, though its symbolism and purpose she had yet to determine. Beyond the dryness of her mouth, sensations that couldn't be explained were surging through her with uncommon vigour — she couldn't imagine how she was being supported, for she became wholly unaware of her legs, and all because a woman, whom she found both thrilling and frightening was beginning to advance toward her. Claire struck a pose before Mary Willow and tilted her head such that her eyes were able to meet those of her diminutive guest, but Mary Willow's eyes had travelled nervously downward so that they were resting on the floor. Claire let on that she was mildly amused by the fear and timidity of her guest, but was most tender when sweeping a tendril of hair away from Mary Willow's face.

"There," she said, "now I can better see your pretty eyes." Mary Willow's face went flush from the unexpected compliment. Claire extended a hand in order to lift up her chin and to see the flushness in her face.

"You're not frightened, are you?" she wondered.

"Should I be?" was Mary Willow's whispered return.

Claire Damien's smirk lent little in the way of confidence that her guest either *should* or *shouldn't* be afraid. She remained vague as always — conquering with uncertainty. She was the ultimate card player, never tipping her hand and leaving Mary Willow the burden of trying make sense of what was transpiring between two women who essentially were still strangers, never mind that the tender manner in which Claire swept away a tendril of her hair seemed to be leaning toward some level of intimacy.

"I can't stop thinking about the other night," Mary Willow managed to admit. "I — I just can't."

"You do realise that you were scared out of your wits?" Claire Damien reminded her. "But, then, maybe you enjoy being frightened. Some do, you know."

This time when Mary Willow's eyes travelled to the floor, it was more from embarrassment than any trepidation that might have been mounting. She was unable to pretend having lacked any understanding of what Claire had implied. *Am I a masochistic fool?* she wondered in silence. She was irked by the question, though she was fairly certain of the answer. Also, she was still holding firm to the note — the all important *validation* was haphazardly folded in her hand, yet missing from the scene was any true sense of welcome, or welcome that possessed any true sense of warmth — only a philosophy on the virtues of wine and roses delivered rather coolly had thus far transpired. Mary Willow wanted badly to assert herself — to do something without being told — to utter words without elicitation — anything that could serve as a warning to Claire Damien, that she wasn't some sort of plaything with which one could amuse themselves whenever one so desired. But she had long since reconciled her weaknesses, or for years at least tried. Some of those weaknesses, though, remained unsettled. Nevertheless, Mary Willow was no match for Claire Damien, and this she knew. If she was to assert herself at all, she would need to take the initiative by way of submitting before it was demanded. She raised her eyes up from the floor, allowing then to journey slowly up Claire Damien's impressive form until having reached her face. "Shall I undress for you again?" she asked.

It wasn't Mary Willow's intention to sound as if she was seeking permission, but her words were peeped as if having come from a child, who for the certainty of knowing the answer was begging her instructor to call upon her. She appeared a bright-eyed youth thirsting for acceptance and whose small, upturned face possessed all the innocence of a child. Indeed, she had all but pleaded with Claire Damien to require that she undress. Mary Willow carefully set down her glass on a nearby table and prepared to do what for days had caused her to act restless and distracted. But her effort was thwarted before it had the chance to begin, and by Claire herself, who informed her: "If undressing for me is something you feel strongly about, then by all means go right ahead; I won't stop you."

This surely wasn't what Mary Willow had hoped for, nor expected — to stand naked before Claire Damien and for no one's benefit but her own. And despite what only moments ago was implied, she didn't fancy herself a seeker of sexual torture, be it physical or psychological. Her desire was to have an experience that was both felt and shared equally, not have her passion offset by Claire's indifference. Though, should a tortured mind be the means by which Claire Damien achieved arousal, the experience, in fact, would be as desired. Still, Mary Willow was of the discernment that her presence, naked or otherwise, was no longer in favour. At once, her mind became a muddled mess of notions that were going nowhere but around in circles and were concluding nothing. She stepped away from Claire Damien as though the woman and her imposing form were impeding her from breathing. When doing so, she appeared a bit tottery — the way one often does when they're about to come undone. "Fuck it!" she went on to shout. "Just fuck it, already! Slit my throat and castrate me if you so desire, but fuck it!"

Claire Damien took a seat and looked on with what appeared to be only a passing interest. She lit a cigarette and occasionally put her glass to her lips. Mary Willow became ignorant to her host's indifference and continued with her rant, while gyrating crazily about the room. And the more she ranted the less coherent were her words — the more agitated were her gesticulations — until, at last, she found herself naked and kneeling at the feet of Claire Damien. The sudden surge that passed through Mary Willow endowed her with wildness never before imagined, never mind experienced — and with this wildness she became strangely emboldened and she felt more powerful than ever. In turn, these mostly unfamiliar feelings afforded her the unbrokered authority to lunge forward after having parted Claire's legs, and then to begin lapping away at her womanhood in a manner that would a ravenous animal when ripping away at a fresh kill. Indeed, she had transformed herself into a beast — a carnivore who would show her teeth dare anyone but her try and own the moment; it was hers and hers alone. How many nights had she lain in bed and in her mind grovelled before those who would never give her a second glance? How many years had she spent living as an outsider — an utterly disconnected soul out on the fringe of the world and holding on for dear life? In Claire Damien, though, she found and seized her vindication, and with uncommon hunger she baptised herself in the loveliness of the woman's sex. No longer able to remain a casual observer given to indifference when it came to ranting, Claire Damien stiffened, and then looked down at Mary Willow with eyes that by the second were growing wider. She observed a girl, who with a measure of fury began to roll herself in her wetness as if owning to an insatiable need to immerse herself entirely. Despite the feral display exceeding the actual sensation, and finesse giving way to ungainliness, both women were rendered breathless. Mary Willow sat back on her haunches and looked up at Claire Damien, as would a child seeking approval or affirmation that it had performed to whatever was the expectation or set standard. She reflected only mild disappointment when informed that she was "hurried" and that having been hurried caused her to become "reckless". She blushed when asked if it was her first experience — mostly because Claire Damien posed the question in a manner that suggested that she already knew the answer, which was often the case with Claire — she had a habit of posing questions (in a smirky, confident sort of way) regarding subjects of which she was already in the know.

Mary Willow leaned in with the idea of redeeming herself, and although Claire Damien was delighted by the girl's eagerness to please, she extended an arm which thwarted the effort. "Come," she said.

Mary Willow got to her feet and was led into a bedroom, where she was then skilfully guided onto a mattress. She was surprised by the sway of a waterbed — she had never laid on one, though chose not to say as much. She permitted her eyes to travel about a room that she found strangely masculine, with its oversized artefacts and abundance of dark hues and right angles. Everything was massive and too blatantly direct to inspire tranquillity — nowhere was there softness of any kind or anything that could be described as feminine. The space was indicative of someone who clearly enjoyed being in charge, or at least tried to project as much.

Claire put her lips to Mary Willow's ear and whispered, "I'm going to teach you." She leaned over Mary Willow such that her hair fell forward and began caressing her breasts. Mary Willow closed her eyes as tendrils from Claire's lovely mane danced atop her skin and swept along its smooth bareness, until having travelled the entire length of her form. Next, she felt the warmth of soft lips upon her — lips that were much fuller than her own, and this was followed by the moistness of a wickedly skilled tongue. So unhurried, so under control was Claire Damien — she performed as would an artist owning the innate facility to paint or sculpt actual sensations; and, as Mary Willow, a never before played upon canvas was learning, Claire possessed a virtuosic prowess equal to that of Elijah when brandishing his flute. Though, where Elijah had stirred her spirit, Claire Damien was stirring that which so longed to be awakened. Mary Willow lay there, transported by lust and reverie brought about by another's artistry. Claire had transformed that which was always thought to be earthly plainness into a laser beam possessing the most brilliant kind of light — a light that's bound only by the limits of imagination. She soared and soared until having achieved a rarefied space, where omnipotence and powerlessness, vulnerability and superiority, converge to produce uncommon sensations; and for the second time in the course of the same evening, Mary Willow was rendered breathless. Claire Damien leaned over her subject and gave her what by then had become her familiar smirk. Its conveyance was clear, that she was victorious in providing Mary Willow with her most impactful experience. What happened next came quite unexpected and was also a terrible disappointment — for Mary Willow, that is: Claire gave her hair a playful tousle and then informed her that it was time to go. Nary a moment of afterglow was permitted before she was instructed to dress and to take her leave.

"I have an appointment in precisely one half hour," Claire Damien told her.

"An appointment? At this hour?" Mary Willow couldn't hide her disappointment, nor help a note of indignation, as she leapt to the assumption that Claire Damien was dismissing her in favour of another love interest.

"Don't look so cross, it's only business," Claire informed her. "*You*, Mary Willow, are my pleasure." A moment ago Mary Willow was all but reduced to a sulky child with an edge of defiance, but upon told that she was Claire Damien's pleasure, she went soaring through the universe like a boundless laser beam whose illumination couldn't help but to dazzle. Claire kissed her fully and deeply on the mouth, and then instructed her that she was to "come by a week from tonight at the same time."

With an effort, Mary Willow resisted a frown. *A whole week*, she thought. But after already having been accused of crossness, she didn't wish to leave Claire Damien with the notion that her lover, "her pleasure" was too much a child.

"Oh, Mary Willow, one more thing before you go running away," said Claire. With arms folded and while wearing her familiar smirk, she moseyed over to Mary Willow, who by then was standing at attention in the doorway. Mary Willow felt the sudden inclination to remind

Claire that she wasn't running away, but was shooed, but ultimately elected to remain quiet. Besides, she was thrilled to have been awarded additional time and attention, despite somewhat wary of what *one more thing* could mean. "I'm curious," said Claire. "I want to know how you feel about penetration." It was the most disarming question that Mary Willow was ever asked — or, could remember being asked. Moreover, it was the sort of question that one might squeeze out one syllable at a time with more than its share of awkward pauses, or at the very least with some humility. But Claire shot from the hip, blew on the gun smoke, and then shoved the firearm back into her holster. Despite its unclear intentions, be it discovery or curiosity, Mary Willow found the question a probing one delivered in a manner that was jarring and intrusive. Claire wasn't merely *wondering* aloud as some have the habit of doing; nor had the question seemed a *casual curiosity.* There was no trace of *oh by the way* in her tone — instead she wanted to know clearly and decisively Mary Willow's view on penetration. This caused Mary Willow to become terrified that she might fail to tender an appreciative reply. *Does she wish to know if I desire to be penetrated? Penetrate her? Or how I feel about the subject on the whole?* Claire seemed to loom large over her — even larger than when she was forced to stand naked in the middle of the floor while examined under the harsh glare of light.

"May I have time to think it over?" Mary Willow timidly peeped. "Perhaps I could answer you tomorrow or the next time we're together?"

"No," replied Claire. Her *no* was firm and decisive. "I don't want you to have hours or days to formulate the answer that you think I want to hear. I want to know how you truly feel. So which is it? Is it something you favour or not?"

"What happened between us tonight is what I favour," said Mary Willow. There was wavering and hesitation in her words, which Claire might have taken for diplomacy, for her reply *was* a most careful and diplomatic one. But Claire chose instead to believe that any wavering and hesitation that surfaced came mostly from nervousness. She stepped back to allow Mary Willow more space to breathe and to not crowd her thoughts, and in doing so her smirk became a genuine smile — her posture, less rigid. These most welcomed gestures caused Mary Willow to sigh, and her shoulders, which were tightly wound, to gratefully slump.

"Good answer," said Claire. "For if I were one with an inclination to *strap* something on in order to penetrate a lover, then God should have seen to it that I came equipped with a penis. But He didn't, and so I refuse to foster His failures and oversights by behaving, of all creatures, like a man. And if it was my desire to *be* penetrated, I'd just go out and fuck a man, which would be fine for the man — most men are so base they would welcome the notion of being used for sex. But you see, Mary Willow, I don't merely *favour* women, I *despise* men. I despise that they're unable to truly see us — that for many of them, we're a collection of parts which they feel entitled to gawk at, and which they have also rated by way of some moronic scale or system. And clever species that they believe themselves to be, often they'll take the time and trouble of assigning names to our parts, and all before the exchange of a simple hello. Believe me, I've known men that are so ill-equipped regarding social graces that it seems they've scarcely begun to evolve. So I say let them name their poor pathetic penises if they wish, but for God's sake leave *us* alone! A woman, if nothing else, should possess the right to be free from men's adolescent stupidity. Don't you agree?"

Before Mary Willow could offer a reply, which would have been to concur without waver, Claire went on to add: "I also despise that the mystery of femininity can't be enjoyed without first being conquered. The truth is, men's bestial nature is how they cover up their inadequacy — their weakness — and their weakness, I find grossly objectionable. But more to my point, I despise penetration because it begs the notion that one must decide whether they're a "top" or a "bottom". *Really*, has our species become so degenerative that an individual must now define herself by what she deems a favourable position? Lovemaking should be an art form free from boundaries and requisites — an endless exploration, where never a decision is made." She paused, for she sensed her monologue was wearing thin, and then closed by adding, "I've always been far too liberated for such nonsense. I say leave it all to men. What say *you*, Mary Willow?"

"Of course, Claire. I want to be liberated — entirely, like you." Claire smiled. It was a genuine smile, not a smirk and it roused Mary Willow to spring forward and to embrace her. After sweeping the hair away from Mary Willow's forehead, Claire kissed it and then dismissed her. As Mary Willow made her way back to Bloomsbury, she pondered over what became an unrelenting curiosity, which then blossomed into a concern, for without fail it went to the trouble of resurfacing, and with each time that it resurfaced it hovered longer and closer until nothing else could penetrate. This incessant disquietude begged to know, was she in fact involved in a relationship — or, merely a series of appointments owning to the likelihood of resulting in sex, albeit of an artful variety? This deliberation was then brought to her bed, where an effort was made to determine *was there in fact a difference?* Throughout a mostly restless night the only resolution that *was* or *could* be reached was that the "relationship's" course and ground rules would be wholly dictated by Claire Damien. Of this fact, however, Mary Willow was already sensitive, for her body was consumed with tingling and the tingling was followed by an onrush to want to leap with joy or dive to the floor at the feet Claire Damien — either would have been more than an adequate display of gratitude for having been told, "*You*, Mary Willow, are my pleasure". But in the very next breath she was ready to crumble when told not to return for another week. Indeed, she had thus far, and would continue to rise and fall with Claire Damien's whims; and moreover, how she was perceived by the dangerous beauty would become paramount. But she wasn't a fool — not altogether — for she understood quite fully the precarious nature of her position. For so very long, though, she hadn't meant a thing to anyone. So what would it matter to the world, or to anyone, or for that matter, even to herself if she willingly and knowingly became Claire Damien's obedient lap dog? What would it matter? When Mary Willow took her leave of Claire, she did so without having asked how she was so easily tracked down, despite that it had been her intention to do so before the night began. As it turned out, though, she had decided for the time being that it was prudent to set the subject aside and move on to something far less disturbing, such as expressing gratitude for a bouquet of roses. Afterward the thought never resurfaced, at least not while in Claire's company. The following day she decided to reciprocate and she sent Claire a bouquet consisting mainly of daisies, foxgloves, bluebells and poppies — it was quite a profusion of brilliant colour. She chose all her own favourite flowers with the notion of lending brightness and softness to Claire's dark, geometric environs. Along with the bouquet came a note of remarkable contrast to the one that was sent her.

Dear Claire, You are the most capable of teachers. How very fortunate for me. I'll be counting the days until I can show you how well I retained all that you have taught me.

Most sincerely,
your pupil, Mary Willow

It wasn't necessarily Mary Willow's objective to outperform Claire Damien by way of submitting an example of how one should express oneself when using the written word. Her motive was much more self-serving, as her true desire was merely to remain in the forefront of her lover's mind. She chose her words carefully and with the hope that her lover would share her longing and perhaps summon her before a week's time. She was of the notion that, should she have to endure an entire week of waiting and wondering, reaching the point of utter madness was all but a certainty — there was no amount of work into which she could immerse herself that would help the time to be kind. At last, though, she looked in the mirror and smiled sheepishly back at herself that she was acting too much a child.

Despite the typical long, laborious shift work of a nurse, Mary Willow appeared weightless and unburdened. She waltzed through her days in a manner indicative of one about to embark on a journey illuminated with the thrill of romance and all its possibilities. She rejoiced in the late winter mornings, as the days were beginning to show signs that springtime was just around the corner. In the evenings she sought after Elijah and his flute. She requested that he serenade her with the same Schubert piece that he had a week ago. Elijah was delighted by the request and right away began piping the melody of the second and final movement of Schubert's Unfinished Symphony. Mary Willow wanted Elijah to tell her all that he could on the subject of the great composer, who like herself was believed to have had a kind and gentle soul.

"Of all the great composers, he was said to have been the most poetic," Elijah told her. "And those were the words of Franz Liszt, a great composer in his own right."

Mary Willow assumed that Schubert died before the completion of his eight symphony dubbed the "Unfinished", and was confused when learning that a ninth symphony was composed.

"He said all that he had to say regarding the work and decided to break free of it after only a second movement," said Elijah. "Still, many, myself included, regard the 'Unfinished Symphony' as one of the greatest works ever written. I feel most fortunate that I'm able to present you, albeit, with a small sample of the work."

"Elijah, if that was your idea of a small sample, than you are as modest as Schubert was great," said Mary Willow.

On the following evening Mary Willow asked that Elijah pack up his instrument and accompany her to Ebenezer's Coffee House.

"Please, Elijah," she implored, "grace me with your company, and do allow me to buy you a French mug. I promise you won't regret it."

"Now how could I refuse the entreaty of such a lovely young woman," said the agreeable flutist.

"It pains me to burst you bubble," said Mary Willow, "but I'm afraid, Elijah, that you're about to be seen with an ugly duckling on your arm."

"Nonsense!" the flutist replied. "I bet nothing could be further from the truth."

It gave Mary Willow enormous pleasure to introduce Elijah to Brian. Afterward she became a fascinated bystander, while the two men discussed their respective passions: coffee and music. Finally, an order was placed, and while awaiting their French mugs, as best she could, Mary Willow described for Elijah, Ebenezer's Coffee House. After having been presented with their mugs, she reached across the table and took hold of the flutist's hands. "I'm in love, Elijah!" said beamed. She squeezed his hands, and then confessed, "I suppose that was a bit much — to suggest that I'm in love. Actually, it's more like — I'm enthralled. Either way, though, my life of late has been very exciting."

"You sound as though you've been given the gift of youth and are making bloody well sure that it isn't going to waste," said the flutist. "Whether you are *truly* in love, or for the moment enthralled, happiness of any sort doesn't come easy, so I say more power to you!"

"I have met someone — a rather rare someone, who in a matter of mere seconds was able to discover and understand my nature and has used it to thrill me in the most unimaginable ways," Mary Willow gushed. "Not in all my life have I experienced such vigour. I feel as though I could run like the wind, and if I flapped my arms I just might take to the sky!"

"I guess this is where I'm supposed to tell you to take your time, to be careful, and that you might be opening up yourself to a world of hurt," said Elijah. "Beings that I'm along in years, that's what I'm supposed to tell you — it's what anyone who can't bear to see others happy would tell you. So there — I've told you. But don't you listen, Mary Willow. Don't you dare listen, because it's all poppycock! Remember, you can cheat at cards; you can even cheat a chap out of his shilling if it's in you to do so, but what you cannot do is cheat your own heart. It's not every day one gets to feel what you're feeling, so keep that heart of yours open and just do whatever the music tells you to do. Sure, you might get hurt, and so what? But you're also just as likely to wind up the happiest woman on earth, so the risk is well worth the reward."

"Do whatever the music tells me to do? How perfect a philosophy is that?" wondered Mary Willow. "Elijah, you're brilliant *and* a romantic!"

"When you've had the pleasure of being married to the world's most wonderful woman for as long as I have, you manage to learn a thing or two," the flutist humbly and gratefully admitted. It pleased Mary Willow to learn that Elijah had a life beyond the sidewalk concerts, and that as far as she could tell he was a soul who hadn't a single regret. Had he been given the gift of sight, and therefore able to follow a conductor, perhaps his life would have travelled upon another path entirely, and one that wouldn't have led him to *the world's most wonderful woman*. He seemed perfectly happy to give private lessons for a modest wage by day, and then take his flute into the open air in the evenings.

Despite a bit of mild protesting, Mary Willow escorted the flutist all the way to his front door. They strolled slowly and at a pace that Mary Willow had set. This wasn't to accommodate Elijah, but rather, Mary Willow wasn't all too anxious to be without the flutist's company. "Maybe it's best you're escorting me home," said Elijah, "because now you'll get to meet Marybeth."

"Marybeth? What a lovely name," said Mary Willow. "I named her myself, right after I purchased her," said Elijah. "When they placed her on my shoulder the first word that came to mind was *Marybeth*."

"You named your own wife? After you purchased her?" This was one of those rare instances when Elijah wished he had the benefit of vision in order to fully appreciate Mary Willow's astonishment.

"Of course not," he said, knowing full well that he misled her. "Marybeth's my parrot."

"Elijah, you're a devil making me think such awful thoughts," cried Mary Willow. "And I am sure that Marybeth is a fine parrot, but I'm much more interested in meeting *the world's most wonderful woman.*"

"*Her* name would be Sarah, given to her by her mother," said Elijah. "But if it wasn't for Marybeth I never would've met my Sarah. I was all but seventeen that day when I was standing just outside Forney's Pet Shop and playing Stravinsky, when this girl came running out and complaining that one of the parrots was squawking something awful. Who knew parrots were such music critics? Anyway, I followed her inside the shop and began playing a Brahms lullaby and Marybeth became as docile as a lamb. Sarah told me that since Marybeth had such reactions to music, it only stands to reason that she should belong to a musician. She sold Marybeth to me for half price with the stipulation that I would come by from time to time and serenade her. She, too, tries to tell me that she's an ugly duckling and that she's the lucky one; but she can't fool me, and neither can you."

"My, aren't we the perceptive one?" were Mary Willow's cheeky words. She took her leave of Elijah feeling better off having met *the world's most wonderful woman,* Marybeth, and for having the opportunity to spend a bit of time with a couple that was every bit as in love as the day they took their vows. What struck her, though, as she was making her way home, was that Elijah had wished her and her lady friend luck with their relationship. Mary Willow was certain that she hadn't revealed that her involvement was with another female. She wondered whether the flutist was showing off his perceptiveness for which he seemed so proud, or whether in the course of conversation she had inadvertently referred to Claire Damien by way of a female pronoun. She was well aware that when one is lacking a sense, the others, intuition in particular, can become more acute. If that in fact was the case, she found Elijah's *sixth sense* remarkable to the extent of alarming.

A week which saw Mary Willow's confidence surge and wane had at last come to an end. She stood in the corridor outside Claire Damien's door, still a bit timid, but mostly excited. She was a fresh face ingénue eager to show Claire all that she had learned — she was aching to perform. At the beginning, Claire looked on as would a third party observer whose charge was merely to critique a performance, but then soon discovered herself overwhelmed by Mary Willow's new found and perhaps unexpected adroitness. Afterward, Mary Willow sought Claire's approval and went on to intimate relishing the roll of the eager-to-please teacher's pet to her lover's poise and authority. Claire gave the favourable critique that was so dearly desired, along with endorsing the rolls into which they were each settling. What she didn't do, however, notwithstanding Mary Willow subtly hinting her to do so, was in any way acknowledge the lovely bouquet that was sent. *Surely she couldn't have found my reciprocating with flowers objectionable?* Mary Willow thought to herself. Claire ended the evening just as she had a week ago, by rather coolly informing Mary Willow of another commitment that needed to be kept.

"It would be nice if sometime we could spend the whole night together," Mary Willow peeped.

Claire agreed, and also submitted that "Business can be a nuisance that at times can pop up unexpectedly."

"I'll tell you what, though," she added with the thought of being kind and to send her lover away happy, "I'll come by your place tomorrow night." She then informed Mary Willow, who right away began fishing through her bag to locate a pen with which she proposed to write down her address: "That won't be necessary."

"I take it then, you already know where I live?" Mary Willow swelled with curiously.

Claire answered with her customary smirk that at times Mary Willow found irksome, but mostly caused her to want to fall to her knees.

"You found out where I work and now you know where I live?" Mary Willow made certain that her words possessed both timidity and reverence, but she wasn't able to conceal entirely that it disturbed her that Claire was able to acquire information so easily. "Claire, please forgive me if in any way this sounds evasive, but what if by chance you found out something about me that I wasn't yet prepared to tell you? Shouldn't I first be given the chance?"

"You must forgive me, Mary Willow," said Claire, "but there are certain occupations that require one to have eyes in the back of one's head. Surely you can understand as much? But since you're not a Communist, a Nazi, a spy, nor a criminal, I suppose I have no need to investigate any further."

"Please, Claire," begged Mary Willow, "you know all too well that I'm easily overpowered. Just tell me that I don't need to be afraid and I'll believe you."

Claire Damien advanced toward her frail lover and took her anxious little face into her hands. "There is no need to be afraid," were her firm words. Then she drew her lover's mouth to her own to form a kiss possessing reassurance and promise mere words might have otherwise lacked.

"We *are* in a relationship, are we not?" Mary Willow begged to know.

"There is only you, Mary Willow." There was no smirk or smile, but an unbroken stare that inspired utter confidence.

Mary Willow was halfway to Bloomsbury before having realised that Claire never bothered to mention what time she would be coming by. *Tomorrow night* was very vague; but thus far much about Claire Damien was vague — a fact Mary Willow was trying to reconcile or perhaps convince herself it was alright to overlook. At last, she decided, what did it matter about the time, as she would be entirely too anxious to do anything else but sit and wait for her lover. She went strolling by the spot where Elijah often played, but the flutist had already gone home to the world's most wonderful woman.

Mary Willow was of the notion that Elijah was a gift — a treasure, and that in a world given to misery and dysfunction there existed a blind man who was able to see souls and to pour into them his own unique brand of kindness, along with the tenderness and poetry of Schubert. She was grateful for every second that she was able to spend with him.

It was eight o'clock on the following evening when the doorbell had summoned Mary Willow. It couldn't be said that she sprang up from a chair, for she had been busy nervously gyrating about the room, while obsessing over every inanity that came to mind, including whether her cocktail napkins should be folded into a triangle, rectangle, or simply left alone. "A pupil after my own heart, I see," remarked Claire Damien, when spotting a bottle of Pinot Noir and two glasses resting atop a table and awaiting their involvement.

"Your *only* pupil," Mary Willow respectfully corrected her lover.

"Of course, Mary Willow; my *only* pupil," Claire agreed. Claire Damien was just beginning to become acquainted with the character of the well chosen spirit, when she noticed her lover's restlessness. "I can't say that your eagerness doesn't please me," she admitted, before her mouth creased into that all too familiar smirk.

Mary Willow fell to her knees, where she gratefully confessed to having been rendered incapable of taking a single step or keeping a thought in her head without wanting to bury herself in her lover's womanhood. At first she began lapping hungrily at her lover, with wildness and with abandon, forgetting all that she had learned, but then Claire reached down and took gentle hold of her face, and in doing so she brought her back into form. Afterward Mary Willow leaned back on her haunches and looked up at Claire as if begging to be judged and hopefully told that she had pleased her poised and authoritative lover. It wasn't until the two women returned to their glasses, that Claire noticed the starkness of Mary Willow's surroundings.

"Did your interior decorator die the day you hired him?" she wondered. "There isn't an artefact or adornment to be seen! The walls, shelves, and table tops are all completely bare!" Claire wasn't disturbed by the starkness and absence of anything that could qualify as personal, but she found it curious and had more than a passing interest of why.

"You might say I've been in sort of a transitional phase," Mary Willow told her.

"*I'll* say you are," said Claire. "I've known the most brutish of men who were entirely incapable of getting in touch with their feminine side that have done better than this."

"I do have one artefact," said Mary Willow. "Or rather, you might say it's a memento. It's very precious, though."

Before Claire could ask to have a look-see, Mary Willow took her by the hand and led her into a short hallway — at the end of which, Claire was introduced to an equally stark bedroom, save for the singular "memento".

"Why, it's an old photograph," she cried out while peering over Mary Willow's shoulder. Her interest in the photograph seemed genuine and this pleased Mary Willow, for she didn't wish to bore her lover — though how bored could one get when only forced to look at a single photograph; Mary Willow hadn't any albums to pour over; this one memento was all that remained of her childhood or any part of her past. "And how enchanting!" Claire added. "It's like how I always imagined the world to look in fairy tales."

"We're standing in the secret garden of Sudeley Castle," Mary Willow told her. "There aren't many days in one's life like a fairy tale, but that surely was one."

Claire examined the photograph more closely. "Mary Willow — the flowers in the garden — they're the very same as the flowers in the bouquet you sent!" This, Claire cried out as if having made a great discovery.

"They've been my favourite flowers ever since that day," said Mary Willow.

"That day must've meant a great deal to you," said Claire. She took possession of the photograph and held it up to her eyes. "Am I to assume that you're the beautiful young girl that's positively sparkling in this adorable frock?"

Mary Willow turned away as though modesty had rendered her incapable of replying. Claire shot her a curious look, and then moved on to the twin boys in the photograph.

"Their names are Colin and Douglas Broxton," Mary Willow told her. "And yes, just like their mother, Delia, they were beautiful to look at."

"And who is this darling little boy holding onto your hand and the two monkeys?" Claire asked her.

Mary Willow turned away — not from any sort of modesty, but rather, her countenance suddenly appeared quite solemn. It was her hope that Claire would be so charmed by the beautiful twins, the lovely girl in the frock, and the garden and castle in the back ground, that she would have overlooked the little boy entirely, as he was the least impressive subject in the photograph. Mary Willow seemed hesitant to want to talk about him.

"The little boy — he's the reason you still keep this photograph around, isn't it?" Claire seemed to press her lover. "It's not at all about the lovely garden, or the enchanted castle, or day like a fairy tale, it's about the little boy. There's not a single shred throughout this entire flat that says a thing about you, but I guessing that's not so of this boy."

"Do remind me, Claire, to commend you on your perceptiveness," was Mary Willow's sharp return.

"There's no need to be cross," said Claire. "We can talk about it, can't we?"

Mary Willow emptied the contents of her glass into her mouth, and then looked about for the Bottle, which had been left behind in the other room. Claire seized her agitated lover by the shoulders and guided her to a seat on the edge of the bed. She stroked her hair until some serenity was restored.

"His name was Jimmy Philips," Mary Willow began. "His mother, Catherine Philips, and Delia Broxton, the mother of the twins, were sisters. Jimmy's parents didn't travel often, but when they did he was sent to the Cotswolds to stay with the Broxton's. His cousins, Colin and Douglas were more than just twins, though; they were like one person split up into two bodies. That sounds crazy, I realise, but they were absolutely of one mind and as evil as they were beautiful, and they *were* beautiful. And because they looked like angels we kept trusting them, Jimmy and me, and they would do the most awful things to us. Not the sort of childish pranks that most of us at some time in our childhood must endure, but things that were wicked and unimaginable. Delia Broxton was the loveliest of the lovely, but she was never able to see her sons for what they were. Early on, I was of the notion that it was Colin who was mostly responsible for their malevolence, but as time went by, I came to learn that it was shared quite equally. Jimmy and I wanted what they had, to share a soul and to become of one mind. We loved each other so, we did. It wasn't a sexual love, though, and rarely did we as much as embrace. I loved his heart and especially his thoughts, for his voice beamed with such loveliness whenever he shared them with me, which was often. We shared everything, he and I — even that which is scarcely said aloud when there's only (you) to hear it. We desired to exist wholly on this imaginary plain, where we could become one another's thoughts. I like to think that we almost made it — that we were *this* close."

"What happened?" Claire asked.

"One day Jimmy was found beaten and left for dead in the woods," Mary Willow went on. "I knew it was Colin and Douglas that did it. Who else, but those capable of evil, could crush the life of one so lovely — so pure. It never went to trial — there was never even an arrest made." For Mary Willow, this was a fact that could never be reconciled. "Delia and I were close, but for a long time I couldn't look at her. Perhaps in a way I blamed her. Later, whenever I visited it was when I knew for certain that Colin and Douglas wouldn't be there. After a while it became all too obvious, though Delia went out of her way not to hint as much. For one another's sake we did everything possible not to mention Jimmy, unfortunately our talks arrived at dead-ends quicker than we would have liked, and trying not to mention Jimmy became too much of a strain. As time went by my visits became less frequent until they stopped altogether. For awhile we corresponded with cards and letters, but even that has come to pass, though it's a bridge I hope one day to rebuild."

"It's so strange," said Claire, "but there's something familiar about Jimmy — something in the manner in which he's holding your hand and looking up at you and clutching those monkeys. I feel as if I know him."

"Fish and Chips," said Mary Willow.

"Fish and Chips?" said Claire, with a queer sideways glance.

"Those were the names of his monkeys," said Mary Willow.

"No wonder you loved him so," said Claire. "Who couldn't love a young boy who named his stuffed monkeys Fish and Chips?"

"There's so much tragedy in the world, and so much of it is senseless," said Mary Willow. "Stay with me, Claire. Please say you'll stay the night."

Claire eased her lover back until her form was resting comfortably atop the bed. She rained whisper soft kisses all over her face and mouth, then lay next to her and stroked her hair. "Of course I'll say with you," she said, then thanked Mary Willow for sharing a painful part of her past. Reaching for a lighter moment, though, she alluded to the "business of the bottle in the other room" which she went directly to fetch. As Mary Willow observed, Claire's long, shapely legs went liltingly such, that they gave the impression that she was waltzing away from the bedroom. Claire's sudden whimsy seemed largely out of character, though Mary Willow found it delightful that beneath her lover's dense layer of poise and coolness, there existed a soul who hadn't nearly the aversion for impulsiveness as was once believed.

"The Pinot Noir grape was first *cultivated* in Burgundy, France, which you might have already guessed," Claire stated upon her return. "But did you know that grape itself goes as far back as the 1st century AD?"

"As a matter of fact I did," was Mary Willow's proud and surprising reply.

"Really?" asked Claire. She couldn't imagine that someone who freely admitted to an unsophisticated palate would know such an obscure fact.

Mary Willow smiled and a moment later her smile turned to laughter. When she saw that her lover was quite bemused, she confessed to having asked and received a brief but helpful education on the Pinot Noir grape from a well versed man named Walter at a place called the Wine Cellar where she made the purchase. "I wanted to impress you," she admitted.

"I'm flattered that you went to the trouble," said Claire.

"I know a man named Brian — in fact, he owns Ebenezer's Coffee House, and he talks of coffee similarly to the way you talk of wine," Mary Willow went on. "You don't merely know that a particular grape has a particular character, but *why*. Brian talks of climate and elevation as it pertains to coffee beans. I believe we take far too much for granted, and I'm starting to want to learn things. We mindlessly open bottles and cans and packages without ever giving but a thought to all the craft and preparation that goes in to all that we enjoy."

"Nothing could be more true," agreed Claire. "But I must confess, although I've always had an interest in wine, much of my passion and knowledge stems mostly from a monetary attachment that was formed a few years back. I'll now let you in on a little secret: I have a 10% share of a vineyard in Burgundy. Perhaps this summer we could travel there, and while we're traveling the countryside I can check on my investment. What would you say to touring a vineyard?"

"Oh, Claire, that would be wonderful!" cried Mary Willow. "I never travelled anywhere before. As a youngster I was always getting left behind. My parent never allowed me to travel with them, and they were always going to the most interesting places, such as Budapest and Singapore, but they never travelled to France— at least not that I know of."

"My dear, sweet Mary Willow," said Claire. "My eager-to-please teacher's pet Mary Willow, I have so much to show you." Claire smiled, and like her lover moments ago, her smile also turned into laughter. She, too, had the opportunity to watch her lover swell with bemusement. However, *her* confession was that she was entirely incapable of saying only a portion of Mary Willow's name. "I can't even think your name without putting it together as if it was one word — Marywillow. It's like a tree, whose dainty and fragrant blossoms are beyond compare — Marywillow; or a flower whose loveliness couldn't be described with mere words but with flutes and violins — Marywillow."

Mary Willow smiled brightly as to acknowledge that Claire wasn't alone on the subject of her name. "Never have I gotten just *Mary* or *Miss Willow*, except with patients, who simply call me *'nurse'.*" She fell back on the bed and invited her lover to "please" come join her. The two women lay together and for awhile talked of the virtues of those things which pleased them, including one another; although it appeared to pain the more modest Mary Willow to have her virtues cited aloud by another. She leapt to the notion that Claire was looking for virtues where none existed in order to have as much to say.

Claire, in turn, scolded her self-depredating lover by insisting, "As it stands, the world is already looking to cut us down every chance it gets; let us agree to not help it along, shall we?"

How could Mary Willow disagree with such near flawless logic. And whether she had gravitated to Claire or was ripe for the picking or some combination of each, why not rejoice behind the protective cloak that seemed to be her poised and authoritative lover? Why not graciously accept the virtues that were cited and infuse herself with Claire's strength to better glare back at a world that in the past has displayed the willingness to tear her to pieces? Why not?

"You're so right, Claire," she said. "The world doesn't need any help; least of all from me." Claire enjoyed hearing all about Elijah and *his* virtues and expressed genuine interest in meeting a musician able to play as remarkably well as Mary Willow had maintained. Mary Willow was impressed that Claire was familiar with numerous Schubert compositions, with "Death and the Maiden" and "The Trout Quintet" being two that she cited as her favourites, whereas she herself regrettably admitted to not knowing either.

"I didn't always know them," Claire told her, "I learned them as I went along in life, and so shall you." There was much to Claire Damien to learn; and whether big or small, Mary Willow saw each new discovery as an unparalleled thrill. Then she took hold of her lover in a manner which urged that she come lay on top of her.

"There, I want to feel you all over me," she whispered. She then wrapped her arms around Claire, whose long and sinuous form all but eclipsed her much slighter one. They found each other's eyes and for awhile were fixed on as well as fascinated with one another's lustful gaze, but no words of any kind were exchanged. Then Mary Willow began to draw Claire further up onto her body as though she were urging that her mouth become straddled by Claire's long, shapely legs. "I can't taste you enough. I want to know what it's like to lie beneath you — to feel all your loveliness pouring down over me," were her whispered moans. She began lapping away at her lover, rejoicing in her wetness and the desire to become drenched in her sex. She let go of everything in her past that pained her and went spiralling through the galaxy, not caring when or if she would land or with what she might collide, and all the while she was wholly embracing and relishing the dominion over her which her beautiful lover so soundly possessed. She wanted to scream out, *it's for this I exist! To lie helpless before you!* She felt Claire thrusting above her mouth, the rhythm of which served to intensify a hunger already possessing fury and urging that fury to become near savage-like — to burst through every set boundary and to lose all understanding of all earthly discipline. Claire found herself unexpectedly overwhelmed by her lover, and so unlike before, when in possession of some control, she was rendered powerless to reach down and bring Mary Willow back into form. She, too, was spiralling through the galaxy, like a meteor shower with no fixed destination and with no purpose other than to burn.

Mary Willow could sense that her lover's body had become rigid. She reached down and felt for her own sex and began masturbating to the thought of Claire's wetness oozing down onto her face and into her mouth — the mere notion alone would have set her ablaze, but the reality was indescribable. What followed was concert and accord rarely achieved. In pleasuring both herself *and* her lover, Mary Willow discovered remarkable control — it was as though from her back she had become the most capable of maestros guiding players through a symphony's final movement and on to its riveting climax. At last, the bodies of both women became rigid — their thrusts short and quick in their near vibratory oscillation. Then, in a second that seemed an eternity, there was stillness together with the uncertainty of whether pain or pleasure would accompany a pinnacle that could only be described as singularly uncommon. And within the realm of these burning entities, there existed a shared sense that, if unleashed, be it pain or pleasure, the world about them would tumble like dominos.

When their bodies at last became separated, they stared at one another as if utterly astounded by the sheer power of their sex. For Claire, lovemaking was an art form — a series of movements coming together as poetry and as limitless as language itself, not a reckless, primal act born out of the baser nature of wantons — but neither had occurred, and for awhile both she and Mary Willow elected to simply linger and remain quiet, with each attempting to gain some sort of understanding of what they were creating. It was Mary Willow who first spoke; though not of the experience, for she was sure to find the adequacy of mere words both crude and limiting. In fact, neither wished to hear, nor apply overused superlatives or platitudes to that which exceeded all imagining; to have had such uttering's expressed and consequently heard would have been regarded as a gross intrusion sure to have adversely affected the perfection of the current atmosphere.

When Mary Willow did speak it was simply to intimate the desire to be held until put into what she hoped would be a peaceful and satisfying slumber. Of this overture, Claire was all too obliging, and she went and lay down beside her lover. She drew her close to her bosom, and there they remained. Despite her lover's warmth and the arms that strived to offer comfort, Mary Willow lay wondering, was this all that was missing from her life? Was laying in the arms of a beautiful lover following a riveting climax the pinnacle of love and contentment? Was she at last standing atop the summit of all that truly mattered? She so desired to bask in the serenity of a moment brought about by a shared experience, but understood all too well the tenuous nature of having discovered love and happiness in another. She had the fleeting notion to beseech Claire never to leave her alone in the world and to share ten thousand more nights, like the very one which was now peacefully slipping away, but she understood to even think such thoughts was affirmation that she herself in many ways was less than complete, and that without Claire, she would once again descend into nothingness. She didn't wish to become nothing, to ever again feel like nothing, as she did in childhood and on all those Sunday mornings in the corner of a coffee house. It was painful enough to remember; she didn't wish to go back. At last, she let it all go — her lover, her own incompleteness, her fear of being set adrift, and in her now weary mind she turned on her virtuoso flutist and imagined him piping out Schubert for the world's most wonderful woman. *What could be more perfect*, she thought. Elijah understood what it was to feel complete — the sort of completeness that didn't come by way of an earthy climax, Mary Willow knew. Then again, he had been given a gift that helped him to better acknowledge God, and it was mostly *through* God that Elijah found and understood whatever sense of completeness he had achieved, for passions aroused by physical beauty were all but unknown to a blind man. She also understood the depths of physical love to be shallow, albeit the perversities that can sometimes drive such love were all too overpowering. Nevertheless, she allowed the serene nature of spirit to be overtaken by these forces, and the loveliness of Elijah's flute to be driven from her head. At last, there she lay, no longer in the arms of her slumbering lover, but nestled between her long, shapely legs and once again prepared to pay homage to her womanhood.

Toward morning, Mary Willow began to stir and when doing so she let out soft yet audible moans. Claire woke and placed a caressing hand on her chest hoping it would return her to what had been a peaceful slumber. Instead, Mary Willow sprang forward into a sitting position and let out a terrible scream. Claire also sprang forward, though with rescuing arms, as her delicate lover appeared to be fighting for her breath.

"Mary Willow, you're having a nightmare!" Claire cried. "It's alright, Mary Willow, I'm here with you, I'm holding you! Mary Willow!"

"Claire! Oh, Claire!" she cried out. Then she collapsed in her lover's arms.

"Shhh, it was just a bad dream," Claire assured her. She guided her head back to her pillow, then stroked her hair, and placed whisper soft kisses on her eyelids in an effort to inspire calm.

"I'm sorry to startle you so, Claire. But you'll stay with me again, though, won't you?" was Mary Willow's hopeful entreaty.

"Of course I'll stay with you again," Claire told her. "Tomorrow night, if you like?"

"I have bad dreams sometimes, Claire. Awful dreams, in fact," confessed Mary Willow. "There are things that have occurred in my past that keep resurfacing — things that manifest themselves in these reoccurring nightmares."

"None among us is pure, Mary Willow. We're all sinners in this world, and for that reason we all have our demons to battle," Claire assured her. "Do you wish to tell me about yours? Not your sins, of course; I don't profess to be anyone to whom one should confess their sins, but you could tell me of your demons. There's no need to be afraid, you know. If you'd like, I'll hold you while you tell me."

For the first time Mary Willow looked at Claire Damien, not merely as someone capable of thrilling her beyond all imagining, but as someone who could care for her, and with whom she could grow to understand love on many levels.

"There's this one particular demon," she began. "He comes to me only when I'm in the deepest of slumbers. His hands are huge, monstrous even, and with them he seizes me and then holds me down under the water. At first I'm unable to see him, but can only hear his voice, which is lovely, and he uses the loveliness of his voice to lure me to the river. Once there, he reveals his ugliness to me — his cruelty. He's a terrible brute whose might is great, yet I still struggle against him for all the good it does. From below the surface I can hear his hideous laughter, and the more I struggle, the harder and more hideously he laughs. He allows me to come up for a breath, but then right back down I go, for he enjoys toying with me — he's the most sadistic of demons, who pleasures himself in my fright. Sometimes I wish he would hold me down until I am no more, so that I need not ever again be afraid."

"Colin and Douglas — they're the demons — the ones who held you under the water?" Claire wondered.

"No," answered Mary Willow, "it wasn't me whom they submerged, but Jimmy, my dear, sweet Jimmy. But it might as well have been me, for I was able to feel all his pain, just as he was able to feel all mine. Yes, pain, pain, pain," she agitatedly repeated, "it's a wonderful thing to share until you discover that you're all alone and have to bear the burden … *all* alone. The price of love and a gift from the grave."

"But you're not alone, Mary Willow," Claire reminded her. "Not anymore."

Mary Willow smiled weakly, and then went on to add, "Jimmy truly loved his Aunt Delia, you know. But one day, when laying down together in the meadow — I remember it so well, it was such a swelter that day — he told me that I was his only hope. I thought I knew what he had meant, that I was the only person to whom he could tell things, truly intimate things, but then he asked me if I could imagine him as a man. Jimmy was frail — so truly lovely and frail that it was difficult to imagine him all grown up and a man. So I told him, 'I don't want to think about what the world might be like in five years or maybe in ten; I want to enjoy who you are right now, today, and in this very moment, because this moment that we're sharing is our only guarantee.' Jimmy knew that I was trying to avoid telling him *that* which *I* believed he didn't wish to hear. But the truth was he *did* wish to hear that I couldn't imagine him as a man, because afterward he told me that he believed that God had made a mistake and that the world might make much more sense to him if he were more like me on the outside. He asked, 'does knowing that about me bothered you?' I never as much as batted an eye. I told him that it didn't matter, that I loved his heart, and that was the truth … then *and* now.

"You see, Jimmy revered women. In fact, his reverence was such that, except for his Aunt Delia and me, women terrified him — he could never even think of approaching one. It was all his mother's doing, though — Catherine Philips. She never showed him even a pittance of affection the whole time growing up, and Lord knows Jimmy worked hard to try and win her heart. I can't imagine how it must feel to have to try and win the heart of your own mother and actually fail. You would think a young boy would grow up to become a misogynist, but he went the other way entirely, holding women in such regard that he saw himself as unworthy of their affections. It didn't matter how I loved him, *or* his Aunt Delia, the damage that Catherine had done was too severe. And I'm fairly certain that if Jimmy was still here he would not be a man. And what would it matter; his heart would still be his heart, would it not?" She looked to Claire for a sign of concurrence or affirmation to her last remark, and Claire, in turn, nodded to intimate that she was stirred by the depth of Mary Willow's own heart; though she was also trying to understand the true essence of her lover and her lover's dead friend as they once existed. What she knew of Mary Willow, and as Jimmy had been described, they seemed to her interchangeable entities, as identical on the inside as Colin and Douglas Broxton were on the outside.

"I wonder, though," asked Mary Willow, "had Jimmy lived — had he followed through with what he had intimated to me on that hot summers day in the meadow, would his reasoning have been as simple as the old adage, *If you can't beat 'em, join them?"*

"Before you asked that question I was already thinking about a particular Sun Tzu quote — something that perhaps goes much more to the heart of the matter," said Claire.

"What, Claire? What was the quote?" Mary Willow swelled with the hope that her lover had some special insight that she was about to share. She knew that Sun Tzu was a philosopher in the Spring and Autumn period of ancient China, and that he was perhaps quoted nearly as often as Winston Churchill, and as was the case with Churchill, his quotes were well documented.

"To know your enemy, you must become your enemy," Claire told her. "Perhaps Jimmy saw his own mother as his enemy. Imagine, becoming that which you don't understand in order to understand it. I imagine one would be wholly unable to do such a thing if they lacked courage."

"You're as wise as you are beautiful, Claire. And believe me, I'm not patronizing you — I wouldn't dare — I'm very sincere. I can't even begin to fathom the amount of envy that has followed you around all your life. I wonder how much of that envy you yourself have bothered to notice. But then again, why would you notice? When the perception of others has always been favourable to the extent of bordering on worship, I would imagine that after awhile it becomes a matter of routine and therefore as indifferent as white noise. Maybe that's a good thing, or maybe it's bad — I couldn't begin to know. But what I do know is that after awhile we become the perception. We can't help it." What followed Mary Willow's words was silence, with each woman trying to imagine what is was like to be the other. Then Mary Willow went on to add, "My flat wasn't always so stark like this, Claire. There was a time not all that long ago, when it was well decorated with lots of trinkets on shelves, pictures on walls, and knickknacks on table tops. But I once heard it said that, a person's décor should make some sort of statement of who they are. Well, I never knew who I was — not entirely." She frowned as one would when having become quite dismayed with themselves. "Who am I kidding," she jeered. "I scarcely knew myself at all. In fact, knowing myself was an issue that I've struggled with all my life, until most recently. So one cold winter's night I came home and took everything down from the walls, shelves, and off the table tops, placed it all in bags and then threw it all away."

"I must say, Mary Willow, you're becoming more complicated by the moment," said Claire. "In fact, every minute that you haven't been eagerly at my vagina, you've either been morbid, complicated, mysterious, or a downright *bummer*, as they say."

"I'd say that's a most rectifiable dilemma," said Mary Willow. "Wouldn't you?" She gave Claire a dose of her own medicine by emulating her smirk.

"Yes," Claire agreed. "Though I must inform you, should you follow through with your devilish intentions, you would hold the distinction of being the very first to bring me to the promise land four times in the same evening."

"Well, if that isn't incentive, I don't know what is!" laughed Mary Willow. "I might even have a T-shirt made up to say as much. The front could read *Claire Damien's Sex Slave* and on the back I'll have the statistics of my epic performance."

"Now wouldn't that be the cat's meow," Claire added. After Mary Willow positioned herself for the evening finale, her thoughts turned to the blind flutist, who no doubt was laying in a peaceful slumber next to Sarah, the world's most wonderful woman. *How gentle were their souls*, she thought. *How pure were their hearts?* She was all at once seized with the notion that loving Claire was like cheating. After all, how difficult was it to love a beautiful, poised, and authoritative woman with a fierce intellect? In a crowd, Claire was like an elegant mare among overworked mules. To say she loved Claire was no different than saying that she loved an autumn sunset or Schubert. Nevertheless, the guilt passed and she went on gorging herself, until her thoughts at last turned to a young woman whose body was laid to rest some years ago in a cemetery in Bibury — darling Mary Willow was what Delia Broxton use to called her. She wondered how much longer such a charade could be stretched — a year, perhaps ten, or maybe forever? Again came an onrush of guilt — this time over a woman who rescued her from oblivion.

Sometime during the course of all this weighty pondering, Claire was brought to a climax. Mary Willow pretended to rejoice for having pleased her lover, but was gripped with hatred toward the Broxton twins for taking away the one person with whom her soul had intertwined. Mary Willow squinted into the early morning light that was breaking through the scantily dressed window. Despite a night-time that was filled with confessions, discoveries, and the delight of a sexual odyssey, she woke feeling remarkably refreshed and alert. Claire, meanwhile, took the liberty of rummaging through cabinets until a bag of ground coffee labelled *Ebenezer's Coffee House* was discovered. When she returned to the bedroom with cups and saucers, Mary Willow frowned, for her lover was already dressed and all put back together and looking no worse for wear. This wasn't to be the tousle-haired, droopy-eyed morning after a slumber party for which she had hoped, as Claire seemed all too eager to get along and was hurrying through a cup of coffee — the goal of which was only to provide a measure of alertness, otherwise it was considered extraneous and an imposition. "But Claire," wined Mary Willow, "I thought since you stayed the night that we might spend a bit of the day together, if only the morning."

"It's a good thought, Mary Willow, and there's nothing I'd like more, but duty calls," Claire told her disappointed lover.

"Of course … duty," grumbled Mary Willow. "And what sort of duty would it be this morning?"

"You shouldn't ask questions if you're not all too sure that you really want to know the answers," said Claire.

"Well, *that* surely wasn't very encouraging," Mary Willow complained. "After last night I thought that perhaps I might deserve, at the very least, a speck of disclosure."

"Forgive me, Mary Willow, it wasn't my intention to sound quite so callous and abrupt," said Claire. "But …"

"Then take me with you, Claire!" begged Mary Willow. "I'll sit up straight, fold my hands, keep my mouth shut, and you can introduce me to all you associates as your valet!" A smirk slowly formed on Claire's face, as if she was finding the idea a somewhat attractive one and was giving it its due consideration. She paced about the bedroom in a contemplative silence, while occasionally sipping from her cup. At last, she set the cup down on the window sill and went charging across the room. She appeared determined, as if having reached a revelation that infused her with great strength and vigour. Mary Willow had but a second to determine whether she was about to be thrashed or forcibly made love to — it was only these two notions that were considered — and before a conclusion could be reached, less was there a chance to turn away from the apparent fury, she found herself seized by the shoulders and pushed backward until her frail little form was pinned to the mattress.

"Are you in love with me, Mary Willow?" Claire demanded to know. From flat on her back Mary Willow's eyes widened, and if permitted, her frail little form might have shrank, as the question and the authoritative manner in which it was posed took her quite by surprise. Nevertheless, she managed to peep that she believed she *was* in fact in love — or at least in love as she knew "in love" to be.

In the past, she merely ached and hungered, but remained a damaged wanton existing on the fringe of society, trapped somewhere between convention and rebellion — but in love? She understood attachment, and had experienced what she believed all along was an unparalleled attachment, but "in love" was new ground.

"And would you submit to being my slave, Mary Willow — and would you do all that I ask, even if there are times you don't find the going agreeable?" was Claire's additional demands.

"I *am* your slave, Claire," Mary Willow professed. "At least I believe I've already proven myself as such — have I not?" It wasn't until Claire eased up on her grip, that she realised how firmly she had taken hold of her frail little lover's shoulders. She took a step backward, and when doing so she noticed the deep impressions that her hands had made. For this she didn't *voice* any regret, but her own shoulders slumped and the severity had all but vanished from her face. Mary Willow had shown the willingness to surrender from the very night they met, and upon their second meeting, without reservation or fear of consequence, she placed her being and foremost her nakedness at Claire's feet; it was redundant by now, she thought, for Claire to demand that she pledge servitude and obedience, though she didn't dare express as much.

"Well, don't just lay there like a lump," said Claire. "The morning's getting along and we have a bit of a drive ahead of us — we need to get on the road lickety-split!"

Mary Willow jumped to attention, saluted her lover, and like a whirling dervish she managed to pull herself together in the little bit of time that Claire afforded her. Claire, meanwhile, had returned to her coffee and observed the effort as though it was a terrific source of amusement. Once outside, Mary Willow's eyes widened like those of an excitable child on their birthday or Christmas morning, when she spotted sitting curb side a shiny, white Porsche. "One thing is for certain, you're not a nurse," she said rather drolly. "We don't command the sort of salary that affords us much in the way of luxuries."

Claire placed her frail but excitable little lover in the car and then drove off.

"Can we roll the top down!" Mary Willow clamoured. "I've never driven in a convertible before!"

"It's still March," Claire reminded her. "We'll catch our death. Perhaps in a few weeks time we can go about with the top down."

Mary Willow swelled with excitement when learning that their destination was St. George's Hill. She jabbered on about Ringo Starr, Elton John, Tom Jones and other famous people that she heard lived there; she also wondered about the possibility of sighting a celebrity.

"You'll hardly find them outside mowing their lawns, or walking their dogs," Claire informed her.

Still, Mary Willow's enthusiasm continued to soar as she began to jabber on about the virtues of a sports car to which she alluded, "Must cost three times my annual wage!" It took some time, but at last she was able to settle down enough to where she could enjoy the sensation of the ride. With the city in the rear view mirror and the open road ahead, she found herself gazing at Claire and wondering what it was about herself that this stunning creature found so fascinating that night at Bruno's Café. She was inclined to ask, but figured Claire was owed a bit of silence — that for awhile she should be permitted to enjoy the sunshine, the road, and her own thoughts without a voice in her ear. At last it was decided that she didn't wish to know — that whatever attribute was owed to procuring the fascination of one Claire Damien should remain a mystery. After all, should she discover as much, there existed the likelihood of becoming exceedingly mindful of something which had occurred instinctively, and the further likelihood of her trying too hard to play a particular role — the contrivance of which might cause her to become a caricature of what it was that attracted Claire, and in due course it could become irksome.

"Well, we're here," said Claire.

Mary Willow's open mouth gaze was near comical, while she attempted to contemplate the kind of wealth it took to own such property, but being of such naivety as she was (she was familiar with the old world charm of the Cotswolds, but found St. George's Hill astounding), such wealth was unimaginable.

"I can't wait to see the inside!" she clamoured.

"Mary Willow." Claire purposely sounded grim in order to temper her lover's enthusiasm. "I'm afraid you're going to have to wait in the car."

"But, Claire!" Mary Willow became sulky and her shoulders slumped as would a child's when informed of a punishment they believed was too severe per the infraction. "It's been such a lovely morning," she went on. "Do say you're not serious?"

"I'm afraid I am," Claire told her. "But it won't always be like this; I promise. For now, though, I have to keep you on a bit of a short leash."

"A short leash? How very lovely," hissed Mary Willow. "Maybe I'll turn about for you in tight little circles while I'm on my *'short leash'*. Or, maybe I could roll over so you could scratch my belly? You don't happen to have any treats on you, do you? A pup likes to be rewarded you know. And just think, afterward I can give your hands and feet a thorough licking. You'd like that, wouldn't you?"

"Mary Willow, please don't be cross," pleaded Claire. "It's true, many of my clients are of a certain wealth and privilege, but I can tell you firsthand they're not all well behaved, and for that reason I need more time to prepare you. But you'll see; we'll be partners before you know it."

Mary Willow let out a few *arfs* and *bow wows* to assure he lover that she would be quite content to wait in the car and enjoy the view. After having watched Claire disappear inside a remarkable edifice that caused her to gawk, she permitted her eyes to rove about a landscape belonging to one of the wealthier suburbs in all of England, and while doing so, she contemplated the current state and vicissitude of her existence: the Porsche, its stunning owner, St. George's Hill — it seemed all too unfathomable and this caused her to feel far removed from those with whom she worked and who were of a similar station. Far away, too, was the needfulness and fear of the sick. But most of all, the blind flutist no longer seemed of the same world — the same blind flutist whose true essence, in Mary Willow's estimation, far exceeded any tangible wealth. It always pleased Mary Willow to think of Elijah — and so she closed her eyes and allowed the melodious strains of Schubert to creep into her head, where aside from providing a measure of delight, the imagined music helped her to overlook the fact that there was still much to Claire Damien that remained a mystery.

Mary Willow and Claire Damien spent a great deal of time together in the days ahead and shared many a night. When darkness came, they were the most splendid of lovers, with Claire playing the part of the consummate artist, who explored with the elegance of a ballerina, whereas Mary Willow was the ever insatiable gorger of flesh. Mary Willow maintained that their lovemaking transcended Heaven and Earth; for Claire made love as though they were *in* Heaven and had an eternity to rejoice, whereas she herself played the role of a back-alley prostitute always ready for a command performance and cognizant of the fact that time was money. Though when all was said and done, it was laying in one another's arms that was craved. By day, they each allow the other to penetrate further into their respective worlds; though the process was a careful one, where nothing yet was learned that made either of them wary.

A drive to the Cotswolds was made one Sunday, which included a tour of Sudeley Castle and a stroll through its secret garden, which was beginning to perk up with the early days of spring. They snapped photographs of one another in the vibrancy of the early season and asked that a bystander capture them posed together. Perhaps it was hopefulness that was blooming along with the flowers of springtime, or the sun shining down on a wide open space that seemed immeasurable in its delight, but surging within them was a sensation that they could exist entirely un-tethered from the world of conformity — therefore when they posed, they did so in a manner that made no bones of the fact that they were lovers. Afterward, Claire thought since they were already in the Cotswolds, that it might be a good idea to visit Delia Broxton — or, as Mary Willow referred to her, *Aunt Delia*. But the proposal, as Claire plainly observed, caused Mary Willow to become squirmy, and the light in her eyes that throughout the day had been ever present became dim. She went on to protest, "The Broxton's aren't the sort of people that enjoy being dropped in on." Despite the untruth, it came off sounding like a viable reason not to drive anywhere near the grand old Tudor.

"Mary Willow, if my memory serves correct, and I believe it does, I clearly heard you mention that Delia Broxton was a bridge that you wished to one day rebuild," Claire reminded her squirmy, out-of-sorts lover. "And you know what they say? There's no time like the present."

"Naturally, there's no time like the present, that's why it's called present; the past and future are hardly adequate for mending fences ... or bridges ... or for that matter, any structure. But thanks just the same for the life lesson. And, as always, Claire, your memory is spot on."

It was rare, but there were instances when a particular attribute of Claire's (and there seemed an abundance) annoyed Mary Willow — and whenever she became annoyed she was given to being ironical, but then immediately afterward she would offer a fairly sincere apology, which she did now before adding: "I promise to work on that bridge — diligently, in fact — but just not today. Beginning with the earliest rays of the sunrise, today has been perfect, and I don't want to run the risk of spoiling perfection, but Aunt Delia is an initiative I'll one day take. But I want today to belong only to us."

Claire seemed satisfied, and so not another word was mentioned on the subject, and the perfection that Mary Willow alluded to was fully restored. Whether sharing a bottle of Pinot Noir, taking car rides in the country, or strolling the numerous squares of London in the evening, Mary Willow spoke often of the kind of love that inspired poetry and great literature — it was as if by her effort alone she was trying to will her and Claire to such loftiness. At times she seemed to be forging ahead in an effort to create the perfect space and climate in which they could exist. Claire permitted such folly, but she wasn't necessarily encouraging. Although, when in times of repose, it pleased her to listen to Mary Willow, who read beautifully, recite the love poems of John Keat's and inspiration passages from romantic literature. When in public places, Mary Willow quickly became accustom to the way men ogled her lover. Then again, what choice did she have? Claire was an eyeful, and anyone who lay eyes on her was of the notion that she must be *some*body — a celebrity of *some* sort. Even men who had women securely draped on their arms were driven to utter distraction. At first, though, Mary Willow found the attention all too unsettling, which caused her to act clingier than Claire liked, but then she subsequently learned to covet her envious position. Once, when knowingly ogled during a cool evening stroll, Claire turned to her lover and kissed her deeply on the mouth. "There," she said wickedly, "that ought to send him home with something to think about."

"Claire, you are an absolute devil!" cried Mary Willow. "Come morning the poor chap will have worn away all his foreskin."

"Serves him right," said Claire. "If there's one thing I despise, it's when a man looks at me as though my being a lesbian is a waste."

Mary Willow made a genuine effort to at least *sound* magnanimous in her concern for the *poor chap* and the future state of the poor chap's foreskin, but her effort accentuated the farce and therefore served to heighten the hilarity of the remark, and this ultimately caused both women to erupt into a chorus of laughter. There were passersby who took a moment to pause and wondered what was so humorous, but the giddy pair dismissed the cause of their laughter as too private and perhaps too offensive for general consumption. Still, Mary Willow was all too cognizant that having been publicly devoured was for her own benefit — that it was, in fact, Claire's not so subtle way of reassuring her that, no matter how many lecherous eyes coveted the prize, her envious position was well secured. Before leaving Sudeley Castle and its secret garden, to brighten the mood she nearly dampened, Claire reaffirmed the promise of a trip to Burgundy and the tour of a vineyard of which she was part owner. Over a French mug at Ebenezer's Coffee House, Mary Willow beamed with delight on the very subject to Elijah; although, the virtuoso flutist confessed to an uneducated palate regarding the virtues of wine.

"I once heard that alcohol dulls the senses," he went on to say, "and being that I'm already a bit deficient in the senses department, I figure I'd be doing myself a huge disservice by indulging." Nevertheless, the flutist, who regarded his senses with tongue in cheek, managed plenty of enthusiasm that Mary Willow would be gaining the opportunity to visit a place of interest, and Burgundy, France certainly qualified. "It's good to travel, to treat the senses to new adventures. From time to time, whether they realise it or not, a person needs to see the world under a different sky, to hear new voices, to eat different food, and to smell new smells. It's good for the soul. And when you return, you may discover a renewed appreciation for what you already have; although, from what I can gather, nowadays you're doing just fine in *that* department."

"How right you are, Elijah! How very right you are! But now I must insist that you allow me to walk you home so that I could spend some time with Sarah and Marybeth."

"Ahh, just using me for my wife and parrot, are you?"

"Of course," said Mary Willow. "Why else would I force myself to muddle through Schubert and such terrific conversation?" Elijah needn't have been gifted with sight to know the delight that illuminated in Mary Willow's smile.

That very same night, when Mary Willow returned to her flat, she discovered a contemplative Claire Damien seated alone in the dark. She became startled when she turned on the lights. She wasn't expecting company; nor had she spotted Claire's car parked anywhere on the street; although her mind was so occupied with Marybeth, who had learned to say her name in that squawking sort of parrot speak, *Mary Willow Mary Willow*, that she might have overlooked the shiny white Porsche. Nevertheless, by then it was understood that Claire didn't need an invitation; she was free to come and go as she wished.

"What a pleasant surprise," Mary Willow chirped, as she tried to hide that discovering her lover alone in the dark and looking more contemplative than she had ever seen her look before was unsettling. "I was just talking about you with Elijah. As it turned out, one thing led to another and the next thing I knew I was gushing about our trip to Burgundy. So why were you sitting in the dark?"

"I think better in the dark," Claire told her. "I think better in the dark, particularly when I'm forced to think about things that I find unpleasant."

"Unpleasant?" said Mary Willow, who, although unfounded, she right away leapt to the notion that the unpleasantness that Claire was forced to ponder was in some way related to her, and their relationship — that perhaps Claire had tired of her and decided that the relationship had already run its course and she was sitting alone in the dark reaching for the softest language imaginable to say goodbye to her frail little lover. "Would you prefer that I turn the lights off?" Mary Willow cautiously asked Claire.

"That's no longer necessary," Claire replied. "I've already done all my thinking; now it's time to act." Both Claire's words and the dispassionate tone with which they were delivered, frightened Mary Willow, and she as much as told her so. All at once, the evening strolls through London's many squares that sparked numerous nights of splendour disappeared into a misty cloud of uncertainty, as too did the weekend drives in the country that brought about an exhilarating sense of freedom that was so well enjoyed, along with bottle after bottle of Pinot Noir that led to intimacy so artful, that even Claire herself confessed to new ground having been breached. Now, all that seemed to remain was the Claire Damien, who when she entered Bruno's Café, was met by all with reverence — the same dangerous femme fatale who both fascinated and intimidated Mary Willow — who promised to slit her throat and threatened castration, and in doing she so caused Mary Willow to shrink in her barstool. "I need you to come with me tonight," Claire told her frightened lover. "Only this time you won't be waiting in the car."

Claire expected Mary Willow to act pleased, that at long last she was invited to become further involved with business — that she was *that* well loved and trusted. No lover of Claire's had come so far nor was trusted this much — a fact that she made known to Mary Willow.

In the past, Mary Willow had sulked when only permitted to come along for the ride. Afterward, when alone in the car with only her own thoughts with which to amuse herself, she would ponder the gravity of her lover's suspected issues with trust. Now, when at last informed that she was needed — words which she longed to hear — instead of acting pleased, she appeared frightened as one does when drowning in a sea of uncertainty. All at once she returned to that first night, when she was ordered by a strange woman to remove her clothes and stand naked upon examination. The shame and thrill that surged through her then was immeasurable, as it led to, if not discovery than the reaffirmation of the submissive lover she suspected herself of being should she ever become a lover. But tonight she didn't seek shame, nor thrill, less have them collide to form the core of her sexual wantonness; and although such discovery *or* reaffirmation never failed to feel new in their essence or in their capacity to thrill, tonight she was in need of other sensations — among them love and reassurance.

With less expectation than she could have hoped to possess, she went and placed her head on Claire's chest and held on to her as though she were pleading for love and reassurance — that the part of her lover, which thus far had remained a mystery, when revealed, wouldn't destroy them.

"Mary Willow, I need you to be strong tonight," Claire firmly demand of her lover. "I need you to do exactly what I say without thought — without question. Do you understand me?"

"Yes, Claire, I *do* understand," said Mary Willow. "I understand perfectly." A faraway look came over Mary Willow, and when she spoke it was in a tone that was barely audible, and her words, although they were exactly what Claire wished to hear, contained little in the way of conviction.

Not a word was exchanged on the way to the white, shiny Porsche, which was parked under a street lamp, where it was beautifully illuminated in all its splendour; how could Mary Willow have missed it earlier? Claire was fleet of foot and was in possession of a temperament that made her appear somewhat hurried, though not agitated. Mary Willow was ushered to her seat, though not in the gentle way, which in the past had been the custom. When she heard the car door slam shut and Clair's stunning heels pound decisively on the street, she was reminded of how it felt the first time she stood in the corridor just outside Claire's door. Once again she was experiencing the sensation of being seated in the first car of a rollercoaster slowly ticking its way up its initial incline on the way to its rousing plummet. And just like on that night, she was in full possession of an intuition dowsing her with tones of warning that whatever uncertainty was about to unfold, it might be more than she was able to bare. As Claire turned the ignition, Mary Willow made a thorough examination of her lover's countenance. The engine rumbled impressively, then off they drove. Claire didn't roll the top down, nor did Mary Willow ask her to; this wasn't to be a drive in the country, she realised — certainly not at such an hour. Claire also kept the windows rolled shut; evidently, wherever was the destination, which thus far she hadn't revealed, she wished to arrive unruffled and with every strand of her lovely mane perfectly in place.

By now, Mary Willow had determined that this was no longer the Claire Damien with whom in public she shared a rollicking laugh following a lover's kiss. Nor was this the same woman whose hand she held in the secret garden of Sudeley Castle — but rather, this was the dark, dangerous beauty whom Bruno once warned her of. For weeks, Mary Willow had foolishly given way to the notion that *that* Claire Damien — the dark and intimidating femme fatale — the woman whom Bruno seemed all too proud to have claimed knowing, was all but *loved* away — that her softer side had been set free to blossom and had all but supplanted a woman known to make strong men shudder with a mere glare. Mary Willow was so transfixed on Claire's countenance, that she was unable to hazard a guess as to how much time had elapsed or distance was travelled before at last informed that their destination was Camden Lock — a place many consider the tattoo, neon-coloured hair, and body piercing capitol of the western world. So soon after sharing coffee and delightful conversation with Elijah, she was in no mood to be placed so far out of her element, but she elected not to intimate as much. Besides, at this point there was nothing to gain by informing Claire of how she felt about Camden Lock or any other destination. And despite the impressiveness of St. George's Hill and what ended up the loveliest of days — how she wished to have never clamoured to penetrate so far into Claire Damien's world.

"We'll be meeting a fellow named Calvin," Claire told her quiet, apprehensive lover. "He's an interesting sort, who has an irresistible interest and attraction for petite, vulnerable Caucasian women; he assumes that any woman petite and Caucasian must also be vulnerable."

That Claire pointed out that Calvin's appetite was mainly for "Caucasian women", caused Mary Willow to leap to the conclusion that Calvin was a black man, which he was; though on this matter she didn't bother to seek confirmation. "I'm not sure what gets his juices flowing more freely, the sensation of the conquest, or the notion that he's rescuing them. Either way, some men would have been so much better off had they been born without penises, and Calvin quite clearly is *one*."

"You'll look out for me, though, won't you, Claire?" Mary Willow begged to know.

"No matter the circumstances, no matter how dicey things become, do as I say at all times and everything will be fine," Claire told her. "You simply have to put all your trust in me; I can't make that clear enough." Then she reached over and squeezed her hand. Mary Willow displayed much more reassurance than was truly in her heart, though she felt much better than she did a minute ago. She closed her eyes and willed the loveliness of Elijah's flute into her head and managed to keep it there until they reached the carnival atmosphere that was Camden Lock.

"Not exactly St. George's Hill, is it?" remarked Claire, as she drove through a crowded market place known as the hub of their destination. "But, unfortunately, none of us has the luxury of handpicking our clients. I'm sure you must have had at least *one* patient whom you found utterly repulsive, yet had to administer the same level of care as you would to a bobby socked cheerleader. And look on the bright side; when you get back to work, you can tell all your co-workers how you went slumming."

Mary Willow gawked at what was more eccentricity and honky-tonk than she had ever imagined existed, as the market place and its unique flair seemed to be where all those worshipping all things considered *the alternative* had flocked. The colourful menagerie was comprised of tattoo parlours, body piercing shops, and clothing boutiques able to accommodate the fairy princess aspirant, to the vampire, and every sort of eccentric in-between.

The marketplace was a human jungle of nonconformity; but when thought of in that essence, Mary Willow discovered herself celebrating the cluster who had chosen to recognise and to cling to their own uniqueness and spirit over the societal rules that declare that it should do otherwise. It occurred to her that it wasn't necessarily the fairy princesses or the vampires who were the wannabes — that the true wannabes where those coasting by and trying hard not to be *too* obvious when gawking from behind closed windows of automobiles. Coasting was all that could be done, though, when driving through the marketplace —especially at night, as both the sidewalks and street belonged to those on foot. Call it an unwritten rule or eminent domain; either way, it was an accepted practice, but one that wasn't always appreciated. A bare-chested man with a shaved head and an unnaturally dark, full beard strolled in front of the shiny, white Porsche. He purposely slowed his gait in order to sneer at an automobile that he saw as the most offensive result of capitalism imaginable.

"Just what we need — another half-baked radical, who thinks we should all stop what we're doing and plant daisies," Claire uttered with disgust. The man smirked back at Claire, and then turned his back, revealing a tattoo of Jesus — it covered his entire back. It wasn't the baby Jesus, or the crucified Jesus, but Jesus amid a dissipating cloud, looking contemplative, and holding a modern guitar. Behind His head was the sun with a multitude of spires stretching out from its orb. Mary Willow let out a gasp, after which, Claire remarked rather drolly: "Were you expecting Batman?" Mary Willow ignored the remark, as she was so entirely taken aback by the bald, bearded man; though she was unable to determine whether it was the man himself strutting about so boldly with his religious passion tattooed on his bare back that moved her, or whether it was the most emotionally stirring Christ that she had ever seen? She was perfectly aware that the remarkable likeness of the king of Christendom was a tattoo, though done by a supremely capable tattoo artist — but Christ seemed to be calling her, compelling her to look deeper, and that perhaps if she looked deep enough and trusted what she saw, the mystery of faith and mankind, at least as it pertained to her, would be revealed.

The man faced forward and nodded to Claire, as though he truly believed that in some way he had enlightened her. "Alright, you made your point, now move along," she said. The man took a bow. It wasn't until he returned to an upright position, that Mary Willow noticed that his well-defined chest and flat, firm belly were also shaved to better display three roses of Jericho — one on each breast and a much larger one that covered much of his belly; perhaps it was supposed to be a representation of The Father, Son, and the Holy Ghost. Mary Willow inadvertently let out a sigh, when at last Claire brought the car to a stop. The show was over; it was now time for business. Thought it was clear from her posture, which appeared drawn and more frail than usual, that she was overcome with reluctance, and on her face was more than a mere suggestion that, whatever was about to take place, made her very afraid. Despite receiving another pep talk, she appeared rigid when faced with the task of extracting herself from the car — the maneuver seemed to take a maximum amount of effort, with each movement carefully calculated.

Claire asked for her hand and together they weaved their way through the crowded marketplace. Mary Willow walked with her head down — she no longer wished to see Jesus — not even his tattooed likeness. At last they dipped into an alleyway that led to the back of a building. There, Mary Willow winced when accosted by the stench of vomit and urine. Claire found it curious that she would react so strongly to odours, which for a nurse, must be considered routine — but then she considered her lover's anxiety, which ebbed and flowed, but never was unapparent since leaving Bloomsbury. Also in the alleyway were two men and a woman — at least it was believed that the third person in question was a woman, she was *that* wretched; although the men that flanked her were no better representatives of their gender. All three of these woe begotten creatures were gathered around a trashcan in which they built a bonfire with whatever was available; although whatever it was that they decided to burn couldn't overpower the stench of vomit and urine — which all three, as Mary Willow ascertained, had an equal hand in creating.

"Calvin lives here?" the grimacing Mary Willow wondered aloud, as though she was wholly unable to imagine how someone alleged to be of such meagreness could in any way be connected to the likes of Claire Damien.

"He rents the space above the tobacco shop and uses it as a sort of headquarters, you might say," said Claire. "He lives on the other side of Camden — a fact, of which he doesn't know I'm aware. I make it my business to learn things about my clients that they themselves aren't likely to disclose." She then winked at her lover when through touting her proficiency. Mary Willow sighed and was alleviated of at least a portion of her anxiety, as she was now of the notion that Calvin was someone over whom Claire possessed a decided edge; after all, Claire knew things about Calvin (including what brought him to arousal) that Calvin surely didn't know about Claire, and knowing one's opponent was half the battle, assuming that Calvin was considered an adversarial acquaintance. Either way, Claire wasn't one to show her cards.

Claire located the correct back door that led to the flat above the tobacco shop. She twisted the handle, and with her shoulder she gave the door a good nudge as in order to gain entry. With Mary Willow still holding on to her hand, they climbed the stairs that led directly to a second storey door. There, nothing other than the twist of a hand would be required. The door was left unlocked, as Claire was expected. The door opened up to a sea of glass, chrome, and white leather. When Mary Willow took in the scene, she found it cold to the extent of jarring and it gave her a peculiar sense of unrest; she had never been anywhere (not that she was able to readily recall) that was in such need of warmth or in need of properties capable of absorbing the glare that the wide open space seemed to create all on its own. She heard a voice imploring Claire to come in and to make herself at home, which, incidentally, Claire was already beginning to do, and would have regardless, as she wasn't one to wait for permission to do anything, never mind make herself comfortable.

Next, a plump man accessorized in such a way that he would have been well in accordance with the marketplace below (Jesus freaks included), made an appearance. Mary Willow never actually *saw* Calvin enter the room, but, nevertheless, there he was standing in full form amid the perceptible confusion of glass, chrome, and white leather; Calvin was wearing a dashiki, and Mary Willow likened him to a knickknack or some other type of adornment one thoughtlessly purchased as a housewarming gift before ever bothering to find out the decor. Her eyes then went straight for Calvin's bleached hair, which was striking against his brown skin — then they moved on to his round, moonlike face, which she determined was much too boyish for the multitude of piercings that adorned it.

Her initial impression was that Calvin was a hardcore wannabe, who was much better suited for business attire — or, better yet, crewneck sweaters; and although his face was remarkably round and boyish, and he possessed an adolescent pudginess that made him appear unappealingly doughy, he also exuded a strange sense of menace, and one which led Mary Willow to the notion that Calvin was no one on whom she would turn her back.

Next, what struck her as being even more remarkable than Calvin's appearance was that for someone so plump — so utterly lacking of an athletic form, he was exceptionally light on his feet and moved about with an agility that was nothing less than astounding. He sashayed across the room as though he were ballroom dancing with an imaginary partner. This astonishing grace continued until he reached an all glass and chrome bar, where he stopped to mix drinks, which he did like an artist or magician steeped in the deceptive skill known as *sleight-of-hand*. Afterward he pirouetted with the grace of a ballerina and presented Claire and Mary Willow each with the result of his effort. "My latest concoction," he declared, before grandly stating: "Jesus may have turned water into wine, but *I* can turn vodka into pure heaven!" He followed his grand but droll statement with a laugh that, not only was it *not* infectious, but Mary Willow found it irksome. She winced, whereas Claire had no reaction at all — not even a polite chuckle did she offer to her host.

Mary Willow found Calvin's concoction favourable but far from heavenly. The same could not be said for his overabundance of confidence, which was nearly as irksome as his laugh. Still, she was polite as always and she acted gracious when she and Calvin were properly introduced. Claire, meanwhile, maintained that Calvin outdid himself, giving this latest concoction a slight nod over the last, which at the time she had dubbed "unsurpassable". Along with understanding Calvin's weaknesses, Claire also knew just how to butter him up. Though if truth be told, she tolerated Calvin's concoctions, for she preferred straight vodka poured over ice — the slightest divergence was viewed as a desecration of a perfectly good spirit. Claire was one who preferred things in their true essence: Coffee was taken black, liquor was drank straight, and never, Heaven forbid, should a wine fizz or sparkle! Once, though mostly in jest, she described Mary Willow's French Mug as a "bastardization of a perfectly good substance" but not loud enough for Brian to have overheard her. By the third sip, though, she moved off her rigid stance and admitted that the French Mug was "a worthy concoction".

After a few sips of her drink, Claire moseyed on over to a seating group that was surrounding a coffee table, and on which upon her arrival she had lain her briefcase. She was anxious to move beyond vodka and all that could be achieved with it, be it Heaven or some other blissful environ, and get down to the matter of business.

Mary Willow, however, wasn't nearly so anxious, for she was quite wary of what was hidden away inside the briefcase. She would have preferred to have finished her drink, and then another, and perhaps a third, until she no longer cared what was inside the briefcase; but everyone seemed to be playing by Claire's rules, which was no surprise. When the moment of truth arrived, Mary Willow tried, though with little success, not to gape at the kilos of white powder that earlier on were transported across town, weaved on foot through a crowded marketplace, and now had at last been unveiled. Calvin's mouth slowly creased into a grin that nearly stretched the entire width of his moon shaped face, and his eyes became all aflutter. It appeared to Mary Willow that nothing other than what Claire had unveiled could have pleased him more.

"Ahh, Ms. Damien, you made ol' Calvin, here, a happy man. A happy man, indeed," he crooned. "And the locals will surely be happy little plebeians." The term *plebeians* as it was used made Mary Willow cringe with disgust. "And, as for ol' Calvin himself? He'll appear nothing less than heroic. In fact, as it now stands, all the little girlies *already* call me daddy. It kinda gets me right here." Calvin pointed to his heart, and in doing so, his finger made a deep indentation into his pudgy, adolescently doughy chest. There was further cringing from Mary Willow, which Calvin either chose to ignore, or was too much in the thrall of the white powder to have taken notice. Then Calvin produced a razorblade, straws, and hand mirror, and then informed his guests that it was time to do a bit of sampling before completing the matter of business. "Calvin never backs away from the opportunity to party with beautiful women," he grandly declared. "No siree, my mama didn't raise any fools."

Claire sounded genuinely regretful when informing their host that she and Mary Willow needed to be getting along — that before the night was through they had other business to conduct and that it would require a clear head.

"A woman's work is never done," she said with a sigh.

Despite the politeness of her decline, and the authenticity of her charade, Calvin produced a fairly substantial firearm, which he proceeded to slam down on the glass table before bellowing, "Forgive me, for perhaps I haven't made myself clear; but when Calvin says it's time to party, that means it's time to party!"

"Oh, Calvin, don't be such an old bore," Claire uttered, rather glibly. "And really, must you always refer to yourself in the third person; after awhile it becomes awfully tiresome." She sank into the white leather sofa and with a sigh she added, "*Men* are so tiresome."

Claire's casual and relaxed attitude further incited Calvin's ire. He stood and began waving about his pistol.

"You got no right to show up here with this sweet, little thing, and then tell ol' Calvin that it isn't time to party!" he went on to bellow. "Ms. Damien, just what kinda game are you trying to play!"

"Careful, Calvin," warned Claire, "she's not that kind of girl."

"*I'll* decide what kind of girl she is," was his sharp return.

"By all means, Calvin; you're the *big* man with the *big* gun," Claire conceded, though she was clearly mocking his authority, or whatever authority he believed to have possessed. "So clearly *you* get to decide."

She went reaching for her drink, which was resting on the glass table, then sank back into the soft white leather and crossed her legs. She viewed Calvin as though she were mildly curious as to how far he intended to take his idiotic display of manliness. Her glibness, however, served to frustrate her host.

"That's right, Claire; I got the gun!" he ranted. "So *I* decide!"

"Yes, Calvin, that's already been established, and quite painstakingly, I might add." Claire followed her remark by letting out the sort of sigh that indicates the loss of patients. She gave her host a casual shrug of the shoulders and wave of the hand, and then she put her still nearly full glass to her lips. Calvin held a lecherous eye on Mary Willow, but it was Claire to whom he directed his words.

"A young girl needs a proper upbringing; isn't that right? They need a good man to show them how things ought to be done."

From her knees, and while held at gunpoint and about to perform for a man whom she found utterly repulsive, Mary Willow looked to Claire, her poised and authoritative lover — her eyes were pleading for her to somehow thwart this foulest of transgressions.

"Mary Willow!" Claire was stern and direct when she spoke. "Remember what we talked about. Everything will be fine. You only need to trust me. Do you understand?"

At that very moment Mary Willow hated Claire Damien — and moreover she hated that she allowed herself to be dragged into Claire's diseased world, and that it was she herself who was now paying the price, while Claire, with one long, shapely leg draped over the other, sank into the plush, white leather of Calvin's sofa and casually sipped her drink. She appeared as though whatever was about to take place was purely for her benefit — her entertainment — like a queen in her court with nothing to do but await the minstrels and jesters to come and amuse her. What was worse, Mary Willow had no one to blame but herself; for it was she, on the morning after that wonderful night of splendour, which saw Claire taken to the *promise land* four times, who like a child clamoured to accompany her lover. It was she, who blindly surrendered and pledged servitude. Mary Willow never heard Calvin's words of encouragement, which to be kind, weren't at all clever, *and* in fact were most typical of what a man might say to a woman when he wants her to do something that she finds grossly objectionable. Still, Mary Willow accepted Calvin into her mouth, though when doing so, she was at once transported. One by one, in what amounted to a flash, the days of her life began flittering away, until at last she found herself hovering above a familiar meadow. Below, and clinging to one another, for they were trying so dearly to smother one another's pain, were fifteen-year-old Mary Willow and ten-year-old Jimmy Philips. Like Colin and Douglas Broxton, they aspired to be as one — of one mind and of one soul, and to a degree where, there would no longer exist any distinction between the girl who was raped and the tormented boy who was locked away in the cellar and was forced to watch. She felt Calvin begin to pulsate in her mouth, and still she had no clear sense of who she was — her identity had blurred. How many tormented nights were spent in the darkness of a closet? How many times had a body been violated, and in how many ways? She had the notion to cease what she was doing — this objectionable act that she was forced to perform, and subsequently put an end to Calvin's pulsating and moans. She would do this with the fleeting hope that Calvin would discharge his firearm, and at last silence all her demons and the ordeal that had thus far been her life. Claire uncrossed her legs and rose up from the plush, white leather sofa. Leaving her drink behind, she advanced on Calvin. When at his side, she placed a long, graceful arm across his broad, doughy shoulders in a manner that could only be described as friendly and perhaps bordering on affectionate.

"She's very good, isn't she?" she remarked. "That's why I keep her around, you know. No one has ever served me nearly as well as she has. Perhaps, Calvin, you're the sort of man who would appreciate a little demonstration? I hear that sort of thing drives men near the brink of madness, to watch a beautiful woman have her vagina serviced by the capable tongue of another female."

"God bless you, Claire Damien, you're a woman after my own heart," Calvin managed to mutter.

"Calvin, you're getting a bit goggle-eyed," said Claire. She tickled the back of his neck as to make light of his arousal. "Oh, and by the way, Calvin … say goodnight … and may God have little or no mercy on your miserable fucking soul."

Mary Willow felt Calvin shrink in her mouth and then disappear altogether. She straightened up on her haunches and let out a deafening shriek before alertly putting her hands to her mouth. She became horrified when viewing Calvin's body, which for a few seconds convulsed before it lay motionless on the floor, as Claire Damien knew just where to insert her knife in order to render a man lifeless with one swift blow. Mary Willow seemed to lapse into a sort of hazy twilight when regarding Claire; she couldn't imagine where on her long, sinuous form, which was clad in a dress that complimented it beautifully, such a weapon was concealed — never mind how deftly she was able to employ it! After severing Calvin's jugular, which spouted like a geyser, for good measure, so that Calvin couldn't locate anything to apply pressure to what ended up the fatal wound, Claire took the point of her knife and pierced his eyes. Three precise wounds in a matter of a second! Mary Willow's eyes returned to Calvin, who right away reminded her of Bruno several weeks ago when he tried to warn her, or rather, *school* her on the legend of Claire Damien. Her hazy twilight began to fade and she shrieked, "My God, Claire, he's dead! You've killed him!"

"Mary Willow, get a hold of yourself!" Claire ordered. "Of course I killed him. Did you really think I would allow this reprehensible creature to deposit his revolting semen into your mouth? Did you think I would stand for that?"

"Revolting semen? I've been either raped or tortured my whole life!" Mary Willow cried out. "This was hardly a reason to kill a man! And what if he tried to fuck me, Claire? Really; what if he had been fucking me? Given your views on penetration, what if he nearly deposited his "revolting semen" into my vagina? What then? Or was it only my *sweet little mouth,* as you like to refer to it that concerned you?" The notion that Calvin's death wasn't necessarily an unscripted calamity was beginning to formulate in her head.

"Colin and Douglas? The twins? They raped you?" Claire wondered aloud.

"Oh, what does it matter, Claire," Mary Willow went on. From her knees she waved her armed about in dismay. "What can it possibly matter at this point; you're a murdering drug dealer, for God's sake!"

Silence was what followed Mary Willow's coarse and sobering words. (The words were coarse where Claire was concerned; sobering for Mary Willow.) Mary Willow was looking up at Claire as if hopeful that an alternative explanation for the valuable and highly sought after white powder, along with a dead man, would be offered. Claire frowned. She never thought of herself as a murderer. She had killed before (twice), but only when it was required of her — or, in other words, when it was for the betterment of business as it was foreseen. Nor did she think of herself as a drug dealer; *Calvin* was a drug dealer — a peddler; he and other sorts like him dealt with the "plebeians", whereas Claire was in charge of regional distribution, a position within a drug empire that, in her estimation, although only one step higher up on the food chain than Calvin, it was a step that was decidedly higher — infinitely higher; she saw a vast gap between herself and the likes of men like Calvin. As for her St. George's Hill clientele; by no means were they traffickers — they were buyers, whose purpose was to use and to entertain other well-to-do users. They were the sort, who wouldn't run the risk of getting caught within a kilometre of men like Calvin, but a sophisticated, beautiful businesswoman was perfectly acceptable, so they dealt with Claire directly, and she always made sure that they were presented with the very best and the cleanest narcotics available.

Claire reached down for Mary Willow, who was still kneeling. She took her by the hand and guided her over to the plush, white leather sofa. "I didn't kill Calvin because of what he was forcing you to do," she confessed. "Although it would have been more than reason enough for me; I'm not particularly fond of the idea of sharing you, especially with of all things, a hideously ill-mannered man. But the fact of the matter is, it wasn't even my idea to kill Calvin; the order to do so came to me many weeks ago and from a bit higher up in the food chain."

Mary Willow scooted away from Claire as though she could no longer bear to be near her. "My God, Claire, weeks ago!" she cried. The notion that Calvin had an irresistible interest and attraction for petite, vulnerable Caucasian women was what raced through her mind. "The night we met at Bruno's Café — the threats — the ordering off of my clothes at your flat — it was all a damn test, wasn't it! You were recruiting me, weren't you! You were recruiting me for this very night! Tell me, Claire, were you watching me when I entered Bruno's; and from behind the wheel of your shiny, white sports car did you say to yourself, 'Now there goes a pathetic little waif; I think I can make good use of *her*.' Well did you?"

"I don't deny it," said Claire. "You were a vulnerable young girl, who wandered into the wrong bar in the wrong part of town. And knowing Calvin as I do ... or *did*, you were just what I needed. But that as then, and it all seems an eternity ago. Since, I've come to care for you a great deal, and I've grown more fond of you than I ever have of anyone. If you never allow yourself to become convinced of anything else, at least believe *that*."

Mary Willow got to her feet and began backing her way toward the door; occasionally she stumbled as she went.

"Mary Willow!" Claire called to her.

"I must get some air," she implored. "Please, Claire, don't try to stop me." By the time she reached the door tears were trailing down her cheeks and she was quivering as though she might convulse — her words were also tremulous and were driven by the depth of her emotions. "Incidentally, Claire, you weren't the only sinner in the room tonight — not by a long shot." Claire's eyes travelled to the pool of blood in which Calvin lay perished. "Not him," said Mary Willow. "He's nothing compared to you and me; we take the cake. Oh, indeed, Claire, I can match you sin for sin; and on that front I suppose we deserve one another. But I want to become someone who deserves more. Dear God, how I *need* to become someone who deserves more!"

Mary Willow went rumbling down the stairs and burst through the door. The door swung open with such force that it startled the woe begotten trio that was still huddled around the bonfire, which was still being fed with whatever material the alleyway provided. Unlike earlier, Mary Willow was oblivious to the stench of vomit and urine, which was every bit as generous as before, and thanks to the trio (the woman included) the alleyway was introduced to fresher samples of urine.

"Ay there, Missy, come join us, won'tcha," the woman offered in the most guttural English Mary Willow ever heard. "We're goin' first class tonight. That's why we're back here in the alley, ya know; we don't want no one to see us. Well, go on, Freddy, show her, already!"

The man whom the woman called Freddy, was hogging the bottle of Fireball Cinnamon Whiskey — a spirit whom the judging Claire Damien would have disapproved of and dubbed *cheap and disgusting*. (But even vagrants are entitled to their booze and an occasional bonfire.)

"Have at least *one* swig," the woman urged. "If you don't mind me sayin' so, you surely look like you can use one."

Jack, the third party that made up the trio, looked cross, that Alice (who qualified as the woman among them) was offering the coveted spirit without first gaining his approval.

"Thanks, but no thank you," said Mary Willow. It wasn't Jack's crossness that caused her to decline; nor the cheapness of the spirit (she wouldn't have known Fireball Cinnamon Whiskey from Chevis Regal; Claire hadn't taken the time to school her on the virtues of whiskey); it was her fear that Claire would any second appear, and should she have remained in the alleyway, Claire would assume that she was waiting for her, or that she was afraid to venture off alone, and if only to herself, Mary Willow needed to prove otherwise. She was gracious when having begged off of the trio's company, then went stumbling through the alleyway.

"Careful, Missy, the world can be cruel, you know," Alice warned.

"Let her go," said Jack. "Besides, there's still the other one to come down."

"It's most likely the other one that's got that poor girl all upset," said Alice. "It don't take no genius to figure that one out."

"Who cares," said Jack. "If I won the lottery, I'd give half of it away just to have a good hour at the other one's cunt."

"Fucking ay," concurred Freddy, who was still hogging the bottle.

When Mary Willow first took to the marketplace, her eyes were dissecting the crowd as she went in search of Jesus. She had no idea what she hoped to gain, or what revelations might transpire from gazing at a tattoo. Did she truly expect Christ himself to manifest from the ink that a tattoo artist, albeit an enormously talented one, needled onto the back of a Camden Lock radical? There were countless likenesses of Jesus the world throughout; why was this one so important? She hadn't taken but a few more paces, when it occurred to her that she was mainly curious of whether or not the man would recognise her and remember her as the passenger in the shiny, white Porsche for which he had shown such contempt — or, had he only noticed Claire and was never even aware that someone else was in the car?

She began to weave her way through the dense crowd as one would when filled with the urgency of a fixed purpose. It was no longer Jesus or the anarchy worshipping radicals of the marketplace that she craved, or in which she wanted to lose herself; it was Elijah's company that she was now craving — it was his voice and flute that she so desperately longed to hear, but he was miles away and it was late. At last, there were no more bodies through which to weave — no more shoulders to brush up against, as she had cleared the marketplace entirely and was going off alone to dissolve into the darkness of night. Had Claire merely hurt her by allowing another lover between them, Mary Willow would have returned. Again and again she would have returned and from her knees begged to be loved, not as she wished to be, but by any means Claire saw fit. *I'm yours entirely, Claire; do with me as you wish.* However, that their relationship sprang entirely *not* merely from a deception, but from one so egregiously afoul, was a notion that she was unable to wrap her mind around, less reconcile. She was also waking up to the notion that, Claire Damien in her life was made possible by her *own* transgressions — her own inability, *or* unwillingness to disclose. But this was a fact to which she was just beginning to awaken. For months she had been living in the moment. She would soon awaken fully.

For sure, the misery of her childhood and of the many years that followed could be laid at the feet of others. But the life that she consciously decided to lead, beginning from the last time that she knelt down before a particular grave in Bibury, was the tortuous cause of her unravelling.

CHAPTER VI

THE DESSERT TRAY

"You're awake, I see," said Sister Ignatius. She wasn't nearly as surprised as she had sounded that Finn had awakened, but she was, nonetheless, glad for it. Despite their contentious exchanges earlier, with all that was happening back at the camp, along with the abhorrent state of the shack which they currently inhabited, she became enlightened to the fact that any company was better than no company.

"If you can call sitting here like a groggy lump of redundant protoplasm being awake, then I guess I'm awake. How long was I out, anyway?" wondered Finn. He wasn't certain whether he had dozed or had fallen into a deep sleep.

"Not for very long," replied Sister Ignatius. "I needed to give you a mild sedative for the pain, and so that you wouldn't fidget so much while I dressed your wound. You were becoming quite agitated, you might remember."

"Yes I *do* remember, and no I *don't* need any reminding. But if my memory, which didn't take the bullet, serves me correct, you were more than holding your own." Sister Ignatius frowned, for Finn was correct, she had easily matched, and in some instances surpassed his passion and level of agitation when their discussion blossomed into argument. "So how bad is it?" wondered Finn. (He was referring to his gunshot wound, not the state of affairs back at the camp.)

"Just try to relax and remain still," the sister urged him.

"That wasn't exactly the answer that I was hoping for," said Finn. "Although well meaning, when someone tells you to relax, they may truly *believe* that they're being cavalier and shouldering all the burden of worry, but in fact, those words tend to have the opposite effect. *Relax* or *don't worry* is the same as saying, 'I'm sorry, you poor bastard, but there's more to worry about than you realise'."

"You think too much, Mr. Finn. Perhaps it would be better if you tried prayer," the sister told him.

"Prayer?" said Finn. He had a vision of his mother as she appeared thirty years ago; she was kneeling in the pew, and evident in her countenance and comportment was her fear of God, love of Christ, and reverence of Father McKinley. All three of these manifestations united to form a singular manifestation, which served to overwhelm the young boy kneeling beside her. However, before that young boy had reached an age when one was capable of understanding why one would give themselves entirely to God, Christ, and a priest, *he*, like the Clockmaker before him, was showing signs of becoming indifferent toward religion. "Prayer?" Finn repeated. "You might as well inform me that I have but an hour left to live!" Whether Finn himself believed in them, his meagre views on the power of prayer and the reasons why one should bother praying, caused Sister Ignatius to frown and then momentarily look away. When she turned back toward her patient, she put a cup of water to his mouth, then took a towel and patted down his face. "I assure you that the water is good and very well appreciated, but you didn't happen to grab the Chevis Regal, did you?" Finn asked his caregiver. "It was in Mr. Somersby's backpack. He's a man, who among all things believes in being prepared — a real boy scout, you know."

"Under the circumstances, as you perhaps may remember, Mr. Finn, whatever was in Mr. Somersby's backpack wasn't the highest of priorities."

Sister Ignatius's irony prompted Finn to retort: "Speak for yourself, Sister; it's in times like these that the palate needs a little reminding that the art of being a human being is to *live* and not to merely survive."

"Very well put, Mr. Finn." Sister Ignatius was genuine when making her admission. "But I believe that I'm speaking for the both of us when I say, I grabbed only what was necessary, and even with *that*, we were fortunate to have escaped with our lives." Finn let out a long, exaggerated sigh — partly because he had a bullet lodged deep within him, but mostly because he was reminded of how it got there and the wild frenzy that Kalma was turned into. It wasn't bad enough that it became necessary for ninety-thousand people to be herded into what fast became perhaps the world's largest refugee camp; now these people were forced to endure the same sort of abhorrent acts and tactics that landed them there in the first place. Nothing like adding insult to injury, he thought.

"Okay, so we have no booze, nothing with which to toast, for lack of a better term, 'the occasion'." Finn's words came out sounding much more sulky than how he was truly feeling on the subject of having no Chevis Regal. The irony which he had strived for never did surface — not even a trace. Then, of all things, Finn asked, as though he was reaching for something that would hold Sister Ignatius's attention (perhaps he believed that the bullet lodged in his body was no longer sufficient, or he had momentarily forgotten about it): "But please do tell, Sister, was it always your ambition to become a nun?" The question drew a timid chuckle from the sister, who assumed that Finn was merely making small talk and wasn't necessarily probing for information that he regarded as pertinent. After all, what should it matter to Finn why Sister Ignatius chose to become a nun? Since that night by the Acacia tree, which involved a discussion on the drawings of Darfuri children (two in particular); the state of affairs in Darfur as it pertained to genocide; a peek into one another's souls; and lastly the consumption of black market spirits with unfortunate results, only once had Finn masturbated to the thought of Sister Ignatius's slim, shapely ankle, among other parts that made up her collective composite of delicateness. And because of the respect Finn came away with that night for Sister Ignatius (her vomiting notwithstanding), he went out of his way to imagine Caroline at night when all alone and his eyes were too tired to bother with Dostoevsky's saintly Prince Myshkin. But just before he was about to climax, it was the soft, pretty eyes of Sister Ignatius that had invaded — it was under the watchfulness of those soft, pretty eyes that he felt most vulnerable, and in those brief instances of vulnerability he climaxed like never before.

"We've been here together in Darfur for several months now, and have known one another for nearly as long," the sister pointed out. "Why, suddenly, are you so interested in my religious ambitions? Not to suggest, mind you, that I find your interest objectionable. Quite the contrary."

"Maybe I've always been interested," said Finn. "Maybe I always wondered about it, but there never seemed to be a right time to ask."

"And now is?" the sister wondered, as though under the circumstances it seemed in every respect absurd that such a trifling curiosity was aroused. Though, she also understood that, when one asks a nun or priest about their religious ambitions (particularly when the one doing the asking is a man), what they're in effect asking is whether or not those in question truly understand all that they have given up in order to fulfil their ambitions.

"Forgive me, Sister," said Finn, "but I'm of the inclination that, if I'm going to bleed to death in front of you, I might as well know something about you — something much deeper than the fact that you're proficient at dressing wounds."

"Where you're concerned, Mr. Finn, I haven't exactly been a closed book — or, have you already forgotten our little debacle?" Sister Ignatius raised an eyebrow which caused her to appear stern. She seemed to do that often when around Finn — raise an eyebrow and appear stern. She wondered whether

Finn went out of his way to provoke her — that perhaps her ire led to his arousal— Finn was beginning to wonder it as well. "It wasn't all that long ago, you realise — our night by the Acacia tree, and all that was exchanged. But alright; you're wanting to know more about me is fair enough. Although I can assure you, Mr. Finn, nobody has *always* wanted to become a nun — *or* priest. It's not a dream or ambition, you see, but something that comes upon us — like a moment of clarity. When it passes, we're left with a greater sense of understanding."

"Greater understanding?" asked Finn. He seemed agitated, for he had leapt to the notion that, because Sister Ignatius had what she referred to *a moment of clarity*, she knew and understood things that were out of his reach — that is to say until *his* moment of clarity arrived. Though, not all that long ago Finn believed that he had experienced several moments of clarity. However, when strung together they formed a hodgepodge of ideologies that ultimately cost him his relationship with Caroline, the only woman whom he professed to have loved. Caroline was able to appreciate each moment or ideology separately and on its own merit, but they all began to run together and it made Finn unbearable to live with. It wasn't' until after Caroline had gone, that Finn realised a moment cannot be searched for (else one ends up adopting every philosophy ever known to man), it must arrive on its own.

"Do forgive me, Mr. Finn," implored Sister Ignatius. "You mustn't feel offended. I wasn't insinuating that I have a greater understanding than you do of heaven and earth, *or* of the world and the universe; even if that were true, which it is not, I would never be so bold. I merely gained a greater understanding of what I once had of *myself*, of who *I* am."

"Ah, I see," said Finn, who found the sister's explanation not only satisfactory but well stated. "And there for a moment I thought you once again had found a clever way to mock the fact that I'm an arrogant American."

"Even if that were so, that *you are* an arrogant American, I would do all that I could to not judge you as such, less mock the fact," said Sister Ignatius. "Though there are *some* who have shown the innate capability of testing my resolve."

Finn grinned the way one would when having been politely scolded by someone of authority — perhaps an elementary school teacher. "No, of course you wouldn't' *judge*," said Finn. "It wouldn't be humble or very *nun-like* to judge and especially to mock. What*ever* would the sisters back home think?"

"*Now* who's doing the mocking?" asked Sister Ignatius. She frowned, and her eyes appeared weighty and had become downcast when looking away from Finn. This caused him to feel albeit just a twinge of remorse.

"My apologies," he said. "It surely wasn't very wise on my part to mock the only caregiver in the room, especially when *I'm* the one receiving the care. And I must say, Sister, despite that it is your duty, you have shown me remarkable care and compassion, never mind that you weren't alert enough to wrestle away the Chevis Regal from Mr. Somersby's possession. But do tell me, though, Sister, and I beg that you not become offended: Have you ever explored a man, or permitted a man to explore you? I mean, you said so yourself, that nobody has *always* wanted to become a nun, and since I wouldn't give you a day over thirty-five (Sister Ignatius was thirty-eight), more than half your life, I imagine, was spent secularly, and for many of those years you were sexually viable — or one might assume."

"I'm sorry to disappoint you, Mr. Finn, but I'm afraid that I have nothing to reveal on the subject, either way. That moment of clarity of which I spoke earlier, it came to me before one should act upon such impulses." Finn had no reason to doubt the sister's claim that there had been an absence of a sex life and that her *moment* came too soon, but her tone was a bit too supercilious for his liking. Whether there was a sex life or not, Sister Ignatius would have approached the subject with utmost modesty, he knew — but instead, her words reeked of disingenuousness. *Why would she lie*? he wondered.

"That's too bad," said Finn. "Not that you became a nun, that is — especially a missionary sister; Lord knows it's worked out quite well for me for the past half hour or so. But what I mean to say is, without first knowing a man — without giving it a chance, how can you be so certain that you made the right choice?"

"Ahh, at last, the question is finally asked," Sister Ignatius hissed. "Poor Mr. Finn; you've been sitting on that bombshell for how long now? How burdensome must it be to have such a question occupy your poor little head?"

"Why take such offence?" wondered Finn. "It's perfectly natural to be curious about such a thing."

Finn was right and Sister Ignatius knew that he was. It *was* natural to wonder, and under the current circumstances and given proximity, it was even natural to probe, to challenge one another's ideas, if no other reason than to feel alive and normal in a land where war and terror has become business as usual.

"I think maybe I should try and return to camp and salvage whatever supplies and water I can find." In both her countenance and tone the sister seemed solemn.

"Please, don't run off, Sister," Finn begged her. "Not just yet. It's still too dangerous, and I wouldn't want anything to happen to you on my account. If I die here, then so be it, but you still have many lives to save."

Whether Finn was acting magnanimous or was simply afraid to be left alone, Sister Ignatius knew that he was right; returning to camp was entirely too risky and would be for some time. Dust was still being kicked up from the Janjaweed, devils on horseback, and gunshots could still be heard; though there was no longer the spray of bullets that had prompted them to flee the camp. But Finn knew that the sister had deflected from her sex life — that perhaps she hadn't truly intended upon running off and leaving him for the sake of supplies that in all likelihood were either destroyed or had been looted.

"Look, sister, I don't mean to press you," he continued. "I'm sure you made the right decision and it has made many grateful. This I know, as I've watch you work near and from afar. But you did mention that your moment of clarity came before one should *act* upon such impulses, not that you didn't *have* impulses. And whether or not you truly believe that your moment came to you too soon, it still must have come when as a young woman, not as a young girl — so surely, if only within the realm of your thoughts and your own imaginings, you must've allowed your womanhood to flourish."

Sister Ignatius blushed at the near poetic manner in which Finn had suggested that, in the past, and perhaps even now in the present she had masturbated. "I'll bet you were a typical pigtailed English girl, gawking at all the boys at school," Finn went on.

"I did no such thing. Gawking wasn't the sort of thing that was in my line." Sister Ignatius acted huffy that Finn had dared to suggest such a thing. "But I'd be willing to wager that *you*, Mr. Finn, were quite the gawker."

"And you would be quite right," Finn proudly admitted. "In fact, if they gave out medals for gawking, mine would be gold! You see, my dear Sister Ignatius, as far as I'm concerned, a woman's body with all its curvaceous and interesting parts is like a dessert tray ..."

"It isn't possible that I need to hear this," the sister alertly interjected.

"Oh, it's *quite* possible, and you *will* hear it," said Finn. "So go on and widen your eyes, flare your nostrils, and get all your hissing done and out of the way." Finn cleared his throat as he prepared his monologue "Now, before you became a missionary sister, you must've had some experience eating in fine restaurants. You ate you soup, hors d' oeuvre, or both, then a salad, during which time you may even have had a drink or glass of wine… am I right?" Sister Ignatius's eyes travelled to the floor, which Finn took for an admission. "Finally, here comes the main course, after which, you swore that you couldn't eat another bite. But then the waiter, who perhaps had more charm than any of the men with whom you happened to had been dining, wondered whether or not you've left room for dessert. You had no intention of ordering any dessert, because you were quite full, which you no doubt made known to the waiter by making all the customary sounds and movements, like sighing and reaching for your belly. And being as you are, a petite woman — and it's always the petite women who are fussiest about their waistlines — yet still you must see the tray with all it sinful selections. At your request, the waiter dashes off to fetch it. Then like magic, just as he returns and you've taken a moment to gaze longingly at his tray, your appetite magically returns. Now, not only do you crave *a* dessert, but you're unable to make a selection, because if truth be told, your wish would be to have a taste of everything on the tray!"

"Really, Mr. Finn, can it truly be possible that this is your perception of the twenty-first women … a dessert tray?" The glower that accompanied the sister's indignant words was a clear indication that she was no longer hiding the fact that she was judging her fellow missionary, and furthermore, was finding him a bit distasteful.

"Indeed it *can* be and in fact *is* my perception," Finn went on. "I see a young woman's perky breasts as two perfect mounds of tartufo in a light cinnamon glaze surrounded with drizzles of raspberry sauce! Have you ever had tartufo, Sister? There's this place in Philadelphia I know called Varalli's; they have the best in the city! Ahh, and a young woman's heart shaped bottom … most definitely a bowl of ambrosia! Her vagina …"

"Mr. Finn, please!" implored Sister Ignatius.

"Oh, enough with this Mr. Finn business," Finn protested. "Call me Charles — or, if you prefer, Charlie."

"Very well, then," said Sister Ignatius, who was nearing the point of exasperation. "Charlie!"

"Now, where was I?" asked Finn. "Oh, yes, her vagina. Her vagina would have to be the crème Brule. Wouldn't you agree, Sister, that a woman's vagina *must* be the crème Brule?"

"I must redress your wound, Mr. Finn," said Sister Ignatius. She seemed more disturbed by Finn's antics than perhaps she should have been, but more to the point, she became grim in both her demeanour and countenance. "Blood is beginning to seep through the bandage."

"I truly meant no disrespect, sister," said Finn. "I was just having fun trying *not* to think about the bullet that's lodged inside me."

"I should have known, Charlie," said Sister Ignatius. "I'm sorry."

"Sister?" said Finn. Concern registered on his face, for he noticed that Sister Ignatius's tone had become sombre and she appeared as if that any second she might burst into uncontrollable sobs.

"You were away from the camp that afternoon, Charlie; perhaps you were in Nyala." The sister was unable to raise her voice much above a whisper. "They brought her to me, this poor woman. The pain, the terror, the violation — no matter how many times you see it — a thousand times, a million times — it cannot be gotten use to, and yet there's not a second to act shocked or surprised by the most abhorrent kinds of human depravity, because care and comfort needs to be administered swiftly; there's no time to ask God why certain acts are permitted to go on. This woman — it wasn't enough that she was raped repeatedly and was severely beaten; her vagina had been mutilated — butchered. Dear God, Charlie! Oh, dear God! There was nothing that could be done to save her. Morphine was administered, and I held her hand until she finished bleeding out. It didn't take long. So much for crème Brule."

Both Finn and the sister chose not to utter a word all throughout the redressing of Finn's wound. Each had determined that a few reflective moments spent in silence would be wise. During this time, Finn looked away; not that he was all that squeamish regarding blood, even his own, but he found surveying the meagre accommodations of the abandoned shack in which they had hidden themselves away more pleasing than his own mangled flesh. Without meaning to, Sister Ignatius let out soft grunt. This, Finn chose to believe was from the effort it took to rebandage the wound, not from the disconcertion the sister was no doubt feeling when appraising the state his health.

After checking his vital signs and the clarity in his eyes, the sister gave Finn another mild sedative. "It's best that you rest and try and remain calm." She didn't bother to mention to him that while asleep he would bleed less. She put the cup of water to his mouth, again she patted down his face with a towel, then urged him to be still. Afterward an idyllic expression formed on Finn's face, which Sister Ignatius mistook for delirium, though he had yet to become feverish or hypoxic.

"Do you believe in destiny, Sister?" he wondered. "Do you believe that it's by some fantastic quirk of fate, that a boy from Philadelphia and a girl from England, one day should end up in an abandoned shack in Darfur, Sudan, otherwise hell on earth? I once read about things like this — that two people an ocean apart, each did something at the same time that years later caused their paths to cross. I wonder what *we* did?"

"Surely, Mr. Charles Finn, you wouldn't happen to be suggesting that our intertwined destinies should result in *me* becoming one of those tempting items on you dessert tray, would you?" Whatever idyll that had formed on Finn's face was replaced by a satisfied smirk, which revealed the amusement that was brought about by Sister Ignatius's suspicion. Her suspicion and guardedness always seemed to bring Finn pleasure; it was the classic battle of class clown versus the scolding teacher, and anytime Finn managed a rise out of Sister Ignatius it was considered a victory — sometimes resounding, at other times marginal.

"You can't blame a guy for trying, can you, Sister?" Finn asked in return.

"I suppose not," said Sister Ignatius. "But while we're on the subject of destinies seemingly shrinking oceans down to the size of brooks, I once heard that a butterfly can flap its wings in India, thus setting off a chain of events, with each event becoming more impressive than the last — each one growing in size and strength, until half way around the world the result is something wondrous — *or*, horrific. We could allow ourselves to become engrossed for hours and perhaps even days imagining the many ways the world could change and how the course of lives could become altered because of those changes, and all as a result of a single flap of a wing."

Finn began to wonder whether he *had* hours never mind days in which to ponder the cause and effect of seemingly innocent actions that days, months, or even years down the road could grow into something else entirely.

Sister Ignatius suddenly appeared despondent when adding, "God only knows what sort of creature flapped its wings that ultimately set off the Khartoum government, which brought forth the Janjaweed and all this senseless slaughter."

"Whatever sort of creature it was, may it be damned to hell, or let us hope that it will soon become extinct," said Finn. "The world couldn't bear for it to stir, never mind go flapping its wings again. The Janjaweed are devils! Butchers! They are the souls of every evil man that has ever been afforded time on this planet manifested into one godless tribe!" Finn's sudden rage caused him cough and appear as though he might convulse. Pain was shooting everywhere and it felt like he was on fire. With some effort, he managed to hold himself still and temper his breathing, and when he was at last fully settled, he added more calmly, "Why do you now look away from me, Sister? With all that you've seen, could it be that my suffering upsets you so? *Or*, could it be that you don't agree with my assessment of the Janjaweed? So which is it?"

"Is this your idea of resting and remaining calm, Charlie?" the sister asked.

"There you go, Sister, always deflecting whenever the going gets tough — whenever someone strokes your fur the wrong way." This wasn't the class clown Finn trying to provoke the scolding teacher who was talking; this was a man whose intention was to challenge Sister Ignatius.

"Like or not, Charlie," the sister returned, "the Janjaweed are of the very same god as the sedentary farmers and villagers that they have slaughtered — the very same god as "civilized westerners" like you and me, in fact! (It was clear to Finn, that Sister Ignatius had mocked him when stressing the words *civilized westerners*.) I can't explain *why* there is evil in the world — *why* the world is so corruptible! I can't pretend to know why *this* land can produce fruit but *that* land cannot, and why after centuries and centuries of *so-called* civilization, we haven't come up with a system to accommodate this well known fact! Yes, the *actions* of the Janjaweed are godless, but *they* themselves are not, and one day they *will* be judged …"

"But not by men?" Finn was quick to interject. "Your assertion is that their day of reckoning shouldn't come while as men, but later on by a much higher order? How very unfortunate for Hadil, his family, and the rest of the sedentary farmers and villagers."

"Only God can know absolute truth, Charlie!" the sister cried. "Only He can see the world as it truly is!"

"Thank you, Sister, for that wonderful example of how to rest and to remain calm," said Finn. "I'm sure I'll do much better now.

Sister Ignatius's face reddened before she turned away and sheepishly uttered, "Oh, Charlie."

"Please, Sister, if you would allow me to set aside theology and remain on point for just another moment," begged Finn. "I think we can agree that it takes quite an effort to cultivate land — to devise and implement, no matter how crude it may be, systems of irrigation. For sure, it involves months of planning followed by a lifetime of effort and maintenance — which is perhaps more planning, effort and maintenance than some, like for instance the Janjaweed, who would much rather scorch the earth and poison wells, are willing to undertake. Also, it's much easier to take by force from others, who have displayed what I call 'that good old can-do American spirit', all that they have managed to develop." Finn was nothing less than haughty in his last remark, and acerbic when adding, "So explain to me once more why such violent perpetrators shouldn't be punished by *men*?"

Finn's caregiver frowned then looked away, which was becoming a familiar theme whenever his thoughts or opinions (particularly if they were sexually or religiously motivated) disappointed her. If he challenged her socially or politically, she was perfectly willing to wage a dispute. In this instance, although the subject was religiously and politically transcendent, and therefore likely to inspire either the familiar frown or wage a dispute, Finn felt prompted to further add, "Forgive me, Sister; sometimes I simply cannot resist flexing my American arrogance." He sighed and his shoulders slumped, which was his way of indicating that he was finished on the subject of whether God or man, religion or politics should punish the Khartoum government and the Janjaweed. The self-deprecating remark, for which Finn painted himself as an arrogant American, caused him to laugh hardily, his arms flailing about. Sister Ignatius found the delayed reaction to a remark that wasn't all that humorous, curious. She was quick to remind her patient of his wound, that it would begin seeping though the new bandage should he refuse to keep still. (For the moment the bandage was unstained; perhaps the bleeding had slowed or was beginning to clot.)

"If I have to bleed to death in an abandoned shack in the middle of the Sudan, at least let me do so with a smile on my face," implored Finn. "That way when you're finally able to return to camp, you can tell all the others, or whoever is left, that good ol' Charlie Finn laughed himself to death — and you watched him do it! It'll be one hell of a story to tell amid all this atrocity. On second thoughts, be sure and tell Mr. Somersby first and let him be the one to retell it. You know what an engaging storyteller he can be; he'll have them choking on their aseede, gurassa, and makhbaza, not to mention that gasoline they call beer!"

"Oh, Charlie," Sister Ignatius said, with her familiar frown — her eyes downcast. She got up and walked over to a window — a pane-less opening it was, though still there remained a four panelled frame with tiny shards sticking out from the grooves. The broken window put her in mind of the dark, shambled alleyway that led to the second story flat above a tobacco shop that belonged to the ill-fated Calvin. Thousands of miles away and thirteen years later her nostrils filled with the stench of vomit and urine. It was a night that she tried hard to forget, but learned to reconcile and eventually embrace — even the revulsion of Calvin filling her mouth. She could still see the faces of Freddy, Jack, and Alice huddled together around the bonfire, though she regretted not lingering long enough to have learnt their names. After all, it was Calvin, Claire, and she who were the true miscreants of the night; the three in the alleyway were merely part of a sector known as the harmless woe-begotten.

Sister Ignatius used her foot to sweep aside the broken glass on the floor, then searched the floor for the rocks and other objects she first assumed might have been used for the vandalism, before arriving at the likely conclusion that a spray of bullets would better explain the missing glass. *Someone*, she concluded, must have inhabited this dwelling and was driven away — or worse! It wasn't the home of a villager — the village was on the other side on the camp — the shack was on the way to Jebel Marra, the mountainous region. The shack might be sitting on what was once farmland, but given the current state of its environs, to suppose that would only be a guess. Finn was beginning to settle down, his shoulders were further slumping. Sister Ignatius had the sense that he was close to succumbing to the sedative that she had administered upon redressing his wound.

"Sister," he called weakly. "If you knew for sure that this was going to be it … I mean, if you knew this day would be your last … *our* last … would you want to leave the world a nun or a woman?"

"Oh, Charlie," why must you ask me such things?" (Again, the familiar frown and downcast eyes that usually accompanied her feeling threatened whenever asked to reveal information that she in no way was prepared to reveal.)

"I not trying to challenge you, Sister, believe me. And I'm surely not just trying to make talk — I'm much too tired for just *talk*. More than anything, I really wish to know." There was sincerity and true vulnerability, the sister observed, in Finn's entreaty. She hadn't seen it until then and wondered where this side of his character had been hiding for the past several months. The sister was never oblivious to the fact that Finn was handsome and possessed a wicked sort of charm, but at this moment she found him truly appealing.

"If it was to be, that I must leave the world today, I would plan to do so just as I am — a religious missionary who serves God, and this noble cause." There was more superiority and dignity in her tone than had been intended and it provoked Finn, despite the sedative, into becoming surly and agitated.

"You would *plan*?" he asked, clearly accusing the sister of being a bit too haughty in her proclamation. "You mean to suggest that, when the hour of reckoning has arrived, you'll be reading from the playbook of nobility? Ahh, a real trooper, I see; true blue until the bitter end, we are. Only look around, Sister; in case you hadn't noticed this isn't a convent! And if you die today, it surely won't be from natural causes! When the wolves are at our door, you won't look into my eyes and want me to love you as you once were … a mere woman? Or hold you like a man who's desperately in love? You can honestly say that you wouldn't want to leave this world a woman having perfectly touched another human soul— having wrapped yourself around it so entirely, that if ever parted the world thereafter would be unbearably desolate and there would be nothing left to desire *but* death? I should say, dear sister, as much as anything, *that* would surely qualify as a defining moment — *or,* as you're fond of saying, 'a *moment of clarity*'!"

"Perhaps you're right, Charlie," said Sister Ignatius. There was no frown or any looking away with downcast eyes; this time the sister had held her gaze on Finn all throughout his tirade. "Perhaps I was being a bit too hasty when I answered. How can one determine what their perception of the world and of one's own self would be at such a time? No matter how steadfast one claims to be in their faith and convictions, there are things that cannot be known unless experienced. Maybe I *could* be a woman for you, Charlie. Maybe I'll even wish it and pray that God will see it as a deed and not a betrayal."

"Please forgive me, Sister, for my vehemence, and earlier on for my dubious dessert tray," begged Finn. "Many of us are in possession of, and unfortunately are stuck with our perversions — myself included. Many of those perversions, I admit, are more unique than others — as you have had the opportunity to discover. But only a fool would drone on as though *his* were of any real interest to another."

Sister Ignatius went and sat next to Finn. She lifted his hand and pressed it to her cheek. She held it there until he was consumed by the sedative. Then she kissed it and whispered, "If you only knew, Charlie. If you only knew."

CHAPTER VII
GOD'S LOST AND FOUND

The notes flew effortlessly from Elijah's flute, and then they took wing by way of the warm summer breeze that was carrying though the square, until gently settling in the ears of their listeners. Some had gathered in the square to listen to the Bach Sonata in E, BWV 1035 (most had only recognised the piece as *belonging* to Bach, not the specific opus); the tender, somewhat plaintive tone of the first movement, the adagio ma non tanto, seemed to so well echo the feel and mood of a warm summer evening. The final three movements, *allegro, siciliano, and allegro assai* are all in the binary form of a dance and provide a delightful sampling of Elijah's virtuosity.

While many were attentive listeners, some merely slowed their pace so that their ears could capture, albeit a small sample of the music's essence. Then there were those who rushed on by, apparently in much greater need of their destination than the sound of good music filling the air and restoring them to a sense of calm and balance. Soon after the rushers disappeared, so too did the aroma of food served by the street venders positioned around the square. The earth had turned and day became night, and through the trees, many watched as the sun dipped below the horizon. The restlessness of the square ceased, and all that remained were those sitting on benches and reclining on blankets with the desire to hear music under the stars of a London sky. The stars and moon were ushered in by Bach's Sonata in B minor, BWV 1030 — a work considered a masterpiece among the great composer's flute music. Breaking from the traditional form, it's a three movement sonata, beginning with an unusually long but beautiful *Andante*. The movement is highlighted by a spacious refrain, *or Ritornello,* which is reminiscent of the great master's Passion music, particularly "Erbarme dich", an aria from the Saint Matthew Passion. The final two movements, *Largo e dolce* and *Presto*, may not match the *Andante* in expression, but are a worthy compliment. A man lying on a blanket had whispered to his lover, that from the *Andante,* to the Fugue that made up the *Presto*, "Bach transitioned from the majesty of the spiritual to the wonder of nature." Had Elijah heard the man's whispered words, he would have agreed. Elijah enjoyed Bach's flute music in the summertime — there're many passages in each sonata that were nimble and buoyant and appealed to the sensibility of how the blind flutist had always imagined the summer season to appear. Elijah relied largely on his sensibilities; though at this stage of his life he couldn't be certain whether music helped cultivate his sensibilities or his unique sensibilities helped him gravitate toward certain works of music. He never bothered to wonder how accurate were his perceptions of nature and seasons and of other earthly forms; he was already blind, and to doubt these perceptions — his *own* sensibilities —in a sense he would be constructing his own cage into which he would retreat and surrender the spiritual freedom and the freedom of expression he so well enjoyed.

Sarah never once accompanied the flutist to the summer concerts in the squares; she already knew (most of) the music by heart and much preferred to hear all about the evening as it was described to her by the flutist himself — she would rely on his imagination and perception, which often was kinder than reality. It would have broken Sarah's heart to learn that the virtuoso was only playing for derelicts (not that she believed that derelicts were undeserving of experiencing good music) who made the squares their summer home. Then one afternoon in the pet shop, she overheard a fellow say to another, "You should've been in the square last night; a blind flutist played *'The Lark Ascending'*. Never had I heard more beautiful music!"

Sarah was very familiar with the Vaughn-William's work; for months Elijah had been working on it in-between students and whenever else he had a free moment. She was cleaning out a hamster cage when the fellow began to speak so highly of the blind flutist. She tried to control herself, but knew that it was useless. At first, her eyes welled and she began to quiver, but in seconds she was overwhelmed with more love in her heart than she ever knew could exist. She wept openly. She wept openly as though she would never stop. Patrons of the pet shop rushed to her side, including her employer, Mr. Forney, who asked whether everything was alright with Elijah. (Mr. Forney had grown fond of Elijah, particularly since the day the flutist had charmed Marybeth with his playing and as a bonus got Sarah to fall in love with him.) The fellow, who thought that the solo flute version of "The Lark Ascending" was the most beautiful music he ever heard, was examining the hamster cage, though he couldn't imagine anyone experiencing such a heartfelt cry over a dead hamster. The other fellow, the one who hadn't the privilege of being in the square for the Vaughn-Williams gem, noticed that all the hamsters were moving about quite nicely, and furthermore ascertained that Sarah was shedding tears of joy, though he elected to keep this to himself. Sarah, meanwhile, didn't bother disclosing to either fellow that her husband was the flutist in the square who had treated everyone to "The Lark Ascending". Mr. Forney walked away mumbling something to the effect that hormonal women are likely to cry over nothing. The crying incident was thirty years ago — Sarah was a twenty-one year-old bride of two years, and Elijah was going through his Vaughn-Williams\Elgar phase. Since then, Sarah always had a cup of tea ready when Elijah returned from those night-time concerts in the square. She was eager to learn what he had played, and he would treat her to a passage or two from each work, and from those passages, she was usually able to guess. They would sip tea together and he would tell her how many folks had lingered and listened; he would also describe the fragrances that he detected on some of the women, and repeat the comments made by the musically astute.

On the night of the Bach sonatas, it was mostly friends from the university and couples from Bloomsbury that had gathered in the warm, moist summer air that had settled thickly in the square; though one woman had come alone and had been the first to arrive. A starry night sky, lamplights softly illuminating the square, and a flutist and his audience — altogether it filled the air with a sense of enchantment, and those fortunate to have gathered, felt insulated from the rest of the bustling city, along with their own bustling lives. Even when Elijah was through playing and was packing up his flute, there were those who chose to linger in the peacefulness of the square and to consider how they were touched by the beautifully wrought music of a great composer, brought to them by a most capable soloist. When Elijah began walking away, he heard footsteps just beside his own that he thought sounded apprehensive and reminded him of a friend of more recent times — a friend who was given to act demure and timid, and who in the past had inspired the flutist to play Schubert. Elijah knew scents and he knew voices, as any blind man does, but he was also able to recognise footsteps; perhaps his blindness and musicianship in combination helped him to become intuitive to any and all things that occurred in intervals. He stopped, and without turning toward the footsteps, he uttered, "Mary Willow?"

"I forgot just how sharp was your sixth sense," she uttered in return.

"I know your scent," said Elijah. (He didn't wish to boast that it was more her tentative footsteps that gave her away.) "All night long I had a feeling that you were nearby, that you were somewhere in the square." He was inclined to wonder how long she had intended to walk alongside him before taking the initiative of identifying herself — perhaps she had no intention of doing so — but the flutist elected to keep his wondering to himself. "I haven't heard from you in some weeks. Don't tell me that all this delightful summer weather that we've been having has chased you indoors?"

"Hardly," said Mary Willow. "I enjoy the summertime as much as anyone." Elijah could sense a *but* coming, but elected not to interject on behalf of that notion — he permitted Mary Willow the full length of what he sensed was an agonising pause. "But I guess you could say that I've made a big change in my life — perhaps the biggest I have ever made."

"Last we left off, as I remember, you were very much in love. We were celebrating!" No sooner the words flew from the flutist's lips, he had a clear sense that Mary Willow didn't wish to be reminded of all that they discussed during their last encounter.

"I certainly *was* in love, wasn't I," was her solemn admission. Elijah needn't have been blessed with the gift of sight to know that Mary Willow had looked away with downcast eyes.

"But not so anymore, and you were too ashamed to come and tell ol' Elijah all about it," the intuitive flutist remarked.

"I suppose I was," Mary Willow guiltily admitted. "I was very ashamed to have been such a fool — to have made such an egregious error in judgment."

"Shame on the world, Mary Willow, *not* shame on you. Come what may, we're meant to walk the world over with our hearts wide open. We need to learn to embrace our pain along with our pleasure, because there're days when all you'll feel it pain, and if you don't learn to embrace it, it'll turn you into a surly old sort — you'll wind up a piece of fruit that no one has picked and that's rotted on the vine. So don't change who you are. After all, how would we know what happiness is if we didn't have sorrow to compare it to. Anyway, I'm all ears," said Elijah, "and there's still plenty left to the evening."

"Well, then," said Mary Willow, "I suppose you should call *the world's most wonderful woman* and inform her that your silly friend, the nurse, has returned and intends to wear out your poor ears. No doubt, she'll be in a great rush to thank me."

"Ah, but while we're on the subject of the family, I'd be remiss if I didn't inform you that Marybeth has missed you as well," Elijah told her. "Squawks out your name all the time, she does!" The notion that a parrot had missed her, made Mary Willow smile. "Simple pleasures," Elijah added to her smile. "Simple pleasures."

Mary Willow *had* felt ashamed to approach Elijah and divulge to him who Claire Damien truly was and how easily she had been taken in — *or*, allowed herself to be taken in. On an evening earlier in the summer, she had enveloped herself in the crowd that was hurrying through the square and on to its evening destinations, just as Elijah was beginning to play. On another evening, she lingered long enough to see the square settle to where, all whom remained were those who came prepared to listen. She made it through the first movement of *Summer* of Vivaldi's "The Four Seasons", when she became restless and began to pace about. She was aware that she had become a distraction to the university students who were clustered together, and to the couples lying on blankets, who came to hear music while gazing at the stars. She walked away, and in doing so figured that those who took notice of her dismissed her as an unsophisticated sort who lacked fondness of good music, and furthermore was in no mood to become enlightened.

A week later, she walked by Elijah's home. On all three occasions she lost her nerve, and on the days that followed she prayed in earnest. "My life was going nowhere fast," she confessed to Elijah, "and I suppose that I had reached a point in time where I was looking to give myself away to someone — *anyone*. I entered Bruno's Café wanting *something* to happen — to connect with *someone*. Claire was so beautiful and she seemed so empowered. I was dazzled by her light and also lured by her darkness. She was whom every woman wishes to see when looking in the mirror, and whenever I was with her, it felt as though my status had been elevated to a place it had never been." As she spoke, she tried to imagine what Elijah might be thinking, that she entered an East End café a pathetic wanton and became an even more pathetic hanger-on — a grovelling sycophant; but Elijah wasn't judging her — he was merely listening with an ear pointed toward compassion. "I had come to matter to someone so well admired — or perhaps feared — and it was thrilling. And yes, I knew very well the dangers and pitfalls of allowing my whole being to dissolve into another, and still I submitted … freely and entirely."

Friday night was a happening night at Ebenezer's Coffee House: Friday was the night when musicians were invited to come and test their wares, permitting they booked in advance and obtained Brian's approval. Bloomsbury's leading coffee barista wasn't a music critic, he just didn't wish for his patrons to have their heads blown off by a full-sized rock band. Soloists of any instrument were most appreciated; duets, he also favoured; anything larger, he wanted to know the instruments involved and the genre of music. (A four piece rock band, versus a four piece folk band, decibel-wise, are two entirely different animals. After all, Ebenezer's was a coffee house, not a concert hall.) By the time Mary Willow and Elijah had entered Ebenezer's, a young musician (Mary Willow placed the dark, ringlet-haired man in his early twenties) who was sitting on a stool with a microphone at his guitar, was already well lathered from having skilfully picked and strummed his way through Francisco Tarrega's *"Recuerdos de la Alhambra,"* Joaquin Rodrigo's *"Concerto de Aranjues,"* and Isaac Albeniz's *"Suite Espanola-Leyenda"* (Asturias). Interspersed with those formidable Spanish pieces (Spanish guitar was the young man's forte) was a Fugue by Bach, and an Introduction & Fandango by Luigi Boccherini. Also, the young man had opened with a fiendishly clever rendition of *"Eleanor Rigby"* that he learned from American Jazz guitarist, Stanley Jordan. Mary Willow had hardly opened the door enough to permit her own passage into Ebenezer's, never mind Elijah's, when the flutist recognised the strains of Isaac Albeniz. "Show off!" she said. They managed to find a table in the crowded coffee house, and over a French mug, Mary Willow described for Elijah the events of her last night spent with Claire Damien. She wept openly when reliving the horror of Calvin holding her at gunpoint and his subsequent murder. As she wept, the opening strains of Manuel de Falla's *"The Three Cornered Hat"* was filling the ears of those in the crowded coffee house.

"It was if I had been placed inside someone else's nightmare and was unable to move about or breathe. There was so much blood! You can't imagine! Although, I don't think Calvin was ever aware of what hit him; for all intents and purposes he was dead before he hit the floor. Claire's proficiency saw to *that*. And yes, he was a foul and objectionable sort, was Calvin, and what he made me *do* was foul and objectionable; but by night's end, I arrived at the painful conclusion that I hated Claire more than him. She murdered a man, and to look at her afterward, it seemed no more bothersome a task than taking out the rubbish or ironing a shirt! But I also hated myself; that much I knew for sure. And believe me, there was enough blame to go around for how I ended up in that room above that alleyway. Looking back on it, there was much that I pretended not know — about Claire, about the world, about my own culpability."

There are deceptions, and then there are *deceptions*: The night at Camden Lock, in a room atop an alleyway that stank of urine and vomit, Mary Willow didn't understand that *her* deception — *her* transgression was no less egregious than Claire's. (Perhaps it was less dangerous, but no less egregious.) This was a fact that she had only awakened to, but unlike the present, she had yet to fully understand. But even now, so many weeks later, it made her shudder to think that someone whom she professed to have loved, and with whom she so splendidly shared a bed, regarded the taking of a life (Calvin notwithstanding) as so trifling a matter that it wasn't worthy of a pause in a conversation. So many nights she woke with the sensation of Calvin pulsating in her mouth, and half expecting his "revolting semen", as Claire had described it, to explode down her throat. For awhile, there were nights thereafter that she wished Calvin had pulled the trigger. But in time, she learned to embrace the revulsion — to embrace the terror, and from embracing that which she dreaded, strength was gained. If the night in Camden Lock came with a regret, Mary Willow wished that she had lingered in the urine and vomit laden alleyway long enough to have learned the names of Freddy, Jack, and Alice — the three woe begotten creatures of the night, who were huddled together around a bonfire and sharing a bottle of Fireball Cinnamon Whiskey. Alice's offer that Mary Willow join them was a genuine one, though her claim that they were hiding out in an alleyway because they didn't wish for others about the marketplace to know that they "*were goin' first class*" (She had urged Jack to flash Mary Willow the bottle as proof) was not. Alice was well aware that they were drinking bottom shelf whiskey in the most unbecoming of settings — a setting many would find deplorable; though her invitation to Mary Willow was issued with the hope that someone of a loftier ilk — a higher station, as Mary Willow was supposed to have been, would see her not as a lowly wretch, but as a human being. Weeks later, Mary Willow returned to Camden Lock and the alleyway (the scene of the crime) hoping to find the woe begotten trio — to learn their names, to sip their whiskey, and to confess that it was *she* who was unworthy, and that it was her, Claire, and Calvin, who were the true miscreants of the night. But all she found was an empty alleyway filled with broken glass and the stench of vomit and urine.

On the first night that Mary Willow had departed the alleyway, having left behind Alice, Freddy, Jack, their Fireball Cinnamon Whiskey and warm fire, along with the bloody mess that Claire Damien made of Calvin, and Claire as well, she swiftly but jerkily weaved her way through the marketplace — the denseness of its humanity appeared to be racing toward her with alarming speed and with a blur of harsh light and many moving parts — more parts than she could count and more light than her eyes could bear. Within the blur there existed a menagerie in uproarious celebration, or so it appeared. The human jungle had further enveloped her, making it difficult to negotiate a path (or so she thought), and all that she could do, or wish to do, was beg to know *where was Jesus?* Where was the guitar playing *Christ in the clouds*, whose soft, beautiful eyes, she knew, could pierce harmlessly through her mortal flesh and seize her eternal soul and show her the way? But Jesus had moved on. To where, she didn't know. The harshness of the lights — the marketplace with its eclectic collection of humanity — together it grew into a monstrous swirl that seemed to swell, and as it did it gathered strength, until it became a singular entity all of one mind that was preparing to wage an assault against the one person perceived an intruder — the one person who dared to pierce their universe and upset its harmony. *Where is Jesus? Where is Jesus?* She was once again a five-year-old child, who stood awestruck while gazing up at the grand old Tudor, and who had hoped that the loveliness of Aunt Delia was the *real* world and that everything else known was a false representation. But every face in the marketplace became the faces of Colin and Douglas Broxton — the evil twins as they appeared as ten-year-olds were everywhere! Aunt Delia was *never* the real world, she was always the exception — an exception unable to understand evil, and therefore unable to recognise evil where and when it manifested. *Where is Jesus? Where is Jesus?* The world was closing in all around her — once again it had become a place where loud, angry voices raged and reduced her to a frightened young boy who once hid himself away in a dark, lonely closet, clutching to Fish and Chips, his monkeys. The marketplace, the world, her *life* — it had all meshed to become a farcical masquerade, whose roads claiming to lead to peace and calm were mere deceptions, and those deceptions led to more deceptions, until all that existed upon an un-navigable landscape were treachery and confusion. There was nowhere that she belonged, or so she felt. *Where is Jesus? Where is Jesus?*

Much of Mary Willow's fear and confusion was manufactured, but her urgency was quite real (her desire to be free of Claire and the massacre that had been made of Calvin were her main objectives) — and it was because of her urgency that she quickened her steps — the result of which, caused the banging of shoulders with some, while others alertly managed to dodge a pathway that was becoming less predictable and more agitated with each step. Some in the marketplace excused her, assuming that something had caused her to become legitimately hysterical, while others openly reproached what had been interpreted as overt and unfounded rudeness. She paid no mind to either, but instead, maintained her determination to break free from the cocoon of loud and unsettled humanity. At last, she had cleared the marketplace, but was entirely without thought as to where she might be heading; nor was she cognizant in which direction she was walking. Her only objective was to place herself as far away from Claire Damien as her legs would allow. Her home wasn't an option, for she knew that it would be the first place that Claire *would*, and, in fact, *did* look. After tidying the scene of any evidence that she was there, Claire packed up her briefcase, along with the money for which it was supposed to have been exchanged. She looked down at Calvin with her familiar smirk, and then flicked an ash from her cigarette, which settled onto his chest. "Sorry, Calvin," she said, as though the corpse in the room was poised to reply. "It's nothing personal, but I had my orders, which meant, *your* number was up." She left the dead body on the floor and went thumping down the stairs and out into the alleyway, where waiting for her, were Alice, Freddy, and Jack, still gathered around the bonfire, still sipping Fireball Cinnamon Whiskey.

"There she goes," whispered Freddy.

"Well, go on, ask her to join us," Jack urged Alice. Alice didn't say a word; she had felt utterly worthless when Jack claimed that, if he were to win the lottery, he'd give half of it away just to have an hour at Claire Damien's cunt. It made her frown even more so when Freddy concurred. Claire heels pounded through the alleyway on the way to her car. She drove straight away to Bloomsbury. Mary Willow had a head start, but she was on foot and she wasn't necessarily walking in the direction of Bloomsbury. In Mary Willow's flat, Claire sat just as she had in the beginning of the evening, alone and in the dark. Occasionally she flicked her lighter to better see her wristwatch. Come 2:00 a.m., there was still no Mary Willow. Claire rose to her feet and entered the bedroom. There, she went reaching for the one artefact in her lover's life — the only item Mary Willow chose to keep. Claire flicked her lighter to better see the youthful faces of the Broxton twins, the beautiful girl in her summer frock, and the little boy who held her hand, while clutching his monkeys. Claire had always suspected there was more to the photograph than Mary Willow had divulged, but she couldn't quite put her finger on it, nor ask the right question. What Claire did know, however, was that the photograph's value to Mary willow was beyond any earthy treasure, and that Mary Willow would do whatever she had to do to protect it. Claire began to suspect that her lover would not return — not tonight; but kidnapping the photograph was a guarantee that she would see her lover again. Indeed, Mary Willow would come looking for the photograph, and Claire would gladly hand it over, providing that she was given an opportunity to make amends for what had been the worst of nights.

The dark ringlets of the Spanish guitarist were glistening with perspiration. To the applause of the coffee house, and the admiration of Elijah, the capable, young musician strummed and plucked his way through the *Introduction, Afternoon, Fandango, The Corregidor, and The Miller's Wife,* of Manuel de Falla's, *"The Three Cornered Hat".* He was about to begin the second suite of the same piece, which he saved for the encore, when Mary Willow reached across the table and seized Elijah's hands. She leaned in and began: "I got to sip the best wines, sampled the best food, and took lovely drives in the country in a fancy sport car. I even had my head filled with trips to vineyards in France! I realise those things are shallow and hardly an excuse for being so blinded as I was. I suppose that my *only* excuse, if it could be considered an excuse, was that my life until Claire was more sheltered than I realised, because it all seemed so fantastic. On the surface, being with Claire was akin to being in possession of the winning lottery ticket. Funny thing, though, about the surface; you can live on it for so long, then it tends to wear away, and when it does, look out!"

While Claire was on her way to Bloomsbury, Mary Willow was at times recklessly, but always assertively vanishing into the darkness of the night. Step after step after block after mile she trekked — hour after ponderous hour. (There was much to ponder, and she tortured herself with all that there was to ponder, beginning with what had been a broken childhood, which led to a fractured and confused adulthood — an adulthood that began with the most heartfelt tears she would even cry, as she fell to her knees at a grave in Bibury.) She felt herself slipping away as one does when all sense of reality has been blurred. She began to doubt who she was and what she became; her motives, whether manufactured of born out of need, became a whirlwind of confusion. Was she merely a living tribute to a young woman who was laid to rest in Bibury? Or, was it simply a case where (sexual orientation excluded), the world would make more sense to her as a woman? In the darkness of night, the line dividing sexuality and sexual identity became as blurred as the faces she saw in the distance along her journey. As she continued to move swiftly through the night her pondering waned; no longer did she burden herself with Catherine and Nigel Philips or the Broxton twins; nor did she desire the loveliness of Aunt Delia, who supported her (financially) throughout her transformation; not even the young woman who was resting (perhaps fitfully) in Bibury was occupying a portion of her mind. All her pondering had subsided in favour of a higher order: *Where is Jesus? Where is Jesus?* The cool night air had become thick and moist, as the morning was approaching. By then she had grown numb and could no longer hold a thought in her head. Still, she trekked onward. The blackness of night became a murky blue, and the murkiness began to dissipate from the sky and it gave way to the earliest morning light; although by then it mattered not, for she was no longer able to keep her eyes open. Still she trekked onward with eyes closed or at times barely creased, and she did so until at last having collapsed on the cool, damp grass of the Holy Trinity Minories.

With each movement, Elijah was growing more impressed with the young musician, whose specialty was Spanish guitar. Mary Willow watched his dark hair shake vigorously, the perspiration fly from his well formed ringlets, as *The Miller's Dance* or *Farruca* of Suite No. 2 of the *"Three Cornered Hat"* was being brought to its conclusion. Next would be *Jota*, or *The Final Dance.*

"He's not reading from sheet music, is he?" Elijah asked Mary Willow. It wasn't actually a question; Elijah was merely asking Mary Willow to confirm what he already suspected.

"No, he is not," Mary Willow told the flutist. "He has no music stand, nor any sheet music. How did you know?" Mary Willow examined the young musician more closely; she was now of the notion that she was perhaps so engrossed in her own story that she might have overlooked the young musician's blindness; but upon her examination she saw that that wasn't the case at all. Meanwhile, Elijah smiled the sort of self-satisfied smile one flashes when their intuition is deadly accurate.

"How did I know?" he said, repeating Mary Willow's question. He could have cited the fact that, he had been seated in the coffee house for forty-plus minutes and thus far hadn't heard a page turn, but it was the sense of freedom and abandon with which the young guitarist played that led Elijah to his intuitive conclusion.

He turned toward Mary Willow and squeezed her hands, which prompted her to continue: "It was Sister Augustine, who later that morning discovered me. She tends the gardens, you know — and when I felt the touch of her soft, youthful hand on my face, it was if I was experiencing warmth and love for the very first time! She has these long, graceful fingers, does Sister Augustine — the kind a pianist would kill for, but she prefers to put her lovely fingers into the soil. But more than just *experiencing* warmth and love through her touch — the touch of an angel — I had at long last come to an understanding of their true nature. Never shall I forget the feel of Sister Augustine's hand on my face that morning. It nearly made me afraid to open my eyes and discover that I was dreaming, and that the feeling would be lost forever, unless I were ever fortunate enough to dream the same dream. But when I did at last open my eyes, I saw her kind face, and suddenly everything made sense — the whole universe became crystal clear, as did my entire being in relation with it. And then, just like that, all the torment that for years had been accumulating and consuming me left my body — I could actually feel it leaving — it was as though it were seeping through my pores and dissipating in the morning air, and all that remained on that cool, damp grass was the essence of serenity. I knew right away that something extraordinary had happened, for it was more powerful than any drug or night of splendour — and if Claire had been standing in the garden at that very moment, I would have found the strength to rise up and embrace her with forgiveness that was both earnest and bountiful."

"Are you alright, Miss?" asked Sister Augustine. "Are you injured? Were you attacked?"

The serenity that had settled in Mary Willow's opened eyes provided the answer. Sister Augustine, quickly got to her feet and went dashing off to alert the others of the unlikely guest that had been dropped into their bosom. Her enthusiasm seemed almost childlike, and she ran with a child's abandon — the way one would suspect a child to run on the last day of school, when at last released into the perfection of a summer's day. Mary Willow tried to call after Sister Augustine, but was too weak, and thus unable to raise her voice much above a whisper. She laid her head back down against the soft, dewy grass and closed her eyes. In remembering the gentle touch of Sister Augustine's hand, and the angelicness of her face, she thought that she could be in no place other than the secret garden of Sudeley Castle. In the thickness of the morning air, she could smell the fragrance of summer flowers. The morning sun had finally found her face and its warmth was delightful. She wasn't certain of how long she lay there, when once again she looked up and saw the kind and angelic face of Sister Augustine. Accompanying the sister were three other sisters, whose morning prayers were interrupted by an overly enthused colleague. The three sisters all huddled around Mary Willow; bent at the waist they peered in at her as though they were making every effort to determine who she was and how she might have ended up either having slept or having passed out on the grounds of the Holy Trinity Minories. The three sisters, Therese Marie, Frances Olivet, and Mary Agnes, all helped Mary Willow to her feet, while Sister Augustine clamoured that the strange woman, whom they've yet to learn anything about, should be brought to *her* bed in order to rest, or if necessary, convalesce. All three sisters rolled their eyes as they often did whenever Sister Augustine became overly enthused regarding affairs that they believed weren't worthy of such stimulation. Nevertheless, they did as the younger Sister Augustine had suggested; although it wasn't until the task was completed that all four sisters became mindful of their presumption, *and* of the fact that Mother Odilia had yet to become informed of their *latest accommodation* — or, as Mother Odilia often referred to them, *stunts*. It was Sister Augustine, naturally, who was unanimously elected by a committee of three, to go running off and explain to their superior the newest state of affairs.

"I feel I know her. Like … we're kindred spirits!" Sister Augustine told Sisters Therese Marie, Frances Olivet, and Mary Agnes.

"Had she said anything to you? Anything that would lead you to such a conclusion?" Sister Therese Marie wondered. Sisters Frances Olivet and Mary Agnes stood with folded arms and were frowning; they were posing as though they knew the answer would be a *no*, and also that the explanation for why Sister Augustine believed that she and the strange woman, who decided to use their lawn for lodging, were kindred spirits would be a foolish one, if not entirely outlandish.

"Not a word," Sister Augustine reported. "But there was something in her eyes that told me all that I needed to know. You know when you get a feeling that something must be so? I got that feeling!"

"I suppose, at least for the time being, it wouldn't hurt for us to trust your instincts," said Sister Therese Marie, who after looking down at Marry Willow went on to murmur, "If nothing else she appears harmless enough." Sisters Frances Olivet and Mary Agnes subscribed to the theory that no one, particularly a frail young woman who was well-dressed, spends a night having slept outside in a place that's somewhat removed from society, unless she was in some sort of danger or was trying to escape a dubious involvement. However, before Sister Augustine ran off to alert Mother Odilia of their guest, they were all in accordance with the notion that, by herself, Mary Willow would likely prove to be a harmless acquaintance.

The young guitarist brought Manuel de Falla's masterpiece, *"The Thee Cornered Hat"* to it riveting conclusion, then quick reached for a towel to mop up the perspiration on his face and hair. The coffee house erupted with applause.

"Would you take me to meet him?" Elijah asked of Mary Willow. But Mary Willow was way ahead of the flutist; she wouldn't dare let the young guitarist depart Ebenezer's without first acquainting him with Elijah. The young man's name was Jarrod Mingues, and as Mary Willow had suspected, he and Elijah had plenty to talk about. The young guitarist left, but not before he and the flutist agreed to collaborate on Antonio Vivaldi's *"The Four Seasons"* and Joaquin Rodrigo's *"Fantasia For a Gentleman"*, two pieces that they each believed would be served well with flute and guitar, and which they promised to soon bring to Ebenezer's Coffee House. Mary Willow escorted Elijah back to his seat.

"If you hadn't come by the square tonight to hear me play, I never would have met that young man," he told her. "It's funny how things turn out. But where were we?" Mary Willow was so thrilled to see Elijah connect with a fellow musician that she had all but forgotten that she was in the middle of a story.

"They permitted me to stay and to convalesce, did the sisters, and to take as long as I needed," she continued. "All the sisters were very kind, but it was Sister Augustine who routinely came to check on me. She took a great interest in my wellbeing. When I at last was in possession of enough strength, I began to help her with her garden. She taught me a great many things about the earth, and how with hard work and with the right preparation it can give back. The garden became my cathedral, you might say; and aside from working in the garden with Sister Augustine, it was also where I went and prayed most earnestly. Sometimes Sister Augustine and I would pray together. I would never ask God for anything — not even for strength — but over and over again I would thank Him for what I already had.

"The sisters took me in, and I ate with them and prayed with them. Then one night at dusk, I was in the garden, kneeling and giving thanks, when I felt Mother Odilia's firm hand on my shoulder."

"From what I can gather, Sister Augustine has taken quite a shine to you," said Mother Odilia. "Of course, one never needs to guess what's on *her* mind, does one?"

Mother Odilia's remark drew a smile from Mary Willow, who said, "And I, of her. I've become most fond of Sister Augustine. In fact, I've become very fond of *all* the sisters."

"You might say that Sister Augustine is our resident child; she finds wonder in the most rudimentary of things," said Mother Odilia. "Once she came rushing in and was spinning like a top to report on how blue was the sky on a particular day. Another time she was beaming over having interacted with, of all things, a ladybug! I see in you, much of the same qualities that I see in her."

Mary Willow pressed her cheek to Mother Odilia's strong and reassuring hand. "For the innocent," she began — "for the ones who see the thrill of small wonders, or what most take for granted, the world can be a daunting place — a place where to merely exist can require more courage than at any one time can be summoned."

"You've had such experiences?" asked Mother Odilia. The Holy Trinity Minories superior felt moisture on the hand that was presses to Mary Willow's cheek.

At first, Mary Willow wept silently, and then she shook with sobs that alone could have told the story of her life. When she at last was able to speak, she began: "I was five-years-old when my parents sent me away to the Cotswolds for two weeks to stay with my Aunt Delia and Uncle Peter, while they vacationed in Vienna and Budapest. It was the best two weeks of my life; it was also the worst two weeks of my life. My twin cousins, who I had never met before, and who were twice my age, tortured me. But I never knew what true loveliness was until I laid eyes on my Aunt Delia. The second day I was there, Aunt Delia gathered us all together and took us on a tour of Sudeley Castle. But before we went, she told us the most fantastic story about Queen Catherine, and how Queen Catherine became separated from her child, and that there's a legend that her ghost has been spotted walking the halls of the castle in search of her lost child. For two weeks I could scarcely think of nothing else but this poor lost child all alone in the world without her mother. In many ways I felt that I, too, was a lost child, and that if I could find *Queen Catherine's* lost child — if I could somehow reunite mother and daughter, *I* would feel better. I was five; I suppose that's how five-year-old children think.

"When my parents came for me, I was very excited to tell them all about Sudeley Castle, and Queen Catherine and her lost child. My father, being quite the historian that he was, proceeded to inform a five-year-old that the lost child whom I'd developed such an attachment for was Mary I, otherwise known as *Bloody Mary!* Indeed, I got quite a history lesson that day. I learned that Mary I resented the Anglican Church that her father, King Henry VIII helped to establish. She strongly resented England's break from Rome, and thus ordered the execution of hundreds of Protestant leaders, including the Archbishop of Canterbury. 'It was a real reign of terror,' my father had said. 'England hadn't seen anything like it, before or since.' I was devastated. I was sitting in the back seat of their motorcar, when my mother turned to me and said, 'So how do you like your poor lost child, now?' Why my father chose to deliver such a history lesson, I don't know. Perhaps he thought I'd be better off if I were well informed. At him I was angry, but my mother, I hated. I could see as plain as day the satisfaction on her face, that my childlike sense of reality had been shattered. I never did understand my mother's cruelty. I suppose in order to understand cruelty, one must first become cruel themselves, and that's not something that I was willing to let happen."

"You were right earlier when you said to merely exist or to remain true to our nature, when the world is all but forcing us to do otherwise takes courage," said Mother Odilia. "Sister Augustine is of the belief that your turning up here was anything but random. She's quite earnest in her belief that, your life thus far has been a journey that has led you to us. But now begins another journey — one which will require you to be more steadfast than you ever imagined — a journey that will test your faith and resolve in ways never before tested. Some here are of the notion that you're well ready to give yourself to God and our mission. But what say *you*, Mary Willow?"

"Everyday I'm learning more and more of what it means to be a Franciscan," Mary Willow told Elijah. "And with each passing day I grow happier and happier. I have moments when I can feel my spirit soaring and filling up with the hopefulness of springtime and childhood, until it's so full I fear it might burst! Surely, Elijah, it must mean that my feet have been set upon the right path."

"If you're filled with feelings of springtime and childhood, it can't mean anything *but*," the flutist told her. Mary Willow permitted her eyes to travel about the coffee house, beginning with Brian, who despite only minutes away from closing time was still busy at his craft. Next, she rested her eyes on to the table where once sat the quartet of girls from the university. They had long since moved on did the quartet, who were never made aware of how they tortured a soul in transition, as did the fellow, who on Sunday mornings was given to sourly drone on about what he considered bad politics of the day. At last, a place that was both lofty and humble, where torment and ignorance could no longer exercise its dominion had been reached. She was free. Indeed, the little boy who, for years would hide himself away in the darkness of a closet had sprouted wings and was now prepared to take to the sky. Lastly, her eyes came to rest on Elijah. She found it ironic that, since the ill-fated young woman from Bibury, it has taken a childlike nun and a blind man to see into her soul. The flutist and the woman who would one day soon become Sister Ignatius departed Ebenezer's Coffee House. They were off to see Marybeth, a parrot that was given to a sidewalk piper a decade before Mary Willow was born, and Sarah, the world's most wonderful woman.

CHAPTER VIII
SAINT JIMMY IN PARADISE

"Writing our memoirs, are we?" wondered Finn. His slightly creased eyes took notice of the pen in Sister Ignatius's small, unattractive hand. She was either thoughtful enough while under siege to toss a pen into her backpack, or she found it rummaging through the abandoned shack, Finn thought. She was taking the pen to a tablet of paper; no doubt the tablet had been in her backpack all along, Finn assumed, but wasn't curious enough to ask. The sister's hand was moving at an alarming speed, as though her thoughts needed to be captured on paper before forgotten and perhaps lost for good. *This* made Finn curious.

"Ah, we're awake, I see," said Sister Ignatius. "And, to answer your question, *no*, I should think my life and times are hardly worthy of memoirs."

"To answer *your* question, *yes*, I'm awake," said Finn. "Perhaps not fully, but awake enough to be my usual engaging self. In other words, I haven't kicked the bucket just yet. And only a nun would be so self-effacing as to deem that the life of a missionary in such a place as Darfur, wasn't worthy of *some* documentation. I would gladly toot a horn or wave a banner on your behalf if I didn't think it would cause me to bleed to death faster than I already am."

"I do appreciate the thought, Charlie," Sister Ignatius maintained, "but even if I were to write my memoirs, I doubt very much whether I could scarcely fill but a page."

"Well, then, you must be writing a letter to that old lover of yours — the one whom you refuse to talk about," said Finn. Sister Ignatius frowned that Finn was still trying to pry his way into a part of her past which she didn't wish to disclose. "It's not all that uncommon, you know, to want to reconnect with the past, especially when faced with adversity in the present." He thought a softer approach would persuade her to open up, but he followed his words with a narrowing of the eyes; it was a self-satisfied gesture to convey that, his first guess on the subject of the sister's written words was deadly accurate.

In truth, Claire Damien hadn't been far from Sister Ignatius's thoughts; perhaps it was the danger of Darfur that kept Claire near the forefront of her mind. Once accepted into the abbey, she *had* written Claire. Her words were full of forgiveness and at times were cordial bordering on loving, but with a strong sense that, whatever they had was unmistakably in the past. She had written Claire once more to confess how much from her she had learned. *It was all because of you that I became less afraid and more worldly.* It was Claire, who first flashed through the sister's mind when the Janjaweed were approaching the camp. Once again, as was the case the first time when standing alone in the corridor outside Claire's flat, she was placed on the first car of a rollercoaster slowly ascending to its pinnacle, before making its terrifying plummet.

She quickly but methodically packed her bag, then urged Finn to flee with her. By then, it was no longer Claire Damien that was occupying her mind. Nor was it the spray of bullets and knives that was prompting her to flee. Instead, it was the sheer loudness of the Janjaweed — it was their angry shouts that prompted her to want to run off and make for the abandoned shack — much in the same way her screaming parents had chased her into the darkness of a closet.

"Or," Finn continued, hazarding another guess, "maybe you're writing to your parents, who disowned you because you were their only child, and because their only wish was that you would one day give them grandchildren. *Or ...*"

"I was writing to the sisters back at the abbey in London!" Sister Ignatius emphatically interjected.

"Of course; I should have known," said Finn.

"Charlie, you say that as though you're disappointed," said the sister. "Please don't be disappointed. I'm sorry that I can't be as interesting as you would like."

"Please, Sister, give me something!" implored Finn. "At least tell me why you're here? Why choose *this* life in *this* place? And please, don't recite for me your vows, or the nun's code of duty; *that*, thanks to my mother, I can almost do verbatim. There must be something in your past — something aside from the more current and the obvious that's brought you to this point and has allowed you to accept it with such uncommon honour. Earlier on you mentioned having experienced a moment of clarity, but you never told me what that moment of clarity was."

"I saw Jesus!" Sister Ignatius blurted out.

Finn, who was all puffed up with passion and fervour, began to deflate and then slump. He rolled his eyes the way one does when they have lost all patients or interest in what someone has to say. "That was unexpected," he said.

"No doubt," Sister Ignatius drolly added.

"Sister, for you I've reserved nothing but the healthiest respect and admiration. And, your faith notwithstanding, I always pegged you for a pragmatist — a grounded intellectual, if there's such a thing." That Finn chose an oxymoron to assess the sister, caused her to smile somewhat ironically; though she thought it more becoming when earlier on he described her as a Kafka reading existentialist. "So when someone such as yourself claims to have seen Jesus, I can only assume that you mean *Jesus*, as in *the genuine article*, and that you weren't some half-baked lunatic who ripped their life apart because they saw the formation of the blessed virgin in a slice of bread, or an image of the crucifix in their cup of coffee? I'm hoping that, at the very least, you saw a retro 1960s rock and roll Jesus sometime in the late eighties when you were falling apart, and all a soulless world had to offer were space programs and nuclear energy." Again came the sister's ironical smile, for the guitar playing Jesus in the clouds that was tattooed on a man's back was a perfect depiction of a retro 1960s rock and roll Jesus.

"On night, when at a very low point, while in a crowded marketplace in Camden Lock, I felt Jesus was near. I knew he was near." Sister Ignatius went and knelt down directly in front of her patient. "I *will* give you something, Charlie. I'll *really* give you something. But don't you dare in any way look at me with eyes of pity. Do you understand? Hadil and Mozamel might still be out there, and they only *might* still be alive, and we should be praying for them in earnest, instead of playing armchair psychiatrist for one another. But here goes it: I was weak, Charlie. The weakest of the weak — pathetic, in fact."

"I find that hard to imagine. It's as though you describing a person who no longer exists and perhaps hasn't for quite some time." Finn was genuine when opposing or doubting what he believed must be an overly harsh disparagement of the sister's own character.

"Be that as you believe, but it was *quite* true!" The sister was fiercely resolute in her admission. "I was a frail, vulnerable child, who later became a frail, vulnerable young woman. Within my world there existed those who saw me as a mere *thing*. Can you appreciate the sort of occurrences that can be levied upon a person, when they're surrounded by those who are unable to distinguish them as anything more than a mere *thing*? Need I say more, Charlie?"

"Those beautiful twin boys in the photograph? They were your tormentors?" Finn imagined every sort of abuse that men have waged upon women.

"Jesus said if someone slaps your cheek to give them the other cheek. Well, I would turn the other cheek as instructed, whenever Colin would slap me, but Douglas was always right there to finish the job, and they were *so* very good at what they did. Then darling Mary Willow was taken from me, which all but put an end to dear, sweet Jimmy. And my parents? Well, *they'll* have to be a story for another time. All I had left in the world was a relationship with my Aunt Delia — my lovely Aunt Delia, and that had become nothing less than a strain. Eventually I wandered into a relationship that took me down the darkest of paths. You see, Charlie, when you're all alone and weak, you tend to reach out for whatever comes along — and worse, you allow yourself to be completely taken over. This led to a night that saw me kneeling at gunpoint and forced to do something reprehensible. Once again, I found myself reduced to a mere *thing* — an object that can be bent and twisted however one sees fit. But I had no one or nothing to blame but my own weakness."

"Nevertheless, no one deserves such treatment," said Finn. "Not for any reason."

"We don't get what we deserve, Charlie, we get what we get," said the sister. "It's one of the consequences of *all* human souls given free will. You surely don't *deserve* to be sitting here with a bullet lodged in your body."

"Good point," Finn admitted.

"Anyway," the sister went on, "I look back on that night with fondness. It was *that* night at the Camden Lock Marketplace that brought about my *moment of clarity*. I survived having been forced to my knees and held at gunpoint. That night, with the help of Jesus, I walked away from my lover and did so without a single backward glance. I walked into the night well beyond the point of utter exhaustion. I could feel that my legs were still moving, though I was unable to keep my eyes open. Still I kept pressing onward. I pretended that I was floating in the sea, and that if I stayed afloat long enough eventually I would wash up safely on the shore. Well, I did better than wash up on the shore; I washed up on the grounds of a Franciscan Abbey in London. Sometime had gone by before I was discovered. I can still remember the way Sister Augustine's hand felt when she touched my face. No one had ever touched me like that before; certainly not my own mother. No hand ever felt so warm and loving or made me feel so reassured. The sisters took me in and I gave myself entirely to God. I had at last come home."

"I must admit, Sister, your story has moved me more than I was expected to be moved," admitted Finn. "Unfortunately, its ending has forced me to view you less as a woman and more a nun — a turn of events which pains me terribly."

"You have my sincerest apology, Charlie," was Sister Ignatius's disingenuous reply. "But now it is *your* turn."

"*My* turn? Right; of course; it's my turn." Clearly, Finn hadn't planned on having to reciprocate and so he half-heartedly muttered a reply to his own question, before stalling further by adding: "So you wish to know why *I'm* here, is that it? It's time for good ol' Charlie Finn to come clean; no sympathy for the patient around *here*. But please bear in mind, Sister, it's not just *anybody* who's willing to abandon a land where there exists twenty-four hour a day news and sports at one's disposal — where the roads are littered with oversized vehicles of the most comfortable designs — where, from within the confines of one of those oversized vehicles, one can't drive a block without spotting a sign that reads *All You Can Eat* because of an overabundance of food. Indeed, I left all that behind, and in favour of bleeding to death in an abandoned shack in the middle of the Sudan and in front of a woman sworn to celibacy. To be sure, Sister, for *that* it would require a *uniquely* qualified imbecile!

"But here goes it: (As though someone threw a switch, all the farce and mockery vanished from Finn's countenance, and what appeared in their stead were the soft eyes of one given to wallow in the grimness sincerity.) It all began a few years ago in a concert hall in Philadelphia; I was with my lady friend,

Caroline. The orchestra was playing Shostakovich's 11th Symphony. The work is a remarkable depiction of "Bloody Sunday". Of course, as you well know, human history has surely known its share of bloody Sundays. The one, which on that night was receiving a representation, took place in 1905: Unarmed demonstrators marching to present a petition to Tsar Nicholas II were fired upon by soldiers of the Imperial Guard. The incident sparked a revolution. It's been said, Sister, that within Shostakovich's symphonies lies 'the secret history of Russia'. Aside from "Bloody Sunday" there exists within this particular symphony, his 11th, a sharp condemnation of the Hungarian Invasion, which saw unarmed citizens gunned down in a fashion to that used by the Tsar five decades earlier.

"You know, Sister, if I didn't know any better, I'd say we were a species doomed to repeat our mistakes, and that we have an insatiable thirst for irony, and the more bitter the irony the better we seem to like it. Who could ever dream up such a species? (Sister Ignatius frowned, but didn't interrupt.)

"Anyway, I sat there with my eyes pinned to the stage — not for a second did I look away— neither did Caroline. Charles Dutoit was conducting that night. Shostakovich's 11th is remarkably visual, and at times it can be overwhelming. In the fourth and final movement the music swelled and soared such that, one might have thought the auditorium could no longer hold it — it was *that* powerful. Then all at once, silence — and out of the silence came a clarinet solo. The notes that it played could only be described as a singular voice crying out in the wilderness. The voice was urging ... *no*, not *urging*, but rather it was *imploring* that mankind become a better version of itself. Then it began to weep openly, for it understood that we were no better prepared to act upon its entreaty than we were two-thousand years ago when standing at the foot of the cross. Indeed, Sister, they'll be more bloody Sundays, and more bloody Sundays, and perhaps more than can be counted before the voice in the wilderness at last reaches our ears.

"I sat among a crowd of three-thousand. I don't know how many others, if any, heard the voice, but I heard it and heard it clearly, as if it spoke to me with clear words in a familiar language. But that's the beauty of art; it's transcendent. Well, ol' Charlie Finn walked away from that concert hall certain that he needed to lead a life entirely different from the one that he had been leading. It cost him the woman whom he once thought certain to marry, among other things; but even as he sits here with a bullet lodged in his body, he hasn't a single regret."

Sister Ignatius placed her cheek alongside Finn's so that they were touching. "I love you, Charlie," she whispered. "I love what's in your heart."

"And I love you, Sister, because of what's in *your* heart," said Finn.

For awhile there was silence, until Sister Ignatius uttered, "It's over, Charlie. I must go, now that things have quieted down and it's safer."

"Go?" wondered Finn. "Go where? The stores are all closed, aren't they?" Finn was beginning to lose his grip on where he was, along with the current state of affairs. Sensing this, Sister Ignatius gave his face two slaps — the sort of slaps one gives to make a groggy person more alert when being alert is imperative.

"I must go and fetch Mr. Somersby," she told him. "Be still, Charlie, and together we'll return with a vehicle — most likely that abysmal looking jeep that has served the both of you so well on several trips to Nyala."

"Sister?" Finn faintly whispered, as he was already beginning to miss the feel of her hand in his. Then his mouth creased into a smirk when he added in regard to Nyala, "Boys will be boys. Tis written."

"I'll go as quickly as I can — like the wind I'll run, Charlie," said Sister Ignatius. "You'll see, I'll have returned before you know it."

She placed a kiss on his cheek. It was the sort of kiss one might place when desiring more; but after a brief moment of hesitation, where more than the state of Finn's wound had been contemplated, off she dashed. Finn's wound was at last beginning to clot, though much blood was lost, and the soft tissue damage was substantial.

When the sister returned to camp, still lingering was a sense of urgency, as the air remained filled with the potential threat of violence, while blanketing the ground was the astonishing aftermath of what had already occurred. When coming upon the carnage, she fell to her knees and prayed in earnest. Afterward, she tried to ignore the dead, as they were beyond all earthly hope, then she searched the multitude for Somersby, and while doing so she also kept a keen eye out for Hadil and Mozamel; it was the sister's wish to report back to Finn that the Sudanese gentleman and his brave son had survived and were well. She weaved her way through the dead, the broken, and the anxious survivors, on her way to the Doctors Without Borders clinic; it was the last place that she remembered seeing Somersby. As expected, there wasn't an open bed or chair to be had, along with a multitude of wounds yet to be treated. She realised how very badly needed were her services, but Finn's situation had grown dire. She gazed into the grim faces of the wounded and she wondered, *how can I abandon all this for one man?* Never had she felt so torn. The multitude of the desperate and fearful were weighing on her; they were human beings — a human parade of misery, who deserved so much more than their fate. They were men, women, and children with the divine gift of a soul, but they were also a nameless, faceless multitude, whereas she had just come from having been granted access into a soul and with the freedom to navigate; she had travelled a man's life and embraced each stage along the way, and by journey's end she understood it as a gift — *her* gift.

"Sister!" she heard a voice call out. "Sister Ignatius!"

She turned about as though the sound of the calling voice shattered her buffering thoughts, and the sensation of those shattered thoughts helped to cause a scene which, in her current state had seemed muted and unhurried as is often the case in a dream, to magnify and then fall on her with alarming alacrity and clamour. "Sister Ignatius! Over here!"

"Mr. Somersby!" she finally called back. "Oh, Mr. Somersby, your neck! That's some bandage!"

"Just a scratch," he said. "It'll be good as new in a day or so."

"Just a scratch, my eye!" remarked Dr. Soderberg, the handsome Swede. "Another centimetre, my good fellow, and you were a goner; you'd have bled out long before *I* could have done anything to save you."

"What's life, if not a game of centimetres — or, as Mr. Finn would say, inches," remarked Somersby. "You know, Sister, we use to have this saying back at the university: Sometimes you get the bear, and sometimes the bear gets you. It was always good for a laugh, you know. Anyway, they've got me working pretty good here. All hands on deck, as they like to say."

"Mr. Somersby, Mr. Finn has been seriously wounded and is in great need of our help," said Sister Ignatius.

"Mr. Finn?" asked Somersby. "Seriously wounded, he was? But he was standing right next to me when everything got out of hand; I don't recall him getting wounded."

The sister turned to the Dr. Soderberg and implored, "Mr. Finn is a distance from here, perhaps a kilometre, maybe a bit more, and with a bullet inside him. I've managed to control the bleeding, but his situation can only be described as dire. He can no longer walk; he'll need to be transported. Would it be possible to spare Mr. Somersby for a short spell?"

The doctor nodded his given permission, but also wondered to himself how it came to be that Finn was such a distance from the camp. He found the event a peculiar one, but before he could raise a voice to the matter, Somersby and

Sister Ignatius had run off; they weaved their way through the grim scene on the way to procuring a vehicle.

"The old girl has served both Mr. Finn and me very well on our trips to Nyala," said Somersby. "She lacks amenities, as I'm sure you can tell, and she's not all that comfortable, either, but she'll get us where we need to go for sure. In fact, she's just *like* an old girl: loyal and dependable, but nowadays not much to look at."

Sister Ignatius smiled, as she was well aware that Somersby was simply making idiotic small talk in order to alleviate their anxiety.

"It's a kilometre or so in that direction — an old abandoned shack," she said, pointing. "How in the blazes did Finn make it all the way out there if he was seriously wounded?" wondered Somersby.

"I can clearly remember filling a bag with medical supplies and other provisions, but not whether I did it before or after Mr. Finn was hit. When I did realise that he *was* hit, I can remember thinking that we needed to get away from the spray of bullets and the stampede so that I could better dress his wound. I grabbed his arm and urged him to run. Once we were away from the camp and reasonably in the clear, I recalled stumbling upon an old abandoned shack during one of my walks. If figured there we could remain safe. It *seemed* a good idea, but perhaps I used bad judgment. Perhaps it was my fear that overwhelmed Mr. Finn and provoked us to run."
"Mustn't be too hard on yourself, sister," said Somersby. "You made a snap decision in the heat of the moment. There's no way of knowing how such things will turn out when you only have a second to decide. Besides, you don't strike me as the fearful type; whatever decision you made, for better or worse, it must have been with Mr. Finn's best interest in mind. Furthermore, two people such as yourself and Mr. Finn

alone in an abandoned shack, there's no telling what good can come of it."

"Can this vehicle go any faster?" Sister Ignatius complained. Her tone and twisted countenance was a clear indication that she was quite annoyed with what Somersby had implied, and not necessarily with the adequacy of an old jeep that has seen its share of kilometres.

"Bear in mind it's an old jeep, you know," said Somersby. "She won't do much above 40 kilometres and that's if you stand on the pedal, and she's drinks petrol like it's going out of style. Old engines are not very kind on fuel."

"There!" shouted the sister. "It's over there!"

"So it is," said Somersby, who was quite confident that he was well alleviated of any and all dust that had been kicked up in camp and had settled into his ears. He stretched his ears and jaw as though he were attempting release Sister Ignatius's ringing words, which were still reverberating, then he jumped on the gas pedal. He had yet to bring the jeep to a complete stop, when Sister Ignatius leaped from the vehicle and in doing so she was able to hit the ground running, for she had made a perfect landing. Somersby was surprised by her agility. He watched her go sprinting off, and then he parked the jeep and followed after her. When he entered the shack he saw the sister kneeling by Finn and weeping.

"Oh, Charlie," she was crying. In Finn's still and lifeless hand was the letter that Sister Ignatius had written while Finn was under the influence of a sedative — the same letter that was suspected to have been meant for an old lover or estranged parents. On his face, if one was able to see beyond the final moments of agony, as was Sister Ignatius, there existed an expression that could be described as idyllic.

"He heard the voice, Mr. Somersby," the sister said. "He heard the voice and understood it as clearly as I'm speaking to you." She looked toward the heavens before adding, "I know You'll grant this most worthy servant eternal peace."

"Amen," added Somersby. Then he placed what he hoped would be a comforting hand on Sister Ignatius's shoulder. I'm sorry, sister," he said. "I'm sorry for the both of us. He was a damn good fellow, are Mr. Finn."

"Indeed he was, Mr. Somersby," agreed Sister Ignatius. Then she reached for Somersby's hand and asked, "Would you mind kneeling down beside me so together we can pray for the soul of a clockmaker's son." Somersby wasn't a praying sort, but didn't feel that it was the right time to intimate as much; he simply did as the sister asked.

Both Somersby and Sister Ignatius rode back to camp mostly in silence, with the sister contemplating the likelihood of an American boy, who was denied the right to play little league baseball by an overbearing father, dying in an abandoned shack in Darfur, Sudan. The possibilities in life were endless. Meanwhile, Somersby was considering life in Darfur without his colleague. Finn had been an easy acquaintance, who became a friend, and their friendship (perhaps in-part because of the circumstances) was given a higher value than whatever might have been their worldly views. They debated as any two might, but never in a contentious manner; they understood from early on how much they might have to depend upon one another for their own sanity.

When they arrived back at camp, the sister threw herself into the care of the wounded, of which there were many; it was overwhelming. On a calm day, there seemed an endless stream of wounds and rashes, along with the always present issue of malnutrition. Today, and the days ahead would prove to be extraordinary. As the sister steadfastly ploughed her way through the remainder of the day, there were those about who were trying to determine the number of wounded versus the number of those whom had perished, and that the bodies of those who did perish would need to be dealt with expediently for fear of disease. There also existed the issue of replacing the many provisions that were either looted or were set ablaze.

Hours had gone by (though most had lost all sense of time) when at last the sister casted her sight out toward the grim multitude within the camp. With a keen eye, she dissected the crowd, and through the mostly downtrodden mass she managed to spot the sincerest of eyes and noblest of faces. "Hadil!" she cried out. She weaved her way through the crowd until having reach the tall Sudanese gentleman, then threw her outstretched arms around him. "Hadil, you're alright!"

"Yes, I am quite well," he said, "though today the ground of Kalma was stained with much blood."

"And your family?" the sister wondered, though she was bracing herself for fear the blood of Mariam (the wife of the Sudanese gentleman and a Kalma volunteer), Mozamel, and his other two children hadn't stained the hot dusty ground of the camp.

"I am most happy to report that we are all still together and intact," he said.

"Thank God," sighed Sister Ignatius. "Thank God for that."

"Sister, you are crying," said Hadil.

"It's Mr. Finn, Hadil," she said. "He's no longer with us."

"I am most sorry, Sister," said Hadil. "Mr. Finn was a good man. I would have liked to have known him more."

"I was with him up until the very end." said Sister Ignatius. "He spoke of you with fondness and held you in the highest regard."

The sister and the Sudanese gentleman stood beside one another and looked skyward. They shared a pensive moment, with each searching the sky, as though somewhere in the great vastness there existed an answer to all the madness below. They parted company knowing the sun would shine down on them for at least another day. The sister returned to the steady stream of wounded, while Hadil, along with his son, the brave Mozamel, would assist in the demanding task of ridding Kalma of its deceased.

Later that same evening, when Sister Ignatius retired to her quarters, with bleary eyes, she took the letter from her pocket and looked it over. When she reached the end, she became fretful and agitated, until finally she wept. "In death we shed our skin," she cried, "our wretched cocoon of narcissism, which tends to cage our spirit and smother the better angels of our nature. But you're free now, Charlie. You're free."

She went to the window and looked out upon the darkening landscape and a camp that was at last beginning to settle itself. She began to recall her childhood — the dark coat closet in the hallway, the cool river Windrush, Catherine and Nigel, and the Broxton twins, and that to merely exist took courage and perseverance. But she didn't fully understand the true nature of courage and perseverance until she arrived in Darfur, and acquainted herself with men like Hadil. She laughed to herself thinking that to survive in the west takes but a credit card. Indeed, she had come a long way from the days when the female quartet at Ebenezer's Coffee House left Jimmy Philips a tortured wreck. By the light of a candle she revised the final lines of the letter. P.S. The blood stains on this letter belong to a man whom I will always remember as a dear friend; though in truth, I knew him only as someone who came willingly to this godforsaken land, and who, like myself, foolishly carried within him this ponderous affliction known as hope. Together, in his waning hours we forged a friendship that became his final act of humanity. His name was Mr. Charlie Finn, a clockmaker's son, and as long as I am alive I shall carry within me his final act and always look upon it as a divine gift.

Afterward

The idea of "The Courage of Existence" came to me years before ever attempting to write word one. It would have been my second novel had I not wisely recognised that I wasn't a seasoned enough writer to deliver such a narrative. Still, I allowed it to occupy a portion of my mind while ploughing forward with other writing projects. "The Courage of Existence" began life as *Saint Jimmy in Paradise*, but it was decided that was too revealing. Later it became *The Missionary*, which was determined revealed too little. Later hitherto, it became *Confliction,* for in one way or another, there was conflict throughout. But it was told to me by someone whose literary prowess I respect, "Confliction is too harsh a word". Besides, I don't usually favour one word titles. Finally, it was settled that *The Courage of Existence* would do, as it gave some insight that somewhere within the novel, *or* throughout, to merely exist requires a measure of courage. To a greater degree, this notion is illustrated by the life of Sister Ignatius. However, both she and Charlie Finn, two souls in utter conflict — conflict with themselves, one another, the world at-large, and lastly, were dropped in a place of conflict (Darfur), perform admirably in a region that requires uncommon courage. I began first by typing out the letter that preludes the novel, then leapt forward to what would become chapter six, titled *The Dessert Tray*. It was there that my difficulty began, as the dialogue (what little there was of it at the time) was uninspiring and deadly dull. Once again I came face-to-face with the notion that I lacked the ability to deliver such a narrative. I had two choices, neither of which were satisfying: Plough forward knowing full well that my aim would fall short of whatever were my lofty intentions — or, abandon the project altogether. Luckily I had what some like to refer to as *an epiphany*— or, as Sister Ignatius might say, *a moment of clarity*. Afterward it became unimaginable that Sister Ignatius began as an American, and Charlie Finn, an Englishman. Once their geographies were set straight, the sea parted, and it seemed as if the story began to write itself, leaving me a mere bystander permitted to peek in from time to time on the lives of these quirky characters.

Once these two adversarial subjects were properly assembled and set into motion, so began my fascinating odyssey down the pathway of human sexuality. In the beginning it was uncertain the extent of such a journey, or how much weight it would carry throughout the novel. Even today, as I write these words, the motives of Jimmy's transformation remains a mystery. Was he of the notion that he could better gain access into the world of women? Did he truly believe that he could live more effectively as a female? Or, did he at last arrive at a threshold where, spiritually, he saw his being a mere extension of Mary Willow, and therefore became Mary Willow? None would be the wrong answer, and all would be correct, singularly and in combination, along with other motives for such a character that I myself have yet to conceive.

In my research, I confess to having learned that sexual orientation has little to do with gender identity. Along that aspect, I would hope "The Courage of Existence" on some level is perceived a celebration of our complexities. There is nothing all too heroic about a bullied English boy. There is nothing all too virtuous about an Englishwoman, who, like a piece of clay, allows the world to shape her however it sees fit. However, *heroic* and *virtuous* are two words that seem to go well with Sister Ignatius. Still, the sister is never without a trace of the vulnerability that once afflicted the boy in the closet. And, as far as her virtue was concerned, one could easily arrive at the opinion that, Darfur was her atonement for having dared to alter the form that God created for her, and that perhaps she herself saw it that way, and therefore embraced her new life. Whenever I think of Sister Ignatius, I am able to somehow separate her just enough from the demons and complexities that led to her radical alteration, to see her emerge as a heroine. It also pleases me to believe that, with each rebuke of Finn's overtures, and with each conflict they attempted to resolve, respect was gained and friendship deepened. Lastly, I was left with the impression, had Sister Ignatius shown any inclination to succumb to Finn's overtures, that alone would have satisfied him, and from there he would have taken the moral high road.